C. L. WILSON

CROWN of CRYSTAL FLAME

AVON
An Imprint of HarperCollinsPublishers

AVON BOOKS
An Imprint of HarperCollins*Publishers*
195 Broadway
New York, NY 10007

Copyright © 2010 by C. L. Wilson
Map by C. L. Wilson
"Eternal Song" copyright © 2010 by Arabella Hancock
"Shadow's Eyes" copyright © 2010 by Jennifer Huizar
"My Shei'tan" copyright © 2010 by Janet Reeves
"Tairen's Chant to His Beloved" copyright © 2010 by Ashley Denman
"Dahl'reisen's Lament" copyright © 2010 by Rebekah Lyness
"Dahl'reisen's Plea" copyright © 2010 by Ashley Denman
"Shei'tanitsa Sonnet" copyright © 2010 by Helen Thompson
"Call to War" copyright © 2010 by Colleen Billiot
"Flight of the Tairen Lovers" copyright © 2010 by Phyllis Bright
"Majestic Flight" copyright © 2010 by Janet Reeves
ISBN 978-0-06-201896-0
www.avonromance.com

First Avon Books paperback printing: November 2010

Avon Trademark Reg. U.S. Pat. Off. and in Other Countries, Marca Registrada, Hecho en U.S.A.
HarperCollins® is a registered trademark of HarperCollins Publishers.

Printed in the U.S.A.

HB 03.22.2024

For Kevin.
My one true love.
Ver reisa ku'chae. Kem surah, shei'tan.

Acknowledgements

The publication of this book brings to a close the dream I have pursued for over a decade. I first met Rain and Ellie in 1999 in between contract jobs as an IVR programmer and B2B marketing specialist. Their story consumed me. I fell in love with them, their friends, their world. I'm so glad you did too.

Thanks to my wonderful family—my husband, Kevin; my daughters, Ileah and Rhiannon; and my son, Aidan—for supporting me and all the long hours of writing and writerly stuff. Special thanks to my mother, Lynda Richter, and my sister, Dr. Lisa Richter, for the tireless hours of reading half-baked manuscripts and helping me make them better, and to all the CP's over the years who've had a hand in making Rain and Ellie's story the best it could be, especially my starfish pals: Christine Feehan, Kathie Firzlaff, Diana Peterfreund, Betina Krahn, Sheila English, Carla Hughes, and Sharon Stone. Thanks to my dad, the incomparable Ray Richter, for being my web guru all these years. A very special thanks to my agent, Michelle Grajkowski, and my former editor, Alicia Condon, because four years ago, you both took a chance on an unpublished writer and a monster manuscript no one else in publishing would touch. Last but not least, thanks to my new editor, Tessa Woodward, and my new publisher, Avon Books. I look forward to what I hope will be a long and fruitful relationship.

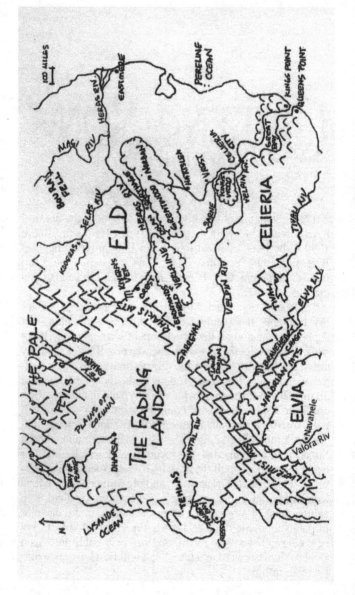

PROLOGUE

Northern Celieria ~24th day of Verados

Death raked like a knife across Ellysetta Baristani's empathic soul. Talisa Barrial diSebourne was dead. Killed by the tairen venom in the red Fey'cha her husband, Colum, had thrown at her Fey truemate, Adrial vel Arquinas.

Of Colum diSebourne—Talisa's husband—there was no sign.

The scorch of ozone, the odor of powerful magic released with explosive force, still hung heavy in the air. No one needed to draw Ellysetta a picture. She'd felt Colum's hate-filled fury, felt Talisa's death. Adrial's wild, deadly Rage. She'd sensed the moment Colum's anger turned to terror, seen the unmistakable explosion of Adrial's magic, and then . . . nothing. A vacuum of emotion, the utter stunned silence of disbelief, followed at last by grief and accusation and a chaotic whirl of unchecked thoughts and feelings.

Colum had discovered his wife returning from the forest with her Fey lover, and he'd set into motion the series of events that had led to this: Talisa and Adrial dead. Colum . . . simply *gone*.

"My son." Great Lord Sebourne—Colum's father—stepped into the open space where his son had been. His eyes swept the clearing. His jaw thrust out aggressively. "Where's my son?"

"He's gone," Talisa's father, the Great Lord Cannevar Barrial, answered in a bleak voice. "They're all gone." His sons Luce, Parsis, and Severn stood in stricken silence beside him. He swiped at the tears brimming in his eyes and glared at his neighbor. "I hope you're *jaffing* satisfied, Sebourne."

Kneeling on the ground beside the bodies of Talisa and his brother, Rowan vel Arquinas fixed his grief-stricken gaze on Ellysetta. "Please, Feyreisa. Save them. If anyone can, it's you."

Rowan's ragged plea spurred her to action. She crossed the field and dropped to her knees beside the fallen truemates.

"Rain, try the Shadar horn on Talisa," she commanded. A gift from the Elf King, Galad Hawksheart, the curling horn from the magical horses called Shadar was reputed to be an antidote to any poison—even irreversibly lethal tairen venom.

"Ellysetta." Rain, Ellysetta's unbonded truemate, laid a hand on her shoulder. "It's too late, *shei'tani*. They're already gone."

Her gaze shot up, pinning his. "I have to at least try to save them," she protested. "You know I must."

Compassion and understanding softened his expression. Her mate, the King of the Fey, who had once scorched the world in a fit of grief-stricken madness, was no stranger to death or the desperate desire to prevent it. "There's nothing to be done. They have passed beyond the Veil. Even if you could call their souls back into their bodies, you would only summon them as demons, not as the friends we knew."

The sounds of shouting made them turn. Lord Sebourne and Lord Barrial were at each other's throats, swords drawn. All their men had blades in hand as well, ready—even eager—to spill their own countrymen's blood.

"What are you thinking?" Ellysetta cried. "Haven't you had your fill of death?"

Though the Fey-Celierian treaty that prohibited Fey from manipulating mortal thoughts with their magic—and though that was precisely the crime for which Adrial vel Arquinas had been sentenced to death—Ellysetta still did it. She spun a weave of peace upon the enraged men, stealing the raw heat of their anger.

"Sheathe your swords," she commanded, infusing her voice with compulsion. "There will be no more killing here today. Lord Barrial, Rowan, tend to your dead. Lord Sebourne, mourn your son. For the sake of the dear ones each of us have lost, let there be peace between us."

Though Sebourne sheathed his sword, not even Ellysetta's weave was enough to still his anger completely.

"Peace?" he spat. "There will be peace when Celieria and her king are free of Fey manipulations and control." He turned to the king, and declared, "Sebourne will not fight beside these Fey *rultsharts*. I will not spill one more drop of Sebourne blood on their behalf, or trust them at my back. I pray gods you soon find the strength to cut free of their strings."

Raising his voice, Great Lord Sebourne shouted, "Warriors of Sebourne! Mount up. We ride for home!"

CHAPTER ONE

I watch my loved ones weep with sorrow,
death's silent torment of no tomorrow.
I feel their hearts breaking, I sense their despair,
United in misery, the grief that they share.

How do I show that, I am not gone . . .
but the essence of life's everlasting song
Why do they weep? Why do they cry?
I'm alive in the wind and I am soaring high.

I am sparkling light dancing on streams,
a moment of warmth in the rays of sunbeams.
The coolness of rain as it falls on your face,
the whisper of leaves as wind rushes with haste.
> *Eternal Song*, a requiem by Avian of Celieria

Celieria ~ Kreppes
24th day of Verados

"The bodies of Talisa and Adrial have been sent back to the elements," Rain said.

After Talisa's and Adrial's deaths, the King's Army continued marching to the great walled city-fortress of Kreppes to prepare for war. Rain and the Fey had stayed behind with Great Lord Barrial and his sons to say their final good-byes and return the bodies of their loved ones to the elements from whence they came.

Now, as he and Ellysetta stood before Celieria's king in the chambers Great Lord Barrial had surrendered for Dorian's use, Rain feared that the deaths of Adrial, Talisa, and Colum diSebourne on the fields of northern Celieria today had destroyed far more than three lives.

Only one month ago, the Fey had learned that the evil High Mage of Eld intended to unleash a terrible army upon Celieria. An army one of his Mages had compared to the mythic Army of Darkness, a world-conquering force of millions. Rain and Ellysetta had spent weeks trying to cobble together an alliance to combat the threat, but now, thanks to what had happened with Talisa, Adrial, and Colum, the small army they'd managed to assemble was in danger of coming apart at the seams.

King Dorian X of Celieria, who had not risen when Rain and Ellysetta entered, continued to scan the sheets of parchment in his hand as if Rain had not spoken, leaving the king and queen of the Fey to stand before him like chastised children summoned to the schoolmaster's office.

Irritation flickered through Rain. Dorian had a right to his anger—and Rain knew he deserved reproach for hiding Adrial's continued presence in Celieria City from Celieria's king—but he would tolerate no discourtesy towards Ellysetta.

"The Fey stand ready to fight," Rain announced, speaking to the top of Dorian's bent head, "but before this battle begins, King Dorian, the Feyreisa and I must know what impact our recent mutual loss will have on our alliance."

The hands on the parchment froze. The Celierian king's head lifted. Eyes hard as polished stones clashed with Rain's gaze.

"It's a little late for such concerns, don't you think?"

The quiet venom in Dorian's tone came as a surprise. Since

meeting the descendant of Marissya and Gaelen's sister, Marikah vol Serranis, Rain had never regarded Dorian as much more than a too-weak, too-mortal product of a great Fey bloodline. Fey in name only, with little to recommend him as either a strong leader or a seasoned warrior. But there was a new edge to Dorian that Rain had never seen before. A flinty glitter in his eyes and resolute hardness to his jaw.

Trusting, accommodating Dorian vol Serranis Torreval had grown steel in his spine—and with it a decidedly less favorable view of the Fey.

Rain spread his hands in a placating gesture. "King Dorian—"

"You knew!" Dorian kicked back his chair and surged to his feet. "All this time, you knew about Adrial and Talisa. You knew Adrial and the others hadn't gone back to the Fading Lands. Knew they were using their magic to hide their presence from Talisa's husband. You knew, and you condoned it. Not only that—you participated in their deception!" He jabbed a finger in Rain's direction. "You, who posture and pride yourself on Fey honor, intentionally set out to deceive me, the Sebournes, and the Barrials."

Rain's skin flushed. "I know how this must seem—"

"*Seem?*" Dorian gave a harsh, humorless laugh. "You spoke so eloquently about honoring our customs, holding our marriage vows as sacred as your own, and all the while, you plotted to rob a man of his wife. Is this the measure of Fey honor? Is this how low and worthless it has become—or is it merely an indicator of how low and worthless *your* honor has become?"

At Rain's side, Ellysetta bristled, but he silenced her with a small touch of his hand. «*Nei shei'tani. Dorian has a right to his anger. I* did *intentionally deceive him.*»

"You counted on my trust . . . on my belief in your honor," Dorian continued hotly. "You manipulated me like the puppet my own nobles have accused me of being. You used my faith in the goodness of the Fey—even my love for my aunt, Marissya, and my ties of kinship to the Fey—to deceive me. You are the reason three people died today! How I wish I'd heeded Tenn v'En Eilan's warning about you!"

"That's enough!" Ellysetta exclaimed. Her green eyes shot sparks. "How dare you lay full blame for today at his feet? You, who bear as much blame as he?"

"Ellysetta, *las*." Rain pulled her closer, half-afraid of what she might do to Dorian. "Dorian has a right to his anger. I *did* manipulate and deceive him. And I will bear the weight of Adrial and Talisa's deaths, as I bear the weight of all the lives lost to my sword and to my flame." Silently, he added, *«Perhaps Tenn was right, and I truly have lost my way.»* The leader of the Massan, the Fading Lands's governing council, had accused Rain of that when he banished Rain and Ellysetta for weaving the forbidden magic, Azrahn. Had he fallen from the Bright Path and been too blinded by his love for Ellysetta and his hatred of the Eld to realize it?

She whirled on him, anger eclipsed by shock and repudiation of his silent confession. *«Rain, nei. Don't even think that way. You are a champion of Light. Don't you ever doubt it.»* She clasped his face in her hands and stared fiercely into his eyes, as if, by sheer force of will, she could make him believe her.

Turning back to Dorian, she said in a calmer voice, "In his sorrow and guilt over today's terrible loss, my *shei'tan* allows you to heap blame upon him without protest. But I will not. What great evil has he done? He allowed a dying man to spend the last months of his life watching over the woman he loved. If that is a crime, you should pray to the gods you would have the heart to be as guilty as he!"

For the first time since they'd entered this chamber, Dorian looked uncertain. "Vel Arquinas was dying?"

"Ellysetta," Rain murmured a low warning. The high price of *shei'tanitsa* was a dangerous truth Fey never revealed to outsiders.

"Aiyah, he was," she confirmed. *«I'm sorry, Rain, but it's long past time he learned the truth. He is part Fey, after all.»* To Dorian, she continued, "From the moment you

upheld Talisa's Celierian marriage, Adrial's life was over. You did not realize it, but by denying him his *shei'tani*, you condemned him to death."

"Don't be ridiculous." Dorian scowled and began to pace. "Despite what the poets say, a broken heart never killed anyone."

"Perhaps not among mortals, King Dorian," Ellysetta said, "but the same is not true for the Fey. Once a Fey finds his truemate, he has only months to complete the bond, or he will die."

Dorian stopped in his tracks. He turned, glancing uncertainly between the pair of them. "Is this true?" he asked Rain.

Rain sighed, then nodded. "*Aiyah,* it is true."

"But you have yet to complete your bond with the Feyreisa. Are you telling me *you* are dying?"

"I am."

Nonplussed, Dorian leaned back against the window, his hands gripping the stone sill. "How long do you have?"

"Not long. Weeks perhaps. No more than a month or two." Ellysetta's hand crept into Rain's. He squeezed her fingers gently.

"If this is true, why is this the first I've ever heard of it?"

"Ellysetta once asked me the same question. My answer to her was the same as it is to you now: If you had so great a vulnerability, would you let it be known to those who might wish you harm?"

Dorian bristled. "You think I wish you harm?"

"You? *Nei.* But you are king of a people who have shown increasing animosity towards the Fey. It seemed wiser to keep our secrets safe."

"Knowing this," Ellysetta said, "can you now understand why Rain acted as he did? It's true he allowed our Spirit masters to weave the illusion of Adrial and Rowan leaving the city while they remained behind with Talisa's quintet, cloaked in invisibility weaves to avoid detection. And, *aiyah*, he kept the secret of their presence from you so that no blame would fall upon you. But he didn't do it so Adrial could steal another man's wife. He did it so Adrial could spend the last days of his life close to the woman he loved."

Dorian recovered his composure and regarded them both with a mix of suspicion and defensive ire. "Even if vel Arquinas was dying, that doesn't excuse him. To manipulate diSebourne's mind the way he did . . . to run off with the man's wife. Those are not the actions of an honorable man—Fey or mortal."

"Nei," Rain agreed. "They are not. And that is precisely why Adrial would have embraced *sheisan'dahlein,* the Fey honor death, and why no Fey will attempt to avenge him. What Adrial did was wrong. None of us will deny that. But his brother Rowan tells us he was going to do the honorable thing. He was going to leave his *shei'tani* with her husband and return to the Fading Lands."

Dorian's shoulders slumped. "You should have come to me. Trusted me. If I'd known the price of the matebond, I could have tried to do something to spare vel Arquinas's life. Now it's too late. Three lives are lost—one of them the only heir to a Great House. Sebourne and his friends will make certain I regret my indulgence of the Fey."

"I do understand, Dorian, and I will do all that I can to make amends, but we have a far greater threat than Sebourne's vengeance to worry about now. Hawksheart warned us the Eld would attack tonight."

"Tonight? I thought you said the attack would come next week?"

"Apparently, things have changed."

"How many Elves did Hawksheart send to our aid? If the attack does come tonight, will they get here in time?"

Rain hesitated. This, even more than Dorian's anger, was the part of this meeting he'd been dreading. "The Elves are not coming."

The king's brow furrowed. "Lord Hawksheart thinks the Danae alone will be enough against an army as large as the one you expect?" Weeks ago, after warning Dorian to marshall his troops and march to Kreppes, Rain and Ellysetta had traveled south to plead for military assistance from the Danae and the Elves.

"We never met with the Danae. Hawksheart's Elves intercepted us before we crossed Celieria's borders. He promised he would speak to the Danae on our behalf, but even if they agree to come, it will be days, possibly weeks, before they reach Kreppes."

"Then we are doomed." Dorian began to pace again.

"The keep is heavily guarded, and the shields are strong," Rain said. "Between your twelve thousand men, Lord Barrial's two, and my three thousand Fey, we'll give the Eld a good fight. The Mages will not claim one fingerspan of Celierian soil without paying a high price."

"Don't patronize me," Dorian snapped. "I've read the legends about the Army of Darkness. It was millions strong, they say."

"Legends often grow over time."

"Yes, but even if this Mage has built an army only a tenth that size, our seventeen thousand would still be outnumbered twenty to one. If the Elves and the Danae had agreed to fight, we might have stood a chance. *Might*. But now . . ."

"Now, if this Mage truly *has* built an army to rival the legend, the best we can hope is to hold back the tide and kill as many of them as possible before we are overrun," Rain agreed baldly. "And pray our defeat will spur the Elves to action, as our pleas for aid could not."

"You must hold out some hope of success," Dorian insisted. "You would never bring your *shei'tani* here if you thought defeat was certain."

"She is here because I am, but if the situation becomes dire, her quintet will take her to safety."

At his side, Ellysetta went stiff as a poker. *«Rain, I'm not leaving you.»*

«We will talk later.» He would not look at her.

«Nei, we won't. Because there is nothing to talk about. I won't leave you. You're mad if you think I would.»

The corner of his mouth quirked, and despite the seriousness of their situation, he cast her a quick glance that sparkled with wry humor. *«I believe we've already established that, shei'tani, and I'm getting madder by the day.»*

She glowered. *«That's not funny.»*

Thick swaths of embroidered velvet hung across the glass, buffering the room against the chill of the north's snowy winters. Dorian pulled back one of the hangings and peered out across the torchlit northern battlements into the darkness of Eld.

"It is late. My scouts have reported no armies on the horizon. My generals have already sought their beds. I suggest you do the same. If an attack does come tonight, 'tis better we face them rested and ready to fight." Dorian returned to stand beside his desk. "Lord Barrial's servants have prepared a suite for you and the Feyreisa. Her quintet may stay with you, of course, and you may post another quintet to stand watch with the tower guard. But have the rest of your troops make camp outside the walls. I am not the only Celierian unsettled by today's events. Emotions are running high, and I prefer to avoid any potential conflicts."

"Of course." Rain gave the brief half nod that served as a courtesy bow between kings and held out a wrist for Ellysetta's hand. "We have no wish to cause you further distress."

After leaving the king, Rain and Ellysetta went out to the Fey encampment—Rain to meet with his generals and Ellysetta to ease what she could of Rowan's grief. One of Lord Barrial's servants was waiting for them upon their return and showed them to a spacious suite in the inner fortress's west wing.

Now, secure behind her quintet's twenty-five-fold weaves and Kreppes's own impressive shields that self-activated each night at sundown, Ellysetta lay in Rain's arms in the center of the room's opulent bed. A warm fire crackled in the hearth, illuminating the room with a flickering dance of shadows and firelight.

"How is Rowan?" Rain stroked a hand through her unbound hair.

"Devastated." Her head rested on his chest. She snuggled closer, needing the feel of his arm around her, the sound of his heart beating beneath her ear. "The loss of his brother eats at his soul. Bel offered to spin a Spirit weave to Rowan's sister, but that only made things worse. He couldn't bear the thought of telling her their brother is gone. He blames himself for Adrial's death. I don't know how he could possibly think that. None of this was his fault."

"Grief isn't always logical. And with a Fey, it's never mild. Our kind do not love in half measures."

The Fey did nothing in half measures. That intensity of emotion was part of their appeal. It made them the fiercest warriors, the staunchest allies, the most passionate lovers. The most devoted mates.

"I wove what peace on him I could," she said, "but I'm worried. There is a look in his eyes . . . a shadow I've never seen before. Almost as if some part of him died with Adrial, and the rest is only going through the motions of living. When this battle starts, I don't think he intends to live through it."

"I will talk to him tomorrow."

"Thank you." Rain knew loss. He knew what it was to wish for death. Ellysetta traced a pattern across the skin of his chest. She ran a hand down his torso, fingertips stroking the silky-smooth skin. All she had to do was touch him to set her world to rights. "Rain . . ."

"Aiyah?"

"About what you said earlier to Dorian. The bit about my leaving if the battle grows grim."

He caught her hand, stilled it. "I've already commanded your quintet to take you to safety, when the time comes."

She rolled away and propped herself up on one elbow so she could see his face.

"Lord Hawksheart said we should stay together," she reminded him. " 'Do not leave your mate's side,' he said. 'You hold each other to the Light,' he said. And he said we could only defeat the Darkness together."

"He said many things. Most of which I don't trust."

"I see." Ellysetta freed her hand from his and lay down on her back to stare up at the ceiling. "So we kept information from Dorian for our own purposes, yet you expect him to forgive our transgressions and trust us as if nothing has ever happened. But when it's we who are deceived—when it's Lord Galad keeping information from the Fey for his own purposes—somehow that makes *his* every word suspect?"

Dead silence fell over the room, broken only by the snap and pop of the logs on the fire.

Rain sat up, furs spilling into his lap as he twisted to face her. Silky black hair spilled over his muscled shoulders. His brows drew together.

"You think I have treated Dorian the way Hawksheart has treated us?"

She met his gaze. "I think we decided which truths to tell him and which to keep secret, just as the Elves have done to us. So now he distrusts us. Just as we distrust the Elves. Yet somehow you think he should just forget our deceptions and heed our advice without question—while you will not trust Lord Galad."

Rain scowled. "The two are not remotely comparable. Hawksheart left your parents to suffer a thousand years of torment. He sent gods knows how many people to their deaths. He refuses to fight the Darkness he *knows* is coming."

"And three people are dead because we let Adrial stay with his *shei'tani* and hide his presence from the Celierians. And now, though you've been told we must both face the High Mage together, you want to send me away and ensure our defeat."

"You are twisting the facts. I want to keep you alive! How is that so wrong?"

She sat up and put her arms around him. "I don't want to die, Rain. But I won't be sent away so you can sacrifice yourself. You need me." She stroked her fingers through his hair, smoothing the long strands back from his beautiful face. The bond madness was upon him. He fought it every moment of the day, and without her close by, the battle was more difficult. "And I need you, just as much."

The last three weeks, they'd been each other's constant companions, never apart for more than a few chimes, and to-night, when he met with his generals while she went to heal Rowan, she'd felt his absence acutely. She'd come to rely on the strength she drew from him when he was near, just as she'd come to rely on Lord Hawksheart's magical circlet of yellow Sentinel blooms to keep the Mage out of her dreams when she slept. Just this last bell apart from Rain had left her feeling stretched thin. She'd found herself constantly reaching for him through their bond threads, drawing his emotions to her and soothing him with her own. Needing to know that he was close, that he was well, that she was not alone.

It frightened her, a little, how much she needed him.

"Sending me away won't save me, Rain. Without you to keep me strong, it's only a matter of time before the High Mage claims my soul." She already bore four of the six Mage Marks needed to enslave a soul, shadowy bruises upon the skin over her heart, invisible except in the presence of the forbidden Dark magic, Azrahn. Two more Marks, and she would be lost forever. "You know that, even if you want to deny it."

His face crumpled. "I can't lose you."

"And that's why you can't send me away. Because the only way you could ever truly lose me is if the Mage claims my soul. Besides," she added softly, "if you sent me away, where would I go? You're the only family I have left."

Ellysetta was, essentially, an orphan. Mama—Lauriana Baristani, her adoptive mother—had been killed by the Eld. Papa and her two sisters, Lillis and Lorelle, were lost in the magical fog of the Faering Mists. Her Fey parents, Shan and Elfeya v'En Celay, whom she had never met, were prisoners of the High Mage of Eld, and had been for the last thousand years. Except for Rain, she had no other kin.

His head bowed. *Shei'tani.* The word escaped his battered mind, filled with sorrow and despair. "I need to keep you safe."

"The safest place for me is at your side. Whatever happens, we face it together."

His eyes closed and he nodded. "*Doreh shabeila de.*" So shall it be. She pulled him close, stroking his hair and back, and he kissed her tenderly. But when tenderness blossomed to passion, and he would have borne her down upon the bed, she stopped him.

"If this is to be our last night together, *shei'tan,* I don't want to spend it here, in a strange room in a cold castle on the borders."

His brows rose. "Then where would you have us go?"

"To the Fading Lands." When he frowned in confusion, she lifted a hand. The lavender glow of Spirit, the magic of thought and illusion, gathered in her palm. "I want to spend our last night in Dharsa, with our friends and family around us and the tairen singing from the rooftops and the scent of Amarynth in the air."

Rain's lips curved in understanding. "I think, between the two of us, we can arrange that." His weave joined her own, threads merging and spilling out across the room. The walls, the bed, all of Celieria faded away, replaced by the perfect beauty of Dharsa and the gardens near the golden Hall of Tairen. *Faerilas,* the magic-infused waters of the Fading Lands, burbled in exquisite marble fountains, and the air was redolent with the scents of jasmine, honey-blossom, and Amarynth, the flower of life. The Fey were singing, the music rising into a soft evening sky. Fairy flies winked and glittered amidst the flowers and trees.

And there, standing in the great marble arches, stood El-lysetta's family. Mama and Papa and the twins. Her Fey parents, Shan and Elfeya, healthy and whole and free, their faces alight with love. Kieran and Kiel, Adrial and Talisa, and Rain's parents, Rajahl and Kiaria. Even sweet, shy, gentle Sariel, Rain's first love, was there, dancing the Felah Baruk with the joyful Fey maidens and fierce-eyed Fey.

Rain and Ellysetta joined them. They danced and they sang, and as the night deepened, they walked out into the perfumed gardens and made love beneath the stars.

And overhead, the sky was filled with tairen.

And the world was filled with joy.

The Faering Mists

Lillis Baristani had never been happier in her life. She didn't know if she'd died and gone to the Haven of Light or if the Faering Mists was a magical place where dreams came true. Either way, she never wanted to leave. Mama, who died in the Cathedral of Light this summer, was here. And Lillis spent every day glued to her side, sitting beside her on a wooden swing in the misty garden, cooking and laughing with her in the kitchen, lying with her head in Mama's lap as Mama read to her at night. Everything she'd missed since Mama had died. Everything she'd wished she could do again.

Every moment seemed perfect, enchanted. And Mama was even more wonderful than Lillis could ever remember her being. It was as if whatever had happened that day in the Cathedral of Light had changed Mama, stripping her of the fear and disapproval that had so often darkened her eyes.

Tonight, Lillis and Mama cuddled together on the suspended wooden swing Papa had installed on the back of their house, rocking gently as they watched the fairy flies dance across the garden, trailing glittering fairy-fly dust in their wake. As they rocked, Lillis heard herself confess that she and Lorelle had revealed their magic to Papa and to the Fey.

The chime the words were out, she clapped a hand over her mouth and wished them back, but instead of delivering the sharp chide Lillis expected, Mama only smiled and stroked Lillis's hair.

"It's all right, kitling," she said. "I should have told the truth myself long ago, but I was afraid."

That made Lillis's eyes go wide. Mama? Afraid? But she never feared anything. Lillis was the scaredy-cat of the family. "What were you afraid of, Mama?"

"Oh, many things." Mama sighed. "Mostly I was afraid to face the truth about myself. And afraid that what happened to my sister might somehow happen to you or Lorelle or Ellie."

Lillis leaned back to look up at her mother in surprise. "I never knew you had a sister."

"She died long ago." Mama's eyes were dark and sad. "Her name was Bessinita . . . my sweet little Bess . . . and I loved her more than anything in the world." Then Mama had told her how Bess had been a Fire weaver, too, like Lorelle and Mama, only when Bess was two, she accidentally burned a neighbor's house down. The villagers had insisted on winding Bess—taking the baby out into the dark Verlaine Forest and abandoning her there to die.

"What did you do?"

"There wasn't anything I could do. I wasn't even as old as you are now." She rested her chin on the top of Lillis's head. "I prayed and prayed that someone would find her before the *lyrant* did, or if nothing else, that the Bright Lord would send his Lightmaidens to carry Bess away to the Haven of Light."

Tears turned Lillis's vision hazy. "Poor little baby. Poor little Bess."

"That was why I was always so afraid of magic, kitling. Not because I thought you or Lorelle was horrible for having magic, but because I'd been taught that magic was evil, that it could make the people who had it evil, too. I was so afraid of what people would do if they knew."

"But you're not afraid anymore?"

Mama smiled gently. "No, kitling. When I let love be my guide, fear lost its power over me."

"So you're not mad at us for telling?" Lillis asked.

"Of course not." Mama pressed a kiss in Lillis's curls. "I'm very proud of you and Lorelle both, and I'm proud of Ellie, too. I love you all more than I can say."

"I love you too, Mama." Lillis snuggled closer and closed her eyes in bliss. Her arms squeezed tight around Mama's neck, holding her close, and she breathed deep of the special scent that was Mama's own, the scent of home and love and security, where bad people never came, and monsters never howled. "I never want to lose you again."

Mama caressed Lillis's hair in slow, rhythmic strokes, and the beat of her heart thumped reassuringly beneath Lillis's ear. "I'll always be with you, Lillipet. No matter what. If ever you're feeling alone or afraid, just remember that. And remember this, too: We are all the gods' children. All our gifts come from them. It's what we do with those gifts that determines whether we walk in Light or Shadow. The choice is ours. When you see Ellie again, will you tell her that for me? And tell her I said to let love, not fear, be her guide."

"You can tell her yourself. Once Kieran and Kiel get here, we can all go find Ellie together."

Mama smiled. "I think she'll understand it better if it comes from you. Will you promise me, kitling?"

Lillis frowned a little but agreed with an obedient, "Yes, Mama."

"And you won't forget? No matter what?"

"No, Mama."

Her reward was a kiss and another hug. "That's my sweet Lillipet."

Lillis burrowed into her mother's arms, closing her eyes in bliss as Mama's love and warmth enveloped her.

CHAPTER TWO

Celieria ~ Kreppes
25ᵗʰ day of Verados

As the watchtower of Kreppes rang six golden bells, the guards fresh from the dining hall and a good night's sleep climbed the steps to replace the night watch. Soft light from the rising Great Sun lit Celierian fields untouched by war and the perfectly aligned rows of creamy canvas tents fanned out to the west and south of the castle walls. Across the Heras River to the north, the dark fir- and spruce-filled forests of Eld remained empty of all signs of an approaching army.

"Are you so sure they *are* coming?" Dorian asked Rain, as the two kings toured the ramparts. "You claimed the attack would come last night, yet it did not."

"Hawksheart said the attack would come last night," Rain corrected. "I don't know why he misread what he Saw."

"What if you're wrong about *where* the attack is coming, too? What if Celieria City is the real target? I've effectively emptied the city of defenders. I marched half my armies here and sent the other half to King's Point with my son on your word that an attack was imminent. I left only a few garrisons to protect the city itself. Please, tell me I have not made the most colossal mistake of my lifetime."

"Celieria City was neither the target specified by the Mage we captured nor the target Hawksheart warned us to protect," Rain said.

"And yet, here we stand, and there is not an enemy in

sight." The Celierian king folded his arms over his chest. "Or is there perhaps some other important little tidbit of information you've been keeping from me? Some reason you wanted me here that you thought I'd be better off not knowing?"

"*Nei,* there is not. I have always spoken true. I may not have told you everything, but I've never lied to you."

"Oh, right. You don't lie. That would be dishonorable. Instead, you just manipulate and deliberately mislead."

Rain's muscles drew tight as his temper rose. Dorian had a right to his suspicions, but this was deliberate insult. "Are you going to throw that in my face every time I advise you? The enemy may not have attacked last night, as Hawksheart said they would, but there remains no doubt in my mind that they will. There is no doubt in my mind that we are facing the deadliest battle of our lifetime. Our ability to strike any sort of significant blow against this High Mage's army will depend on how closely we can work together, how much we can trust each other."

"Perhaps you should have thought of that before you chose to deceive me." A hard north wind blew Dorian's blue cloak back off his shoulders and tugged strands of dark hair from his queue to whip about his face.

"Spit and scorch me!" Cursing under his breath, Rain stalked to the crenellated edge of the battlement. He grabbed the edges of the stone and held on as tightly as he was holding the fraying edges of his temper.

Ellysetta was down in the encampment with her quintet, checking on Rowan and making the rounds of the Fey and Celierian armies—ostensibly to see if any of the warriors needed healing, but really to start mending fences and rebuilding damaged trust. As important as that was, Rain should have known better than to take this walk with Dorian without her. Thanks to his encroaching bond madness, his ability to control his temper proved elusive when he strayed too far from Ellysetta's side. Even the smallest conflict sparked his tairen's ire—and considering that a tairen's idea of diplomacy was to flame-roast his opponent and eat his smoking carcass, that was not particularly helpful.

Rain stared across the river at Eld and counted to ten. The enemy, he reminded himself, lay there—across the river. Not standing here beside him. He clung to that truth and used it to force back the growing threat of his tairen.

"I've already said I was wrong," he told Celieria's king. "But do not forget—the decision I made came after a summer full of difficulties dealing with your people. I warned you war was coming, but you and your Council ignored my concerns and rejected my warnings until the Eld attacked the Grand Cathedral of Light and tried to capture my *shei'tani*." Ellysetta would have been proud of how calm and controlled he sounded, how neatly he laid out his argument, when all he really wanted to do was grab Dorian by the throat and shake some sense into him. "The anti-Fey sentiment so prevalent amongst your nobles—your Queen, among them—was still fresh in my mind."

"All Annoura and those nobles ever did was warn me that Fey would manipulate mortal minds. It seems to me that all you did with the whole Talisa and Adrial fiasco was prove them right!"

Rain drew a long, deliberate breath. "As I told you," he reiterated slowly, "I did what I thought best at the time. Adrial remained with his *shei'tani*, but I tried to make certain that if his presence had been discovered, you would be absolved of all blame."

"So you lied to me—manipulated me—for my own benefit?"

"You and I are kings, Dorian. You know as well as I do that in politics, truth is often the first casualty. I doubt you can claim with any shred of honesty that you've never manipulated facts or obfuscated in order to avoid a conflict or do what you believed was right." When Dorian did not immediately reply, Rain knew the thrust had struck home. "Fey do not lie. That puts us at a severe disadvantage when dealing with mortals who have no such scruples. So, we have learned to dance the blade's edge of truth, to veil truths we do not wish to share. It is a survival tactic we have found necessary when dealing with your kind."

"I *am* your kind—or so I always believed myself." Dorian was the descendant of Marikah vol Serranis of the Fey, Gaelen vel Serranis's twin. "But apparently my blood is not Fey enough for you to feel the same—or to trust me as I have always trusted you."

"*Setah,*" Rain rumbled. "Enough." His hands slashed through the air with curt command. "What is done cannot be undone. Will you allow hubris to keep us at each other's throats, or can we agree mistakes were made on both sides and move on?"

"Hubris?" Dorian's brows rose. "Is it hubris to want to know how far I can trust an ally?"

"You can trust us to defend Celieria from the Eld!" Rain snapped. "You can trust us to stand against our common enemy and give no quarter. To die by your side. You can trust that the Fey will not leave this battlefield so long as a single Eld soldier stands with weapon in hand. Can that not be enough?"

"I suppose it will have to be."

Ill-humored and grudging though it was, that was the sound of capitulation. Rain closed his eyes for a brief moment and drew another long, deep breath of the icy northern air. His nerves felt as if he'd just spent a full day being scoured and pummeled by the Spirit masters of the Warrior's Academy. His head hurt, and every muscle in his body was clenched tight with the effort he'd expended to keep his dangerous temper and wayward thoughts in check.

"*Beylah vo,* King Dorian."

Dorian put his hands on the cold stone and leaned over one of the deep crenels as he gazed northward into Eld. "So you do truly believe they're coming?"

"There's not a doubt in my mind. The Mage we Truth-spoke said the attack would come this week. If the Eld have been watching our buildup here at Kreppes, it's possible they may choose a different place to cross the river, but let us wait at least this week before we assume our information is wrong."

Dorian considered the request, then gave a curt nod. "Very well. We wait. But if there is no sign of attack within the week, I will have no choice but to redeploy my armies. There are other locations of greater strategic importance than Kreppes."

"Agreed," Rain said. "And I will send my warriors wherever you need us most. Until then, I think it best to continue our preparations for battle. As we learned in Teleon and Orest, just because we can't see the armies of Eld doesn't mean they aren't there."

"I will inform the generals to give you whatever assistance you require."

Rain started to leave, then paused. "And Dorian? For what it's worth, if I had to do it over, I would tell you about Adrial. You are right. I did you a disservice by keeping that truth from you."

Celieria's king—the mortal descendant of an ancient Fey line—nodded without turning. Rain left him there, standing on the ramparts, solemn and solitary, morning sunlight glinting on his crown, the bright Celierian blue of his cape snapping in the wind.

In a small tent in the heart of the allied encampment, Ellysetta sat beside Rowan vel Arquinas, holding his hand and sharing his grief over Adrial's death. Tears spilled, unchecked, down her face. Adrial and Rowan both had served on her first quintet, back in Celieria City, before she'd known she was Fey, in a time when all their lives had been happier and more carefree.

Since the day she just met them, the brothers, Rowan and Adrial, had done everything together. And though to mortals, the seventy-year difference between Rowan's age and his brother's might have seemed insurmountable, by Fey standards they were practically twins. They'd even looked alike, both black-haired, brown-eyed, full of mischief and laughter. Rowan, especially, had an almost tairen-fondness for playing pranks.

The Fey who sat beside Ellysetta now was a shadow of his former self. All the happiness, the laughter, the mischievous glint in his dark eyes was gone. In its place lay a cloud of such overwhelming grief she didn't know how he could even move.

"I failed him," he whispered, his voice cracked and broken by all the helpless tears he'd shed.

"Oh, *nei*." Her chin trembled on a sudden swell of emotion. She wrapped her arms around him as if comforting a child. "*Nei*, Rowan, *nei, kem'ajian*. You didn't. He would never want you to say that—not even to think it."

"But I did. My *mela* told me to look over him. To keep him safe. And I didn't."

Ellysetta didn't mean to pry, but with her arms around Rowan and her empathic senses so enmeshed with his, she couldn't block out the vivid, memory of the day Rowan's mother had placed the precious, squirming little Adrial in his arms for the first time.

"Rowan, my son, meet your brother, Adrial," she'd said.

And Rowan had oh-so-carefully held his brother and gazed down at him in awestruck wonder. Baby Adrial's bright, inquisitive brown eyes had been wide open and sparkling with hints of what would become great magic. A tiny, waving hand had caught the tip of Rowan's finger and curled around it in a tight fist. In that touch flowed a warm, bright haze of wordless emotion: security, trust, and most of all, perfect innocent joy. Rowan had been little more than a Fey youth himself—the blood of his first battle had yet to wet his steel—but with that first touch of radiant, untarnished innocence, he had known he would suffer any fate, pay any price, sell his soul to the Dark Lord himself, if it meant he could keep his brother safe.

Yet here he stood, still alive, and Adrial was gone. Rowan

had failed him. Failed the promise he'd made to their mother to always keep his brother safe.

Tears gathered in Rowan's eyes and spilled over in a flood. Harsh sobs racked his warrior's body. He could have taken a sword to the chest with naught but a brief gasp, but this loss ripped his vulnerable Fey heart to shreds.

Holding him, sharing his pain, Ellysetta wept, too. He needed to grieve, so she grieved with him. Sharing his memories, sharing his torment, taking it into her soul and giving him back what small measure of peace he would accept. She stayed with him, soothing him, singing to him, weeping with him, until together they had drained enough of his sorrow that he could sink into the much-needed peace of the sleep she wove on him.

When she finally emerged from Rowan's tent, Rain was there, waiting. Wordlessly, he opened his arms, and with a fresh spill of tears, she fell into them.

"Oh, Rain." She closed her eyes and clung tight to him as if she could absorb some measure of his strength. And perhaps she did. He was her rock, her haven in the storm, and it was to his soul, his love, that she'd anchored all the happiness left in her life.

If anything ever happened to him . . . The mere thought made her shudder.

Eld ~ Boura Maur

The Tairen Soul and his mate were in Kreppes.

An unexpected thrill of anticipation curled in the High Mage Vadim Maur's belly when he received the news from his assistant, Primage Zev, one of the handful of Mages who had been with Vadim since their earliest days as Novice greens. Of all the Mages now living, Zev was the one Vadim mistrusted least. He was an experienced Primage who knew his limitations—one of which was a lesser command of Azrahn than Vadim possessed.

"How many tairen are with them?" he asked.

"Just the Tairen Soul, Most High."

"Elves?"

"No sign of them."

Fezai Madia had been bragging that the harrying tactics of her Feraz on Elvia's southern border were keeping Hawksheart and his minions occupied. Perhaps she was right, after all.

"Primage Soros?"

"Awaiting your orders, Most High."

"Excellent." Vadim rose from behind his desk and stretched, enjoying the youthful tug and pull of supple muscles in his new, virile body. Gethen Nour, the Primage whose body Vadim Maur now inhabited, had tended his form well. Pity he had not been so conscientious about tending his work. "Zev, old friend, it's time to prepare for conquest."

"Yes, Most High."

"Come with me." Vadim strode from his office, and Zev hurried close behind. Purple robes and blue swept over black stone as the two Mages ascended to the uppermost level of Boura Fell. There, in a large room fitted with skylights that traveled up through more than four tairen lengths of rock to the forest floor above, a hundred Feraz, recently come from Koderas, had assembled. On the far side of the room, brightly garbed *fezaros*, Feraz cavalry, crooned to their caged *zaretas*, the swift tawny cats of their desert land that they rode into battle. Nearer to the door, twenty Feraz witches sent by their leader, Fezai Madia, amused themselves by trying to ensnare the Mages and soldiers Vadim had set to guard them.

When the witches caught sight of Vadim, six of the sloe-eyed beauties headed his way, hips swaying, bright silk veils fluttering, ankle bells jingling an exotic invitation with each step. They surrounded him and trailed silken, perfumed hands over his chest, his arms, his back. The air around him grew heavy, warm and sweet and intoxicating.

"At last, they have sent us a handsome one."

"Look at his hands. Such strong hands." Smaller, feminine palms brushed perfumed skin in a simulated caress. Breasts rubbed against his arm. Moist lips skimmed across his neck, his jaw, his ears.

"Are you so strong everywhere, *zaro*?" Nimble fingers darted under his robes and reached for the fastenings of the silk trousers he wore beneath.

In his old body, Vadim had been mostly immune to the seductive enchantments of Feraz witch women, but the lust surging through his new, youthful body as the witches worked their wiles made it clear that was no longer the case. And it gave him a new understanding of Gethen Nour, the Primage who had inhabited this body before Vadim. He'd always despised Nour's endless carnal indulgences—a powerful Mage controlled his urges; he did not let his urges control him—but if this ravenous hunger was a force Nour had constantly battled, no wonder he'd given in so often.

Now, however, was *not* the time to surrender to such urges. What the Mages did with Azrahn—enslaving the souls of the weak—Feraz witches achieved through seduction. When a man surrendered to the sensual spell of a Feraz witch, she could bind him to her will, enslave him with her touch, her scent, her body, until he would rip his own flesh apart to please her.

With more effort than he cared to acknowledge, Vadim suppressed the lust screaming through his veins and caught the wrist of the witch unfastening his trousers.

"Enough," he said. "In a battle of power with me, my dear, you would not like the outcome. Ask your Fezai Madia what happened to the last witch who tried to bend Vadim Maur to her will."

The witch in his grip went still, and most of the sultry promise blanked from her beautiful face, leaving a look of wary suspicion. "You are *Chazah* Maur?"

"I am."

"But I was told *Chazah* Maur was an old man. Not one so young and"—her gaze swept over him—"*dazoor.*"

His lip curled. Like most of the Feraz language, *dazoor*

was a word with many meanings. When applied to an object, like a house, it meant sturdy, well built for its purpose. When applied to a man, it meant much the same thing, but considering that Feraz witches considered men good for only two things—muscles and mating—the connotation translated to something more like "strong and mountable."

"I'll take that as a compliment to my new form, Fezaiina, but rest assured, I am the same Mage—with the same power—as before. So I suggest you and your sisters save your seductions for the Celierians and the Fey. I need my men and my Mages clearheaded and under my control. I will not take it kindly if I find you've interfered with that."

"Zim, Chazah." The witch lowered her lashes and inclined her head. "As you command."

"Good. Now give me an update on the potion you have been working on. Is it ready?"

"The potion has been tested and approved by your Primage Grule in Koderas," the witch said. "My sisters and I are waiting on the rest of our supplies, then we can begin preparing the potion in the quantities you require."

"How long will that take?"

"Once we receive what we need? Three days, *Chazah.*" Then, because no Feraz witch could help herself for long, the Fezaiina trailed a hand across his shoulder. "Time enough for other things, hmm?"

He caught her wrist again and this time wrenched it hard enough that the sultry seduction in her eyes became a dangerous glitter. "Do not press me. I will see that you get what you need. You see that you do what you've promised." He thrust her away from him.

The Fezaiina rubbed her wrist and regarded him from beneath her lashes. *"Zim, Chazah."*

"Watch them," Vadim told Zev when they exited the room. "Make sure no one goes near those women without first being warded against Feraz witchspells. And don't let the same men guard them more than once."

"Yes, Most High."

"Be sure they get what they need for their potion. I want twenty barrels of the stuff in four days' time."

"Yes, Most High."

"And see to it our friend Lord Death gets well fed. I want him strong and healthy by the end of next week. I have a feeling I'll be needing him soon."

Zev bowed without question. "Of course, Most High. I'll see to it immediately."

When the call came for the feeding of Lord Death, the High Mage's oldest and most treasured prisoner, the *umagi* Melliandra made sure she was the one chosen. A full week had passed since Lord Death had nearly slain the High Mage, and though she'd practically had to tie herself to the wall to keep from going to him, she'd deliberately stayed away until now. She couldn't afford to draw attention to herself by constantly being first in line to tend the most powerful prisoner in Boura Fell. The Mistress of Kitchens would get suspicious, and Melliandra's careful, quiet plans for freedom would be ruined.

Tray in hand, Melliandra hurried down the winding stairs to the lowest level of Boura Fell and down to the last door at the end of the long, dark corridor. There, behind a *sel'dor* reinforced door, inside a narrow cage forged of floor-to-ceiling spiked *sel'dor* rods, his body pierced and manacled and weighted down by more *sel'dor* than any other prisoner had ever survived—and *still* guarded twenty-four bells a day—Shannisorran v'En Celay, Lord Death, the greatest Fey warrior ever born, lay captive.

He remained hidden in the shadows in the corner of his cage when she entered. She knew why—and it wasn't the same reason *umagi* darted for cover when a Mage approached, or tunnel rats fled when a torch drew near. Lord Death didn't hide in the shadows because he was afraid. He lurked there because he was a predator, blending into his surroundings as he stalked potential prey and calculated the probabilities of a successful attack.

She should have feared him. She wasn't sure why she didn't except that she needed him.

"They tell me you haven't been eating." She set the tray down and pushed it towards the cell bars. She hadn't been able to hide her surprise when the Mistress of Kitchens put an enormous, steaming bowl on the tray and commanded that Lord Death must consume every drop. The usual fare for prisoners was cold, fatted porridge, leftovers from *umagi* meals. Today, however, the food on the tray was a savory stew, thick broth swimming with plump grains, chunks of real meat (which did not look like or smell like tunnel rat), mushrooms, and chopped tuberoots. Melliandra had never had fare so rich. She'd never even been this close to such a feast. Her stomach growled loudly, something it had been doing since the moment she picked up the tray.

"Sounds like you need the food more than I." Lord Death's low voice rasped from the darkness.

She licked her lips. The temptation to sneak a taste was so strong she could hardly bear it. She closed her eyes and breathed in the heavenly aroma. "It's hot. It smells too good to waste. Come, eat. You need your strength."

"Why? Because you need me strong enough to kill the Mage for you?"

"Ssh!" She shot a look over her shoulder. The door to the cell was cracked open. "Voices carry in this place." Thankfully, the guard wasn't listening. Judging from the blissful sighs and sounds of slurping, the cup of stew she'd given him from Lord Death's bowl was holding the guard's full attention.

She turned back to Shan. "And yes, that's why. You nearly killed him last week. I thought for a moment, I was free."

Like a *darrokken* springing on its prey, Lord Death exploded from the shadow, crossing the cell in a single leap. His hands curled around the spiked cell bars. Eyes glowing bright, teeth bared and savage, he snarled, "You should have let my mate die. You should have let *us* die. Why didn't you, for pity's sake?" Then, as abruptly as it had come, his fury faded. He slumped against the bars of the cage, and his whole demeanor changed from anger to despair. "What have we ever done to you that you should keep us in such torment?"

She looked away. Pity was a stranger to her, shame even less familiar. But she felt both now.

"I couldn't let you die," she whispered. "You're my only hope." Her voice almost broke then, and she had to stop and clear her throat. *Don't be such a mush-hearted fool, Melliandra. You'll destroy everything.* But she could practically feel his pain as if it were her own. She knew what it was to be caged, to long for freedom that never came.

She gave herself a mental shake and sat up straight, steeling her resolve. She needed this man to keep his promise, and not just for herself. For Shia's son, too. Only if the High Mage died could they be free.

"You're the only one capable of killing the High Mage. He fears you. Everyone in Boura Fell knows that. The only thing he fears more is a Tairen Soul, and since it's unlikely a Tairen Soul will make an appearance here anytime soon, that leaves you. I need you to kill him. It's the only way."

"The only way what?"

"The only way to be free." A lifetime of caution stopped Melliandra from mentioning Shia's child. She even tucked away all thought of him in that secret place in her mind where even the Mage could not go. "So long as the High Mage lives, there's no life, no freedom for me. He owns my soul."

"Then how is it possible you are here, asking me to kill him for you? I thought no *umagi* could plot against his master."

"That's none of your business."

"If you want my help, you'll make it my business."

She glared at him in stubborn silence.

His brows rose, and he crossed his arms. "I have nothing but time, little *umagi*."

She huffed a frustrated breath, then dug a small cup from her pocket and thrust it through the cell bars. "Fine. Eat your stew, and I'll tell you."

Shan tilted the serving cup and shook more of the stew into his mouth. It was good. *Jaffing* good. The best food he'd had in years, possibly even centuries.

"So there's a secret place in your mind where you can hide thoughts from the Mages?" he repeated as he chewed the flavorful chunks of meat. The little *umagi* had told him about how one day she'd discovered that she could keep secrets from the Mage, and how she'd been testing it over the last months. "So where did it come from? How did you create it?"

"I don't know. One day it was just there. And I realized that what thoughts I keep there are private. The High Mage can't see in. It's like a room protected by privacy weaves, and it gets larger the more thoughts I keep there. That's how I can have this conversation with you and know he will never learn of it." She watched him dip his cup into the bowl again, and when he carried it to his mouth, she licked her lips.

Despite a thousand years of horrendous torture, despite a soul-deep enmity for the Eld, the Fey called Lord Death felt his heart squeeze with pity. Poor child. Those big, hungry eyes of hers had been tracking every move of the serving cup since he'd begun to eat, and even the hand pressed hard against her stomach hadn't been able to quiet its growls. If her presence was another of Vadim Maur's twisted games of torment, it was the best attempt of the millennia. Because, gods help him, he had fallen for it.

"Do all *umagi* have this secret place?" Shan drained the cup in two mouthfuls.

"I don't think so. I think I'm the only one."

"The stew is very good. You should have some yourself."

He offered her the serving cup and nudged the half-eaten bowl of stew towards her. "Go on. Every child deserves a treat now and again."

Her eyes flashed up, molten silver and full of sudden ire and cynicism. "I'm no child. And treats are just bait to trap the stupid."

"No bait here, child. Just a shared cup to seal our . . ." he started to say "friendship" but realized the little *umagi* would probably ruffle up some more, so he settled on a different word, ". . . agreement." It hurt his Fey heart that any child should be so misused she suspected a trap in even the simplest kindness. "*Teska*. Please. It's really quite delicious."

The offer was too much temptation to refuse. She snatched the cup from his hand, dipped it in the bowl, and poured the still-warm stew into her mouth. Her eyes closed in bliss. Judging by the look on her face, she'd probably never tasted anything so good in her life. That realization hurt, too. His heart wept for her—almost as much as it wept for the daughter of his own blood whom he'd never seen, never held.

"In the Fading Lands, *kaidina,* you would have been cherished and pampered every day of your life. Not a chime would go by that you did not know how greatly you were loved. Your father would have carried you so proudly in his arms, and sung young songs from ages past to make you smile, and rocked you to sleep spinning Fey-tale weaves of beautiful *shei'dalin* maidens and their brave *shei'tans,* while fairy flies sparkled in the gardens outside your window. And every warrior of the Fey would willingly lay down his life to save you from the slightest harm."

Rather than growing misty-eyed by his maudlin confession of fatherly dreams, the little *umagi* took umbrage. "I am Eld. Your warriors would have killed me on the spot and left my bones for the rats." She handed his serving cup back through the bars. "So will you kill the Mage, or won't you?"

Shan understood. She was an Elden *umagi,* brutalized since birth, suspicious of the slightest kindness. She did not need or want his useless dreams of a Fey-tale childhood. She did not need or want his friendship. Very well. He would not let his Fey heart be softened by the vulnerable appeal of too-big eyes in a too-thin face.

"I need my *sorreisu kiyr*," he said. "My Soul Quest crystal. I tried to kill your Mage without it and failed. If you want me to kill him, you need to get me that crystal."

CHAPTER THREE

Celieria ~ Dunbarrow Manor
27ᵗʰ day of Verados

Damn the Fey! Damn Dorian and that Fey-lover Barrial!

Grief and rage writhed like snakes in Great Lord Dervas Sebourne's chest. He paced the confines of his study in Dunbarrow on unsteady feet. Small waves of sea-green Sorrelian *quist*—a highly intoxicating liquor distilled from a fermented blend of sweet sea grapes and deadly moonshade—sloshed over the rim of the crystal tumbler clenched in one fist.

Dervas lifted his glass and tossed back its contents in a single gulp, barely feeling the fiery burn as the potent liquor slid down his throat. This wasn't his first glass of *quist* tonight, and it wouldn't be his last. When a man lost his only son and saw the end of his Great House looming on the horizon, his soul craved a stronger balm than pinalle.

Dervas harbored no illusions about his future. King Dorian would not leave unpunished the Great Lord who had spat defiance and insult, then taken his men and ridden away from the coming battle with Eld. Sebourne had broken with the king, and Great House Sebourne would soon sink into disfavor and, ultimately, into obscurity.

And with it would go the power he'd meant to pass on to his son.

His only *son*.

His *dead* son. The son who'd been murdered, his body so completely destroyed there wasn't even a corpse over which Dervas could mourn, as a father should. Nothing. Just emptiness where a life had been.

All because of the Fey—and that weak, spineless puppet

of a king who sat on the throne of Celieria while the Fading Lands pulled his strings.

Damn them! Damn them all! He hoped the Eld slaughtered them and left their corpses for thistlewolves and *lyrant* to feast upon. Renewed fury seized him, amplified by intoxication. Dervas shot to his feet and hurled his glass of *quist* into the hearth. Crystal exploded. Flames leapt with a roar as the potent liquor ignited.

The blast of heat and the sudden change in attitude left him overwarm and swaying on his feet, so he stumbled to the window that looked out over Dunbarrow's western fortifications and threw open the sash. Cold winter air flooded in. He thrust his head out the window and took a deep breath.

The moons overhead were both three-quarters full, the Mother waning, the Daughter waxing. This week, the brightest nights in the last three months signaled the last hurrah of Light before both moons went new two weeks hence.

Something about that was important. He frowned and rubbed his temple as a band of pain tightened around his skull. With a groan, he pressed the heels of his palms against his bloodshot eyes and staggered away from the window, only to freeze when he saw a dark shape move in the corner of the room. Suddenly, the air in Dervas's lungs grew short. Each breath became a labored gasp, and his heart beat a rapid tattoo. Shadow flickered at the edges of his vision, and a strange, sickly sweet smell filled his nose. For an instant, he wasn't standing in his study in Dunbarrow, he was back in Old Castle Prison in Celieria City, watching in mute horror as a figure wreathed in icy shadow stepped towards him.

The image of Old Castle faded, but the shadowy figure remained. It stepped into the light. Blue robes gleamed richly in the candlelight, and dark jewels glittered on a silken sash that hung from the intruder's waist.

Dervas reached for his sword, but his waist was bare, his weapons belt lying useless in his bedchamber. "Who are you?" he demanded. "What are you doing here? What do you want?"

Gloved hands pushed back the robe's deep cowl, revealing a ghostly-white face and eyes like the blackest pits of the seventh Hell.

"Nerom, umagi," the creature uttered. "Remember."

Dervas squeezed his eyes shut and shook his head, but invisible floodgates flung open in his mind, pouring out decades of suppressed memories in a wild deluge.

The shadowy figure who'd come to visit him in Old Castle assumed a face—Lord Bolor, a newly invested minor lord who'd recently come to court. Only Lord Bolor wasn't a Celierian at all. He was an Elden Mage masquerading as a Lord to gain access and influence over the Celierian court. And he'd come to command Dervas, on behalf of the High Mage of Eld, just as other Mages had come to command Dervas in the past.

Just as Mages had commanded every Great Lord Sebourne before him—ever since the minor lord Deridos Sebourne, vassal of the Great House Wellsley, had traded his soul in exchange for power and wealth three hundred years ago.

In return for Deridos's soul, the Mages had engineered and released the Great Plague that had wiped out the Wellsley family, along with half the inhabitants of northern Celieria. When, in the resulting fear and chaos, Deridos not only successfully defended Moreland from an Eld attack but also "discovered" the cure for the Great Plague, a grateful King Dorian VI had raised House Sebourne to Greatness and granted to it the vital border estates previously entailed to Great House Wellsley.

The Eld had been using Sebourne land as their Celierian base ever since. Over time, every inhabitant of Sebourne land, from infant to elder, peasant to Great Lord, had been bound to the Mages of Eld. Dervas had surrendered his own infant son to the Mages when they came calling, as had every Great Lord since Deridos. Those who married into

Great House Sebourne surrendered their souls as well—
some willingly, others less so.

Dervas shuddered as his Mage induced "memory" of his
wife dying in childbirth along with their second son was replaced with a clear vision of his wife weeping, arms clasped
protectively around the small mound of their unborn child,
as she stood on the battlements of Moreland Castle. The
day was Colum's first birthday, and the Mages had come to
claim him and his mother, Great Lady Sebourne.

"You call yourself a Great Lord?" she cried. "You're nothing but a slave to an evil master. Worse, you've damned our
son to the same enslavement! Well, at least this child will be
free! And so will I!" And with that, she leapt to her death
rather than accept a Mage Mark for herself or her second
child.

Now, standing here, stunned into sobriety by those memories, he realized she'd been right. He wasn't a Great Lord.
He wasn't any sort of lord at all. He was a *slave*. A witless,
unsuspecting puppet of the Mages.

Oh gods.

The Primage smiled. "Oh god," he corrected in lightly
accented Celierian. "Seledorn, to be precise, the mighty
Dark Lord, God of Shadows. And, yes, I hear your thoughts.
There is no part of your mind I cannot enter. No thought or
action I cannot control. I am the Mage who claimed you, and
all that you are is mine."

Sebourne's stomach clenched in a tight knot, and the
blood rushed from his face. With a choked cry, he spun to
one side and retched into the waste bin by his desk until
nothing remained in his belly but bitter gall.

"Clean yourself up, *umagi,* and come kneel before me."

Dervas didn't give his body the command, but his hands
wiped a cloth across his face and his feet began walking.
He tried to fight it, tried to make himself stop, but it was as
if he were merely an observer trapped in some other person's form. He circled the desk and crossed the room, then
dropped to his knees before the Mage.

"You see?" The Primage shook his head. "Still you wish to rebel. You always do." He sighed. "Very well. Go to the hearth—no, on your hands and knees. You are my dog, *umagi*, and I am your master."

Weeping, but unable to refuse, Dervas crawled.

"Your right hand offends me," the Mage said when he reached the stone hearth. "Put it in the fire."

"No, please!" But his hand was already reaching for the flames. "Please!" Then, because now he remembered all the times before, the prices he'd paid for his attempted but never-successful rebellions over the years, he cried, "Please, master! Please, master, forgive your worthless *umagi*."

His hand stopped moving towards the fire, but he was still close enough he could feel the heat licking at his skin. Unless the Mage released him, his hand would slow roast. And the Mage would make sure Dervas felt every torturous moment.

"Will you serve me, *umagi*, of your own volition, or must I force your obedience as I am doing now?"

"I will serve! Please, I will serve!"

"Then speak your vow, Dervas, son of Gunvar, and speak it with conviction."

Dervas closed his eyes and spoke the mantra of surrender and obedience he'd been taught so long ago. "This *umagi* serves you willingly, master. Whatever your command, he obeys without hesitation. This life and this body are yours to use or destroy."

"You may rise."

Dervas dragged in a sobbing breath of relief and rose on shaking legs. "What is it you require of this *umagi*, master?"

The Primage smiled. "It is time for you to fulfill your purpose."

Celieria ~ Kreppes
27th day of Verados

The hooves of a thousand horses thundered in the night. An army of men, outfitted for war, rode across the fields and

woods of northern Celieria, Great Lord Dervas Sebourne
at the lead. The army moved swiftly, covering the miles between Dunbarrow and Kreppes without stopping.

*You will ride to Kreppes with your army. You will beg
an audience with the king and throw yourself on his mercy,
pleading with him to forgive your anger on the day your son
died. Grief and your distrust of the Fey drove you mad, you
will say. Remind him of his own son and how he would feel
should Prince Dorian perish.*

*But you have had time for that first rage to pass. You are
a Celierian, and loyal to your king. You request the honor
of fighting by his side. Above all, you beg to be near because
you do not trust the Fey.*

*Remind him of how they lied to him, how they manipu-
lated him into believing what they wanted him to believe. Are
those the actions of a loyal race? Trusted allies? No, they are
not. Lord Barrial may trust the Fey implicitly, but would it
not be better for the king to keep at least one advisor by his
side who is not so blind to the possibility of Fey duplicity?*

Lord Sebourne's army reached the perimeter encampments around Kreppes before the tower watch struck nine
silver bells. Campfires burned across the fields around the
fortress, illuminating the rows of neatly ordered tents, both
Celierian and Fey. Amongst the Celierian tents, pennants
from the King's Army fluttered alongside those of the Border
Lords who'd sent troops in answer to their king's call, Great
Lord Barrial, the new Great Lord Darramon, all of the lesser
lords from hundreds of miles around.

Dervas noted the familiar crests as he left the bulk of his
army waiting at arrow point on the outskirts of the encampments while he and a personal guard of six men rode, under
escort, towards the city gates.

And if the king does not grant me an audience?

*You'd better hope he does, umagi. Else you will cause
such as scene you will get thrown in the castle jail. One way
or another, I want you inside that fortress where you are*

supposed to be. Where you would be had you not ridden off in a fit of pique after the Fey killed your son.

Yes, master.

Good. Now, Primage Nour gave you a necklace when he visited you in Old Castle Prison, did he not? Fetch it.

Torches burned on the sides of Kreppes's great gates. Bowmen stood at attention on the tower, their arrows nocked and aimed at Dervas as the gatekeeper and his companions approached.

"I am come to see the king," Dervas informed the gate-keeper with cold command. "Tell him Great Lord Sebourne requests an audience."

The guards at the gate made him wait. Two pikemen blocked the way while a runner went for permission to admit Great Lord Sebourne and his entourage into the castle.

Dervas sat tall and proud in the saddle, staring down his nose at the king's men. He had come garbed for war, but that did not stop him from looking as resplendent as a Great Lord ought. His armor gleamed to a mirror polish. A thickly furred cape attached to his epaulets, flowing back in regal splendor over the scale-armored rump of his mount. A thick gold chain circled his neck, the heavy, jeweled links carved with symbols of protection, each link growing larger and more elaborate as it neared the jewel's set piece—two gleaming white stones, one round and a smaller, crescent shape to symbolize the Mother and Daughter moons, set above a sparkling amber crystal surrounded by a ring of stylized waves suggesting the radiance of the Great Sun's corona.

You will keep this necklace with you at all times. Waking, sleeping, in the bath. You will not take it off for any reason, understood?

Yes, master.

Good. There is one particular danger you must watch out for. The Tairen Soul keeps one who was once dahl'reisen by his side.

Yes, master. Gaelen vel Serranis.

They say he can detect Mage Marks. If they discover you are Mage claimed, they will either put you to death or put you under such great guard as to be useless to us. So if vel Serranis is summoned to check you for Mage Marks, speak the word Gamorraz *to activate the larger of the two white stones.*

What does the stone do? Is it a weapon?

Of a sort. Just keep it close and use it if you must to keep from being discovered. The amber crystal will let me hear your thoughts, while warding against all but the most deliberate attempts by others to do the same.

The runner returned and whispered in the gatekeeper's ear. The gatekeeper turned to Lord Sebourne and said, "His Majesty will grant you the audience you have requested, Great Lord Sebourne. But you and your men will not be permitted to bring weapons into the castle."

Sebourne drew back. "I've come to defend my country against invasion, and I am not permitted to carry a weapon?"

"I'm sorry, my lord, but not into the castle. Your weapons will be stored in the armory and returned to you in the event of an attack. His Majesty prays you will understand the precaution."

Dervas caught sight of a Fey warrior beyond the gate. The Fey was clad for war, his black armor bristling with a full complement of silvery Fey blades. "A Great Lord of Celieria must surrender his weapons, but Fey wander the castle freely, carrying enough steel to slaughter an entire regiment? Where is the sense in that?"

The gatekeeper didn't even have the courtesy to look embarrassed. "King's orders, my lord. You must surrender your weapons here at the gate."

Dervas capitulated with ill grace. He turned in the saddle and nodded to his men. They all immediately began unbuckling their sword belts. Dervas tossed his to the gatekeeper, then bent down to remove his boot daggers and hand those over as well.

"Two swords. Two daggers. Shall I surrender my shield,

too? Who knows, I might bludgeon someone with it in a fit of rage."

The gatekeeper ignored the sarcasm and answered with studied politeness, "If you wish us to hold your shield, my lord, we would be happy to do so."

"Bah." Dervas waved a gauntleted hand.

"If you and your men will dismount, my lord, we will stable your horses."

Dervas dismounted and handed his reins to one of the guards. With his men at his heels, he walked through the gates of Kreppes.

Once you are in the castle, you will make note of everything you see. Troop counts, location of the guards, artillery on the battlements, entrances and exits, defensive positions, any weakness that can be exploited. There is nothing too large or too small for you to consider.

And finally, once you've had your audience with the king, you will make it your business to discover where in the castle the Feyreisen and his mate are lodged. Every detail you noted about the castle, you will also note about their location. Where it is, all the ways to access it, what time they rise and retire, how many and which warriors guard them, anything and everything you can think of. You will find a way to secrete this stone in their room or just outside it.

The guards escorted Dervas across the outer courtyard, which housed stables, secondary barracks, training fields, as well as houses and workshops for the small, walled city that was Kreppes. A second gated wall surrounded the pentagon-shaped inner castle. Dervas noted the towers every two tairen lengths along the battlements of the crenellated second wall, the location of the armory and second barracks, each set of stairs leading up to the battlements, the number of guards standing the walls.

Only a handful of Fey stood among the Celierians on the walls, and that surprised him. Dorian was such a Fey-lover, he'd hand over the keys to the kingdom if he could.

"Great Lord Sebourne?" They had reached the main

building entrance. A young soldier wearing the Celierian blue-and-gold tabard of the King's Guard stood on the steps. He bowed deeply. "I am Lieutenant Arvin, my lord. My men and I will escort you to the king." Another six Guardsmen stood just inside the arching doorway with its wide, steel-reinforced door. Arvin nodded to the gate guards, who saluted and headed back the way they'd come.

"I apologize for the armed escort, my lord," Arvin said, as they walked through the keep. "Tensions are high. I do hope you understand."

Dervas wanted to snap that he understood a great many things, including the fact that the Fey had poisoned the king's mind, but he held his tongue. He was here to mend fences and salvage what he could of his power and his standing in the court.

"If surrendering my weapons and submitting to armed escort will set my king's mind at ease, then I surrender and submit gladly," he lied. They crossed the main hall. At the back of the hall, a stairway led up to a second level. There were two doors on the left and an open archway on the right. Two of the King's Guard stood beside each of the doors and the archway.

"Thank you, my lord. I appreciate your gracious understanding." Lieutenant Arvin stopped beside the second door on the left. "The king has granted this audience to you alone, my lord. Your men must remain here."

Sebourne motioned for his men to step back.

"There is one final thing, my lord. I have been commanded to search you before you enter the king's presence."

Sebourne's brows shot up towards his hairline. He had accepted every slight with grace, but this was too much. His ire spewed out before he could check it. "Search me? What in the gods name for, boy? Do you think I have a sword stuffed up my ass? I am a Great Lord of Celieria! I was asked to surrender my weapons, and I have done so. You have my word I carry no other weapon on my person. That should be more than sufficient for you!"

The lieutenant would not be swayed or intimidated. He remained instead, polite but firm. "Please, my lord. I must insist. King's orders."

Dervas huffed and snorted and glared—and muttered in a dark voice about the end of the civilized world—but in the end he submitted to the abominable indignity of a search. He knew exactly why he was being subjected to it. Dorian meant to humiliate him, to put him in his place, to remind him there was no right or power even Great Lord Sebourne enjoyed except by the consent of the king.

What of the king, master? When we were in Celieria City, Master Nour said that when we reached Kreppes, I was to kill Dorian.

That was the original plan, but now that the Feyreisen and his mate have come, the plans have changed. Your new mission is to assist in the capture of the Tairen Soul's mate.

Yes, master, of course . . . but Dorian . . . please, I would still like the honor of killing him . . . now more than ever. For my son.

And so you shall, but locating the Feyreisa is your first priority. And it is to that aim that you will devote all your efforts. Once you have provided me the information I require and put that stone in place, your reward will be the honor of killing Celieria's king.

After a thorough pat down, the lieutenant led Sebourne through the door and down the connecting hallway. They passed five doors, three on the left, two on the right, before the hallway made a thirty-degree turn to the right. Two more of the King's Guard stood at attention beside the fourth door on the right. The door led to a small, windowless interior sitting room, fairly bare by court standards, though the two couches and chairs that occupied the room were of obvious quality. There was a closed second door at the back of the room, flanked by more guards.

"Make yourself comfortable, my lord. I will let His Majesty know you are here." The lieutenant bowed deeply a final time, went to rap softly on the back door, then slipped inside.

Dervas cooled his heels in the small sitting room for the better part of a bell. Though several people came and went through that guarded back door, no one came to summon him. No one came to look after his needs or offer him refreshment. No doubt the waiting and the deliberate lack of polite comforts were more small punishments.

And now, my umagi, I am going to erase all memory of this conversation until it is time for you to fulfill your task. This is for your sake as well as ours. With your memories gone, even a shei'dalin as powerful as the Tairen Soul's mate could Truthspeak you but still learn nothing of value.

At last, after what seemed like an eternity, the door opened again. King Dorian's valet, Marten, stepped into the sitting room. "Great Lord Sebourne? His Majesty will see you now."

"That dimskull Dorian has reinstated Sebourne."

Ellysetta looked up at Rain in shock as he shed his golden war steel and prepared for bed. "What?"

"Aiyah. Told me so himself half a bell ago." Rain dragged a hand through his hair in a distracted gesture and sighed. "I suppose I shouldn't call Dorian a dimskull. We're desperate for troops. I can understand why he did it." He met her gaze. "But I have a bad feeling about this, Ellysetta. I don't trust Sebourne."

"You think he will betray us?"

Rain shrugged. "I don't know. I told Dorian he should at least let Gaelen check Sebourne and his men for Marks, but he wouldn't hear of it. Sebourne is still a powerful, well-connected Great Lord with many supporters. He fears that alienating Sebourne—especially after what happened with Colum—would spark a civil war."

"He may be right."

"I know." Rain slid under the covers and pulled Ellysetta into his arms. "But I still have a bad feeling about this."

Rain's bad feeling left Ellysetta just as unsettled as he was. It took her a while to get to sleep, and when she finally did, she dreamed. Images flickered across her mind. Charred and broken stone, shattered glass, the ruins of a building. A dark hole ripped into a wall. Stairs leading down into a windowless room. A sconce lit, revealing a very large, dark oval mirror perched on a column of stone.

As Ellysetta watched, the dark oval of the mirror began to glow with silvery-blue light, just like the phosphorescent mirror pool at the heart of Grandfather Sentinel in Elvia. The surface seemed to ripple, and a face rose from the glowing depths. A Fey face, strong and stern, with pale-blond hair and eyes like deep green wells.

A strange tug of recognition pulled at her. The Fey in the mirror was a stranger . . . but something about him struck a deep chord, as if she should know him—or once had. She reached out a hand, but before her fingers could brush the mirror's surface, the mirror dissolved. The dreamview became a white blur.

When it focused again, she was walking in a grim, denuded landscape. The glare of a harsh white sun blazed down on a world leached of all color, alien and yet somehow still familiar. A river flowed in the distance, its surface still and black—the Heras. The tumbled ruins of a stone fortress lay scattered before it. From the shape of the hills and the destroyed fortress, she recognized the ruins as Kreppes.

The ground beneath her feet was covered in a thick layer of what she first thought were broken shards of sun-bleached shells. She stumbled on a rounded bulge hidden beneath the shards, and pain darted up her leg as her ankle twisted beneath her weight.

Ellysetta nearly fell to her knees, but she managed to catch her balance. She turned to see what had tripped her, and her stomach clenched with a sudden surge of nausea.

The rounded bulge was a skull . . . a man's skull.

White teeth grinned in a macabre smile beneath the gray-white shadows of empty eye sockets.

She took a stumbling step backward, away from the skull, and the shells beneath her feet crunched and snapped. Only then did she realize these were not stones, nor shells. They were bones. Shattered as if by some god's terrible hammer. Bleached white and brittle by the sun.

The remnants of what had once been living, breathing people.

Thousands of people.

And in the center of that barren landscape, upon that graven sea of the dead, Ellysetta stood alone. Garbed in scarlet from head to toe like a splash of blood on the snow-white field.

And she knew, with a certainty she could not explain, that every person whose shattered skeleton lay beneath her feet had died because of her.

Ellysetta's eyes opened. The brittle white boneyard of her dream became the night-dark ceiling of the room she and Rain shared at Kreppes. She could hear the low voices of her quintet just outside the bedroom door.

She sat up, and out of habit turned to check the Sentinel blooms beneath her pillow. The flowering sprigs were still in place, as they had been every night since leaving Elvia. Not a Mage-sent dream then.

Beside her, Rain stirred. His hand flexed against the bed-sheets, seeking her. *Shei'tani.* The sleepy call drifted from his mind. Not Spirit, merely an unchecked thought.

She brushed back the silky spill of hair that feathered across his brow. *"Las, kem'san. Ruliath."* Peace, my love. Go back to sleep. A push of encouraging Spirit accompanied the words, a gentle weave that she laid upon him without guilt.

He was so weary. The fact that her dream had woken her but not him was proof of his utter exhaustion. He had been so strong for so long, but his vast power was beginning to flag. Madness—both from the trauma of war and from their uncompleted truemate bond—was chipping away at the powerful barriers that held back the torment of his overburdened soul. Yesterday, his thoughts had been so loud her quintet had heard them on several occasions.

Since the moment she'd called him from the sky, he had taken care of her, looked after her, put her safety before his own. Now it was her turn to give him back a fraction of that devotion. She loved him so. No longer because he was the hero of her dreams but because he was the Fey, flawed and yet so fine, who had won her heart. He was a king, a great and noble leader of the immortal Fey, but he was also just Rain, her beloved, hers to protect.

And she would protect him . . . just as fiercely as the tairen defended the pride.

When she was certain he was well and deeply asleep, she rose from the bed and dressed quietly, drawing a thick, furlined velvet cloak over her gown. There would be no more sleep for her tonight. The strange, disturbing dream hadn't terrified her, as her dreams often did, but it had left her tense and unsettled all the same. She needed to get out of this room and go for a walk to clear her thoughts.

In the antechamber outside the bedroom, she was surprised to see the five warriors of primary quintet instead of her secondary.

"What are you doing here?" she whispered, closing the door behind her. "Shouldn't you all be asleep?"

"Shouldn't you?" Gaelen countered.

She arched a brow, then had to smile. "*Mei sorro.*" The phrase, which meant well struck, was one Fey warriors used in training when their sparring partners hit a good blow. It was a phrase she'd become quite familiar with since Gaelen and her quintet had begun training her in the use of Fey weapons. She was getting better at hitting precisely where she aimed but still had work to do to improve her own defenses.

"More dreams?" Bel asked softly. He watched her closely, his gaze filled with a mix of certainty and concern.

"Aiyah." She grimaced, then confessed, "I'm beginning to question the real reason Lord Galad gave me those Sentinel blooms. They seem to make me dream more, not less."

"You're starting to learn the true nature of Elf gifts," her uncle Tajik muttered sourly. "When an Elf gives you a rose, always look for the thorn."

She turned to the red-haired Fire master with a puzzled frown. "Why do you hate the Elves so?" Her uncle never had a kind word to say about his woodland kinsmen.

"I don't hate all Elves," he clarified. "Just their king."

"What has Lord Galad done to earn your wrath?"

"You mean besides sentencing my sister and her mate to a thousand years of torment?"

"You were bitter before you learned that." She pinned him with a level gaze.

Tajik looked away. "I loved once. An elf maid named Aliya. With her brother's consent, we would have bound ourselves to one another in *e'tanitsa."* He shrugged. "Instead, he sent her to her doom."

Ellysetta's hand flew to her throat. "Aliya was Lord Hawksheart's sister? Tajik, are you saying Galad Hawksheart sent his own sister to her death?"

Tajik nodded. "I could have saved her, but he made sure I didn't. Had she lived, it would have changed a Verse in a minor Song, but he said that one change might have rippled to a greater, more important Song, and put its outcome in danger. He wasn't willing to take that risk. Her death ensured that change wouldn't happen."

"Oh, Tajik." No wonder he harbored such enmity towards the Elf king. If Galad Hawksheart had intentionally sent Rain to his death, no power on earth, the Seven Hells, or the Haven of Light would have spared him from her wrath. She laid a hand upon her uncle's arm. *"Kem'san avi i ver'baloth."* My heart weeps for your sorrow.

"Beylah vo, kem'jitanessa." He covered her hand. "Now perhaps you will understand that when I say you be wary of Elf-gifts, it is no idle warning. I know just how far Hawks-

heart will go to protect his precious Dance. If he thought tormenting your dreams with those Sentinel blooms would benefit the Dance, he would give them to you without a qualm and never tell you their true purpose."

Was it possible? Could the Elf king have gifted her with the Sentinel wreath not to protect her from the Mage's dream-attacks, as he had claimed, but rather to open her mind to prophetic Elvish dreams?

Your Elvish blood awakens.

The memory of Hawksheart's words echoed in her mind. Since the moment she'd drunk the Elves' liquid sunlight and placed her hand on the Elf king's Mirror, her dreams had not stopped or grown less frightening. Instead, they hummed with a sense of veracity she could not shake, no matter how much she wished to.

The dream she'd just had, and several others before it, were no Mage-spawned nightmares sent to torment her. They were potential verses of her Song, brutal, vivid visions of the dread future that awaited her if she did not find a way to complete her truemate bond with Rain and defeat the High Mages' evil plans for her.

Ellysetta pressed the heel of her palm to her heart. The walls felt like they were closing in, as if the weight of the world were pressing down upon her, oppressive and suffocating.

"I need some air," she said, and bolted for the door.

Except for the guards standing at their posts and the occasional footstep of a watchman going about his night duties, all of Kreppes lay silent and still beneath the starry, moonlit winter sky.

After rushing from her suite in the west wing, Ellysetta climbed the stairs to the ramparts, where the cool air and open sky made her feel less closed in. She walked along the northern battlement in the company of her quintet and looked out over the river into Eld. She didn't know what she was expecting to see. Some sign of malevolence, perhaps, or approaching evil, but all she saw was the unbroken darkness of Eld's great forests, stretching across the horizon, and the silvery shine of moonlight reflecting on the swirling confluence of the mighty Heras and the Elden river Azar.

"Doesn't look like such a threat, does it?"

She turned to see King Dorian step from the shadows of the wizard's wall, the raised walkway spiked with high, open-roofed towers set back from the main battlements.

"Your Majesty." She inclined her head. "Forgive me. I didn't see you there. I did not mean to intrude."

"Your presence could never be an intrusion, Feyreisa."

The compliment flowed off his tongue with both courtly ease and surprising sincerity. How strange it seemed. She'd grown up all her life seeing this man's image on the coins that passed from one Celierian hand to another in commerce, and now, here he was, standing beside her on a silent night on the eve of war, offering the pretty charm of a courtly Grace. Master Fellows, the Queen's Master of Graces who had taught a woodcarver's daughter the ways of Celieria's royal court, would have beamed with pride.

"It is strange, how peaceful it looks." The king continued, nodding towards the vast, shadowy forest to the north. "I have fought in three wars before this. Always, I could see my enemy approaching. I never realized what a comfort that was." Hands braced on the flat surface of the stone crenel, he scanned the dark horizon. "I keep looking for the campfires, the ships, the troops that experience tells me must be there, yet, my reports say this enemy can simply appear, with no warning, and in great strength. This . . . nothingness . . . is very unsettling."

"Perhaps the waiting is actually the first part of the attack." A chill breeze blew through the fortress's night shields. She drew her velvet robes tighter and plumped the fur collar higher about her neck. "To constantly be on your guard, knowing your enemy is stalking you, but not knowing how or when the next blow will come . . . such torments are one of this Mage's favorite weapons."

"No doubt because it is so scorching effective." Dorian pushed back from the wall and turned to face her. "Is that what it's like to be Mage-Marked? To feel as if you're constantly waiting for an attack?"

The question took Ellysetta by surprise. No one had ever asked her what it was like, to be Mage-Marked, and though Dorian had always treated her with impeccable courtesy, he'd never invited personal confidences.

"I suppose it is, in a way," she answered. "The pressure is always there, but it doesn't just come from without. It also comes from within."

"How so?"

"Well, he doesn't just attack you. He also tries to trick you into betraying yourself. Sometimes, the tricks are very persuasive." All her life, she'd battled the Mage and the nightmares he sent to torment her. Since coming into her power, that torment had only grown worse. "I doubt I could have lasted this long if not for Rain. He is my strength."

Dorian looked away. "You are very lucky to have a love so selfless and steadfast."

His glum tones made her empathy flare. The sense of loss—even despair—that had surrounded him these last days, spurring his temper, fanning his anger, suddenly made sense.

"I know how blessed I am to have Rain," she agreed. "All my life, I dreamed of a Fey-tale love. My mother always tried to discourage me. I was an unattractive child." She smiled a little, remembering. "She no doubt meant to spare me the pain of lost hopes, but I didn't realize that at the time. So when she'd tell me to set aside my dreams of Fey-tale love, that such great loves weren't meant for mortals, I'd remind her that she had found such a love with my papa—" She hesitated, then admitted softly, "—and that you had found such a love with the queen."

When he said nothing, she added, "I'm sure that whatever difficulties may lie between you now, they will not last. I have seen the great love you bear her."

He glanced at her with sudden suspicion. "Are you reading my thoughts, Feyreisa?"

"*Nei,* King Dorian. I and every Fey in Kreppes have done all we can these last days to shield ourselves from mortal thoughts and emotions. But not all thoughts require magic to detect."

He grimaced. "I suppose not. Especially when one isn't being particularly subtle."

"If you need to talk, I would be glad to listen. About anything." She started to reach for his hands, but drew back before she touched him. The moment her skin touched his, her promise to leave him the privacy of his thoughts and emotions would be broken.

"You have never much cared for the queen."

"I—" His statement caught her off guard and left her scrambling for an appropriate response. She wanted to deny his remark, for his sake, but Fey did not lie.

"No." He smiled. "You haven't. It's all right. Most people don't. She is not an easy woman to like . . ." He looked back towards Eld, ". . . or to love."

"But you do. Love her, I mean."

"More than life." He rubbed his face, weariness apparent in every line of his body. "So much that the break between us weighs on me more heavily than this war."

Ellysetta had to fight to keep herself from touching him, from weaving peace upon him. His emotions had opened up so much she could not hope to block them. The ragged, aching hole, the emptiness, as if part of his soul was missing. The fear that his wife's love might be lost forever.

"Your Majesty . . . Dorian . . ."

"Some people believe I don't see her flaws," he continued as if he hadn't heard her, "but I do. I simply love her in spite of them. Or perhaps because of them. She is a princess of Cappellas. There's not a more deceitful, conniving, heartless land in all the mortal world. Intrigue, betrayal, murder: They're a way of life there. No one trusts anyone—not even their own family. And she grew up in that. Can you imag-

ine? A child, a beautiful, innocent little girl, raised in that
. . . that *darrokken* pit of a Hells hole. Ah, gods."

He leaned back and shook himself, as if trying to shake
off the overwhelming emotion. "She didn't let it break her,
though. She was too strong. So strong she could live through
all of that and still allow herself to be vulnerable enough to
love me."

The words kept tumbling out, as if he needed to say them,
to hear them. As if he needed to remind himself.

"She is vain, I know. And she plays her game of Trumps
with the members of the court, making them dance to her
tune so she can control them. She constantly schemes for
ways to increase Celieria's power and might. But all that is
part of her armor. She learned from a young age the best
way to protect vulnerabilities was through power, and that
power comes from being the most beautiful, the wealthiest,
the wiliest, the most controlling. That is how she defends
herself and the few people she will ever let herself love. In
a way, she is like a tairen. Fierce. Territorial. Willing to
destroy anything or anyone who trespasses on her lair or
threatens the members of her pride."

Ellysetta would never have drawn that comparison herself, but a look at Annoura through her husband's eyes put
a different perspective on Celieria's beautiful, scheming
queen. "I never understood that about her."

"Few do." He gave a melancholy smile. "She doesn't want
people to understand her."

"Because that would make her vulnerable."

He nodded. "There's nothing she fears more than that."

Fear and vulnerability were concepts Ellysetta understood
all too well. She didn't like Queen Annoura. The woman had
never been more than grudgingly gracious, and sometimes
not even that. But King Dorian was a good man with a kind
heart, and Ellysetta could tell he loved his wife deeply—
perhaps as much, in his own way, as she loved Rain. There
must be something worthy inside the prickly queen—some
goodness Ellysetta had never seen.

"I have faith you will find a way to set things right," she said. "Hold fast to your hope. She loved you once enough to overcome what she feared most. A love that strong does not wither easily."

Dorian closed his eyes, rubbing his face in a weary gesture. "So I have always believed. We have had our arguments before, some of them quite fearsome. How could any man not, with such a strong, stubborn woman for a wife? But this time . . ." He shook his head. "This time feels different." Bleak shadows filled his eyes. "I chose the Fey side over hers one too many times. She says I have betrayed her. And the way she said it . . . the look on her face . . ." He shook his head. "I don't know that this breach *can* be mended."

Ellysetta winced. He had trusted the Fey, the way Annoura had trusted him, chosen to support them at deep, personal cost. No wonder he'd been so devastated to discover how they'd deceived him.

"I'm so sorry, Your Majesty."

"As am I, My Lady Feyreisa. As am I." Dorian heaved a sigh and rubbed his neck, rolled his head in a slow circle to loosen the tight muscles. "It's late. Both of us should be to bed. Tomorrow will be another long day."

"Of course." She started to leave him to his solitude, then paused. "Before you go, King Dorian, may I ask you a question?"

He inclined his head. "Of course."

When he turned around, a dark brow raised in patient inquiry, she said, "I know you feel that we betrayed you by letting Adrial remain in Celieria without your knowledge. But if you had to make the decision to come here again—even knowing that we hid the truth about Adrial's presence from you—would you still come?"

He bowed his head, and his chest expanded on a long inhale as he considered the question. "Yes," he admitted softly. His sober gaze lifted, met and held hers, and he reconfirmed in a firmer voice, "Yes, I would. I would command that Talisa

Barrial remain in Celieria City," he clarified, "but the rest, I would do again."

Ellysetta nodded. "*Beylah vo.*" She hesitated. Five months ago, she'd been a peasant, a woodcarver's graceless gawk of a daughter who never could have dreamed she would be standing here on the battlements of a northern castle, garbed in velvets and sharing a midnight conversation with a king. And she had definitely *never* dreamed that she would be bold enough to offer that king her advice. And yet, that was exactly what she was going to do.

She had vowed not to weave magic on him, but she could not stand by and let him continue to suffer, as he clearly was. Her empathic nature would not allow it.

"You should write your queen. Tonight, before you sleep." She said it quickly, before her courage failed. "Tell her you love her. Tell her all the things you shared with me, about the many ways you admire and value her. Tell her . . . tell her that if you had your life to live all over again, you would still choose her above all others to be your queen and the mother of your children. Sometimes women need such reassurances."

For a moment, she thought she had offended him by offering such personal advice. He stood so still, watching her with such an indecipherable expression on his face. But then he bowed—not just the restrained, regal half nod shared between kings, but a deep, courtly bow, a sign of great respect.

"You are as wise as you are kind, Feyreisa," he said when he straightened. "The Tairen Soul is a lucky Fey." He nodded to Gaelen and the rest of her quintet, and continued down the stairs.

"That was well done, what you did back there with Dorian," Bel said, as Ellysetta and her quintet walked back to the suite.

"I didn't do much," Ellysetta denied.

"You got Celieria's king to acknowledge that he still trusts

the Fey military advice," Gaelen said. "That, even knowing how we misled him about Adrial, he still trusts us to
have his kingdom's best interests at heart. That's more than
anyone else has accomplished."

"And you put his mind at ease about his queen," Bel said.
"No man, Fey or mortal, does his best when his heart aches
and regret weighs heavy on his mind. Even if he cannot
mend what is broken between them, for now he has hope
that he can."

"It's most likely a false hope, you know. Queen Annoura
never struck me as a forgiving woman."

"Perhaps," Bel acknowledged. "But to a man standing on
the eve of battle, even false hope is better than none."

Several bells after his walk on the ramparts, with the letter
to his queen lying on his desk, written, sanded, and sealed,
Dorian paced the chamber in restless thought. Pouring his
heart out in the letter to his wife had brought back vivid
memories of how utterly he'd fallen in love with her, how
deeply and completely she had loved him back. Theirs *had*
been a Fey-tale love, just as the Feyreisa said. He'd known
it. His entire kingdom had known it . . . So what had happened? And why? For the first time, he began to examine the
events of the past, attempting to understand how a love so
true could have gone so wrong.

Lady Ellysetta's remark about how the Mages constantly
pushed at her mind, trying to trick her into betraying herself,
had started him thinking about the possibility that Dorian
and Annoura's troubles had not been of their own making.
He knew for certain that at least one Mage had infiltrated his
court, masquerading as the newly entitled Lord Bolor. That
Mage had stood in the presence of Dorian's queen and could
easily have Mage-claimed Dorian's subjects. He'd only been
discovered thanks to the diligent efforts of Gaspare Fellows,
the Queen's own Master of Graces. But what if Lord Bolor
had not been the first Mage to hide in Dorian's court? What

if there had been others? What if those others had been working their evil on Celieria's queen?

Annoura had changed these last years—especially the last six months or so. At first, the changes had been so subtle, taking place over a period of time so that they had not raised his suspicions. A hint of disquiet here. A small jealousy there. A fear amplified. His brave, strong, beloved queen had begun to doubt him, to see rivals for his affections, enemies among friends. It was almost as if she were back in Cappellas again, fighting a bitter, brutal shadowy war for survival and power.

Looking back, he could see it clearly, and the change no longer seemed at all natural.

Annoura wasn't Marked. He took what comfort he could from that, but someone had been playing on her fears. Undermining the love and trust Dorian and Annoura had shared for decades. Rousing all the suspicions bred into her by her Cappellan upbringing. Tricking her into betraying herself, just as the Lady Ellysetta said the Mages tried to do with her. And he, so used to her changeable nature, her manipulations, and the small ways she'd always tested his love, had thought nothing of it.

The more he thought about it, the more he realized that Mage influence was the only explanation that made sense. And since the changes in Annoura had begun before Lord Bolor came to court, that meant Lord Bolor wasn't the only Mage who'd been influencing her.

So who was it? Who had been closest to her? Who could have had the time and opportunity to play on his queen's suspicious nature and amplify her fears?

Jiarine, Lady Montevero, was an obvious candidate— considering that she'd been the one to befriend Lord Bolor at court—but she'd been taken to Old Castle for questioning after Bolor's unmasking. Tortured by some too-zealous prison guard, too, according to his Prime Minister Lord Corrias's report. And she'd known nothing. She was, apparently, as big a dupe as the rest of them.

Annoura's other Favorites were possibilities, including, of course, the oh-so-charming Ser Vale, a handsome, minor noble sponsored to the court years ago by Jiarine Montevero. He'd wormed his way into Annoura's inner circle quickly enough. If Dorian didn't trust Annoura so much, he might have suspected the relationship between her and Vale had become deeper than mere friendship and flirtation.

He scrubbed his scalp in frustration. Did he really think Lady Montevero and that silky-smooth lordling, Ser Vale, were agents of Eld, or was he just an angry, jealous husband trying to blame someone else for the disintegration of his marriage to a complicated and temperamental queen?

Dorian spun away from the window and stalked across the room to his desk. Maybe he was angry and jealous. But maybe he was also right. He needed someone he could trust to conduct an investigation. If there really were still Mages at work in Celieria City, his queen and his entire kingdom lay at risk.

Dorian sat down, pulled a fresh sheet of blank vellum from his paper box, and uncapped the inkwell.

CHAPTER FOUR

Eyes filled with cold blood-red
seeking, enjoying their amusement's dread
Eyes that look forward to bloodshed
anxious, desperate to taste the dead.

Shadow's Eyes, a Fey poem

Celieria ~ Celieria City
29ʰ day of Verados

Hooves thundered down the North Road as a royal courier—
the last in a network of couriers posted every ten miles from
Celieria City to Kreppes—galloped towards the city gates.
As one of the four riders assigned to run the ten miles stretching between the royal palace and the first posting exchange
on the North Road, his face was well-known to every guard
who worked the gate, but he still flashed his courier's flag as
he approached—a bright red square of fabric to indicate that
he carried dispatches from the king. The guards hoisted a
larger version of the same flag over the gatehouse and raised
the gate so he could ride through without stopping.

"Make way!" the city guards cried. "Make way!" They
rushed to clear the crowded city street as the courier galloped past.

Five chimes later, his horse lathered and panting, the courier arrived in the small, private courtyard of the king's dispatch office. Alerted by the signal flags raised at the north gate, Lord Renald, the king's minister of communications, was there to greet him and to take the pouch bearing the king's dispatches. Lord Renald had never trusted vital communications to any servant or underling.

"Thank you, son," Lord Renald said, when the courier handed over his leather satchel. "I will have a return pouch ready to go before twelve bells. Take your rest until then. I understand there are fresh burberry buns and clotted cream in the courier's hall."

"Thank you, my lord." The courier tugged the brim of his hat and grinned. Lord Renald was a favorite among the palace servants. He never spoke a harsh word, and always ensured the comfort of those who served him.

Lord Renald carried the precious mail pouch into his office, closed the door, and sat down to personally sort and log its contents. A bell later, he emerged from his office to deliver the post.

A young serving maid entered the now-empty room to collect the tea tray she'd brought to him earlier. Three letters lay under the linen tea cloth—one written in Lord Renald's hand, the other two sealed and marked with the king's personal signet. She dropped the letters in her apron pocket, picked up the tray, and headed for the kitchens.

Lord Renald was indeed a man of impeccable character and incorruptible loyalty to the crown, but he was also a devoted husband and the adoring father of three young children. And that was the leverage the Mages had used to claim him.

A knock rapped on the door of an apartment in the courtiers' wing. "Morning *keflee*, Ser," the maid called through the door.

A moment later, the door opened to reveal Ser Vale, Queen Annoura's most favored of her Favorites. "Thank you, my dear." He stepped aside to let the servant deliver the tray and flashed his famous, dazzling smile at one of Annoura's other young Dazzles, who was eyeing the *keflee* enviously as he walked by. One of the perks of being a Queen's Favorite—besides the luxury of claiming a slightly larger room in the palace—was the option of having the palace staff deliver meals to one's room rather than being required to eat with the other Dazzles in the queen's breakfast room.

Once the maid had departed and the door to his room was firmly closed behind him, Vale's smile winked out. The charming, sensual, seductive face of Annoura's Favorite disappeared. A different man, much colder, much harder, and infinitely more dangerous, emerged in his stead.

Sulimage Kolis Manza, apprentice to the great Vadim Maur, High Mage of Eld, lifted the linen cloth beneath the plate of burberry buns and examined the three letters. The note from Renald was a brief summary of the correspondence from the king to his ministers and from the generals to their staffs. Kolis opened the sheet, scanned its contents quickly, and set it aside.

He poured a cup of *keflee* and held the sealed letter addressed to Queen Annoura over the steam until the wax seal loosened. An adept slice with a letter opener popped it free, then he unfolded the vellum and read the words Dorian X had written to his queen.

The letter contained no Writs of Authority, nothing that needed to be passed on, just a maudlin outpouring that made Kolis's lip curl. In Eld, the Mages had long ago learned the uses and the limitations of women. They were kept to their place. Baubles to be enjoyed. Tools to be used. Nothing more. For a while, with Jiarine, Kolis had become too attached—and look where that had gotten him. Weeks of torture, terrors that still woke him, gasping and drenched in cold sweat—the punishment he'd earned for failing his master.

He would never fail again.

He tossed Dorian's note to Annoura into the fire that warmed his spacious apartment. He'd worked too hard to destroy the royal couple's marriage to risk reconciliation now. The break between Celieria's royals had been severe, and Kolis meant it to be final.

As Dorian's romantic outpouring to Annoura burned, Kolis picked up the last letter. He frowned at the name written on the outside of the folded vellum. What on earth could the king have to say to the Queen's Master of Graces? Kolis loosened and popped the seal and read the contents.

Halfway through, his hand began to shake.

Gaspare Fellows and his pesky little magic-sniffing cat had brought about the demise of Lord Bolor—the man Kolis knew as Primage Gethen Nour. Now Dorian wanted Fellows to spy on the rest of the court to sniff out other agents of Eld and turn them over to the Fey and the King's justice.

And the first two people the king wanted Fellows to investigate were Jiarine Montevero and the Queen's Favorite, Ser Vale.

Twenty chimes later, garbed in resplendent, fur-trimmed wool and rich brocades, Ser Vale entered Her Majesty's apartments and executed a full, flourishing court bow before her.

"Your Majesty. As always, I am dazzled by your radiance." From another mouth, the outrageous compliment might have sounded laughable and insincere, but Kolis harbored genuine appreciation for the queen's considerable beauty. What might have seemed insincere from another tongue flowed like a bewitching spell from his.

The queen's Ladies-in-Waiting sighed. They all liked Ser Vale, lusted for him in fact. But he had always been careful to keep his dalliances to a minimum. It was much easier to keep the queen's interest if she thought he pined for her in every way.

Of course, it helped that the queen was a celebrated Brilliant in her own right. And today, garbed in shimmering aquamarine, she was the epitome of regal feminine perfection. Her silvery blond hair was piled high atop her head, dusted with iridescent powder, and set with countless pear-shaped diamonds that caught the light and cast dancing rainbows upon the wall with her every move. An enormous diamond pendant hung from a chain of aquamarine-and-diamond flowers encircling her neck.

"I saw the flags go up on the gate announcing word from the king," Vale said. "I hope, Your Majesty, that he only sent you the best of news."

He hid a smile as Annoura's hands tightened into fists in her lap.

A movement at the corner of his eye caught Kolis's attention. He looked up to see the small, elegant figure of Master Fellows entering the queen's chamber, the white kitten called Love perched on his shoulder like a sea captain's bird.

Kolis forced a charming smile when Fellows looked his way, but his mind was busy running through a thousand possible next moves. One thing was certain. Fellows was a problem in need of immediate remedy.

Kolis had no intention of suffering Nour's fate.

Eld ~ Boura Fell

Melliandra had deliberately stayed away from Lord Death for three days, hoping he'd get over the crackbrained notion that she should risk her life trying to steal his Soul Quest crystal from the High Mage. And what was the first thing he asked when she'd accepted the chore of visiting him again?

Did she have his sorreisu kiyr?

Did she have it! As if she could just trot up to the High Mage's office and ask for it to be handed over!

Did the dimskull Fey understand what he was asking her to do? Did he have the slightest clue? Melliandra scowled as she stomped back to the kitchens with her tray.

He was punishing her for saving his mate. That's what this was. Or so she tried to convince herself. Because if he didn't really mean it, she didn't really need to risk herself trying to achieve it.

Melliandra accepted her next assignment—cleaning the refuse bins—without complaint, even though she'd done it two days ago and it shouldn't have been her turn again for at least another five days.

No one really liked pushing the refuse carts. There was never any telling what would end up in them. Noxious poisons, rotting carcasses, and all too often, the bodies of the more unfortunate guests of Boura Fell's Mages.

An image of Shia flashed in her mind. The torn, blood-drained body. The blind, staring blue eyes.

Melliandra shook her head. No, she would not think of Shia. Especially not while pushing a refuse cart through the Mage Halls.

But Shia was on her mind. Ever since Lord Death had spun that sweet picture of a happy, loving childhood, Melliandra had been thinking of Shia, of the songs Shia had sung as she'd combed a young *umagi's* hair and given her the first taste of kindness she'd ever known, and the first name she'd ever had: Melliandra.

It was possible the Fey had plucked those memories from her mind when he'd spun that fanciful Fey tale of a wonderful childhood in an effort to manipulate her four days ago. That's what any Mage would have done. And why she'd let him know it wasn't working.

Even though it had been.

Melliandra, you are such a dimskull.

She reached the stairs and, despite not wanting to go anywhere near Lord Death again today, headed back down to Boura Fell's lowest level. The lower floors were usually the most likely to have the most revolting surprises in their bins, so whenever it was her turn to run the refuse carts, she always preferred to start at the bottom and work her way to the top. That way, no matter what retch-inducing foulness she found in the bins, she could tell herself the next floor would be easier.

It wasn't always true, but at least it gave her something to look forward to.

* * *

When Melliandra reached the level of Boura Fell that housed the High Mage's offices, she pulled the floor's refuse cart out of its storage closet and rolled it along with an almost light-hearted feeling in her chest. She'd just learned that the High Mage was away from Boura Fell. He'd left a little over a bell ago to visit one of the other Bouras—Koderas and his great new fortress, Toroc Maur, if the rumors she'd overheard in the Mage Halls were correct. Apart from the fact that his absence meant his refuse bins would be empty (which was always a great relief; she hated finding those small, lifeless infants whose blood he used to communicate with his Mages afield) the great, crouching malevolence of his all-seeing presence was gone, too, and with it the probing worms of his consciousness, digging into her soul, rifling through her thoughts, poking, spying. Owning.

Melliandra could not recall a single day of her life when Vadim Maur had not been near. But since he'd incarnated into Master Nour's younger, much fitter body (and, oh, the cursing and Rages that had erupted in the Mage Halls over that!), he'd become much less reclusive. Much more likely to be found roaming the halls of Boura Fell rather than simply sitting behind his desk or locking himself away in his spell rooms.

When she reached Master Maur's offices, the guards were standing at their usual posts, but a trio of Primages were arguing beside them. Two of the Primages were attempting to gain entrance to the High Mage's office on some pretext—fabricated, no doubt—while the third Primage, Master Maur's assistant, Zev, was steadfastly refusing to admit them.

"My orders are clear," Zev was saying. "No *umagi* enters unsupervised, and no Mage enters at all until Master Maur returns. If you need something from his office, you may submit your request to me. I will communicate your desire to Master Maur, and if he approves it, I will bring the item to you."

Outraged and grumbling, the two Primages stalked off.

Primage Zev turned, swift as a tunnel snake, and speared her with a sharp look. "Why are you here, *umagi*?" His will, like a dark, suffocating cloud, pressed down on her, tendrils of command and inquiry prodding at her mind.

Melliandra swiftly shoved every free thought and emotion back into the private space in her mind and slammed the door hard shut. She filled her mind with *umagi* concerns. *She was hungry. She'd have to find someone weaker to sit beside at dinner tonight and steal their portion. Who best to single out?*

"Mistress sent me, master." No need to feign that tremble in her voice. She was really frightened. Zev was no Maur, but he was still a Primage, and still perfectly capable of shredding her body and mind if he discovered even a hint of her desire to kill Vadim Maur.

The tension in her chest didn't begin to ease until the Primage grunted and turned to face the office doors. A dark glow massed around his hands, a cloud of shadow shot through with slivers of light, like shining threads in a dark cloth. More threads began to glow about the door. She only saw them for an instant. A strange web of light and dark plaited together in a complex and oddly beautiful pattern. Then she blinked, and the vision went away.

The Primage opened the doors to Vadim Maur's office and motioned her to go inside. "Do what you came for, and be quick about it."

He followed her in and watched her as she crossed the room to the High Mage's great desk. She glanced furtively around the office as she went, looking for more threads of shadow and light. She knew she'd just seen magic: the weave this Primage had spun and the weave he'd unraveled to let her pass. She'd actually *seen* it—the individual threads and their pattern, not just the hazy glow visible to anyone when someone wove strong magic. She recognized it because she'd heard the appearance of magic described many times. The novices in the Mage Halls were young and chatty, and not yet learned enough to spin effective privacy weaves.

She couldn't see any other magic in the room, not even around the door at the back of the office. *Umagi* weren't allowed across that threshold. So far as she knew, no one was. If there was going to be more magic anywhere in this room, she would have expected it to be there, warding that door. But perhaps wards only showed themselves in the presence of other magic?

Aware of Primage Zev's eyes upon her, Melliandra empted the waste bin by Vadim Maur's desk, bobbed a quick bow in the direction of the Primage, and scurried out. She pushed the cart down the hall to the next door, pausing to look back and watch the Primage reseal the wards protecting the High Mage's room.

There. She could see them again. Those shining threads of magic.

Eld ~ Koderas

Vadim Maur walked beside Primage Grule, the Mage he'd tasked with restoring Koderas to its full, pre-Wars capacity. He'd already visited the enormous forges, where blacksmiths hammered *sel'dor* ingots into swords and armor, and the foundries where molten *sel'dor* was cast into barbed arrowheads, spears, and the like. Now, the two Mages passed through an archway and down a series of railed walkways that overlooked Koderas's siege workshops and the various machining and assembly rooms where thousands of *umagi* toiled round the clock constructing the massive battering rams and trebuchets that would be used to grind enemy fortresses into dust. No less than three full rooms were dedicated to the manufacture of bowcannon and their massive, tairen-killing bolts made from tree trunks jacketed with barbed *sel'dor* sheaths and razor-sharp spearheads.

"You have done well, Grule." Praising those who served him wasn't Vadim's strong suit, but Grule's last centuries of effort had exceeded even Vadim's highest expectations.

"Not even during the previous Wars did Koderas operate with such seamless efficiency."

"Thank you, Most High. There is no prize I value more than your approval." A flush of pleasure touched Grule's tanned cheeks. Unlike most sun-bereft Mages, who toiled all their lives beneath the surface of Eld, Grule had spent the last year aboveground, overseeing the start of Vadim Maur's next great achievement.

They had reached the end of the elevated walkway. Grule opened the door at the end of the walkway, and the Mages stepped out of the hot noise of the production floor into a cool, dark corridor. From there, they climbed a flight of stairs that led to a pair of heavy double doors covered with swirling patterns of rune-etched silver and bloodred crystals in the sigils of Seledorn, God of Shadows. Grule reached for the heavy, intricately wrought silver-and-*sel'dor* handle and murmured the words of a release spell while his fingers traced an unlocking weave in the air. Unseen bolts shifted with an audible click.

"After you, Most High," Grule murmured, and with a wave of his hand, the doors swung open.

Vadim Maur stepped over the threshold and into the gray light of the cloud-filtered afternoon sun. He squeezed his eyes closed against the brightness. It was the first time he'd stepped foot aboveground since the scorching of the world a thousand years ago, and even much-filtered sunlight was a hundred times brighter than the dim, sconce-lit shadows of Boura Fell.

"Forgive me, Master Maur." Grule leapt forward to block the sunlight with his body and cast the High Mage in his broad shadow. "Shall I weave screens for your eyes?" He lifted his hands in anxious anticipation.

The old Vadim Maur, trapped in his aged and decaying body, would have snapped in rage. But the newly incarnated Vadim Maur, housed in a body both young and fit, was not so quick to anger.

"No need." Already Vadim's new, younger eyes were adjusting to the abundance of light. He lifted a shading hand over his eyes and squinted at the world around him.

They were standing on a windswept point of land formed by the confluence of two great rivers: the Frost heading down from the Mandolay Mountains in the north, and the Selas, flowing east from its source near the Rhakis. Vadim turned in a slow circle, drinking in this long-unseen world. Behind them lay the mile-long open *sel'dor* pit that housed the new, much-improved, Koderas. Clouds of thick black smoke boiled up from Koderas's great fires. What trees might have once surrounded the pit had long since died away, and all that remained was thick brush, covered in heavy gray layers of ash and *sel'dor* dust.

Vadim's chest swelled with pride. Some who looked upon Koderas might have seen ruin in the ash and soot and poisonous gases choking the life from the surrounding forest. But not Vadim. He saw Koderas for what it truly was: *power*. His power. Raw and brutal and ugly, perhaps, but indisputably great nonetheless.

He turned the final quarter of his circuit and beheld the second reason he had come: the shining glory of Toroc Maur—the first Elden stronghold to extend aboveground since the scorching of the world.

Though little more than a massive outer wall and scaffolding now, when completed the immense citadel would crouch on the banks of the Selas River like a great, horned spider, its gleaming black spires stabbing up from the center of a wide, high-walled and well-defended central keep, towering nearly as high as its foundation, the subterranean levels of Boura Maur, plunged deep. The first soaring *sel'dor* bridge that spanned the river to connect Boura Maur to Koderas had already been built. Flanking the bridge's entrance, two enormous flags of Eld, rich purple embroidered with silvery moons and stars set in the exact configuration of Vadim Maur's birth, snapped in the wind.

Emotions coiled inside Vadim: satisfaction, pride, eagerness. Centuries of planning and toil were finally coming to fruition.

"Show me," he urged.

After touring the existing construction of Toroc Maur and examining in detail the plan for the next stage of construction, Vadim followed Grule up the stone steps to the citadel's high, well-defended walls where cannoneers had assembled beside the bowcannon mounted on the battlements.

"Ah," Vadim said. "The new bowcannon bolts. You perfected the spell?"

"I did. I believe you will be very pleased." Grule nodded to the cannoneers, who immediately began firing the newest weapon—bowcannons bolts spelled by magic to fly faster and higher than ever before—fast and high enough to outpace even a Tairen Soul flying at his top magic-powered speed. The High Mage spent a full quarter bell watching the cannoneers demonstrate the splendid performance of the new bolts.

"Well done, Grule," he praised when the exhibition concluded. "You may well have just ensured our victory. With the skies tairen-free, nothing can stop my Army of Darkness."

"You honor me, Most High." Primage Grule bowed low. "But there is more. I've added a new improvement since my last report. The idea came to me after I read a book of Drogan blood spells. The potential is . . . incalculable."

Vadim arched a brow. "I am intrigued. What is this new improvement?"

"If you please, Most High, allow me to demonstrate. Do you see that *umagi* running in that field there?" He pointed to a tiny spot on one of the distant grounds and handed Vadim a telescoping spyglass.

Vadim lifted the glass and saw a man in tattered rags running for the forest edge. "You are letting one of your *umagi* escape?"

"One of our less valuable prisoners from the battle

at Teleon. I told him if he reached the edge of the forest alive, I would grant him his freedom." Grule gave smile. "I thought he might run faster with a little incentive. Cannoneer Raegus, prepare to fire." He nodded at the cannoneer on the far end of the battlement. The man turned the crank to reposition his bowcannon.

"I don't understand. He is aiming away from the target."

Grule's smile grew wider. "Indeed he is, Most High." He raised his voice and called, "Fire when ready, cannoneer."

"*Ta,* Master Grule." The cannoneer uncorked a small flagon, poured a stream of glowing red liquid on the tip of the mounted cannon bolt, then returned to the firing pad and pulled back the release lever. The thick, braided metal bowstring gave a sharp twang of sound, and the bolt shot into the air. The launch ignited the acceleration spell, and the bolt rapidly picked up speed, just as all the other new bolts had done.

What happened next, however, made Vadim Maur's jaw drop.

The flying bolt, launched in the opposite direction of the escaping *umagi*, took a swift and sudden turn in the air and sped unerringly towards the running man. Moments later, the small dark speck racing towards the forest edge went down.

"I don't believe it." Vadim Maur raised his spyglass to an eye. Sure enough, the bolt had struck its target, cutting the fleeing man in two and pinning the upper half of his body to the ground. He spun to Grule. "How?"

"I used a variation of a Drogan summoning spell to direct the cannon bolt, and used that *umagi's* blood as the base for the spell. Once the cannoneer applied the potion, the bolt was magically drawn to the donor of the blood."

"You mean . . ."

"Yes." Grule was smiling again. He knew he'd done well. "Give me the Tairen Soul's blood, Most High, and I will shoot him from the sky."

"Do that, Grule, and I'll give you your pick of jewels from my own sash. And your choice of seats on the Mage Council." Vadim clasped the Mage's hand in a celebratory handshake. "Well done, Grule. Well done, indeed."

"Thank you, Master Maur. Your praise means everything to me. And now, I'm sure you're anxious to see the real treasure of Boura Maur."

Vadim and Grule took the wide, winding stair that circled down from Toroc Maur into the heart of its Boura below. Descending to levels known only to a select few, and accessible to even fewer, Grule opened the door and ushered the High Mage into the secret rooms that held the real purpose for his visit.

There, in a vast, low-ceilinged hall where the temperature dropped close to freezing, a raised earthen walkway led across what appeared to be an endless sea of mist. Brass ember-pots hanging from the ceilings illuminated the mists with a sickly red-orange glow. As Vadim and Grule stepped out onto the walkway, Grule wove a spell that sent sparks of magic flying across the chamber. Ember-pots brightened, and the mist thinned to reveal a vast series of open pits where masses of grayish white bodies crowded together like maggots packed in a rotting wound.

A dull murmur rose up from the undulating mass, senseless and wordless. A low, rattling moan, like an asthmatic breath dragged through throats choking on phlegm. The disturbing sound would instinctively raise hairs on the necks of the unsuspecting . . . and strike terror in the hearts of those who recognized its portent.

Revenants. Man-shaped creatures spawned from scraps of human flesh and bone, grown like witch-weed in a soupy morass of soil, *magus* powder, and the putrefying offal of both man and beast. Not entirely living, not entirely dead, but rather soulless hulks with a rapacious hunger for live flesh. And despite their current moribund state, when loosed from their pack, they moved with the speed of striking serpents—and the carnivorous ferocity of a *lyrant* taking down its prey.

They were the perfect weapon. Animated by the darkest of

Dark magic, the creatures were all but indestructible. They had no hearts to pierce, no lungs to rob of breath, no veins to drain of blood. Instead, like great, gruesome sponges, they thrived by absorbing the blood and dissolved flesh of their victims. Both their outer skin and the lining of the long digestive tube that coiled from maw to waste duct exuded a corrosive enzyme that liquefied flesh and bone on contact, then soaked up the resulting nutrient-rich goo and shuttled it inward to the rest of the creatures' ever-hungry bodies. On a battlefield, where revenants could gorge and wade through swamps of slain men, even dismemberment only served to multiply their numbers, for a revenant limb separated from its host needed only a soaking of fresh blood to grow again.

Their only thoughts—encoded into every cell of their ravening beings—were to feed and kill . . . and to serve the Elden Mages who held their leashes.

"How many have you grown now?" Vadim asked.

"Three million two hundred thousand, Most High," Grule answered. "Stored cold, kept hungry. When you unleash them, nothing living will long stand in their path."

Three million two hundred thousand. A force like none this world had ever seen, exceeding even the wildest accounts of the mythic Army of Darkness.

"Excellent." The Celierian king had gathered his allies at Kreppes. Vadim's eyes along the border had provided daily reports of their preparations for war, but their efforts would be for naught. Celieria would belong to Eld before the new moons rose on the thirteenth night of Seledos—and after that, the Fading Lands. "You have done well, Grule. You are a Mage worthy of his jewels." He cast a final, gleaming gaze over the revenant pits. "Prepare them for transport."

Celieria ~ Kreppes
30th day of Verados

A knock sounded on Rain and Ellysetta's suite door. When Gil went to answer it, no one was more surprised than Ellysetta to find Great Lord Dervas Sebourne on the other side. The warriors of her quintet went instantly stone-faced, as did Rain, when Gil ushered the Celierian Great Lord inside the room.

"Lord Sebourne," Rain greeted with wary stiffness.

"Feyreisen." Sebourne's voice was equally crisp. "I'll be brief. The king may have decided to overlook your lies and manipulations, but I have not. So do not think my return signals anything to the contrary. For now, I have no choice but to set aside my personal feelings and accept you as a member of this alliance, but when this war is over, I intend to lead the Council of Lords to eliminate Fey interference in all walks of Celierian life. And be warned, war or no war, if I discover you or any of your Fey are using magic to influence or invade mortal minds, I will be the first to call for your execution. Have a pleasant evening."

He gave a curt nod and stalked out.

Ellysetta gaped after him. She turned to Rain, shaking her head. "Did he really just come in here and *threaten* you?"

"It seems that he did, *shei'tani*." Rain's hands dropped to the hilts of the *meicha* scimitars at his hips, and his eyes narrowed on the closed door Great Lord Sebourne had just exited.

In the hallway, Dervas Sebourne dropped a small white stone into the brass wall sconce beside the Feyreisen's suite door before walking briskly back to his own rooms.

Ellysetta was still marveling over Lord Sebourne's inexplicable visit when a loud sound, like the rolling of thunder in the distance, broke the night's silence. She forgot Sebourne's aggressive intrusion in an instant. A bright smile broke across her face.

"They're here!" she cried. "They've come! The pride has come!"

Rain was already heading for the door. Together, with Ellysetta's primary quintet ringed around them, they raced out of the fortress and through the outer gate to greet the approaching tairen.

"Steli! I've missed you so!"

The great, snow-white tairen lowered her head and purred contentedly, blue eyes whirling sky-bright, as Ellysetta flung herself against Steli's neck and stroked the thick, soft fur.

Two other tairen, Xisanna and Perahl, had flown with her from Orest. Rijonn, the Earth master of Ellysetta's quintet, had fashioned a lair for them in the side of one of the newly heightened hills near Kreppes. Small by tairen standards, the lair was nearly as large as all of Kreppes. Rain, Ellysetta, and the tairen fit inside with enough room to move freely about.

«Steli missed Ellysetta-kitling, too. Human city not so fun without you. Too much prey-scent, but Fey-kin says not to eat. Makes Steli . . .» An image of a snarling, slavering tairen filled Ellysetta's head.

"I'm sorry we had to leave you, Steli, but thank you for staying behind to look after Orest for us."

«Mrr . . . scratch there. So good.» The tairen's purring grew so loud the soil around her began to vibrate. Gleaming ivory claws sank into the dirt, and the great cat's sleek tail thumped the ground, raising clouds of dust.

"Why did you leave, Orest, Steli-*chakai*?" Rain asked.

She cocked her head to one side. *«Rainier-Eras and Ellysetta-kitling are here, not there.»* Her tone made it clear she thought the answer should have been obvious to even the thickest skull.

Ellysetta smothered a laugh. The tairen were in a mood for mischief.

Rain sighed. "And if the Army of Darkness does indeed strike here, as we believe, we will be grateful for your presence, but Orest was still under attack when we left. Which tairen will speak to Lord Teleos on behalf of the pride now that you are gone?" Tairen did not, as a rule, speak to humans. They didn't speak to Fey either, except for the Tairen Souls. They considered it beneath their dignity. Steli had only agreed to do it because Rain asked her to.

«Ah.» Steli's nose twitched. *«Fahreeta talks.»*

Xisanna snorted. *«Talks talks talks.»*

Huah. Huah. Perahl and Steli chuffed with tairen laughter.

"You're telling me Fahreeta agreed to stay behind and speak with Lord Teleos on behalf of the pride?" Fahreeta was a proud, preening beauty, the last tairen Ellysetta could imagine lowering herself enough to talk to a human, not even one with as much Fey blood in his lineage as Dev Teleos. "I can't believe it."

«Mmm,» Steli confirmed. *«Fey-kin tells Fahreeta she so pretty, so brave, sooooo beautiful. Fahreeta likes the Fey-kin now. Says she and Torasul will stay, and she will talk to the Fey-kin. She even lets the Fey-kin pet her fur and purrs to him all the time.»* Blue eyes gleamed with sly humor. *«Torasul likes the Fey-kin not so much.»*

"Oh dear," Ellysetta said. She didn't need the perfectly rendered picture of one very large, very cranky Torasul to know what that meant.

Fahreeta was a flirt of tairen proportions. Sleek and beautiful and well aware of it. Her mate, Torasul, had more than a tairen's supply of patience—which was good, else his mate's constant teasing would drive him mad—but, as the Water master Loris v'En Mahr occasionally reminded his own whirlwind of a mate, even the vastest of seas eventually broke upon the shore.

«Not worry. Steli warned the Fey-kin not to pet Fahreeta so much else maybe Torasul decide the Fey-kin looks tasty-tasty.» She snickered and sang an image of Dev Teleos's face as Steli explained that Fahreeta's mate might eat him in a fit of tairen jealousy.

Rain frowned in concern. "Lord Teleos does not understand pride ways. Perhaps I should sing to Sybharukai and ask her to send other tairen to Orest," he suggested. "Just in case Torasul loses his temper."

Huah Huah. The other two tairen fell on the lair floor, rolling on their backs, their great bodies shaking with laughter. The bright, vivid tones of tairen speech filled the lair, so richly vibrant the sounds actually shimmered gold and silver in the air. *«This is a very good joke, Steli-chakai. Rainier-Eras so worried. He thinks Torasul will really eat the Fey-kin.»* Tairen tails swirled and twined together, and large paws batted the air.

"This is a joke?" Rain arched a brow and his arms crossed over his chest. "You are joking?"

Huahuahuahuah. Steli's eyes squeezed shut, and her head bobbed up and down as wheezing snickers escaped through her nose. *«So good joke. So good.»*

Ellysetta clapped a hand over her mouth to hide her rapidly widening grin. "Oh, you wicked cat!" she exclaimed, then ruined the scold with an irrepressible laugh.

«You need to move now, shei'tani.» The command, sent on tight weave of Spirit, came with a tug of Air that pulled her away from Steli's side.

As soon as she was clear, Rain sprang. The sparkling gray mist of the Change billowed out.

"Mraawwrrr!" Steli squawked and tried to scramble away, but she couldn't move quickly enough to avoid Rain's pounce.

Black and white tairen, limbs tangled, wings tucked tight against their bodies, rolled across the floor of the small lair, wrestling for supremacy. The other two tairen, still laughing, scooted to one side and watched with eager amusement, occasionally dodging to miss a flailing limb or tail as necessary.

Finally, Rain had Steli pinned, his fangs clamped around the back of her neck. Instantly, he released her, roared his victory, then padded over to Ellysetta's side, chuffing and blowing smoke in smug triumph. Steli hopped to her feet, sniffed, and went off to a corner of the lair to groom her ruffled fur.

«So what is the truth of the matter, Steli-chakai?» Rain

asked. *«Did Fahreeta truly agree to speak with Lord Teleos for the pride?»*

«Oh, yes. And the Fey-kin did tell Fahreeta she so beautiful. And he did pet, and she does purr. But Torasul not jealous. Jealous of two-leg? Even Fey-kin?» She snorted and shook her head, clearly finding the entire idea absurd.

Abruptly, Steli's mouth opened wide, fangs gleaming, pink tongue curling in an enormous yawn. *«Steli is tired. Long flight from Orest. Needs sleep. Rainier-Eras and Ellysetta-kitling stay with the pride.»*

It was less a question than a command from the First Blade of the Fey'Bahren pride, and Rain agreed.

«Aiyah, Steli-chakai. We will stay with the pride.»

In Fey'Bahren, the tairen frequently slept apart from one another, but here, in this new lair that had no volcanic heart to warm its stones, they piled together in a nest of fur, wings, and limbs, sharing body heat and the comfort of the pride. At the center of the nest, sandwiched on a bed of soft fur between Steli and Rain, Ellysetta slept, too, and even without Lord Galad's Sentinel blooms, she only dreamed good, happy tairen dreams of hunting and flying and life enveloped by the tight-knit love and security of the pride.

CHAPTER FIVE

Eld ~ Boura Fell
1st day of Seledos

Shrouded in the luxurious folds of his purple robe of office, High Mage Vadim Maur sat on the imposing throne of Eld, his body cradled in the cupped black hands of Seledorn, Lord of Shadows, whose colossal body, graven in *sel'dor* ore, towered over him like the vengeful god he was. Massive black dragon wings, the carved stone polished to a glossy sheen, soared up from the god's back and curved forward to form a great, dark protective dome over the Mage's throne. The symbolism of the throne was clear: Seledorn cradled the High Mage in his hands and sheltered him in the haven of the god's divine might.

The sentiment was one in need of reinforcement. Vadim's spies in the Council and the Mage Halls had carried back the whispers that had begun to circulate among the Mages in the days since his incarnation. As gifted a Mage as Nour had been, there were a handful of others who possessed a greater command of Azrahn, and with Vadim now inhabiting Nour's body, those Mages had begun planning to overthrow him.

But the Mages were greatly mistaken if they believed Nour's limitations had lessened Vadim's ability to hold on to power. He was still Vadim Maur, the greatest High Mage in the history of Eld. He was the High Mage who had engineered his own Tairen Soul after centuries of breeding and experimentation.

And soon . . . very soon . . . he would claim that Tairen Soul and bring her back to Eld to serve as the host vessel for his next incarnation. He'd feared her lost when she fled to Elvia and slipped beyond his reach—but now she was back. Though she was still somehow blocking him from her dreams, the great, vast, dark potential of her drew his senses like a lodestone. Her closeness brought his magic simmering to the surface, sending tiny sparks of dark power coursing through his veins until his whole body tingled with electric anticipation.

When the new moons rose over Dark Night, the thirteenth of Seledos, it would be Vadim Maur, Tairen Soul, who sat cradled in the hands of Seledorn, god of darkness, and the world would cower before his greatness.

"My Mages!" he cried to the thousands assembled in the vast cavern of Boura Fell's throne room. Blue-robed Primages had gathered closest to the throne, followed by red-robed Sulimages. Several dozen select saffron-robed Apprentices and even a handful of promising green-clad Novices had been granted permission to squeeze in to the nooks and crannies at the back of the cavern. "My Mages, long have we dwelled here in the darkness, recovering from the devastation of Demyan Raz's lost Wars. Long have we toiled in secret, patiently rebuilding our numbers, silently growing strong again—even stronger than we were before.

"Many of you had barely donned Novice green when Rain Tairen Soul scorched the world. You do not remember a time when Eld was a power to be reckoned with, when Mages walked freely aboveground, and the lesser beings of this world sought our counsel and good favor."

He let his gaze pass slowly round the chamber, resting longest on the older Mages—both those who had been his supporters and, more importantly, those who had not. "The eldest among you remember what it was like to be a Mage in the Council of Demyan Raz. He was blinded by his own ambitions. He underestimated the power of the Tairen Souls. I have not."

He watched the faces of those he least trusted for some flickering look, some smirk to betray their true feelings, but he found nothing. Not because they trusted him; he wasn't fool enough to think that. No, they were simply skilled adversaries, well versed at hiding their thoughts and pretending loyalty.

"Some of you were with me that day when Lord Death—the Fey warrior who had never once tasted defeat in over two thousand years—threw down his swords and surrendered to me without a fight. So, too, will I conquer Rain Tairen Soul, and the Fading Lands will soon follow."

He saw the heads beginning to nod, as those who had been with him remembered his daring plan and their triumphant return to Eld with Lord Death and his mate in tow. Experienced Primages long into their fifth incarnations had sneered at the young Primage Vadim, dismissing his idea as ridiculous nonsense. Those Mages, who had trembled when Lord Death stepped onto a battlefield, thought it impossible that such a great and fearless warrior could be taken alive—let alone brought to heel in such a simple way. And yet he had, and Lord Death's capture had catapulted Vadim high into the ranks of the Mage Council and ultimately earned him the coveted purple of Eld's highest office.

He was the youngest High Mage ever to sit on Eld's throne. And if several of the older, more hidebound Primages who'd opposed his appointment had ended up mysteriously dead in the process, well, they'd served as a cautionary tale. Such was the price of progress in the Magedom of Eld.

"We tested the strength of the Fey at Teleon and Orest, and found them far more vulnerable than we thought." He pinned his gaze on the Mage he suspected of fomenting most of the dissension currently rippling through the Council's ranks. "Their numbers are few, their allies fewer. If not for the tairen, both cities would belong to the Empire of Eld. Best of all, our use of the *chemar* proved a resounding success."

The real victory of Orest and Teleon, though, was that Ellysetta Baristani had left the safety and protection of the Fading Lands. With his four Marks upon her breast, it was only a matter of time before he completed the claiming of her soul. First, however, he had a kingdom to conquer . . . and a trap for a Tairen Soul to set.

"Now the armies of Celieria are divided, their mortal allies still weeks away. They and the Fey are ripe for the plucking. The victory I have long promised you is upon us." Vadim rose from the throne and spread his arms wide. "At last, my Mages, we are ready to reclaim our rightful place in the world. At last, the time has come to unleash the full might of Eld and seize first Celieria, then the world for the glory of Seledorn, God of Shadows!"

Celieria ~ Kreppes

The night was deep. Alone in his bed, dark but for the light of the waning moons shining in through the windowpanes, Dervas Sebourne lay sleeping. Still, unmoving, more statue than man. Outside, the bell tower of Kreppes rang the first small silver bell of the night, and that sound heralded the arrival of the first day of winter, and the first day of Seledos.

Lord Sebourne's eyes opened.

It was time.

He rose quietly and dressed in silence, with slow deliberation. Leather trousers, boots, no chain mail, the sun-and-moons pendant he'd worn all week. A leather vest lined with steel plate was his only armor—nothing to alert the King's Guard of his intent.

He donned the same weapons he'd worn since receiving the king's pardon: a sword sheathed at his left hip, a long dagger sheathed at his right. But just in case someone needed a quick silencing, he strapped on two small wristbows, each loaded with a poison dart and covered by the wide cuffs of his surcoat.

He slipped a vial of extra darts for the wristbows into his surcoat pocket before slipping out of his bedroom and closing the door noiselessly behind him.

* * *

None of the soldiers standing guard in the hallways paid Dervas much mind as he walked out of the east wing into the courtyard. They were used to the folk in this castle taking midnight strolls along the battlements. The week of waiting for war to begin had worn the nerves of even the staunchest soldier.

He made his way towards the shadowy cleft between the fortress and the inner wall that surrounded it. Six of his personal escort, armed as he was, were waiting.

"The others?" he asked in a toneless whisper.

"Dispatched to their locations, my lord," his captain replied. The other six men of his guard had their own tasks to perform this night.

"Then it is time."

They entered the central building where the king was housed. When the battle began, the wide stone floor would be carpeted in rows of sleeping men at night. But for now, all the troops that did not fit in the overflowing barracks spent their nights in one of the encampments outside the fortress walls.

In the otherwise empty hall, six King's Guard stood on duty. Two near the hallway leading to the east wing, two by the hallway to the west, and another two at the top of the stairs. All six watched Sebourne and his men with unblinking eyes as they entered.

"You two, come with me," Lord Sebourne said to his men in a carrying voice. "The rest of you stay here. I won't be but a few chimes."

Leaving four of his guard to wait in the main hall, he and the other two jogged up the stone steps to the second level and the hallway that led to the king's chambers.

The four guards downstairs sat on a table near the guards on the right of the room. Three of Sebourne's men started a game of toss blade with a sheathed dagger—an old Celierian warrior's game fashioned after the Fey Cha Baruk, the Dance of Knives. The fourth man started an easy conversation with the closest guards.

"I don't know about you two, but I'm starting to wish the flaming Eld would just attack already," he said. "I haven't had a decent night's sleep since we got here."

A clatter made both the guards and Lord Sebourne's man glance around to find two of Sebourne's fellows chasing after the sheathed dagger, which had skittered across the hall towards the other two King's Guard.

"Vern, you *dorn*!" one of Sebourne's men complained in a loud whisper. "You're the flaming worst at this game. You can't throw worth a damn." The two reached the fallen dagger the same time Lord Sebourne reached the top of the stair.

"I can throw better than you can *catch*!" The man called Vern raised his voice on the last word.

Lord Sebourne and his men sprang into action. The two men on the right of the hall sprang towards the two King's Guard guarding the eastern corridor. The two chasing the dagger went for the west hall guards. Lord Sebourne and his two companions lunged for the pair at the top of the stairs. Daggers flew. Blades slashed. With their throats slit and chests pierced, the six King's Guard died in a swift, near-soundless instant.

Sebourne and his two companions headed down the now-unguarded second-floor corridor while his other four men quickly dragged the limp corpses of the King's Guard into an empty chamber.

Dorian sat at the small camp desk he'd unpacked and set up in his bedchamber. He would have used the larger desk in the adjoining chamber, but his valet, Marten, was sleeping on the chaise in there.

"Just think of me like a faithful hound, guarding his master's door," Marten had said with a smile when Dorian objected. Had there been a dressing room, Marten would have slept there on a cot, as he did in Celieria City; but Kreppes was an ancient castle, built for war, not fashionable living, and it lacked many of the amenities of newer abodes.

Dorian sanded the damp ink of his third letter to Annoura in as many days. She hadn't answered him yet. Though some part of him had hoped she would, another part hadn't really expected her to. Still, in the small bells of the night, when he couldn't sleep, it comforted him to write to her, to pour out his heart to her as he so often had in their many years together, to imagine her face softening in a smile as she read his tender words.

When the ink was dry, he folded the letter and lit a stick of Celierian blue sealing wax off the flame of his candle lamp, holding it over the folded flap. As the drops of melted wax splashed on the folded vellum, forming a small pool of Celierian blue, he heard the bedroom door open.

"I'm sorry if I woke you, Marten," he said without looking up. He pressed his letter seal into the pool of wax and held it for a moment to let the impression set. "I couldn't sleep."

"You didn't." The voice didn't belong to Marten.

Dorian's head whipped around. "Sebourne? What are you doing—" His words cut off abruptly. His hands clapped to his throat, found the small dart, plucked it free. Poison. Potent and fast-acting. Already his muscles were failing, and he couldn't seem to take a breath.

"Avenging my son," Sebourne hissed. He stared into his king's stunned and disbelieving eyes and rammed his sword home, driving the blade up underneath Dorian's ribs to pierce his heart. "Your kingdom belongs to Eld now. Before this week is out, your son will be as dead as mine. Your wife and the child she carries will be servants of the High Mage, and I will be Lord Governor of Celieria, the newest province in the Empire of Eld."

Cannevar Barrial knew he should sleep. His body was aching. His eyes were raw and bleary. He would be no use to the king or the allies if the enemy struck when he was too tired to lift a blade. He knew that, but except for a few chimes of restless dozing, true, restful sleep had eluded him all night.

His mind was filled with too many memories of Talisa. He could hardly close his eyes without seeing her tear-stained face, her despair, without reliving the shocking moment of her death, when she'd leapt between her husband and a red Fey'cha blade to save her lover. Even now, Cann could feel the strike of the blade as if it had hit his own heart rather than his daughter's back.

Ah, gods. He sat up and covered his face with his hands. He wanted to rail against her death. To believe it had never happened. But he was too much a man of the north. Too much a lord of the borders. He'd seen too much death—and worse—to wallow in grief-stricken denial.

He rose from the soft, feminine bed covered with plush, fur-lined silk comforters in shades of wintry blue and tender spring green. Severn and Parsis had thought him a fool for taking Talisa's suite after offering his own to King Dorian, for torturing himself with her memory. Only Luce had understood. Luce, Cann's wild, sweet, fey child, with eyes that saw more than most. Almost a man now, and so like his mother. Luce realized that his father needed these memories of Talisa's life to make peace with the memory of her death.

He crossed the room to stand beside Talisa's delicate carved dressing table. The table was all-girl, painted creamy white and laid out with brushes, combs, perfumes, and all manner of womanly mysteries. His hand closed around the pot of perfumed cream Parsis had given her for this past year's Feast of Winter's End. Cann unscrewed the lid and lifted the jar to his face, breathing in the delicate aroma of Talisa's favorite flowers—the scent he would forever remember as hers. Bright, warm, sweeter than a spring morning. His eyes squeezed shut. His heart squeezed tight. But as he breathed the scent, he could see her face, alight with laughter, as she and the other maidens from Kreppes and the surrounding villages had danced around the Spring Tree, weaving brightly colored ribbons around the pine pole's carved scenes of winter, trailing flowers in their wake as they went. Such a good day. Such a happy, happy day.

He breathed the perfume again, trying to fix that memory in his mind. When he thought of her, he wanted to remember that—not the other sight that hurt so much.

A sound filtered through the closed door of Talisa's room. Cann didn't even consciously recognize it, but a lifetime on the borders made his body go tense all the same.

In that one instant, his weariness evaporated, and his grief found itself tucked unceremoniously into a tight box, utterly removed from his current consciousness. Cann the grieving father gave way to Great Lord Barrial, the fierce and wily wolf of the borders. He set the perfume pot down, his hands automatically seeking the grip of his swords but finding only empty air in their stead.

"Krekk." His weapons lay atop a bedside table, next to the rack holding the armor he now cursed himself for removing. The studded leather he'd slept in would do precious little to stop an axe, pike, or arrow strike in a full-on battle.

"We'll wake you at the first sign of trouble," his sons had promised when they convinced him to shed the armor. But trouble was here, and they had not come.

And that was troubling in its own right.

Cann raced across the room in swift silence, grateful for the plush furs on Talisa's floor that muffled the sound of his footsteps. The latch on the door began to lift just as he reached the bed. He dropped down behind the bed and slipped one of his daggers from its sheath. He wasn't half as good with the throwing daggers as the Fey, but at a distance as short as the one between him and the door, he didn't miss.

The door cracked opened.

A voice whispered, "Da?"

Parsis. Cann let out a breath. "Here, Parsi." Wary habit kept him crouched where he was, dagger pulled back for a throw.

Parsis poked his head around the edge of the door. Once he saw his father, he stepped quickly inside. Severn came in on his heels, closing the door behind them.

Now sure it was his sons and no one else, Cann rose to

his feet. Both of them here, fully armed and armored, could only mean one thing. "So, it's begun?"

"The king is dead but not by Elden hands. The attack came from within." Parsis's eyes were dark. "It's Sebourne, Da." He moved swiftly across the room to his father's side and reached for the armor hanging on the rack.

"Sebourne?" That was a shock Cann had not expected. He slipped into the chest plates Parsis held out. "You're sure?"

"Luce saw Sebourne's men kill some of the King's Guard."

"Where is Luce?"

"Gone to lower the shields and sound the alarm." Sev knelt to fasten the greaves to his father's legs.

With the night shields up, they couldn't spin a weave to alert the allies. Sebourne would know that and take precautions to keep those shields up, which mean Luce was headed for danger. As his sons helped him into his armor, Cann sent up a quick prayer for Luce's safety and a quick curse for Sebourne's insanity.

"Grief must have driven Sebourne mad." Arrogant, hot-tempered, and power-hungry though he was, Cann had never known Sebourne to harbor treasonous sentiments against the king. But grief could do strange things to a man. "Who the *jaffing* Hells let him close enough to the king to kill him?"

"I don't think they let him, Da. Luce said all the guards in the main hall were dead. And Sebourne's men were taking care to hide the bodies."

The boys fastened the last of his armor in place and handed him his weapons. He buckled his sword belt, slung his quiver on his back, and settled the band of black Fey'cha across his chest. Sev handed him his Elfbow. He strung the bow quickly, curling his left ankle around one end, bending the long, recurved body of the bow across his back, and settling the loop on the end of the bowstring into place. Bow in hand, he nodded to his sons. "Let's go."

His sons pulled their swords, and together they slipped out into the hall.

* * *

The halls of the fortress's central keep were eerily quiet. All of the King's Guard stationed in the central tower were missing from their posts, with only a few drops of blood an occasional sign of disturbance to hint at their fate. Cann and his sons, followed by the King's Guard who had been stationed in the east wing, padded through the silent corridors.

In the king's suite they found the bodies of Dorian X and his valet, Marten, both unmistakably dead. Cann shared grim looks with the others. Even with the eyewitness accounts of his sons, this irrefutable proof of Sebourne's treachery left him stunned.

"When we find him," Cann growled softly, "he's mine."

His boys nodded. Together, they slipped back into the hallway and made their way to the stone steps leading to the central hall.

They found Sebourne and two of his men disposing of the body of a King's Guard in the first hallway of the west wing.

Cann didn't hesitate. With a speed that would have done his Elvish kin proud, he pulled an arrow from the quiver at his back, nocked it, aimed, and let fly. A second arrowed followed a split second later.

Sebourne's two companions dropped without a sound. The Great Lord whirled, blade unsheathed and raised for battle. At the sight of Cann and his sons, Sebourne's lip curled.

"You," he spat. "I should have known."

"*Ta*, me," Cann snarled. "You miserable, *jaffing* traitor." He thrust his bow at his son Severn. His hand dropped to the hilt of the blade sheathed at his hip, and he drew the shining blade from its scabbard.

"Traitor, am I?" Lord Sebourne snarled, baring teeth like a *lyrant* issuing challenge. "Because Great House Sebourne is finally standing up to that puling Fey-lover of a king?"

"Because Great Lord Sebourne is a spineless *rultshart* of an assassin, too cowardly to face his enemy in open battle." Cann crossed the courtyard in a few long strides and took his battle stance, sword raised.

"I'll face you—gladly." Sebourne raised his sword. Torch-light glinted along the blade's fine, gleaming length. "You killed my son. You and those Fey maggots—and that loose-legged slut you called a daughter."

The insult to Talisa did not make Cann charge recklessly at his opponent as Sebourne had no doubt intended. Instead, all his anger, all his grief, shrank down into a hard, icy knot deep inside his core.

"Your son was a weak, spoiled bully," he replied. "I should never have let my daughter waste herself on him. Even on his best day, he wasn't worthy to kiss her hem."

Satisfaction surged inside him as Sebourne's nostrils flared. The Great Lord swung his blade with reckless force. Cann dodged the blow with ease and swung at Sebourne's unprotected back. Dervas spun sharply, raising his shield in time to deflect Cann's blow. He was no stranger to warfare and no easy kill, with reflexes honed by a lifetime of living in the wilds of the northern borders. Like Cann, there were few lords who could best him.

They flowed from one masterful form to another, attacking and counterattacking with blurring speed and steady, relentless prowess. Scissor Blades. Circle of Ice. Death Drop. Ring of Fire. Shield Strike. Helm Cleaver. Neither flinched or faltered.

Cann had appreciated Sebourne's skill a time or two in the past, and they'd spent many a day sparring together in a friendly rivalry. Right now, he heartily regretted those days. Sebourne knew him too well, knew how he attacked, defended, which combinations came most naturally to him.

But, then, he knew Sebourne, too.

He watched for the patterns that inevitably appeared in Sebourne's fighting. And eventually, it came. After a particularly savage series of attacks and parries, a panting, sweat-drenched Sebourne backed off into a lighter attack called Maiden's Dance. The series of teasing blows, though swiftly delivered, carried much less strength behind them. They weren't meant to kill, only to inflict numerous shallow wounds to weaken an opponent through blood loss and shake his confidence.

Cann took more of the wounds than he normally would, hoping that would encourage Sebourne to attempt his favorite next move. And there it was. Maiden's Kiss . . . the glancing blow to the face intended to lay open the cheek or blind an eye. Not a killing blow, just a bloodletter like Maiden's Dance, but to dodge the Kiss—which was often the instinctive response—put a fighter off-balance. The attacker could then deliver a hard blow and a sweep of his boot across the defender's ankle to put the defender down on his back and vulnerable to Final Point, a sword buried deep in a vulnerable throat.

Cann didn't dodge. He spun into the Maiden's Kiss, taking the side of Sebourne's blade across the cheek. He felt the sting, the warm spurt of blood as his skin split. But helm and chain-mail coif saved him from worse injury as he spun into and under the blade, ducking beneath Sebourne's sword arm. Cann's sword bit deep into Sebourne's wrist as he went, while his left hand reached for one of the black Fey'cha strapped to his chest. He sprang up behind Dervas, dagger in hand, to deliver a slicing blow to the vulnerable back of Sebourne's leg

Sebourne went down on one knee, his sword clattering to the courtyard's paving stones.

Breathing heavily, Cann circled back around, kicked Dervas's fallen sword across the courtyard, and thrust his sword under Sebourne's chin. "You traitorous *rultshart*. I should kill you now."

"Then why don't you?" The defeated Great Lord hugged his injured hand to his chest and curled his lip in a sneer.

"Because you don't deserve a quick death, Dervas. Our new king, whose father you slew, will want you punished as the traitor you are." Cann nodded to the King's Guard, then stepped back and sheathed his sword. "May the gods have mercy on your Shadowed soul." Abruptly feeling drained and hollow, Cann turned to rejoin his sons.

"I won't need that mercy, Barrial," Sebourne called after him. Then his voice took on a Dark edge, and he added, "But you will."

Cann saw Sev's eyes widen. He heard Parsis shout, "Da! 'Ware!" just as Sev raised his father's Elfbow, arrow nocked and drawn. Cann spun and dropped to one knee, blade in hand, to see Sebourne lift his uninjured arm. The cuff of Sebourne's sleeve had fallen back to reveal a small bow strapped to his wrist.

Cann's sword, Sev's arrow, and the King's Guards' swords all pierced Great Lord Sebourne in an instant. The poison dart from the wristbow bounced off the wall behind Cann's head and fell harmlessly to the stone pavers.

Mortally wounded, Dervas Sebourne, the last of his Great House, cried, "Gamorraz!" then toppled to the paving stones. Bright streamers of blood spilled from his nose and mouth as his pierced heart pumped the final moments of his life away.

On Seborne's chest the round moonstone in his necklace began to glow.

"What the—?" One of the King's Guard bent down to examine the pendant. The white stone grew brighter.

Cann had no idea what the thing was, but he knew magic when he saw it. And if the magic was Dervas's dying gift to them, it couldn't be good.

"Put it down!" he cried. "Get back! Everyone get back!"

His warning came too late for the guard holding the necklace.

Bright light gave way to rapidly expanding darkness. The guard screamed in helpless terror as the growing blackness consumed his hand and arm and half his torso. The smoldering remains of his body dropped to the ground and convulsed. Howling shadows fell upon his twitching corpse with ravening hunger.

"Demons!" someone cried, and the Celierians scattered.

Screams erupted from all corners of the castle.

"Attack! We're under attack!"

"Da! Look!" Severn pointed back towards the open portal behind them.

Cann looked in time to see a great, tawny cat leap from the well, a brightly garbed and veiled Feraz warrior on its back. The warrior carried a strange urn on a chain that he spun in circles over his head. Some sort of liquid sprayed forth, the fine droplets settling on the fleeing Celierians. The Celierians cried out, some slapping themselves where the droplets had landed on their skin. They slowed, stumbled a bit as if they were disoriented. Several of them shook their heads and rubbed at their eyes. But then, one by one, they straightened and drew their swords.

"The king! Save the king!" they cried.

And they fell upon their fellow countrymen, hacking and slashing their own people.

"Krekk," Cann swore. They were in trouble. If the Eld took the castle from the inside, all the allies encamped around Kreppes would be geese plump for the plucking. "Sev, Parsi—to the gate!" he cried to his sons. "We've got to open the gate! We can't let them take the castle."

They raced up towards the outer courtyard and the main fortress gates, but before they could reach it, a mob of magic-crazed Celierians blocked their way.

Blades flashed and whirled. Cann and his sons were all gifted swordsmen, trained from birth by the *dahl'reisen* who guarded Barrial land. Blood spewed—none of it theirs—but as the droplets splattered on Cann's face, his eyes and skin began to burn and a strange, disorienting fog came over him.

"Da?" Parsis grabbed his arm.

Parsis's face went in and out of focus. He blinked, rubbing at his eyes with bloody hands. A strange scent filled his nostrils, warm and exotic, intoxicating. On the heels of the scent came fervor. Bloodlust. Courage and determination.

The face hovering before him changed. Shadows played across the features, twisting and reshaping them into the face of the enemy. Pale, skin untouched by sunlight, hellish black pits for eyes, evil oozing from its pores.

"The king!" he cried. "Save the king!" And he thrust his sword into the monster.

In Kreppes's west wing, outside the suite occupied by Ellysetta and Rain, the door and half of the corridor-facing wall dissolved into nothingness as a portal to the Well of Souls appeared where the brass hall sconce had been.

Twenty Primages, led by Primage Soros, leaped out of the Well, globes of blue-white Mage Fire spinning in their hands, ready for launch. But the sight of the empty room drew them up short.

"Check the bedchamber!" Soros commanded.

Mages and Black Guard flung open the connecting doors to the adjoining bedchamber and flooded inside, arrows nocked, swords drawn, Mage Fire blazing. Soros rushed in behind them to claim the High Mage's prize. But instead of gloating with victory, his expression darkened to thunderous rage.

The room was empty. The bed still neatly made.

"Sebourne!" he cried. "You worthless *jaffing rultshart!*"

Ellysetta Baristani and the Tairen Soul were gone.

Outside the castle, in the tairen's makeshift lair, Ellysetta came awake with a gasp. Her body was ice-cold and shivering uncontrollably. Something was wrong. Something was very, very wrong.

She reached for Rain. Her fingers closed around his bare arm, gripped tight, shook him hard.

"Rain, wake up. I think it's begun." She left her hand on his arm so he could sense what she found as she reached out in search of the trouble that had roused her. Her empathic senses soared on wafts of lavender Spirit gleaming with golden *shei'dalin's* love.

Suddenly, she grabbed her throat, feeling the barbs of an arrow pierce her throat. She tried to breathe, but her lungs filled instead with bubbles of blood. *The king. Save the king!* Then pain eased, and her body went limp.

Rain grabbed her shoulders and shook her with sudden fear. *"Shei'tani!"*

She blinked. Stared up at him. Feeling returned to her limbs. She pulled back her senses, locking them tight inside herself. "Kreppes. They're inside the fortress. They've taken the castle! They're attacking our camp!"

"Krekk." Rain leapt to his feet. Green Earth swirled as he summoned his golden war armor and steel. *«Fey! Ti'Kreppes! Ti'Dorian! The enemy is upon us!»* He grabbed Ellysetta's arm, and together they raced for the lair's entrance.

The tairen erupted from their makeshift lair with roars and jets of flame, springing from hill to sky, soaring up on wide-spread wings before wheeling back around to dive towards Kreppes.

The Eld had taken the ramparts and were firing the trebuchets and bowcannon filled with shrapnel bolts on the allied camps. Massive hunks of stone, balls of burning pitch, and bolts that separated into hundreds of razor-sharp shards rained down upon the allies. Chaos ruled. Tents were aflame. Burning men shrieked and ran in mindless terror while around them soldiers raced in every direction.

«Kaiven chakor, ti'Feyreisa! Ti'Feyreisa!» Rain cried on her quintet's path. He swooped low over the Fey tents, and Ellysetta leapt from his back and rode a shaft of Air to the ground.

She landed on her feet in the center of the Fey encampment and was immediately surrounded by hundred-fold weaves and scores upon scores of grim-eyed warriors.

"I need cots and tables," she told Bel when he, Gaelen, and the others reached her side. "Tell the *lu'tan* to start bringing me the wounded."

"Nei, Ellysetta," Bel said, "we need to get you to safety, away from the battlefield. Rain's orders," he added, when her eyes flashed. "It's too dangerous for you here."

"I know what he wants, and I know why he wants it, and

I'm not going anywhere. There are wounded men who need my help."

Bel exchanged a speaking glance with Gaelen.

"Kem'falla," Gaelen said, "it's not just dangerous for you to be here. It's dangerous for everyone around you."

She speared Gaelen with a cold glare. "Don't try to play on my empathies, Gaelen. I know what I'm asking. I know that my presence puts everyone in danger, and if there were any other option, I'd take it. But we have wounded—dying men. I can feel them right now. I'm all they've got, and I will not abandon them. Now get those tables and cots—and send the wounded my way. And tell my secondary quintet to attend to me. All of the generals were in the castle with the king. Rain's going to need leaders for this army, and you five are it. You stay close, though, Gaelen. I'm going to need your help for healing."

Gaelen had known her long enough to recognize when she was determined. He gave a curt bow. *"La ve shalah, doreh shabeila de."* As you command, so shall it be.

Bel squared his shoulders and signaled to his brother Fey. "You heard her, *kem'jetos.* Cots, tables, wounded. Gil, you spread the word to send the wounded here. I'm going to track down the Celierians' next in command."

«Bel, Gaelen, have you lost your mind?» Gillandaris vel Sendahr hissed his outrage on the quintet's private path. Of all the quintet's warriors, Gil was the one who believed that guarding her included protecting her from her own stubborn nature whether she liked it or not. *"It will take the Eld two heartbeats to figure out she's here. This hundred-fold weave lights a beacon to lead their way. We need to get her to a more secure location.»*

«Believe me, she isn't going anywhere no matter what Bel or I or anyone else say or do,» Gaelen told the white-blond Fey. *«Or have you forgotten what she's like when she's determined to do something?»*

«Between the five of us, we could make her go.»

Gaelen gave a bark of laughter. *«Good luck with that,*

Fey.» He clapped a hand on Gil's shoulder. *«I'll sing a mourning ballad in your name when she sends your charred and shredded corpse back to the elements.»*

Gil turned to the other two. *«Taj, 'Jonn. Come on, kem'jetos. You know I'm right.»*

Ellysetta's uncle shook his head. *«Nei, Gil. I saw my sister in Ellysetta's face just then—and more than a bit of my bond brother, too. She'd carve out our hearts and eat them roasted before she'd let us drag her away.»*

Gil turned to Rijonn, but the giant Earth master put his head down and went to work spinning cots and tables for his queen.

"Seven scorching Hells!" Gil cursed and kicked a nearby water barrel. "Gods save me from stubborn women!" With a scowl as dark as a thundercloud, he started spinning Spirit weaves to alert the allies where to send their wounded.

Tairen breath and tairen venom combined. Fire exploded from Rain's muzzle, a great, incinerating jet of magic flame that burned hotter than any natural fire. Stone, flesh, bone, magic: Nothing could long withstand the searing fury of tairen fire.

The sky before Rain went dark with *sel'dor* arrows, shrapnel bolts, fiery mortars, all hurtling towards him as he hurtled towards them. Unfaltering, he flew, clearing a path with his flame. The scurrying ants on the wall became people, armored men lifting bows, racing to reload artillery, the oval shapes of their faces illuminated by moonlight. He drew a deep breath, filling his lungs.

The boiling cloud of tairen flame engulfed the western wall of Kreppes, consuming the bowcannon and trebuchets mounted there, along with all the troops that manned them. The tip of Rain's tail raked the northwest tower as he passed, gouging a crater in the tower's outer wall. The supporting wall compromised, the tower collapsed, raining stone and screaming, flailing men into the spike-filled pit below.

Steli, Xisanna, and Perahl strafed the other walls with similar results.

Roaring in fierce triumph, the four tairen circled and dove in for a second run.

In the few chimes' respite from bombardment afforded by the tairens' attack on the castle, the allies regrouped. Bel sent out a massive Spirit weave to locate and summon the men next in the chain of command of the Celierian forces. As the new leaders of the Celierian forces made their way to the Fey encampment, the field commanders gathered their troops, and the chaos of the allied camps yielded to a ragged semblance of order.

In Ellysetta's makeshift healing tent, the first of the wounded had arrived on her tables—men with limbs missing, skin scorched away, screaming in agony.

"Las, las," she crooned, stroking bloody, burned brows. "I am with you. Don't be afraid. Ssh. There is no pain, *kem'storran*. There is only warmth and light. Do you feel it?" A golden glow of powerful magic radiated around her as she worked. The rest of the world, the other wounded, the battle raging less than a mile away: All faded from her consciousness. The entirety of her thoughts, the concentrated power of her great magic, was focused solely on each dying man carried to her table.

Gaelen and her secondary quintet ringed around her, keeping close by her side as she spun her healing weaves.

Despite Ellysetta's orders, Bel and the other warriors of her primary quintet refused to leave her. Instead, to accommodate Ellysetta's commands without fighting the dictates of their *lute'ashieva* bonds, Bel had set up a military command post beside her healing tent, and it was there that he, Tajik, Rijonn, and Gil met with the Fey commanders and the new leaders of the Celierian forces.

A map of Kreppes and surrounding area—modified by Rijonn to show the recent fortifications and topographical changes—lay flat on a large table. The commanders gathered around it.

"Most of our heavy siege was inside the castle," Bel said,

"but we still have the trebuchets and bowcannon mounted on the hilltops." He spun a Spirit weave to mark their locations. "These are within firing range of Kreppes." He indicated the siege directly north of the castle. "We need to reposition them to provide cover fire for the tairen and do what we can to keep the cannon off those walls. Quintets of Earth masters will move the others into position here and here and here." The small, glowing replicas of the siege weapons on the far eastern and western hilltops disappeared from their current locations and reappeared in the formations placed to attack the west, east, and south walls of the fortress. "The rest of the Earth masters will start constructing siege towers and ladders to scale the walls."

"Commander Tarr." Bel fixed his gaze upon the Celierian officer in charge of the king's archers. "I need your archers in position along these lines." He pointed at the map and drew the lines in Spirit. "When the tairen aren't firing the castle, your men should be.

"Commander Nevin, Chatokkai vel Amah, as soon as the towers and ladders are ready, you'll lead your men up the southern wall. Commander Bonn, our Earth masters are working on a battering ram. Your men will storm the gate on my signal. Fifty quintets will accompany each of your attack forces to weave shields and keep Mage Fire off you."

Bel stepped back from the table. "My lords, my blade brothers, we either retake Kreppes, or we bring it down."

In the outlying fields surrounding Kreppes, two dozen men broke off from the mass of Sebourne troops, each taking a different direction into the crowd of allied troops.

There were so many men running hither and yon, no one paid any attention to Sebourne's men . . . or the small white stones they dropped in their wake.

Two young Celierian infantrymen rushed through the crowded encampment towards the area where Commander

Bonn was marshaling his forces. One of the two fell behind, and his companion turned to scold him.

"Get a move on, Kip. The battering ram is nearly done, and Commander Bonn won't wait on us."

"Wait a chime, Jamis," Kip said. "I thought I saw something over here." He took a few steps towards one of the paths between the lines of allied tents, drawing his sword as he went.

"Saw what? Kip!" his companion exclaimed. Kip had disappeared into the shadows between the rows of tents. "Kip!" He started towards the place Kip had disappeared, then stopped when his friend emerged from the shadows. "What was it? Kip? Are you all right?"

Kip had a strange, disoriented look on his face. His sword arm dangled at his side, and his fingers curled loosely around the hilt of his unsheathed blade.

Concerned, Jamis started towards him, only to stop when Kip's eyes suddenly fixed on Jamis's face and the confused look changed to something much more disturbing. Something menacing.

Kip raised his sword.

Rain led the tairen in series of flame runs over Kreppes's ramparts to weaken the enemy shields and keep them occupied while the allies put their plans into action. The bowcannon and trebuchets were gone, not even piles of ash remained where they had stood. The current menace was archers armed with barbed *sel'dor* arrows. That and the Eld were up to the same tricks they'd used months ago at Orest, with portals to the Well of Souls opening and bowcannon firing from within. They kept the sky filled with *sel'dor*, but before the tairen came within flame-reach, the archers would race down the battlement steps, the portals would close, and the fire would splash against the smoldering stone of Kreppes's diminishing ramparts. As soon as the tairen passed, the archers would rush back into place, the portals would reopen, and they would send a barrage of *sel'dor* arrows and bolts chasing after the tairen.

Xisanna had taken a *sel'dor* bolt to her flank and Perahl had a large hole in his left wing. Strafing the Kreppes battlements was getting to be a dangerous game of dodge-tairen.

Rain folded his wings and dropped. Wind whistled past his flattened ears. He held his forelegs tight and streamlined against his body. The tuck-winged dive was one of his favorite tairen maneuvers. He had always loved the speed, the reckless thrill, the sudden breathless jolt as his wings snapped wide and plummeting fall curved sharply into a high-speed glide. And in battle, he loved how small a target it made him on the approach, and what a blur of speed he was as he shot past the enemy, raining fire upon him.

Spewing flame into the onslaught of arrows and bolts, he burrowed a tunnel through the air. But as he drew another breath in preparation for his next jet of flame, a blast of fire from Steli illuminated the figure of a man standing on the battlement, distinctive Elfbow drawn, as he took aim at Rain.

That was no Elden Mage, and no servant of the Dark either.

What in the gods names was Cannevar Barrial doing up there?

His left wing dropped. The straight glide towards Kreppes became a banking roll away from his target just as Cann fired at the spot Rain had been.

«Cease fire!» Rain sang to Steli and the tairen. *«Cease fire!»* he cried on the new Warrior's Path. *«Those aren't the Eld! It's our men in there! Cease fire! Cease fire!»*

CHAPTER SIX

"Cannevar Barrial has been Mage-claimed."

After sighting Lord Barrial on the ramparts of Kreppes, Rain and the tairen had broken off their attack and returned to the Fey command post with the grim news.

"Impossible," Gaelen said. Now that most of the camp had retreated out of range of the castle's weapons, the influx of wounded needing Ellysetta's care had slowed to a trickle, and since the worst of the injured had already been healed, she'd released him to join the rest of her quintet. "*Dahl'reisen* have lived on Barrial land for centuries. They would have known if he'd been claimed."

"Then perhaps the claiming happened in Celieria City, when he was away from the *dahl'reisen*," Rain said, "because that was definitely him on the ramparts, with his Elfbow. Shooting at me."

"Could he have been trying to send you some sort of signal?" Bel suggested.

"Not likely. It's only because I turned away that he missed." Considering how fast Rain had been flying in that strafing run, that was no mean feat.

"Then you should have killed him when you had the chance," Gaelen said. "Terrible as it sounds, death by tairen flame is the greatest boon you could give the soul-claimed. It stops them from harming others, and they can't be called back to serve in demon form."

Rain hunched his shoulders. Everything in him rebelled against the idea of slaughtering friends—especially Cann.

"It just doesn't feel right," he muttered. "I wouldn't have been surprised at all to see Sebourne up on that wall . . . but Cann . . . He doesn't like the Mages. He's worked against them all his life . . ."

"Most Mage-claimed have no recollection of their claiming. That's part of what makes them so dangerous. They're undetectable unless you spin Azrahn to check them for Mage Marks."

"Maybe, but could all of Kreppes have been claimed without detection? Over half the forces in the castle are Barrial men who've been stationed at Kreppes for years. Even if Cann is Mage-claimed, he couldn't have overtaken all the troops in the castle without help."

"Perhaps vel Serranis's *dahl'reisen* friends haven't been quite as observant as he thought," Tajik suggested with an arched brow.

Gaelen cast a withering glance Tajik's way but didn't take the bait. "How many Eld did you and the tairen see on the ramparts?" he asked Rain. "It's possible they came in through portals to the Well of Souls like they did at Teleon and Orest and overwhelmed the defenders."

Rain reran the strafing runs in his mind's eye. How many Eld had he seen? "I don't know. It was dark. They were firing on us and the encampment." His brows drew together. Come to think of it, he couldn't recall seeing any Mage robes at all on the wall.

«Feyreisen! Come quickly.» A cry rang out across the new Warrior's Path. *«Something is—»* The call broke off abruptly.

Rain tried to trace the weave back to its sender, but the Spirit threads had already dissolved. "Who was that?" he asked. Gaelen and the others shook their heads. *«Fey!»* he called. *«Report! Identify yourself? What's happening?»*

A moment later, another call rang out, but it was a different voice this time. *«Fey! Ti'Commander Bonn! We're under attack! It's—»*

The second call broke off as abruptly as the first.

"Where is Bonn?" Rain demanded.

"Here." Bel pointed a finger and threads of Spirit illuminated a position deep in the heart of the allied encampment—well out of range of enemy fire. No attack on that particular location should have been possible without the enemy coming through the surrounding allies.

Unless the enemy had been among them all the time.

Sudden suspicion reared up. "Where are Sebourne's men?"

Squads of Fey went in search of Sebourne's men while Rain and several hundred Fey raced across the allied encampment to Commander Bonn's position. They arrived to find a full-fledged melee in progress. Shouts of "Save the king!" and "For Celieria and King Dorian!" resounded as silver swords flashed in the moonlight.

«Fire masters!» Rain cried. *«Light the sky!»*

Streamers of brightly burning magic shot into the air over the encampment, illuminating the battle below. Shadowy figures struggling in the darkness became Celierians and Fey locked in mortal combat. Rain had suspected he would find Sebourne's men among the group, and he did. But there were others, too—King's army, Barrial men, even Fey, all slashing at each other with grim savagery.

Of the Eld, however, there was no sign.

Not a single *sel'dor* blade or arrow. Not a single Mage robe. Nothing.

"My Lord Feyreisen!" Surrounded by a cadre of armored soldiers, each with shields raised, Bonn was being driven back by a horde of attackers wearing Sebourne colors.

«Fey, form a line. Take out Sebourne's men.» Rain dove towards the beleaguered commander. Fey'cha flew from his fingertips, spinning out in silvery blurs, thunking home with lethal accuracy in the throats of Sebourne's men. He spoke

his return word to call his blades back to their sheaths and threw a second volley even before the first bodies hit the ground.

Reaching Bonn's side, Rain dispatched another six attackers with red Fey'cha to their throats and spun a rapid five-fold weave to shield the Celierian commander.

"Commander Bonn, order your men to fall back behind the Fey. It will be easier for us to deal with this attack if they stand clear."

"My men?" Bonn gave him a harried look. "Most of those *are* my men."

"We were waiting for the Earth masters to finish the battering ram," Bonn explained. "There was a commotion near the tents, and the next thing I knew my men started attacking each other."

"Did you see anything else? A Mage perhaps?" Rain could detect no Azrahn, so if the Mages were controlling the allies, they'd either found a way to mask the signature of their weaves, or they were using some other method of control entirely.

Before Bonn could answer, an armored Celierian infantryman charged the Fey line. "For King Dorian and Celieria!" he cried as he attacked.

Seven Fey'cha hit him simultaneously, and he dropped like a stone at Commander Bonn's feet. The commander stared at the fallen man in shocked dismay. "Avis?"

"You knew him?" Rain watched the commander's face for any sign of deceit or treachery but saw only genuine shock and sorrow.

"He was my Sergeant at Arms. One of my most trusted men." Bonn's dark brows drew together. "There's no way he could have been one of Sebourne's plants."

"Mage-claimed?"

"Impossible." Bonn shook his head in bewilderment. "Vel Serranis checked all my men yesterday at my own request."

Rain skimmed the minds of the combatants with the light Spirit weave Fey often used in melee combat to determine enemy from ally. The only thoughts he could detect came from the allies and were predominately concerned with defending king and country and slaughtering the traitors wearing their own colors. A number of the combatants kept wondering how friends they'd slept, eaten, trained, and worked beside could have turned on them with so little warning.

He tried a different, more probing weave with the same result. Rain could not tell friend from foe.

What the flaming Seven Hells was going on here?

«Bel.» Rain sent the call on gleaming lavender threads. *«Scan the area around me. Tell me if you can sense anything controlling these men.»* Apart from Rain himself, Bel was the strongest Spirit master of the Fey, and with the bond madness making Rain's control of his magic increasingly unpredictable, it seemed only wise to get a second opinion. If there were any subtle weaves controlling Bonn's men, Bel would be able to detect them.

One of the Fey behind him gave a strangled gasp. Rain turned in time to see the flash of the red Fey'cha embedded in his throat wink out as its owner invoked his return weave. The dying Fey gazed at him in an instant of mute surprise, then crumpled to the ground.

Rain spun back around, searching the crowd, finding the soulless eyes, the vivid scar marring the perfection of what otherwise would be a shining Fey face.

«Dahl'reisen!» he cried. *"Dahl'reisen* are among the attackers! Fey! Fall back. Bonn, tell your men to get out of there now!"

"Dahl'reisen?" Tajik turned to Gaelen. "That's three times now we've found your friends in league with the Eld."

"Not every *dahl'reisen* joins the Brotherhood, nor does every one who joins stay," Gaelen answered with a scowl.

"Whoever these *dahl'reisen* are, I doubt they're acting in the name of the Brotherhood."

"You doubt?" Tajik pounced on the opening. "Which is another way of saying you hope it's not them, but you aren't really sure, isn't it?"

"They are *dahl'reisen,* Tajik. The Dark Path's call can be very strong."

"Quiet!" Bel snapped. His eyes were hazy, his mind traveling on weaves of lavender light, probing the minds of the warriors engaged in the melee.

"Bel, something is wrong." Ellysetta walked into the command tent. "No one from this new battle in the encampment is being brought to me. Surely there must be wounded?"

"There are wounded." His eyes narrowed and began to glow as he sent his senses out, away from the protected healing enclave. "They do not come."

"Why?"

"They don't believe themselves badly injured. They are determined not to give up." He blinked, and his eyes lost the soft haze of magic, becoming twin cobalt diamonds glittering beneath ebony brows. "All they're thinking of is fighting, of dying, if necessary, to protect king and country."

"Krekk," Gaelen said.

"What is it?" Ellysetta asked.

"It's a rare mortal who, when faced with his own death, thinks only of king and country. Mortals may believe in the Bright Lord and his promises of a next life, but every one of them I've ever fought beside has clung to this life with his last dying breath."

"Are they Mage-claimed?"

"I doubt it. I checked many of them personally," Gaelen said. "So many would not fall so quickly. And even if it were possible, directing so many Mage-claimed all at once would raise such a stink of Azrahn that every Fey for forty miles would come running."

"Could the *dahl'reisen* be controlling them with a Spirit weave?" Gil asked.

Bel shook his head. "I already checked. It's not Spirit. I don't think it's a weave at all—or if it is, it's nothing I can detect."

Gaelen turned slowly. Thin, questing tendrils of his magic spun out in every direction, and with each quarter turn, the frown on his face deepened. "It must be a spell of some kind. But I can't sense what it is or where it's coming from or how it's controlling them."

"Whatever it is," Tajik interrupted, "it's not affecting only Bonn's men anymore. I'm getting reports from all over the encampment. Our own men are turning on each other. Fey included."

"Scorching Hells!" Rain and the Fey fired Fey'cha without cease to cover their retreat, but the attackers only seemed to be multiplying—and determined to kill them.

"Watch out, Feyreisen!" Powerful air weaves swirled around Rain, batting down a red Fey'cha that had been flying towards him. At the same time, five *lu'tan* loosed their own red daggers. They screamed and fell to their knees in agony as the *dahl'reisen* attacker clutched his pierced chest and collapsed in death.

"*Feyreisen*, I know that *dahl'reisen*." One of the Fey commanders pointed to the body. "He's Paris vel Mirothel, an Earth master who came with us from Dharsa. He's one of our own."

"*Rasa?*" Rain asked.

"*Nei.* Not even close. He was only a boy during the Mage Wars."

Rain's mouth went grim. If Paris hadn't been *rasa*, slaughtering a thousand mortals should not have tipped him into Shadow . . . and yet clearly something had. That could only mean one thing. Paris had either slain one of the *dahl'reisen* or one of his own blade brothers—and then come after the rest of his blade brothers.

"Whatever this is," the Fey commander said, "it's too dangerous to risk its spreading further. Fey are killing Fey. You should have the tairen fire the field."

"Fire the field?" Bonn echoed. "You can't be serious. These are our own men—including some of my oldest and most loyal friends."

"As your Avis just proved, those friends would kill you if they could," Rain reminded him.

"Isn't there some other way to neutralize them until we can figure out a way to undo whatever has taken over their minds?"

A Tairen Soul's first instinct when threatened was to attack, to kill to protect the pride. Even now, he could feel his tairen Eras hissing, growling, unsheathing his claws in preparation for attack. Tairen did not trouble themselves with morality. To them, there was only survival or death. So when a threat arose, they eliminated it—swiftly and conclusively. There was no word in tairen speech for remorse, nor any word for mercy. There was only strength and weakness, predator and prey, survival or death.

But as Rain looked out over the turbulent—and growing—knot of attackers who wore the faces of his allies, he thought of Cann, standing on the ramparts of Kreppes, Elfbow drawn and aimed at Rain, trying to kill him.

A tairen's first instinct might be to kill, but Rain was more than tairen—and these people were friends. Some of them were Fey, blade brothers. No matter how fiercely his tairen half urged him to scorch and shred them, his Fey half rebelled at the thought.

The five bond-threads he shared with Ellysetta warmed with golden brightness, infusing him with warmth. Her voice, as calming as a tranquil summer sea, washed over him in soft waves.

«Las, shei'tan. Ke sha eva ku.» I am with you.

He closed his eyes, absorbing her Light, drawing her gentleness into his soul and knitting her proffered strength into the ragged threads of his self-control. When he was calm once more, he told her what was happening.

«Gaelen believes it's an ensorcelment that's somehow being passed like a contagion,» she told him. *« Bring some of the affected to me. If we can figure out how the spell is controlling them, we may be able to counteract it.»*

Rain hesitated. They didn't know what this evil was or how it spread, and he was loath to let a single possessed combatant within a tairen-length of Ellysetta.

His hesitation must have given him away, but Ellysetta wouldn't permit his over protectiveness. *«Rain, we don't have a choice. If I can't figure out what this is and how to stop it, the Eld will just use it against us again and again.»*

«One,» he capitulated with ill grace. *«One only. Under heavy guard the entire time and slain at the first hint of danger to you. And don't bother trying to negotiate. It's that or nothing. I won't risk you, shei'tani.»*

«Very well,» came her grudging agreement. *«Send me your one . . . but hurry. We're getting more reports from elsewhere in the camp. The contagion is spreading.»*

"My Lord Feyreisen?" Bonn prodded. "What are your orders?"

Rain opened his eyes. "We will try to save as many as we can," he told the Celierian. On the new Warrior's Path, he gave the command, *«Fey, do whatever you must to immobilize them, but don't kill them unless you have no other choice. And shield yourselves. Until we know what this spell is and how it is passed, do everything you can to minimize your risk of being affected.»*

A moment later, the weaves spun out like ropes of lightning, vivid green and lavender and silvery white, shining bright in the darkness of the night.

Weaving enemies unconscious was much easier when those enemies did not include Fey warriors bombarding you with red Fey'cha and countering your weaves as quickly as you could spin them . . . especially when you were trying *not* to kill the ones thwarting you.

In the end, Rain sent three quintets after each ensorcelled Fey, one to stop his weaves, one to stop his weapons, and the last to render him unconscious. Once all the ensorcelled Fey were contained, the *lu'tan* made quick work of immobilizing the mortals.

"Careful, Fey!" he called, as warriors rushed towards the mass of limp bodies. "Don't touch them. Whatever this is, we don't know how it's spread. Use weaves only to bind and move them."

Turning back to Bonn, he said, "Can you point out one of the ensorcelled men who you know is not Mage-Marked? The Feyreisa is going to try to counter the spell that has addled their minds, but I won't take the chance of sending a Mage-claimed to her."

As the Fey lined the still-living magic-bound soldiers on the ground, Bonn searched through the rows of unconscious warriors until he came across a face he recognized. "This one. He's one of Avis's men. He was one of the first vel Serranis checked."

"Kabei. Take him to the Feyreisa." Rain gestured to the Fey, who hoisted the man onto an Earth-weave stretcher and carted him off the field towards the shining dome of magic where Ellysetta waited.

"What shall we do with the wounded, Feyreisen?" the Fey commander asked.

"Have the Fey do what they can to keep them alive, but don't send any more of them to the Feyreisa until they're free of this ensorcelment."

Rain regarded the carnage grimly. Hundreds lay dead and dying. Hundreds more were useless to the allies until a cure could be found. The Eld could not have devised a more effective attack. Using the allies' own men against each other had dealt twice the damage of any conventional attack—and all without the loss of a single Eld life.

He bent over one of the fallen to bind his limbs and seal the deep slice in his side. The puddle of blood that had gathered beneath his fallen form shone like black oil in the waning moonlight. A faint, exotic scent made Rain's nostrils twitch.

"Do you smell that?" he asked the Fey closest to him.

"What?"

"That smell . . . a sweet spice . . . very faint." Rain lowered his head closer to the unconscious Celierian.

On the ramparts of Kreppes, an armored man lowered a small brass spyglass and turned to hurry down the stone steps to the yard below. Though he wore the colors of the King's Army, the pallid skin that had never seen daylight belonged to no Celierian. The man crossed the yard and ducked into the common room of the large barracks, where a blue-robed Primage and a trio of red-robed Sulimages stood waiting.

The soldier bowed to the Mages. "The Fey have contained the infected, master. They have rendered them unconscious and are binding them now."

The Primage accepted the news without expression and waited for the soldier to bow again and exit before he turned to the Sulimages. "You know what to do."

The dome of magic surrounding Ellysetta and the allies' command center parted to admit the Fey carrying the unconscious body of the ensorcelled Celierian. They deposited the man on one of the empty tables set up for the wounded. Unwilling to leave Ellysetta's safety to anyone else, her primary quintet closed around her protectively, and their magic swirled around them and her in visible auras.

When she started to reach for the bound man, Gaelen blocked her. "You mustn't touch him. We don't know what this is or how it's passed," he said.

She stifled a sigh. "Give me a little credit, Gaelen. I wasn't planning to touch him, but I can't examine him from half-way across the room."

Unchastened, Gaelen reluctantly stepped aside.

Ellysetta moved closer and began to examine the unconscious man carefully. He was soaked in blood, both his own from numerous deep cuts as well as splatters that clearly had come from other donors. Gaelen checked him for Mage Marks, just to be on the safe side, before Ellysetta spun protective weaves around her hands and began checking the man's body for clues as to what had taken over his mind.

"We've already ruled out Azrahn and Spirit," she said as she worked. "So how else could a spell of this sort be invoked?"

"Potions or totems are the usual vehicles," Rijonn said.

"If it's a potion, it was most likely added to their food or drink," Tajik suggested.

"But different areas of the camp were affected at the same time," Bel said. "Which means someone would have had to slip the potion into all the cookpots—and if they did that, why would only some of us be affected?"

"If the spell is tied to a totem, the totems could have been hidden in various parts of the camp," Gil said. "The spell could affect anyone within a specific distance of the totem."

"If that were the case, Rain and the others would have been affected when they got near it," Ellysetta said. "We know the spell affected different areas of the camp, which means there were multiple points of origin, but not all occurred at the same time. Whatever it is affects Fey and Celierian alike, and it spreads."

"It could be darts," Gil suggested. "Delivered by finger-bow, wristbow, or even blowpipes. They're tiny enough to be easily missed, and could deliver a potion or poison directly into the blood."

"Or insect stings," Rijonn added in his rumbling voice. "I remember Lord Shan telling us once about a Feraz witch who used an army of buzzflies to attack her enemies."

"I haven't heard anyone talking about darts or swarms of insects," Gaelen said, "so I think we can safely rule those out."

"It burns," Bel exclaimed. Everyone turned to look at him. "When I was scanning their thoughts, looking for what was controlling them, I heard a couple of Celierians thinking about something burning them. I didn't think anything of it at the time. I thought the Fire masters had spun a weave on them."

"Burns how? Their eyes, their throats—ah!" Ellysetta gasped as a sudden chill, like the poisonous bite of an ice spider, raced up her spine. Her legs went weak, and she had to grab the edges of the table to keep from falling.

"What is it?" Gaelen asked with quiet urgency. "Is it the poison?"

Before Ellysetta could gather her wits enough to respond, a cry rang out across the Warrior's Path.

«Portals opening! Fey! Bote'cha!»

Rain leapt to his feet, away from the bodies of the unconscious, as gaping black maws opened up across the encampment. Barrages of *sel'dor* and Mage Fire poured out of the openings, clearing a path before brightly colored *fezaros* leapt out of the Well on the backs of their tawny *zaretas,* swinging not swords but strange pierced pots on long chains.

Fey'cha flew. Most of the *fezaros* and their fierce cats fell quickly, but not before dozens of Fey and Celierians around them went strangely still, then turned on their brethren, crying, "Save the king!" and "For Celieria and King Dorian!"

«It's a potion of some kind,» Rain spun the news to Ellysetta and her quintet as his blades flew. *«Feraz are dispersing it, so their witches are most likely the makers. The potion appears to possess whomever it touches on contact.»*

More *fezaros* leapt through the openings, now protected by growing rings of ensorcelled allies. And behind them, staying to the center of the growing rings, came black-armored

Elden archers, and blue- and red-robed Mages. *Sel'dor* arrows, invisible against the night sky, rained down upon the allies, and everywhere they fell, cries of "Save the king!" soon erupted. Possessed Fey turned on the unconscious infected warriors and began unweaving their bindings. Within scant chimes, the enemy numbers had mushroomed.

"Fey! Five-fold weaves! Get those portals closed and take those flaming archers out! Don't let the arrows strike you!" Rain leapt into the air, Changing and diving for the closest portal. Though he hadn't wanted to fire the field when the only enemy was ensorcelled friends, now that the Mages had made an appearance, it was a different story.

Tairen fire erupted from his muzzle, blasting a knot of Mages and searing the opening to the Well. The Mages threw up protective weaves to save themselves, but the magic of Rain's flame enveloped the archers around them. Lit up like candle lamps and screaming in mindless agony, the archers ran in frantic circles until they dropped. The gaping black maw of the Well winked shut.

Roaring in triumph, he dove after a second knot of enemies.

"I'm fine," Ellysetta assured her quintet who had dragged her away from the healing table and her bespelled patient.

"Ellysetta." Gaelen's voice was stern, but his eyes held only concern. The other four warriors of her quintet straightened from their attack stance and sheathed their bare red Fey'cha steel, but like Gaelen, their level of tension remained high.

"Nei, really. Whatever it was, it's already gone. I'm fine." It was true. The ice-spider sensation had receded almost as rapidly as it had come. "It wasn't the spell. The same thing used to happen to me in Celieria City all the time. Bel can tell you."

"She's right," Bel confirmed. "We never found out what it was or where it came from, but it never seemed to hurt her."

"I don't like it," Gaelen said.

Abruptly irritated, Ellysetta scowled at him, and snapped,

"I don't either, but it's the least of our worries at the moment. Our brothers are killing each other. Whatever this Feraz potion is, I need to figure out how to cure it. That's what's important."

Gaelen instantly clamped his mouth shut, and Ellysetta turned her attention back to the ensorcelled man on her table.

Half a field away from the blazing hundred-fold weaves of the healing tents, Rowan vel Arquinas bared his teeth in a feral snarl. His Fey'cha flew like lightning. Scores of men had already fallen to his blades. Scores more yet would . . . and all of them clad in the colors of Great House Sebourne.

In Rowan's mind, each man that gasped and fell with a shudder as tairen venom shut down his body wore Colum diSebourne's face. He killed the arrogant, murdering *rultshart* again and again and again, as he had not done when it would have mattered, when it would have saved his brother and Talisa.

The memory of Adrial and the sound of his mother's voice echoed in his mind, driving him with whips of Fire. *You must always look out for your brother, Rowan. Protect him.* But he had failed, and Adrial had died. And despite Ellysetta's many kindnesses and her shared love and calming weaves, Rowan's heart was a desert, cracked with pain and guilt and shattering grief.

He channeled that grief into Rage. All he lived for was vengeance. To kill every Sebourne, as he'd not been able to kill the one he hated most. He hated them even more than he hated the Mages. He fed on that hate, gorged on it, thrived on it.

His red Fey'cha flew, finding target after target. And when his Fey'cha harnesses were empty, he simply spoke his return word—which called each blade back to its sheath in pristine condition—and began again.

He didn't even have to foul his hands with Sebourne blood.

* * *

Rain strafed the encampment, looking for knots of Mages and Eld, burning them where he could. Scores of *fezaros* were rampaging through the rows of tents, swinging their pots of mind-altering poison. Mages, secured in their protective rings of archers, sent globes of Mage Fire soaring across the possessed into the ranks of the uninfected.

Sel'dor burned in his chest and wings. He'd developed a workable initial pattern of attack—dive for the knot of Mages, Change to avoid the barrage of arrows, then Change back to Fire the group—but they'd adapted. Now arrows and Mage Fire filled the air in a constant barrage. He'd given up the dodge-by-Changing technique and started taking the flights of arrows and Mage Fire head-on. Tairen fire consumed the bulk of what came at him, but he still took a few good hits.

One of the Water masters or the Celierians had opened the aqueducts to let the waters of the Heras pour into the field. The battlefield became a swamp of mud and blood. Worse, whatever the Feraz potion was, the waters of the Heras did not neutralize it. Instead, the madness seemed to be spreading more quickly.

«Rainier-Eras!» In urgent tones, Steli sang an image of a bowcannon bolt racing at him from behind.

Rain tucked his wings and rolled right just as the bolt whooshed past. His spine curved, wings spread, and he emerged from the banking roll to wheel sharply about. Tairen eyes scanned the battlefield, where several bowcannon were emerging from portals across the field.

The Eld were getting down to business now. They'd brought in the artillery.

Feral magic flared in Rain's body and he bared his fangs in a savage growl. Time for killing.

Why couldn't she figure this out?

As Ellysetta worked on the body of the unconscious, ensorcelled man, she wished Gaelen's sister Marissya were here. A powerful *shei'dalin*, with over a thousand years of healing—and combating enemy poisons and potions—Marissya would have a much better idea of what to do than Ellysetta did.

The bulk of Ellysetta's training had come from those few short months with Venarra v'En Eilan in the Fading Lands, and none of what they'd covered included how potions worked—or how any non-Fey magic worked, for that matter. Give her a warrior suffering cuts, broken bones, bruises, even mortal wounds and missing limbs, and she could knit his broken body back together. Give her a dying warrior whose soul was halfway to the Veil, and she could hold him to the Light and call him back to the world of the living.

But this Feraz potion magic . . . she didn't understand it. And she didn't have the first clue how to stop it. She'd already done everything she knew how to do. Rain said the potion infected the person on contact, but a detailed scan of her test subject's body revealed no traces of any suspicious liquid on her skin. Not, of course, that she would have been able to isolate it even if there *was* such a thing. The man was covered in blood and cuts and bruises and abrasions. His body looked like it had been used as a battering ram.

She'd spun a weave of Water and Air to wash and dry his skin, hoping that removal of the battle grime might shed some light on his condition, but to no avail. Desperate, she sent a probing weave of pure *shei'dalin's* love into his body, healing everything she could find wrong with him, but when her quintet lifted their sedation weave, the man went wild.

Concentrating was becoming more difficult. The battle was worsening, and despite the efforts of her *lu'tan,* the pain of the wounded and the dying was trickling through their shields—as was Rain's increasing battle Rage. Her head was aching, and her skin felt tight, making her short-tempered and snappish. She wove what peace she could on Rain while she worked, but that made it even harder to focus.

All the while, she was intensely aware that, with each passing moment, more Fey and Celierians fell to the Feraz potion or a possessed ally's blade. And though no one would come right out and say it, everyone was looking to her for answers when she had none to give. She was terrified she was going to fail, and thousands would die because she couldn't figure out a way to save them.

Rain swooped over the knot of Mages, fire roaring before him. He held the flame, heeling back to hover over the Mages and bathe them in fire. He wanted those shields down. Wanted those Mages to burn.

Savage satisfaction raced through him as their shields cracked. Mage screams rose, high-pitched and wild, then fell quickly silent in the incinerating heat.

Rain flung his head skyward and loosed a mighty roar of primal triumph.

Death to those who endangered the Fey! Death to those who injured his friends, his brothers! He was Rainier-Eras, Feyreisen, and he was winged vengeance.

«Rainier-Eras!» Steli sang another warning. The images carried on her tairen speech showed a portal opening on his flank and firing a shot right at him.

Rain spun into a sharp roll, but not quite quickly enough. The bowcannon bolt ripped through his hide, slicing deep.

He roared in pain and wheeled around to spew fire at the closing portal, but as he turned his vision went blurry. He faltered. His wings folded, and he fell from the sky, landing on four paws and swaying dizzily.

«Ellysetta . . .» The bolt had been poisoned. Potioned. *«Burns. It burns. Burns in the blood.»* He could feel the potion racing through his veins, merging with his blood, changing it. *«Vision dizzy. Smell . . . spice, like cinnamon growing stronger.»* He growled and shook off the dizziness as he tried to tell her everything, hoping that something he said would make the difference. He sang the sensations to her in tairen song so she could see them, feel them, taste and touch them for herself.

The burning had consumed him now; the potion had

spread throughout his body. The haziness of his vision was clearing. The faces around him were changing. Some of the faces around him smelled of the faint spice. Others did not. And the faces of the others were changing the most . . . changing to monsters. He sang the changes, until he couldn't remember why he was singing, who he was singing to, until he was surrounded by enemies. Enemies that must be stopped.

He was death, winged vengeance.

«For Celieria and King Dorian!» He screamed, and he leapt into the air, flame boiling from his muzzle.

CHAPTER SEVEN

Powerful, brave, graceful you stand
Deadly sword bright in hand
Eternal love protecting my heart
The two of us shall never part
For all time, ke vo san
My soulmate, my life, my shei'tan

    My Shei'tan, a poem by Evia v'En Herran

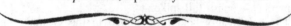

«*Rain!*» Ellysetta cried his name as his tairen song broke off, but there was no response. «*Steli! Xisanna! Perahl! Rain has been infected by the potion. You must bring him down. We cannot let him fly!*»

Confirmations roared across the sky in sparkling notes of tairen song as the three great cats raced across the darkened night to bring Rain down.

"*Kaiven chakor.*" She spun to face her primary quintet. "Help the pride. The tairen will bring him down. You five keep him there until I can figure out how to neutralize this potion."

When they hesitated, clearly torn by their *lute'asheiva* vow to guard her life above all others, she spun buffeting weaves of Air and Spirit and shoved them towards the exit. "Stop him. Nothing is more important. Stop him, or we all die." She filled her voice with every ounce of compulsion she could muster. She wasn't shy Ellie begging them to help her please. She was their queen, holder of their *lute'asheiva* bonds, commanding them to serve her. "Go!" she barked.

They went.

Ellysetta closed her eyes for a brief moment. Gods help them all. Then she drew a deep breath, her eyes flashed open, and she turned the full force of her concentration and determination upon the ensorcelled man strapped to her table.

"Well, my friend," she said grimly, "like it or not, you and I are going to figure out exactly what this is and exactly how to stop it."

Rain howled and thrashed, fire blazing, jaws snapping. His tail lashed like a whip. If he'd been a female tairen, he would have impaled someone—preferably a great many someones—on his tail spike.

Three monsters held him pinned to the ground, their bodies perched on his wings, his back, his neck. Fangs had a grip on his throat and were squeezing just enough that his vision was starting to go dim.

A company of fiendish enemies approached, led by five foul wretches with ghoulish features and long, clawed hands. Ropes of poisonous green magic oozed from their gnarled fingertips. Something hard wrapped around his muzzle, sealing his mouth shut so he could not flame. A hideous miasma enveloped him in choking fog.

He struggled, fighting the monsters on his back, fighting the magic swirling around him. Fighting. Fighting.

But the magic and the press of the fangs against his throat were too much. His vision dimmed. Consciousness fled.

Ellysetta reexamined the images and sensory perceptions from Rain's tairen speech, fixing a keen *shei'dalin's* eye on every tiny detail as she went over the information again and again. *The poison got into the blood, and it burned*, he'd said. Based on the information he'd sung to her, the burning sensation was localized to start with, but spread rapidly as the blood carried the poison to every part of the victim's body.

Whatever was in the blood, however, wasn't something obvious. She'd already checked the test subject's blood and found nothing. Now, with Rain's information and sensory perceptions fresh in her mind, she reexamined her patient, looking at his blood more closely to see what she had missed.

Nearly a full bell later, she finally found it.

She had to hand it to the Feraz. When it came to potions, their expertise was impressive. The active ingredient in the potion wasn't a foreign substance in the blood. It was a slight excess of a naturally occurring element that caused the body chemistry to change and, in doing so, to give off a faint but distinctive scent. That, in and of itself, was harmless, but the potion contained a second ingredient, a chemical that interacted with the sense of smell to alter the way the brain processed sensory inputs. Anyone exuding the faint cinnamon spice scent was perceived as a friend, but everyone lacking the scent was interpreted by the infected brain as a monster and a threat that must be killed.

Once she understood how the potion worked, Ellysetta spent another half bell figuring out the best way to undo its effects and discovered that she could spin a basic Earth weave to extract the excess chemical in the blood and a slightly more complex weave of Earth and Spirit combined to reorient the brain's sensory-processing abilities.

She tested her solution on the Celierian strapped to her table. Within a few chimes of receiving her healing weaves, he sat up, completely cured and back to his right mind.

Ellysetta didn't pause to celebrate or even soothe the man's confusion. *«This is the cure,»* she called on the Warrior's Path, sending images of her weave patterns. *«Every Earth and Spirit master needs to start weaving this now.»* Then she ran for the exit.

"Ellysetta!" Her *lu'tan* cried in alarm as she burst through the protective hundred-fold weave and onto the unshielded battlefield outside.

Inside the healing tent, behind the protection of the hundred-fold weave, the pain and torment of this battle had been muted. The moment she stepped outside those weaves, a wave of agony slammed into her empathic senses. The breath left her lungs on a shocked gasp, and she dropped to her knees.

"Bright Lord save me," she gasped, hunching over, her arms wrapped around her belly.

She thought she knew the pain of battle, of death. But now she realized just how much Rain and her quintet had been protecting her from. There were scores of new *dahl'reisen,* and the unchecked pain of their lost souls spilled out in shrieking waves. Men, maimed, dying in horrible pain, were screaming. Men were burning. Their pain, their torment, their fear bombarded her senses. She'd never really wondered what the Seventh Hell was like, but now she knew. It was like this.

And still, the battle raged.

The Earth and Spirit masters were weaving. Allied combatants were beginning to come back to their senses. That should have been a good thing, but their horror, their self-loathing when they realized what they'd done . . . the friends they'd slaughtered. Men and Fey fell to their knees, clawing at their own eyes and faces, consumed by guilt and grief.

A powerful five-fold weave enveloped her, muting the naked suffering of the battlefield. "*Kem'falla.*" Her secondary quintet ringed around her. "Come back inside the healing tent."

"*Nei.*" She let them help her to her feet, then shrugged them off. "Take me to Rain. I need Rain."

Primage Soros saw the slender figure in red run out from the hundred-fold weave and fall to her knees. He saw the Fey gather around her quickly, but instead of returning to the protection of the hundred-fold weave, all six of them began to run across the perimeter of the battlefield. He scanned the area and saw the Tairen Soul in the distance—still lying bound and unconscious, protected by the other three tairen and five Fey.

Now was his chance.

He summoned his Mages and gave the order. The Eld and Feraz moved swiftly to block her path, while four other groups converged upon her.

As Ellysetta and her *lu'tan* raced across the battlefield, they passed one horrific scene after another. The agony of shattered bodies and shattered minds battered her in endless waves. She could feel her soul separating. Part of her was going numb. Another part of her was writhing and screaming. But a third part, a very scary part, was growing angry.

These were her friends, her people, her countrymen, both Fey and Celierian, and they were being slaughtered all around her. Worse, they were being manipulated by magic into slaughtering their own friends, their own countrymen, their own blade brothers. Their howls of anguish fed her anger.

Something vast and dark was bubbling inside her. She ran faster. She needed Rain beside her, his arms around her.

She didn't see the Eld closing in. One moment, she and her *lu'tan* were running. The next, her spine went icy cold, and her legs went weak. She stumbled and fell. When she crawled back to her feet, a portal to the Well of Souls had opened to her right and left. Mages, Eld, and Feraz were pouring out.

Everything seemed to suddenly slow, as if time had grown weary. Blooms of Mage Fire exploded all around her. *Sel'dor* arrows pierced her *lu'tan*, toppling them.

Someone was shouting, *"Fey ti'Feyreisa! Ti'Feyreisa!"*

A *sel'dor* blade slashed. The Spirit master of her secondary quintet spun, blood from his severed throat splashing across her face. Her Water master's mouth went wide. His hands reached for the place where his abdomen had been before the bubble of Mage Fire cut him in two.

"Ellysetta! Down!"

She dropped to her knees as Rowan vel Arquinas leapt over her, his hands a blur, red Fey'cha flying at incredible speed. But there were too many of them and no *lu'tan* left alive around her to protect his back.

Three *sel'dor* arrows caught him in the back. He stumbled towards the gaping Well of Souls, Fey'cha still flying from his fingertips. Mages and Eld dropped by the dozens. A fourth arrow slammed into Rowan's shoulder, spinning him around to face her. His eyes met hers for an instant.

His mouth moved. "Ellysetta, I—"

A fifth arrow buried itself in his chest. He staggered back and toppled into the Well.

Something snapped inside her. The great, dark anger took hold. Her skin flashed hot, then cold, and she began to shake.

This was too much. Too many friends dead. Too much grief and pain and suffering. No more. Not here. Not this day.

Her fingers clenched in fists at her side. She could feel magic rushing towards her, as if she were a vortex, pulling every bit of energy into herself, feeding off it, growing stronger. The Mages tried to call their magic, but she drew it out of them and poured it into herself. She saw their eyes widen and realized they were afraid, and that made her laugh with savage joy.

The fury inside her roared for release, for justice, for blood. Her mind shot out across the battlefield, throughout Kreppes, finding every Eld, every Feraz, every host of Darkness. And she seized them by the throats with invisible hands, lifting them up off the ground, dangling them in the air.

She lifted her shaking fists. The bodies hanging in the air began to twitch and shake. Gurgling noises escaped from throats as the convulsions grew stronger. Terrified eyes bulged and rolled in purpling faces. Billowing clouds of red mist filled the air as hearts exploded from Eld chests and burst into flame.

"Ellysetta!"

The sound of Rain's voice snapped her out of the strange

furor that gripped her. A loud crack—the sound of thousands of necks breaking in unison—sounded across the strangely silent battlefield. Then came the thuds as the corpses fell from the air.

Ellysetta turned to her *shei'tan*. "Rain, I—" Her voice broke off as her knees buckled. All the energy she'd gathered left her in a whoosh, and darkness filled the vacuum left behind. Senseless, she toppled into his arms.

2nd day of Seledos

The sun shone down upon Kreppes. Its golden light illuminated the devastation of the night's brutal battle. Swords, which Ellysetta had always found such elegant weapons when displayed in the Cha Baruk, were in reality little more than butchers' cleavers. Severed limbs scattered the field. Hands. Feet. Heads. Bodies sliced open like haunches of beef. She'd never seen so much blood. The field was soaked in it.

Alongside the dead killed by the enemy and by the ensorcelled allies lay the scattered remains of all those she had slaughtered.

"Come away, Ellysetta," Rain said. "It's time to Fire the field."

"Nei," she said. "I will watch." She wasn't just a *shei'dalin*. She was a Tairen Soul. War, and its ugly consequences, was her purview now. She could not let Rain and her quintet continue to shelter her, no matter how much they wished to. She was, after all, responsible for hundreds of the bodies lying on the battlefield.

Her gaze skimmed the edges of the battlefield, pausing at the sight of Cannevar Barrial standing beside the empty bier where the bodies of his three sons, Parsis, Severn, and Luce had been sent back to the elements. Deep lines etched Cann's graven face and threads of white now streaked his dark hair. He had aged decades in a single night. Four of

Cann's five children had perished in the span of a week. Almost his entire family gone. Just like that. Worse, Cann suspected his son Severn had died by Cann's own hand when the Feraz magic had consumed him.

Ellysetta had tried to offer what peace she could, but nothing she said or did helped him. Cann was a hollow shell, an automaton driven by a single, searing flame that burned in his dead eyes: the need for vengeance.

She dragged her gaze away from Cann and the pain she could not heal and tried to distance herself from her emotions, like most of the warriors had done.

"Has anyone sent word to Prince Dorian and the queen?" she asked, as the Fire masters walked out among the dead.

Rain nodded. "Bel sent a Spirit weave a few chimes ago."

The Fire masters summoned their magic, gathering the bright orange weaves of their Fire, then spilling it out upon the ground. The Fire burned bright and hot, consuming the bodies of the slain, but there was so much *sel'dor* on the field that their Fire did not consume everything. When they were done, the bones of the dead remained, not scorched by the Fire but bleached white, as if by the Great Sun.

Ellysetta's mouth went dry. Feeling dazed, she stepped away from Rain and walked slowly onto the Fire-cleansed battlefield. She stood there, a *shei'dalin* draped in scarlet, standing in a bleached white field of bones, the remains of thousands of slain, most of whom had died either by her hand or because she'd not been quick enough to find the cure to the Feraz potion.

Her dream had come true.

Celieria ~ Celieria City

"Noooooo!"

The scream ripped through the marbled halls of Celieria's royal palace, punctuated by a series of shattering crashes and sobbing wails. Courtiers stopped in their tracks, gossiping tongues frozen midwag. They turned towards the queen's apartments for a single, hushed moment, then the whispering recommenced, setting the palace hallways abuzz.

"It's true. It must be true. The king is dead."

In her chambers, Annoura swept her arms across another elegant desk, sending crystal candle lamps, books, and statuary crashing to the floor. She shrieked in wild, mad grief and flung herself at her bed hangings, snatching great handfuls of sumptuous fabric and ripping it free of its mooring hooks. Plaster rained down upon her and the puddles of velvet she threw to the floor.

"Your Majesty, calm yourself!" pleaded the minister who had brought her the news of Dorian's death. "Your Majesty, please. You'll make yourself ill. Think of the child!"

"Get out! Get out!" She grabbed part of the broken vase from the floor and heaved it at him, narrowly missing his head. One of the delicate, carved chairs from her vanity followed the first missile. The minister dove out of the way a split second before the chair crashed against the wall where he'd been standing and broke into splinters.

"I'll fetch Lord Hewen," he quavered, and pelted out the door.

With the minister gone, Annoura spun on the Ladies-in-Waiting who were huddled in the corner of the room, some weeping, some gaping in shock at their queen's utter loss of control. "You too!" she shrieked. "All of you, get out! Get out, damn you!" She grabbed the broken candle-lamp stand from the bedside and advanced upon them, jabbing and swinging the lamp stand like a halberd.

Squealing, the ladies fled. An antique porcelain teapot exploded across the gilded door as it closed behind them, drenching the wood, walls, and plush carpet near the threshold with steaming tea and filling the room with the scent of jasmine.

Annoura went through her apartment like a cyclone of destructive grief, shrieking Dorian's name, smashing and rending everything she touched. She ripped pages from books, shattered perfume bottles, tore curtains from windows, smashed mirrors, and slashed paintings. Not a single moveable or breakable object escaped her fury of grief.

When there was nothing left to destroy, nothing more whole than the shattered pieces of her heart, she curled in the ruins of her destroyed bed and wept.

Ser Vale hurried down a servants' stairway to the underpalace, where an entire invisible city worked industriously to keep the palace operating smoothly and Their Majesties' courtiers well served and sated.

Lord Hewen, the royal physician, had been in to see the queen. Vale's informants told him she was sleeping fitfully. There were no obvious signs of distress with the child, though Lord Hewen had not performed more than a cursory visual examination for fear of waking the queen. The ministers wouldn't even allow a single servant in to tidy the mess Annoura had made of her apartments for the same reason.

Vale was perhaps the only person in the court for whom the news of the king's death was neither surprising nor unwelcome. He expected similar news to arrive any day from Great Bay, and once it did, Vale's star in the Celierian court would go sharply on the rise.

It was time to tie up loose ends.

Celieria ~ Kreppes
5th day of Seledos

"I'm worried, Rain."

Ellysetta paced the floor of her room in Kreppes Castle. Ever since she'd stood on the Fired battlefield outside Kreppes and realized that one of her dreams had come true, fear had been a constant companion, eating away at her peace of mind, tormenting her as fiercely as any nightmare ever had.

She'd kept the fear to herself these last days. Rain had been so busy. He and Lord Barrial had spent most of their time scouting Great Lord Sebourne's lands in search of Mages, and at Gaelen's suggestion, Cann had summoned his *dahl'reisen* friends and asked them to check all the remaining Sebourne inhabitants for Mage Marks. In the meantime, armies from the surrounding border estates were sending troops to secure the lands until the new King Dorian could decide what to do with them.

But Moreland was secure now, and Rain was back. Ellysetta couldn't keep quiet any longer.

"I'm worried that if that dream came true, some of my others might, too." Like the dream she'd had last month about Rain dying by Ellysetta's hand while Mage-claimed Lillis and Lorelle danced in a shower of his blood. "I'm worried about all those people I killed and how I felt when I killed them."

Ellysetta dragged her palms over her face and eyes, as if that simple gesture could shut out the world. But shutting out the world—pretending it wasn't there—never solved anything. If she'd learned nothing else, she'd learned that. Hiding from the monsters only made them stronger.

"Hawksheart said I was the double-edged sword. He warned you that I have just as much capacity for evil as I do for good. I believe him, Rain. And I'm so afraid—so terribly frightened—that the evil is winning."

"Shei'tani . . ."

"Nei, Rain. Listen to me. There's something dark inside me—and it isn't all the tairen, and it isn't all the High Mage either. You want to pretend it's not there, but it is. Some horrible, vicious part of me was glad to kill those people . . . . I thrived on murdering them. Worse, I didn't just want to kill them. I wanted to make them suffer. I wanted to hear them scream and beg for mercy. I wanted to see the terror in their eyes and know I put it there!"

"Ellysetta, they'd just killed Rowan and turned our own

people against each other. They made friends slaughter friends. Your Rage was understandable. Do you think I felt any different? What do you think Steli would have done if the Eld had turned tairen against tairen?"

Ellysetta bit her lip. She knew what Steli would do. The fierce white tairen would shred, scorch, and maim every living creature on the battlefield. "I'm not Steli, Rain."

"Neither was I when Sariel died. Yet you've told me so many times that what I did didn't make me evil. Was that all a lie?"

Her gaze shot to his. "*Nei,* of course not!"

"Then how am I to be forgiven for what I did in war, yet you are not?"

She hated when he turned her own arguments against her this way. "You weren't Mage Marked, Rain. You weren't told you'd been born either to save the world or destroy it."

"True. I wasn't born to save the world. I was merely born to slaughter millions."

"You were born to end the Mage Wars," she corrected sharply, "and in doing so to save all those people the Eld would have enslaved if you hadn't done what you did."

His hands cupped her face, and his eyes brimmed with sorrow and love and such understanding she nearly wept. "*Aiyah, shei'tani.* That I was. And though I will never forgive myself for what I did, every day when the doubts creep in, I remind myself that the gods made me for their own purpose. That no matter how seemingly dark and terrible that purpose was, they trusted me to fulfill it. And I remind myself every day, that somehow, I must have proven myself worthy in their eyes because they sent me you, my soul's mate and the beacon that drew me back from Shadow." His thumbs brushed lightly across her lower lip in a tender caress. "Perhaps, *shei'tani,* it's time you began to believe the same about yourself."

Her lashes fell to cover her eyes. Almost since the first moment she'd met Rain, she'd been telling him to forgive himself, to see the Light in his soul that even the Scorching of the World had not been able to dim. Now their roles were reversed, and she was bewailing her own sad plight as if no one in the world had ever walked so Dark a path.

And yet, the doubts were there. She could not deny or ignore them. "What if I'm not strong enough? What if I'm not good enough? What if Tenn and the Massan were right, and I've already done all I was meant to do, and the only way to save the world is for someone to kill me before I fall to Darkness?"

His thumb brushed against her lower lip, and though sorrow shaded his eyes, there was a steady calmness, an acceptance about him, that she'd never seen so strongly before.

"Then we will die together, Ellysetta." The corner of his beautiful mouth titled slightly upwards in a mournful ghost of a smile. "Whatever your fate, I will share it. Wherever your Path leads, there, too, walk I. *Ver reisa ku'chae. Kem surah, shei'tani.*"

She wrapped her arms around him and held on tight, not so much embracing him as trying to merge her body into his until there was no part of them that stood apart. She kissed him with desperate passion, as if his lips could wipe out the pervasive sense of doom that sapped her courage and filled her with fear.

"Kiss me, Rain. Love me."

"I will. I do." He touched his mouth to hers in a kiss of gentle devotion, but she would have none of it. Her lips parted, and she took his mouth with urgent need at the same time her body surged against him. Earth weaves spun from her hands, and his armor dropped from him like leaves from an autumn tree.

He pulled back, frowning. "Ellysetta?"

"Ssh. No more talk. I don't want any more talk. I just want you. I want this." Her nails raked down his naked flesh, teasing him, scoring his skin with a combination of pain and pleasure that made him gasp and his eyes turn bright as stars. She wanted heat, wild and passionate, not tenderness. She called his essence with ruthless command and shared hers in such an unfettered rush that he cried out, barely managing to remain on his feet as every muscle in his body went hard as stone, then began trembling uncontrollably.

She pushed him back onto the bundles of fur that served as their bed, stripping her own leathers with impatient weaves. Naked, she crouched over him. Nails and teeth raked and nipped. He reached for her, but she evaded his hands. Fire and Air danced across his skin in alternate waves of heat and cold. He reached for her again, and she growled a warning in her throat. He bared his teeth and growled back. He caught her in a firm grip, his fingers sinking into her flesh and driving her inexorably towards union.

Passion unraveled the tight barriers in his mind, and his escaping thoughts intruded on her own, memories of the fire and screams of great, winged tairen coming together in the sky in a fierce mating.

She inhaled sharply, feeling the burn in her flesh, the hunger tightening her womb and inner muscles. Hands gripped her hips, and he plunged inside her in one swift thrust, wrenching a ragged cry from her throat. Oh, gods. Her eyes closed. Flames consumed her as her body stretched and burned to accommodate him. His hips thrust again.

"Rain!" She clawed at his shoulders, fought him for control, as a tairen female battled her mate for sexual supremacy until he proved his strength and dominance and established his right to mate her and father her kits.

Stars exploded against the back of her eyes, and it was her turn to tremble uncontrollably as his hands and mouth and magic and the pounding rhythm of his hips drove her to first one peak, then another and another until she could not think, could not speak. Until she could barely even breathe without setting off yet another deep, shattering orgasm.

In the end, even that was not enough. Because when they were spent, and Rain lay sprawled and sleeping beside her own limp, perspiring body, she could still feel within her a spreading black ice deep within her core, chilling her from the inside out.

Celieria ~ Celieria City

Master Gaspare Fellows, the Queen's Master of Graces, held a scented handkerchief to his nose and rolled his eyes. The wharfs. Why did questionable personages always arrange their nefarious assignations at wharfs? Of course, since the nefarious person in question was a ship's captain, he supposed it made sense. But, gods have mercy, the stink of sweat, bodily excretions, and rotting fish offal was blinding.

Then again, would he rather be blinded by stink and battling the heaves, or lying on the floor of his well-maintained palace apartment, clean, perfumed, and utterly dead?

In the days since they'd learned of King Dorian's demise, a string of tragic deaths had afflicted the palace. Lady Nadela, Prince Dorian's betrothed, had tumbled down the marble steps of the grand staircase and broken her neck. She died instantly. Lady Jiarine Montevero, who'd been among the ladies walking with the future princess at the time, had been so terrified of being declared Lady Nadela's murderer that she'd written a hysterical note proclaiming her innocence and hanged herself in her room to avoid being tortured again in Old Castle Prison. Two of the late king's most trusted ministers had perished in horrible accidents.

Gaspare, himself, had narrowly escaped not one, but three, brushes with death, including an attempt to poison himself and Love at breakfast this morning. Only an open window and an unfortunate, hungry thief of a sparrow had saved them. Life in the palace had become a risky business since King Dorian's passing, and considering that Gaspare's breakfast was prepared and tasted by Her Majesty's own servants, he greatly feared that the assassin was someone very close to the queen.

The king was dead, the Fey had left Celieria City, and the queen was possibly in league with an enemy of the crown.

With nowhere to turn in the city, Gaspare had decided his only viable course of action was to leave. That decision had brought him here, to the wharves. Or, more specifically, to the Crown and Cutlass Pub in the wharf district.

Tugging the collar of his greatcoat closer, Gaspare pulled down the brim of his dark hat, ignored the blinding smells around him, and marched towards the Crown and Cutlass. The burning lantern over the pub's door swung in the strong night breeze off the bay, and the wide circle of its light rocked back and forth, like a pendulum, casting the door in and out of shadow as it moved.

"Be brave," Gaspare muttered to himself. "Be brave. Be brave."

"Mmrow?" A small, warm, furry head poked out of the edge of his greatcoat. The little skull beneath the fur nudged his throat as it twisted and turned to get a good look at their surroundings.

"Yes, I know, Love," Gaspare sighed. "You're brave enough for the both of us. Now get back in there. This is not a nice place. The men in here probably eat pretty kittens like you for a morning snack." He pushed his kitten's white head back into his coat and suffered the punishment of her tiny, needlelike claws sinking into his chest.

The pain of Love's displeasure helped him summon the courage to open the pub door and step inside.

Crowded, dimly lit, and smoky, the interior of the pub fit Gaspare's image of a pub of ill repute to perfection. The swarthy, dangerous-looking men idling inside looked up as he entered, as did the blowsy pleasure girls sitting on their laps and leaning low to whisper in their ears. Although, Gaspare noted, the term "pleasure girl" was something of a euphemism in this establishment. He doubted there was a single female in the place under the age of forty. Most were missing several teeth. And likely most of their hair, too, judging by the number of dirty wigs he saw.

"Hallo there, handsome." A hand clapped on Gaspare's shoulder, and he turned to find the grandmother of all plea-

sure girls standing beside him. Gaspare's eye for detail captured the woman's garish caricature of beauty in one horrific
glance. A frizzy yellow mop for hair, greasy eye makeup
that had melted and settled into the lines around her eyes,
flaccid breasts propped up on display by tight stays: The
sight was indelibly seared upon his brain. "Lookin' for some
company?"

He stifled a shudder and tried not to breathe the fetid air
gushing from the woman's red-painted lips.

"Thank you, my good woman, but no," he declined politely. "I'm looking for Captain Sarkay. I was told he would
be here."

"Har!" The woman near felled him with a heave of odor-
befouled laughter. "Eren't you the fancy gent? 'Thank you,
my good woman,'" she mimicked. "More's the pity. Looks
like you could use a good hoist of your mainsail. Ah well,
some other time, perhaps." With a prosaic shrug, she waved
a thin hand towards one of the tables at the back of the pub.
"Sarkay's over there. The handsome one in green."

Handsome was as relative a term as girl, in this place,
Gaspare decided. The only man in green he could see at the
back table was a swarthy giant, with a long black mustache,
bald head, and tattoos curling around every inch of his beefy
forearms.

"Many thanks, madam." Gaspare gave a short bow out
of ingrained habit, then wished he hadn't when he noted
the pub patrons eyeing him with speculation. If he wasn't
careful with his court Graces, he'd get himself clubbed and
robbed and rolled into the alleyway.

He made his way as quickly as possible through the crowd
to the green-clad giant at the back. "Captain Sarkay?"

The giant looked up slowly. "Who's askin'?" Up close, the
fellow was even more intimidating. Black brows arched with
a wicked flare over dark, dark eyes. Scars curled around his
head and down the side of his face—as if he'd stopped more
than one sword blow with his skull.

"The name is . . ." Gaspare racked his brain for a name

that sounded suitably tough and street-wise, " . . . Fist. Ruffio Fist." He started to hold out a hand, then thought the better of it and grabbed the back of a nearby chair instead. "I understand you have a boat for hire? No questions asked?"

The captain arched one demonic brow. "Aye. I've a ship. Where is it you're looking to go, Goodman Fist?"

"King's Point."

"No one sails to the Point these days. There's a war on, haven't you heard?"

"Well then, what's the closest village with an open port before the Point? Take me there. I'll pay extra if we can leave tonight."

"Leave me." Annoura commanded in a cold, emotionless tone.

Her Ladies-in-Waiting instantly obeyed, dropping deep curtsies as they backed out of what had been the king's bedchamber. Since destroying her own bedchamber, Annoura had taken to sleeping in Dorian's. The decision had been a matter of convenience at first, but she realized almost immediately that being here, among his things, soothed her as very little else could these days.

Annoura rose from the dressing table and crossed the room to Dorian's bed. She felt closer to him here. One of his robes lay on the coverlet. She wrapped herself in it and crawled into his bed, laying her head on his pillow. His scent surrounded her, almost as if he were here, holding her in his arms. Hugging that illusion close, she closed her eyes and drifted off to sleep.

As she had every night since his death, Annoura dreamed of Dorian. Not the cold and distant Dorian he'd been their last weeks together, but the Dorian as he'd been when they first met. Dazzling. Seductive. Devoted. The most intensely passionate man she'd ever met. With hazel eyes that could glow like stars and a mouth that drove her mad when he whispered kisses across her skin.

Tonight, like the other nights since his death, she dreamed

they were back in the secluded garden terrace in Capellas, where they'd shared their first kiss. The lilac trees were blooming, as they'd been that day so long ago. Dorian stood on the terrace's stone pavers, older than he had been on the day of their first kiss, but still a dark, lustrous jewel, framed by the lilac's soft hues. The wind ruffled his hair and blew the hem of his rich velvet surcoat about him. He held out a hand, his hazel eyes full of love, and spoke her name. "Annoura."

"Dorian." She reached for him and nearly wept when the warmth of his hand closed about hers and the familiar heat of his mouth possessed her lips. Unlike the day of their first kiss, the dream Dorian didn't simply kiss her and declare his love. Instead, he bore her down upon a bed of soft lilacs, and cool, intoxicating fragrance enveloped her with dizzying sweetness.

Dorian's hands smoothed burning paths down her body. She arched against him, calling his name, pleading with him to join his body with hers. Fearful that, like every other night, the dream Dorian would once again drive her to a frenzy of need, then evaporate, leaving her empty and aching and sobbing into her pillow.

Tonight, however, as her need reached its peak and the Dorian of her dreams started to fade and pull away from her, she clung to him, weeping and pleading for him not to go. "Please, dearling, don't go! Stay with me. I'll do anything, only please don't go. Don't go!"

"Anything, Annoura?" he asked. "Will you give yourself to me, heart and soul, willingly and without reservation? Will you surrender everything you are to me?"

Annoura hesitated. Something in Dorian's voice didn't sound right, and for a moment she could swear his hazel eyes had turned dark—almost black.

Her hesitation must have convinced him she was insincere, because he started to fade again. She could feel him growing insubstantial in her hands, dissolving like mist.

"Wait!" she cried. If she let him go, she would wake and

find herself alone again. And the pain of that aloneness was more than she could bear. She'd do anything to keep him with her, even just as a dream. "Yes. Yes, of course. Anything, Dorian. Only don't leave me."

His hand caressed her face. "Then say it, dearest. You must say the words, so I can stay with you."

She didn't know the words he meant, but suddenly they were there, on her tongue, tumbling past her lips. "I surrender myself to you without reservation. My body and soul are yours to command." The moment she said the words, it was like some bubble of pressure burst inside her, and she drew a sobbing breath. "Now please, Dorian, please stay with me. Please."

Dorian smiled. "Of course, darling." He bent to claim her mouth in a deep and passionate kiss.

As he did, a sudden, piercing coldness stabbed Annoura's heart. She cried out in surprise, and began to struggle against him. Her eyes opened in sudden fear, and her mouth opened to scream.

In the bedchamber of the late King Dorian X, Kolis Manza blew another puff of *somulus* powder into the waking queen's face. Instantly, the scream died silent in her throat, and her beautiful blue eyes went hazy once more. Her naked, struggling body went lax and pliable against his.

"I'm here, darling," he whispered reassuringly. "I'll never leave you again." His tongue thrust deep into her mouth as his sex plunged deep into her body.

And on the satiny, alabaster skin of Annoura's left breast, the shadow of Kolis Manza's first Mark lay like a bruise over her heart.

Elvia ~ Navahele

In the heart of Elvia's ancient Deep Woods, the Sentinel tree called Grandfather, a colossal arboreal giant planted in the Time Before Memory, spread his branches wide across the mossy glens and misty silver pools of the great Elvish city of Navahele. Far, far beneath the surface of Grandfather's island, burrowed into the heartwood of his mile-deep taproot, the Elf king Galad Hawksheart floated in the phosphorescent blue glow of his Mirror pool. Long strands of golden hair floated about his face and shoulders. The cream-colored fabric of his full leggings floated, too, transparent and weightless in the water of the pool. His eyes were closed, their piercing green vision turned inward, as his mind and his soul traveled through the complex webs of the Dance, seeking answers, revelation.

Understanding.

For the first time in his ten thousand years, Galad Hawksheart was blind. The Song—Ellysetta Erimea's Song, to which he had dedicated his entire life and sacrificed countless others—was singing, but he could not See its Verses clearly.

And so he submerged himself in the magical waters of his Mirror, and every chime of the day and night, he searched the Dance for the answers that eluded him.

A familiar sentience brushed his consciousness. Cool and ageless. He recognized her instantly, of course.

His sister, his twin, Illona Brighthand, the Lady of Silvermist. Queen and coruler of Elvia, though she had long ago left Navahele—and, with it, him. She had secluded herself in her palace in the cloud-forests of the Silvermist mountains, leaving the rule of all Elvia east of those mountains to him—along with all interaction in the world on behalf of the Dance. She had never spoken to him again after leaving.

And so they had lived the last two thousand years.

Until now.

Galad. She spoke his name, and her voice was like a crystal chime upon the wind. So pure, so beautiful. Gentle, yet so fiercely unyielding.

Sister. He included no warmth, no surprise, in the voice

he sent soaring across time and space, but she would not be fooled. Of all creatures in the world, she knew him better than anyone, even Grandfather.

Erimea's Song confounds you.

Of course she knew. She had her own Mirror in Silvermist. She left the interpretation of the Dance to him, but that did not mean she did not watch, as he did. She also knew how to follow the faint ethereal traces of his presence, to know which Verses of the Song he had Seen, which he had returned to time and time again.

Most of all, she knew which Verses should have been certain, fixed, unchangeable—and which, now, were not.

She is leinah thaniel. Illona's cool voice whispered across his mind.

You don't know that, he retorted. *The Dark One may simply have chosen to play a different Verse.* That was the one limitation of Elvish Sight. They could never See Shadow clearly except where there was Light. He could watch his cousin Elfeya's torture in Eld because she was of the Light, but Eld activities that involved only other Shadowfolk appeared only sporadically, and then only as murky, constantly-shifting possibilities instead of certainties. Past events were easier to see, but to Shadow-Sung futures, he remained dangerously blind.

You know I am right.

Bayas.

All the denial in the world won't change the truth, Galad. She is what she is.

Bayas, he denied.

Anio. She is leinah thaniel. The Elves must go to war. No matter the cost, we cannot let Shadow win.

CHAPTER EIGHT

Eld ~ Boura Fell

"Master Maur!" Primage Vargus stood at attention as the High Mage strode into the war room in a swirl of purple silk and visible purpose. "Your orders, Most High?"

"It is time. Tell the generals to prepare their men. They attack on my signal."

"Yes, Most High. I'll contact them immediately."

Vadim leaned against the map table, with its glowing vertical display of the armies and battlefields stretched across Celieria's northern border. "And tell Horan to release his pets."

Celieria ~ Orest

"Lord Teleos!" The armored soldier raced from the battlements of Upper Orest into what had once been a lush conservatory overlooking the magnificent falls of Kierya's Veil and Maiden's Gate. The building now served as Lord Teleos's command center, and the soaring glass walls and ceilings provided a perfect panoramic view of Upper Orest and the vast stretch of Eld and Celieria to the east, separated by the wide dark ribbon of the Heras River.

Devron Teleos looked up from the table where he and his generals were reviewing the defense plans for Upper Orest and the hastily rebuilt lower city. The look on the approaching soldier's face brought Lord Teleos to his feet, his spine stiffening with a mix of dread and grim resolve. "What is it?"

"Something approaches in the skies to the north, my lord," the soldier gasped.

Teleos headed to the glass walls of the conservatory. One

of the Celierian generals was already there, spyglass raised and pointed north. "What in the Bright Lord's name is that?"

Teleos followed the man's gaze and saw tiny black specks on the horizon. What appeared to be a flock of dark birds was flying towards them across the forests of Eld. The Fey blood in Lord Teleos's veins had blessed him with a variety of gifts, including the ability to see much greater distances than mortal eyes could. His eyes narrowed, bringing the distant shapes into closer focus. He saw the barbed and taloned wings, the long white fangs, the iridescent sheen of black scales, and the bottom dropped out of his stomach.

"Bright Lord save us," he breathed. "Dragons. Dragons are coming." To the gathered Celierian military leaders, he issued a spate of orders. "Captain Morrow, sound the alarm. Get the women and children to Maiden's Gate. Order every able-bodied man and boy capable of wielding a bow to report to the armories. And light the signal fires. We're going to need all the help we can get before this is over. General Arlon, tell the cannoneers to arm the bowcannon with ice shot."

To the Fey general who had led his men to Dharsa to defend Orest from the Eld, Dev said, "General vel Shevahn, we'll need every Fey you can spare on the wizard's wall."

The Fey bowed his head. "Already done, Lord Teleos. We'll shield as much of the city as we can against dragon fire, but be aware that whatever we do to keep out the dragons will keep the tairen out, too. And we'll have to lower the wall shields each time we fire, or the ice shot will be useless."

"Understood. Do what you can." On threads of Spirit spun intentionally too weak to travel far, he added, *«And call the Feyreisen. I count twenty dragons coming in. The tairen are outnumbered.»*

Celieria ~ Kreppes

Rain and Ellysetta raced for the clearing just south of their encampment. The defenders of Orest were in trouble. Four tairen didn't stand a chance against twenty dragons, even with the Mists to aid them.

Torasul had already sung the call to Sybharukai, and except for two of the great cats remaining behind to watch over the kits, Fey'Bahren had emptied. The entire pride was winging towards Orest to protect their kin and fight alongside the Fey and Lord Teleos's men.

Rain wished he could say the same for the Fey, but a frantic weave to the Massan had proved that blind idiocy still reigned supreme in the Fading Lands' governing council. They were convinced that Rain, not the Eld, were to blame for the war and that Rain's devotion to Ellysetta had blinded him to the danger she posed.

«If not for you, there would be no war!» Tenn accused. *«From the moment you arrived in Celieria, you convinced yourself the Eld were a threat to the world, and you refused to hear a single voice of reason. You beat the drums of war without cease. You convinced Dorian to build up his troops. You built Fey garrisons at Orest and Teleon, built up Fey and Celierian military presence on the borders. Is it any wonder the Eld attacked?*

«You, Tairen Soul, made Celieria the target. You—not the Eld—ordered thousands of fine Fey warriors to their deaths! But the Massan will not endanger more Fey lives by condoning your madness and your senseless war of aggression against Eld.»

«You are a fool, Tenn,» Rain replied. *«I am not the enemy. Perhaps you think I don't deserve to wear the crown your brother once did. But Johr Feyreisen would never have condoned your actions. You bring shame to your family line.»*

«How dare you!»

«I give you fair warning, v'En Eilan. When this is over, and Ellysetta and I have completed our bond, I intend to claim my throne. I suggest you do not stand in the way.»

Magic exploded in a billowing cloud of gray mist as Rain Changed on the run and soared into the sky. He wheeled back and dipped low over the field. Ellysetta timed her mount perfectly, leaping up on a jet of Air and landing in the saddle as he dove past.

«*Bel, Gaelen, gather the Fey and as many Celierians as can be spared and follow us,*» Rain commanded. «*The Massan have refused their support. We're on our own, but we can't let the Eld take the Veil.*»

«*We'll be right behind you, Rain,*» Bel vowed.

«*Steli-chakai, we'll be flying fast. Come when you can—and fly high to keep out of bowcannon range.*»

With a roar, Rain banked in a tight circle, and with a burst of magic-powered speed, rocketed high into the sky, heading west, towards Orest and the gateway to the Fading Lands.

The Faering Mists

"Lorelle, I don't think I like it here anymore." Lillis clutched Snowfoot to her chest so tight, the little kitten mewed a protest and scratched her hand trying to get free. Lillis barely even noticed. The scratch didn't hurt and almost as soon as it appeared, it disappeared again, healed by the magic that filled everything and everyone in this valley.

She wanted for nothing. She and Lorelle had a beautiful bedroom of their own filled with all the treasures and toys they could ever wish for. They had an entire roomful of beautiful dresses to wear and delicious foods to eat—including so many rich, powdery chocolate comfits that they'd practically made themselves sick gorging on them.

But despite her joy at being reunited with Mama, something about this place didn't feel right.

No matter how many sweets they ate, Mama never objected. And Lorelle, who could be so irritating sometimes, had been inexplicably pleasant and good-natured.

Lillis asked about Kieran and Kiel several times now, but each time the beautiful Fey lady Eiliss—or one of the dozens of other beautiful Fey lords and ladies with her—would smile gently, and say, "Patience, kitling. If they survived the battle, they would want you to remain here, where you are safe."

Papa and Mama seemed in no rush to find Kieran either. Or to leave.

"But it's so peaceful and beautiful here," Papa said, when she talked to him about it. "We're all together and we're all safe here. Isn't that enough, Lillipet?"

At first it had seemed so. At first it had seemed perfect. But now, even though only a few days had passed, the perfection was beginning to wear thin. Part of the problem was, they weren't all together. Ellysetta wasn't with them. Kieran and Kiel weren't with them.

And no one but Lillis seemed the slightest bit interested in finding them.

Lillis stroked Snowfoot, then knelt on the floor to nuzzle the kitten's tiny nose and roll one of the pretty latticework jingle balls across the carpet. Snowfoot leapt upon the ball and swatted it with a tiny paw, sending it rolling across the floor. The bells chimed merrily against the pretty white stone in the ball's center.

"Maybe we should try to find Kieran and Kiel on our own," she told Lorelle.

Beside her, Lorelle looked up with a frown, then tossed her own jingle ball for her kitten, Pounce. "Mama and Papa would never allow it. We don't have any idea where we are or how to find our way back. We'd get lost." Pounce leapt for the ball, missed, and went sliding across the polished marble floor with his limbs splayed and an expression of pure bewilderment on his fuzzy face. "Besides, you heard Lady Eiliss yesterday. We should stay put until they find Kieran and Kiel, or Kieran and Kiel find us. It's much too dangerous to go wandering around."

Lillis frowned. "I don't think anyone is looking for Kieran or Kiel at all. If they were, why wouldn't they have found them?"

"We're in the middle of the Faering Mists," Lorelle replied. "It's hard to find anything in here."

"Lady Eiliss found us easily enough. And Papa. And how can Mama really be here?" Snowfoot pounced on his jingle ball again, sending it skittering, and Lillis caught the toy with an idle hand. Her brows knit together. The worry that had been preying on her mind roused again, and this time it would not be brushed aside. "Lorelle . . . do you think maybe we're all"—she bit her lip and whispered her growing fear aloud—"dead? And this is really the Haven of Light? Eiliss looks beautiful enough to be a Lightmaiden."

"Of course not." Lorelle rejected the idea immediately, and for the first time since Lillis had come to this city in the Mists, Lorelle's brows furrowed in a very Lorelle-like scowl. "That's the silliest thing I've ever heard."

Lillis lunged for her twin and threw her arms around her throat in a fervent hug.

"Hey!" Lorelle exclaimed in surprise. "What was that for?"

"Nothing. Everything." Tears sprang to Lillis's eyes. She swiped at them with backs of her hands. "It's just that's the first time you've really seemed like you since I got here."

"You ninnywit." Lorelle gave her a shove.

Lillis rocked back, laughed, then hugged her again, even tighter this time. "Oh, Lorelle, I've been so worried. Everything seemed so perfect, so wonderful. More like a dream than anything real."

"Why is that so bad?"

"It's not." Lillis frowned. "It's just that . . ."

"Aren't you happy here?"

"Yes . . . but . . ." She couldn't put her fears into words. The sense of . . . not exactly wrongness, but more of a not-rightness. She frowned. Lorelle usually knew what she was feeling even before she did. Why didn't she now?

"Just be happy, Lillis, and enjoy this place. We're safe here. Nothing can hurt us. We're with Mama and Papa. We have everything we need—and everything we've ever wanted."

"But not Ellie. And not Kieran and Kiel either."

Before Lorelle could answer, a knock sounded on the door.

Lillis put a finger to her lips and signaled Lorelle not to answer. Lorelle ignored her and called out, "Come in."

The door opened, and Eiliss, the tall, shining woman who had found Lillis, stood in the threshold. She wore a gown that sparkled like snow in sunlight, and her long, golden brown hair tumbled down her back in lustrous ringlets. A circlet of fragrant white Amarynth crowned her head, and her warm amber eyes made Lillis want to laugh with joy and forget all about silly things like whether or not this—and she—were real.

"Come, *ajianas*," Eiliss said. "We have visitors. I think you will both be pleased to see them."

With a cry of excitement, Lorelle bounced to her feet and bounded out. Lillis paused to pick up Snowfoot, then followed more slowly. Eiliss led the way down the corridors of the beautiful building out into the verdant town square, where fingers of mist swirled and eddied around soaring conifers and evergreens, and a central fountain splashed like the melody of a peaceful song.

There, at the center of a cluster of Fey villagers, stood two Fey warriors clad in black leather: one with flowing, waist-length blond hair, the other with shining chestnut. At the sound of Lorelle's excited squeal, they turned in unison, their beautiful Fey faces breaking into smiles of welcome.

"Little Fey'cha," laughed Kiel as Lorelle raced across the square and leapt into his arms. He swung her around in exuberant circles.

"*Ajiana*." Kieran walked towards Lillis, a dazzling smile upon his beloved face, his Fey-bright eyes as blue as skyflowers.

Lillis stood frozen in place. Her heart pounded like one of Papa's hammers in her chest. Kieran looked exactly the way she pictured him from her most treasured memories. Exactly. Tall, handsome, his skin luminescent, his eyes Feybright . . .

. . . with Love the kitten perched upon his shoulder, flicking her stubby little tail against his ear and purring so loud Lillis could hear it clear across the square.

And then she knew, and her nine-year-old heart broke.

"You're not real." Tears blurred her vision. "None of this is real." Mama, Papa, Lorelle, Kieran, Kiel—the family and friends she loved so dearly—all were just an illusion. She turned to Eiliss, sobbing. "Why? Why are you doing this to me?"

"Are you not safe?" the shining Fey replied. "Are you not happy?"

"It's all a lie!" she cried. "I thought Fey didn't lie!"

"Is it a lie to offer you what your heart desires? To make you happy and keep you safe from harm. Here, in the Mists, you can be with your mother. Is that not what you want most?"

Hot tears ran down Lillis's cheeks, and sobs tore from her throat in painful heaves. "But not like this!"

Lorelle—or rather the illusion that wore Lorelle's face—stepped forward. "Listen to Lady Eiliss. You are in danger out there. Here, with us, you are safe. You wanted to be safe, and so you are. You wanted to be with Mama, and she's here. You wanted Kieran and Kiel, and they are here, too."

Lillis backed away. "No! No! I won't stay here. This isn't what I want." Her wild, tear-filled gaze fixed on Mama, standing in the doorway, watching Lillis. She was the only one who didn't say anything, the only one who didn't try to convince Lillis to stay. She simply stood there, watching Lillis with wise and watchful eyes. *It's better to choke on a bitter truth than savor a honey-cake lie.* Mama's admonition rang in Lillis's ears.

Lillis squeezed her eyes shut and clutched Snowfoot to her chest. "Go away!" she cried. "Go away, all of you! This isn't what I want! I want the truth! Show me the truth!"

A hot tingling sensation flashed through her body. The burbling splash of the village fountain and the whisper of the wind rustling through the treetops faded. The pleading voices of Papa, Kieran, Kiel, and Lorelle died away and the world fell into utter silence.

Pain intruded. It started as a dull ache, then accelerated to burning, throbbing spikes of pain jabbing her like knives.

Lillis cried out, and her eyes flew open.

The village in the misty valley was gone. Lorelle, Papa, Kieran, Kiel—Mama—all were gone. She lay buried in a pile of rubble. The world was dark except for a tiny shaft of pale light that illuminated the prison of rocks and dirt and broken tree limbs that lay heaped over her body.

She couldn't move. Could hardly breathe. Something heavy pressed down on her chest. She tried to move her hand, then cried out when bones grated and a sharp pain lanced up her arm.

She coughed, then cried out again. Her chest was on fire. Each breath felt like the stab of a knife. She had no sensation at all below her chest, and she had a terrible feeling she knew why.

Just two years ago, Tomy Sorris's older brother had fallen from the roof of his family home while trying to sneak out his bedroom window and get into mischief with his friends. They said his back was broken and that he couldn't move his arms or legs. His injuries had been too grave for the local hearth witch, and he'd died before a more powerful healer could come.

Was that why the Mists had created that illusion of Mama and Papa and the beautiful city in the valley? Had whatever magic lived here in the Mists been trying to make her last bells as happy and peaceful as possible?

Lillis closed her eyes and let the tears welling in her eyes spill down into her hair. "Mama . . . Papa . . ." This bit of hard truth wasn't just bitter, it was the most awful torment she'd ever known.

She was dying.

She'd thought she was going to die before, when war had broken out at Teleon and she'd seen the *darrokken* racing up the mountainside towards her, but now she knew it for certain. Death was crouching patiently, just beyond what she could see. She could feel its cold nearness in each painful, struggling gasp of breath. Soon it would pounce, just like Snowfoot pouncing on a jingle ball.

Frightened, she tried to call out, but her throat was too dry, her lungs too short of breath to do more than croak raggedly. "Papa? Lorelle?"

No answer.

"Kieran? Kiel? Anyone?" Her weak, raspy call fell like a coin into a bottomless wishing well, swallowed quickly by silence and darkness.

Her head fell back. More frightened, desolate tears spilled from her eyes, and her broken ribs sent jolts of pain radiating through her with each small, ragged sob she couldn't manage to hold back.

For the first time in her life, Lillis was all alone.

And she knew, if someone didn't find her soon, she would die here, lost in the Faering Mists, trapped in the rubble of a shattered mountain.

Eld ~ Boura Fell

A knock sounded at Vadim Maur's office door.

"Enter."

The door pushed inward, and Primage Zev stood on the threshold. "Generals Corag, Grosh, and Daemor are in position, Most High."

"Excellent. And our Celierian friends?"

"Awaiting your command, Master Maur. The Tairen Soul is approaching Primage Fen's position."

Vadim leaned back and touched his steepled fingers to the underside of his chin. "Tell Fen to spring the trap."

Celieria ~ Northern Border

The missile struck without warning.

It came from behind and plowed into Rain's hind leg just below his left hip, detonating an explosion of raw pain. He roared and wrapped Ellysetta in an instinctive buffer of magic as he careened through the air and fought to regain control. Instantly, a new agony seared him, worse than weapon's initial bite. Needles of white-hot pain shot through his veins and stabbed behind his eyes. A familiar bitter tang filled the back of his mouth.

Sel'dor.

«Ellysetta, hang on! We're under fire!» Despite the pain, he maintained his protective weave around her.

A moment later, the sky before them turned black with a barrage of bowcannon spears flying faster and higher than any he'd ever encountered. Rain reared back. A second bolt pierced his chest, near his foreleg, while a third skimmed by so close it tore the edge of his right wing. He roared and banked with desperate speed as a fourth bolt scored his ribs and tore a hole through his left wing, leaving splinters of *sel'dor* behind. With Ellysetta on his back, he could not Change to avoid the missiles.

«Rain! To your left!» Ellysetta spun a dense pattern of Air and slammed it into the volley of spears, batting them away bare moments before they pierced Rain's heart.

«Hold on. Keep low.» His wings flapped wildly as he fought to retain his balance and keep them aloft while he scanned the ground below for the source of the weapons fire. A Celierian Border Lord's castle hugged the bend of the Heras River, and he spied the bowcannon on its ramparts just as they spat a fresh volley of *sel'dor*-tipped missiles.

Tairen breath heaved from his lungs, meeting the fine mist of venom that sprayed from his fangs and igniting just a few fingerspans from his muzzle when the two combined. Tairen fire poured forth in a roaring jet, incinerating the incoming spears to harmless black dust. He screamed a defiant challenge and dove toward the ramparts, raining fire upon the castle walls, consuming one full line of bowcannon and the soldiers scrambling to reload them.

Ellysetta flung weaves and Air and Fire everywhere his

flame had not scorched. She cried out and her weaves cut
off just as Rain felt the prickle of arrows pepper his hide. He
spun away, roaring with fury. She'd been arrow-shot.

«Shei'tani?»

She clung to his back, leaning low over the saddle front.
«I'm fine.»

But she wasn't. Two *sel'dor*-barbed arrows had buried
themselves deep in her back, and he felt them as plainly as
if it were his own back burning with their foul acid. Just the
effort to speak to him on Spirit racked her slender body with
pain.

They had wounded his mate! He screamed his Rage, and
tairen fury turned his vision scarlet.

Before he could circle back and fire the rest of the castle,
a third volley of spears burst from a line of cannon hidden
in the surrounding forest. He banked instinctively in a tight,
northward wheel, but the spears came too fast. Fresh black
agony ripped through his right shoulder and back leg.

He tumbled through the air, losing altitude faster than
he was losing blood. His tattered wings fought for balance,
but every powerful flap shredded muscles against the razor-
sharp shards of *sel'dor* in his flesh. His right wing, impeded
by the spear piercing his shoulder, could not keep up with
his left, and he careened helplessly northward, towards Eld.

«Rain! Look!»

Below, he saw what had previously escaped his notice:
Eld soldiers, thousands of them, massing beneath camou-
flage netting draped between the trees. They raced out from
beneath their cover, and sunlight glinted off their armor and
unsheathed weapons. A company of archers loosed a hail-
storm of arrows. He spun what protection he could around
Ellysetta's own shield and fired a path through the dark
cloud of *sel'dor* missiles. He put on a burst of speed as he
passed the archers, trying to outpace their second volley, but
a Mage must have been accelerating their shots. Arrows tore
through the tattered membranes of his wings and sank into

his hide. He heard Ellysetta's pained gasp as two of the missiles pierced their shields and buried themselves in her leg.

He saw the Eld running in pursuit as he plummeted down a faltering glide path. *«Hold on, Ellysetta!»*

The trees rose up quickly—too quickly—and he cannoned into them, tucking his wings tight against his back as he smashed through the treetops. Desperately, roaring in pain when the *sel'dor* punished his use of magic, he threw a protective web around Ellysetta just before he lost control and went tumbling downward. He felt Ellysetta being flung from the saddle and heard her cry out, but there was nothing he could do to stop her fall. He crashed through the forest, shattering massive trunks with his tumbling body. His wingbones snapped, but even that searing pain was nothing compared to the agony of the *sel'dor* buried in his flesh or the worse agony of Ellysetta's scream as she fell to earth. His paws flexed, claws extending to dig into the trees, the ground, and even solid rock to slow his momentum.

Finally, after what seemed like an eternity of destruction, his battered tairen's body came to rest against a small copse of fragrant brindlewood tree. Tiny yellow leaves drifted down upon him in a shower of bright winter fragrance.

CHAPTER NINE

On dream's whispered breath, I search for thee.
On wings of hope, I soar.
On desire's breeze, I call to thee,
And pray with song and roar.

>   *Tairen's Chant to His Beloved,*
>   a poem by Rainier vel'En Daris, Tairen Soul

The Faering Mists

Stinging little pinpricks roused Lillis back to consciousness and she looked down to find her kitten, Snowfoot, kneading her chest with his tiny, sharp claws. The pouch tied around her neck that had secured the kitten had slung off to one side during her fall, which explained why she hadn't noticed the kitten earlier.

Snowfoot mewed piteously and nudged his head against her hand, the way Love, the kitten, always had when she was hungry or thirsty.

"I'm sorry," Lillis whispered. Her voice came out scratchy and hoarse. "I'm so sorry." More helpless tears trickled from the corners of her eyes. Snowfoot was hers to care for, and she couldn't do any more to save the kitten than she could to save herself.

Lillis started to sob again, then stopped because it hurt too much. She'd never been this alone or this badly wounded or this frightened. Always someone had been there to watch over her and protect her and keep her safe from harm—Mama, Ellie, Papa, Kieran, even Lorelle.

Lorelle would never just lie down and die. Lorelle was the strong one, the fearless one. Lillis could almost hear Lorelle now, irascible and impatient. "Stop sniveling, you ninnywit. What good has that ever done anyone?"

Thinking of her twin made Lillis's tears flow faster. For all that Lorelle could be snappish and bossy, there was no one in the world Lillis was closer to. She couldn't think of a single time in her life when they'd been apart for more than a few bells. Until now.

Lillis squeezed her eyes shut and tried again to contact her twin. *Lorelle . . . Lorelle, can you hear me?* It wasn't magic, exactly. Not magic the way the Fey spun it, in any case. It was more like sharing thoughts—as if some part of them had been united in the womb and never fully separated.

Again and again, she called her twin, but Lorelle didn't respond. It occurred to Lillis that perhaps Lorelle had not survived the destruction of the mountain—that she had perished as Lillis herself was so close to doing—but as quickly as that awful thought surfaced, she shoved it away, out of her mind. No, Lorelle was alive. She had to be. Maybe the magic of the Mists did something to silence their connection. Or maybe Lorelle was living in some happy illusion like the one that had nearly trapped Lillis.

She tried calling Papa, but that didn't work either. She hadn't really expected it to. If Lorelle couldn't hear her, it was highly unlikely Papa would. Her call to Ellie met the same silence as all the others.

Finally, in desperation, she reached out to the last living person with whom she shared a connection: Kieran vel Solande. Surely, if anyone could break the power of the Faering Mists and find her, Kieran could.

Assuming he was still alive.

"You are alive," she muttered. "I know you are. I know

it." *Please, gods, let him still be alive.* She clenched her jaw and gathered her strength, her last ounce of hope, and all the emotions she associated with Kieran: The way he made her feel so safe. The joy when he—or rather the illusion of him—had turned in that city in the valley of Mists and that familiar, dazzling smile had broken across his face. The love that blossomed in her heart whenever he was near.

Fusing those energies together, weaving them into her call the way she'd secretly spun magic all her life, she flung the cry out into the Mists, praying for the gods to grant it wings. *Kieran! Help me. Pease, help me.*

The effort was too much. Darkness closed in upon her. She was so weak. So tired. As if sensing Death creeping near, Snowfoot began to mew more loudly.

A clatter of pebbles sounded overhead, and dirt showered down upon her face. A weak, painful cough racked her frame.

"Lillis!"

A muffled voice echoed in her ears, tinny yet strangely familiar. Light turned the inside of her closed eyelids rosy. With effort, she cracked open her eyes. Images swirled slowly into focus. Faces hovered over her, surrounded by a glow of light. Blue eyes burning with fear and concern held her gaze as strong, familiar hands reached for her.

She breathed his name on a weary sigh as her lashes fell shut again, and the light faded. "Kieran."

Eld ~ The Forests North of the Heras River

Ellysetta sat up and pressed both hands against her head. The world was spinning drunkenly, and she was so dizzy she could barely sit upright. Flung free of the saddle, she'd gone flying through the air and into the evergreen branches of a large conifer. She'd crashed and tumbled through the branches, losing all sense of balance and direction until the ground rose up to smack her in the face.

She spat out dirt and blood, then wiped the back of her hand against her mouth and took inventory of her injuries. Long, bleeding scratches scored the exposed skin of her hands and face, but her shielding weave and leathers had saved her from more serious wounds from the fall. Her hair bristled with leaves and splinters from broken tree limbs.

She started to draw her legs up in order to stand, but pain lanced up her left leg. She cried out and clutched her thigh. Her hand came away covered in blood. The arrows that had struck her thigh and back had been ripped out during the fall.

She held her hands over the gash in her leg and spun a healing weave to stop the bleeding, hissing as fragments of *sel'dor* burned beneath her skin. The barbs from the Elden arrows had broken off inside her leg, but there was nothing she could do about them now. She left the barbs in place and sealed the skin over them.

The instant the leg was healed enough to stand on, she got to her feet and sent out a narrow, questing thread of Spirit. *«Rain?»*

He didn't answer, but his trail was plainly marked by the line of shattered trees and debris from his crashing descent. Pain shot up her leg as she took her first hobbling step towards him, but she gritted her teeth and forced herself to endure it.

She'd seen the Elden army as she and Rain had fallen out of the sky. She knew they weren't far behind, and she knew that the Eld would already be combing the woods. Any chime now, they'd reach this very spot and follow the crash path directly to her mate.

She pressed her palm against her leg and hobbled faster. *«Rain, I'm coming.»* Desperation gave her the strength to ignore the pain and begin to run. She vaulted clumsily over small downed trees and ran around several larger ones.

When she finally caught sight of Rain, motionless, still tairen, covered by a blanket of yellow leaves, her breath stalled in her lungs.

"Rain!" Adrenaline shot through her. She covered the remaining distance between them at a full-out sprint and fell to her knees beside him. Her hands plunged into his thick fur at his neck, seeking a pulse. "Don't be dead. Please, don't be dead."

A rattling breath wheezed out of him. *«Not . . . dead . . . yet.»* Pain accompanied the faltering thread of Spirit, muted but still sharp enough to make Ellysetta clench her teeth.

She smoothed her hands over him, trying desperately to hide her terror as her hands came away drenched in blood. *Sel'dor*-filled wounds didn't bleed, but he'd taken enough glancing blows and external injuries from the crash that the ground beneath him was rapidly becoming a blood-soaked pool.

«Rain . . . can you Change?» She hated to ask. If he were so injured that a simple Spirit weave felt like knife blades on bone, the powerful, concentrated magic required by the Change would likely kill him. *«I need to get you somewhere so I can get the sel'dor out of you and heal you, but we can't hide while you remain tairen.»*

His eyes opened slightly. *«Leave . . . me.»*

She reared back. Did he think her such a coward that she would save her own life at the expense of his? "I can't leave you to die, Rain. I won't."

«I distract . . . you flee.»

"That's not an option. The Fey and the tairen need you." She stroked his face and stared urgently into his pain-dulled eyes. "I need you."

«You can survive . . . my death.» Bloody bubbles foamed at his nostrils. His lungs were filling. He was dying already, and they both knew it. *«Run. Mages . . . cannot take you . . . »*

He meant it. She could feel his sincerity. He wanted her to leave him here to die. He thought she actually could.

"Don't be a ninnywit. I could never—ever—leave you, not for any reason." She smoothed a hand down the soft, thick fur of his massive tairen jaw. "Whatever choices we

make, we make together. Whatever fate, we face it together."
She blinked back tears and infused her voice with what she
hoped was convincing sternness. "So, unless you want us
both to be guests of the High Mage before nightfall, we need
to get out of here. Now, can you Change?" The Eld would be
here soon, and all chance for escape would be lost.

«Nei. Too much sel'dor.» A cough shook his tairen's body.
His eyes closed, and for a moment she feared he was slipping away from her.

"Then I'll have to remove as much as possible so you can."

Several of the bolt shafts and arrows had sheared off
during his crash, but quite a few still remained. They stuck
out from his flesh like obscene quills. The bowcannon missiles ranged in size from spears the diameter of her arm to
the two thick bolts as wide as tree trunks that protruded
from his chest and rear leg.

She stood up and took hold of one of the thinner spear
shafts lodged in a foreleg.

«Must push . . . not pull . . . spears barbed.»

"I know." She'd removed enough *sel'dor* arrows from
wounded warriors to know what to expect. Of course, none
of those warriors had been Rain.

She closed her eyes and drew a deep breath. *Steady, Ellysetta. You can do this. You must do this.* She took hold of
the spear shaft, planted her feet, pushed with all her might.

The spear moved, slowly sliding deeper into Rain's flesh
with a squishing sound that made her stomach lurch. She
tried to weave away what pain she could, but there was so
much *sel'dor* in his body and hers that the attempt only injured them both. *"Sieks'ta, shei'tan. Sieks'ta.* Forgive me,
I'm so sorry."

The spearhead gave a muffled screech as it scraped against
bone. The sound jolted every nerve in her body, and Rain's
pain roared through her. Nausea rose sharply, dousing her
with sudden clammy weakness. She spun away and lost her
breakfast in the dirt.

When she lifted her head a flash of movement caught her eye. The Eld had discovered the swath of broken and shattered trees in Rain's crash path. Black-armored Elden soldiers were pouring from the woods two miles away.

«Shei'tani . . . leave me . . . run.»

"Don't be a dimskull." Ellysetta dragged her arm across the back of her mouth. Grimly, she grasped the spear shaft again, marshaled her strength, and shoved. The barbed spearhead broke past the bone and pierced the remaining layers of muscle and skin.

Ellysetta opened her eyes, then swallowed thickly. The spearhead now jutted out from the front of his leg, just above his wing, a viciously sharp, ugly, black thing that bristled with broken barbs and glistened with Rain's blood. She'd never seen anything so nakedly evil. Rage flared inside her. She grabbed the bloody spearhead and yanked it free.

Rain coughed again, and the sound snapped her back into action. She hurried to the spear in his leg and had to climb up on top of him to inspect the wound. This bolt was not so deeply embedded as the one in his chest. She could see the misshapen bulge of it, just below the surface of his skin.

«Rain, I think I can just cut this one out.»

«Do it.»

She yanked one of the black Fey'cha from the sheaths at her waist, then stared at it in surprise. What a fool she was not to have thought of this from the first. She dragged the sharp edge of Bel's bloodsworn Fey'cha across her thumb. Blood welled from the cut, and she smeared it across the shining edge of Bel's steel.

«Ellysetta?» Instantly Bel's voice sounded in her mind, faint but clear.

«Bel! We need help. We're in Eld. Rain's been shot by bowcannon—he's badly wounded.»

«We're coming. Be strong, kem'falla, and do whatever you must to stay alive.»

"Bel and the *lu'tan* are coming, Rain." But there was no way he or any of the Fey would reach them in time. She glanced over her shoulder. The Eld soldiers were closing the gap quickly.

Rain gave a weak cough, and Ellysetta's attention snapped back to him. They were running out of time. "Hold on, Rain," she said. "This is going to hurt."

She positioned the knife at the entrance wound and dragged it towards her in one swift motion. His flesh parted, and without the thickness of Rain's tairen hide to keep the weapon embedded in his leg, the heavy weight of the spear shaft pulled the buried head free. The spear fell into the dirt, leaving behind a gaping wound.

She quickly attacked the remaining spearheads, pushing one through the tissue of his leg and cutting out the others, until only the massive bolt buried in his chest, near his right foreleg, remained. "I can't get this last one, Rain. It's too large and buried too deep. I can't push it free."

«I'll have to drive it out myself. Step back, shei'tani.» Rain struggled to his feet. A spasm of racking, fluid-filled coughs nearly felled him, but he managed to remain upright. He drew a shallow breath, summoned his strength, and drove his shoulder down, towards the ground. Pain exploded as the bottom of the spear slammed into the ground and the spearhead tore a path through muscle, sinew, and bone and pierced through the skin of his back.

For one long, breathless moment, nothing existed but the blinding agony, but even that was a relief from the crippling mass of *sel'dor*. He rose to his feet and rubbed against a nearby tree until the barbed spearhead caught and he could pull himself free of the bolt's thick shaft. He shook himself as if he could shake off the pain like water clinging to his fur.

"Some of the barbs have broken off inside you," Ellysetta said.

«I know.» The dark metal's presence was impossible to miss, burning like acid within his Fey flesh. Rain cast a grim eye at the approaching Eld. He couldn't fly in his current condition, and even if he could, the Eld and their bowcannon would be waiting for him.

He and Ellysetta were vastly outnumbered. They must run and hide, which they could not do while he remained tairen.

«I need your strength to help me Change. It will be painful, and I will not be able to shield you from it.» All of his energy would have to be directed to completing the Change while the *sel'dor* shrapnel turned his own magic against him.

"Rain, stop talking. Do what you must. I'll be fine."

Pride surged through him. She was so fierce. She had become a warrior of the Fey . . . *nei,* a Tairen Soul, strong and brave.

«Ke vo san, kem'san.» He nuzzled her gently, rubbing his face against her, then stepped back.

He drew within himself, marshaling his strength and focusing his energies inward. The *sel'dor* was there, a distracting, discordant energy, but he did his best to block it.

He had Changed when riddled with *sel'dor* barbs before, as had all of the Feyreisen during the Mage Wars. Most had survived. Some had not. When he Changed, the *sel'dor* would not Change with him. It would remain in his flesh, at its current size and general location, but hopefully not piercing any vital organs.

He summoned his magic.

Instead of the usual, intense pleasure of the Change, the *sel'dor* twisted the sensations. His nerves registered the horrible agony of flesh tearing from bones and liquefying, skin splitting and burning, magic simultaneously crushing him and tearing him apart. Beside him, Ellysetta shrieked and fell to her knees in pain, and her torment nearly drove his tairen to madness.

He held the weave and fed it power, forcing his magic into the familiar lines it now rebelled against. The webs of his magic bucked and writhed, fighting their natural paths.

For one desperate, frightening moment, he thought he would fail, that he would die, and Ellysetta would be left alone and unprotected to face the approaching Eld.

But even as that unimaginable horror seized his mind, she

crawled across the ground on her knees and reached a shaking hand out towards the wildly undulating cloud of gray mist swirling around him. She touched the mist. The bright strength of her power poured through him. He grasped her offering gratefully, weaving her strength to his own dwindling supply. She was there with him, in his consciousness, every thread of their nearly completed bond vibrating with harmonic energies. She was a bright, shining presence in his soul, a vast and endless warmth, stealing his fear and transforming it into confidence and strength enough to force the unruly weaves to his command and complete the Change.

The howling pain of *sel'dor* quieted. The tairen shrank, folding in upon itself, condensing, until once again it was the invisible sentience mingled inside his body with his own soul.

Rain fell to his knees in the dirt, Fey once more and weak beyond belief, his body afire with the barbs of *sel'dor* buried in his flesh. The ones so large they now protruded from his flesh, he plucked out. The others he left where they were. He would not completely heal, nor regain his full strength until the *sel'dor* in his body was removed. Until then, working magic would be painful at best, which gave the Eld a powerful advantage.

Breathing raggedly, Ellysetta knelt beside him and spun what healing she could as she grabbed his arm. "I'm sorry, Rain, I know you're hurt, but we have to go. We have to go now."

"Aiyah." He forced himself to rise and swayed dizzily on his feet. One hand reached out, weaving a Spirit illusion, nothing particularly intricate or strong, but hopefully enough to fool the approaching Eld and give Ellysetta and him a brief head start. "Run. That way." He pointed to the east.

The Eld would expect them to go south, towards the river and towards Celieria, but clearly one or more of the Border lords had either been overrun by the Eld or surrendered himself and his lands to their service.

Rain didn't know how much of the borders had been compromised, but he couldn't afford a river crossing into enemy territory any more than he could afford to take wing here in Eld. They'd have to backtrack towards Lord Barrial's land and cross the river at nightfall. The moons were both on the wane, and for once, he hoped darkness would be their ally.

Eld ~ Boura Fell

Melliandra lay on her thin pallet in the *umagi* den. The sconce lights were low, as they always were, emitting the barest of orange glows. Just enough for eyes accustomed to the dark to navigate the rows of sleeping racks that lined the room from floor to ceiling.

Sleep, in Boura Fell, was a carefully rationed luxury . . . a brief respite in a lifetime of toil granted only because *umagi* couldn't function without it. Each *skrant* was allowed only a few bells per day in a bunk shared in shifts by four other *umagi*. There were no days and nights in Boura Fell. Only work and sleeping. And punishment when you slept too much or worked too little.

But even though sleeping bells were precious and few, Melliandra had been using most of hers to practice her newfound magic.

Every spare moment of the workday, she now spent haunting the Mage Halls, watching the novices practice, listening to them talk amongst themselves, picking up every small scrap of information so she could teach herself to use her newfound abilities. And each sleep shift, she brought what she learned back to the quiet dark of the *umagi* dens to practice.

She closed her eyes, letting the darkness envelop her. She could hear the breathing of the other *umagi*. The occasional cough and sniffle. The shifting of a body in its bunk. She tried to silence those small noises from her mind. From what she'd learned eavesdropping in the Mage Halls, all novice Mages learned to access their magic by first silencing their minds. It was only there, in the darkness and the silence, that a Mage and his magic first truly connected.

Not that she wanted to be a Mage. She didn't. But she needed to know what Mages knew, to better defend herself and Shia's son against them. Most importantly, she needed to know how Mages wove their wards—and how they unwove them—because that talent was the key to all her plans. With it, she could enter Vadim Maur's treasure room where Lord Death's magic crystal and weapons were stored—and with it, she could gain access to the nursery where Shia's son and the other valuable infants of the Mage's breeding program were kept.

Melliandra took deep, unhurried breaths, holding them, letting them out again in a slow, steady rhythm. She breathed in through her nose, held that breath for a count of five, then exhaled through her mouth to the same count. In through the nose and out through the mouth. Inhale. Hold. Exhale. Slowly, as the rhythm took over, her body began to relax, the world faded away.

And there, in the darkness, she found the silence, perfect and absolute. She'd never known absolute silence until this week. It was peaceful. She'd never known that either.

Her breathing continued, slow, steady, and in the silence, she initiated the next step all novices learned. Stretching out their senses, opening their minds to let magical receptors begin to absorb the subtleties of the world around them. In the Mage Halls, the novices had taken turns holding an object, with each novice trying to determine what the other was holding.

"Don't influence, just observe," instructed one of the apprentices who'd come to help them. "Let your partner's senses become your own. If you do it properly, he won't even know you're there."

Melliandra had been practicing that skill every waking bell these last days. What did that *umagi* have in his pocket? What was this *umagi* hiding in the corner? What secret savory had the kitchen mistress tucked away for herself today? She was getting very adept at peering into the brains of the *umagi* around her. Yesterday, she'd had a moment where she'd seen through the eyes of the kitchen mistress— which, she discovered, was a very disorienting practice when the kitchen mistress was walking one way down a hall, and Melliandra was walking the other.

She'd even practiced on the two Mages who'd tried to get into Vadim Maur's office that day last week. She'd heard them talking about the High Mage, about how they'd known the Mage whose body Vadim Maur now inhabited. They'd been talking about how that Mage—Nour—while strong, hadn't been as strong as either of them. There were other Mages, like them, who were growing dissatisfied with Vadim Maur, concerned that he'd lost focus, that his war against Celieria and the Fey was more about some secret personal goal than the triumph and glory of Eld.

It wasn't until this morning, when she'd gone back to listen in on the novices practice again, that she'd heard the apprentice warning the novices not to get too bold with their attempts at eavesdropping.

"Don't try this on a Mage, greenies," he'd warned. "Unless you're more powerful than he is, he's going to know you're there, and he won't be pleased."

And yet she'd tried it on those two Mages—the ones who claimed they were more powerful than the High Mage was now—and neither of them had detected her presence. Just to be sure her success was no fluke, she'd eavesdropped on several other Mages throughout the course of the workday. Not one of them had noticed her in their minds.

Her success gave her courage. And this time, as Melliandra stretched out her senses, she directed them in search of a specific mind, a specific pair of eyes. It was, surprisingly, much easier than she expected, perhaps because the cool, dark path to that mind already existed inside her, forged when she was very young.

In the silence of her mind, unnoticed by her host, Melliandra looked out through the eyes of Vadim Maur.

The Faering Mists

Kieran knelt beside Lillis's body and prayed while the *shei'dalins* worked frantically to save her. Behind him, Lorelle clung to her father and Kiel with desperate fear.

The *shei'dalins*, surrounded by a thinner mist and a golden light, had been the first of the lost party Kieran and Kiel located. Both of the women had already healed each other's wounds from the falling mountain, and rather than heading off blindly into the Mists, they'd decided to wait and send questing calls of Spirit out in every direction. Kiel had stumbled across one of those Spirit threads, and the two of them followed it to its origin. Together, the four Fey began combing the rubble in search of the Baristani family.

Many bells later, they found Lorelle and Sol, both completed covered by a fall of rocks that hid them from view. How they'd found them, Kieran wasn't entirely sure, but he'd followed a sudden feeling that had taken him off in the right direction. Lorelle and Sol were both barely alive—hardly more than a few heartbeats from death, actually—and as the *shei'dalins* healed them, they said that someone or something in the Mists had been holding them to the Light.

It was by tracking the flickering remnants of that Light and the growing sense of urgency pulling at him like a lodestone that Kieran had found Lillis, buried under a pile of rubble, her body shattered, dying. *She* had been the one holding her family to the Light.

There was hardly a bone in her body left unbroken, hardly a fingerspan of skin not horribly bruised and scratched. A large tree limb had impaled her left leg. Sharp rocks had all but sliced off her right arm. Her back was broken in three places.

There was no reason she should still be alive at all—especially after feeding so much of her strength to her sister and father. And yet she was.

The *shei'dalins* couldn't explain how she had survived, and Kieran didn't care to try. He only cared that she was alive, and the *shei'dalins* were here to heal her, and he was with her. Nothing else mattered.

"I'm here, *ajiana*," he whispered, stroking her hair. "I'm here with you. Your papa is fine. Lorelle is fine. You need to stay with us now." Tears gathered on his lashes and dropped onto her cheek, making little paths through the layer of grime coating her skin.

Her eyes fluttered. Dazed eyes found his face. Her cracked lips parted in a faint smile. "I knew you were alive," she whispered. "I knew you would come."

He blinked back more tears and brushed his hand across her hair. "Always, *ajiana*. Whenever you need me, I'll always find a way to reach you. No matter what."

The Forests of Eld

Together, Rain and Ellysetta sprinted through the tall, dense trees of Eld's old forest. Thick, soft moss, layered with fallen leaves and shed needles, carpeted the forest floor. Undergrowth was sparse, but Rain used Earth to thicken the occasional stands of small evergreen shrubs and thin saplings to provide cover from their pursuers. He had to use a light hand. Too much thickening of the brush, and he might as well blazon their path in sun-bright colors.

Ellysetta ran beside him, her footfalls Fey-silent despite the limp in her gait. She more than kept up his pace, but they still weren't running even half Rain's normal speed.

They ran for bells, stopping to rest only when their legs wouldn't carry them another step. Rain wasn't certain how far they had run. Forty miles. Maybe sixty. Still nowhere near close enough to expect rescue from the *lu'tan*.

Rain threw small obstacles behind them. Spirit weaves to confuse and mislead their pursuers: muffled voices to draw Eld attention in a different direction, a flash of Ellie's bright hair to draw their eyes, splashes of blood leading away to the west.

Within his body, the remaining *sel'dor* barbs shifted continually, tearing muscle and flesh, burning, making his every weave a painful exercise. Each time the pain grew too sharp, Ellysetta touched him and stole away the worst of it.

Afternoon turned to evening. They came upon a narrow dirt road that cut a swath through the forest and very nearly stumbled into the path of an oncoming squad of Elden soldiers. Rain grabbed Ellysetta's arm and hauled her back, and they ducked into the shadows of a small rocky outcropping.

«Do you think they saw me?» she asked.

«Nei.» He cursed softly to himself. *«But they're definitely looking for us. See how they're scanning the forest as they march?»*

One of the soldiers stopped to nail something to a tree.

«What are they doing?» Ellysetta asked.

«I don't know.» Rain narrowed his eyes. The man had hammered what looked like a round moonstone on the tree trunk. While farther down, another soldier hung a similar stone on the opposite side of the road. *«Whatever it is, I don't like the looks of it.»*

They ducked back into a small crevice in the rocks as the soldiers drew closer. He spun the barest hint of Spirit to veil the pair of them and make them appear to be part of the stone itself. The weave would not hold up to close inspection, but unless the Eld stood within a few armlengths of them, it should suffice.

He held himself still, hands clenched, as the Eld approached. Rage, his old familiar friend, burned deep within him, hungering for blood and vengeance.

Ellysetta laid a hand on his face, her touch cool and calming.

Rain covered her hand with his. *«I will do nothing to endanger us, shei'tani.»*

«I know you will not.» Her trust in him was simple—and absolute.

He swallowed his hatred, tamping it down as, behind them,

the Eld stopped beside the rocky outcropping. Part of him—perhaps the still sane part—didn't believe her trust was warranted, but he prayed to the gods he would not fail her.

"Here as well," one of the soldiers announced in an authoritative voice.

There was a bit of grumbling. "The Tairen Soul himself gets shot down, and Primage Keldo has us hanging *jaffing* rocks on trees."

"We all do our part, corporal. If it bothers you, perhaps you'd like to discuss it with the Primage yourself?" There was a snap to the squad leader's voice.

"No, sergeant," the corporal replied sullenly.

"Good. Then hang the *chemar* every hundred paces, as the honored Primage has ordered. If the Tairen Soul passes this way, we'll have been the ones to set the trap."

The squad of soldiers moved away, leaving the grumbling corporal behind to finish his task. "Perhaps you'd like to discuss it with the Primage yourself?" he sneered under his breath. "Scorching brown-nose. Bet you wear a dress and bend over any time the Primage gets a stiff one."

From the sack at his waist, the corporal yanked out a small round stone set in what looked like some sort of pendant, then he pulled hammer and nails from another pouch. He slapped the stone against the tree trunk at shoulder height, pinned the nail through the bale loop at the top of the stone, and swung his hammer. His foot slipped on a pile of slick leaves, and the hammer slammed down on his thumb instead of the nail head.

"*Krekk!*" The white stone fell to the ground and skidded across the slick blanket of fallen leaves, down an incline. The Eld soldier loosed a stream of colorful swearing and shook his smashed thumb.

"Son of a pole-shriveling bone-hag. Miserable *chervil-jaffing, krekk*-gobbling *rultshart.*" The corporal stuck his thumb in his mouth and sucked on it as he stomped after the fallen stone, which had come to rest near a small rocky outcropping. "I'll bet they've already found him. I'll bet they're roasting his Hells-flamed Fey changeling ass over Mage Fire right this very moment, and I'm missing out on the lot of it." He snatched up the fallen stone.

He stopped short, his gaze freezing on the shadowed outline of two pairs of booted feet visible within a translucent gray veil of stone. "What the . . . ?" He squinted and stepped closer. The boots were connected to legs and whole bodies. It looked as if two people had been entombed in the stone.

Understanding, unfortunately late, bloomed in the young man's brain as he looked up, straight through the weak Spirit weave into Rain Tairen Soul's glowing eyes.

The *chemar* dropped from the corporal's nerveless fingers. *"Krekk."*

CHAPTER TEN

Eld ~ North of the Heras

Rain's Fey'cha flew true, burying hilt-deep in the Elden soldier's throat. Tairen venom did its job. The young man's eyes rolled back instantly, and he dropped to the ground.

A shout rang out from the squad farther up the road.

"Come on!" Rain grabbed Ellysetta's hand, launched out of their hiding place, and headed due south. The time for backtracking to a safer crossing was over. They needed to get to the river—and fast.

He sent a blast of Fire up the road and whispered his return word to retrieve his red Fey'cha from the fallen soldier's throat. As they sprinted across the dirt road, Earth rumbled to Ellysetta's command, shifting beneath the feet of the squad of soldiers. A chorus of screams rose as trees toppled down on top of them, and another gout of flame lit a deadly bonfire.

One of the white stones on the trees began to glow as Rain and Ellysetta ran past, and a glowing rune appeared in its center, as if written in fire.

"What is that?" Ellysetta pointed at the glowing stone.

"I don't know, but it can't be good. Run faster, *shei'tani.*"

She put on a burst of speed, then faltered as a wave of ice washed up her spine, and her knees went weak. "Rain . . . My legs . . ." Her legs abruptly folded, and she went sprawling into the bracken. Rain circled back and snatched her up off the ground, but her trembling legs would not hold her weight. She collapsed against him, clinging to him to hold herself upright. "I'm sorry."

"Las. There is nothing for which you should be sorry."

He scooped her up against his chest and continued to run. Behind them, the screams of the burning soldiers died out, leaving only the crackling of Rain's Fire.

Ellysetta's trembling increased until her entire body shivered uncontrollably with the familiar sensation of ice spiders crawling up her spine. Her temples ached, and there was a strange pressure at the backs of her eyes, not unlike the burn of unshed tears. She stared over Rain's shoulder as he ran, and watched in horror as a black spot began to widen in the place where the glowing *chemar* stone had been.

"Rain! It's the Well! The Well of Souls is opening!" Her fingers clawed into his shoulders as a sudden, powerful blast of cold, gagging sweetness swept over her. Robed Mages rushed out of the Well, globes of deadly blue-white fire whirling in their hands.

"Run!" she cried. She flung a series of five-fold weaves behind her, but the *sel'dor* weakened her threads, and the Mages easily batted them aside.

Rain clutched her to his chest and raced across the rolling hills of Eld. The exertion opened his barely healed wounds, and drops of bright scarlet marked a trail that would be all too easy to follow. Of course, with Mages at their back, leaving a visible trail was the least of their worries.

Ellysetta didn't think the situation could get worse, then two—no, make that three—new portals opened. She saw one of the white stones with the fiery rune glow bright, just before a fifth portal opened where the stone had been. "It's the stones! They're using those stones to open the portals."

The Eld were gaining on them. Carrying her as an extra burden slowed Rain down too much. She squirmed in his arms. The tingling, ice-spider feeling was still strong, but the initial rush of weakness had faded. "Put me down. We have no chance of outrunning them if you keep carrying me."

He set her on her feet without breaking stride, and she landed running.

«If we can make it to the river, we might have a chance at escape.» The Heras was fed by the powerful *faerilas* Source

at Crystal Lake, and its waters worked like acid on Mage flesh. Even with their magic tightly leashed, Mages avoided wetting so much as their smallest toe in the fierce waters of the Heras. *«The river won't stop the Mages completely, but at least it might slow them down.»*

They raced through the trees, leaping over small rocks and fallen tree trunks. As he approached a final, small ridge, Ellysetta could smell the brisk, clean waters of the Heras and hear the rushing burble of its swift current.

Almost there. Five more tairen lengths, and they would be over that last ridge and speeding down its slope to the protection of the river and away from those gods-scorched *chemar* stones that were spitting out Mages by the dozens.

An arrow slammed into Rain's back, knocking him off-balance and sending him sprawling.

"Rain!" Ellysetta scrambled down the hill towards him.

"Leave me! Run! Get to the river! I'll be right behind you."

"I've already told you, I'm not going anywhere without you." Her eyes went wide, and she lunged for him. "Look out!"

Rain threw himself to one side. The arrow in his back snapped in two as he rolled onto his back, and two more barbed arrows thunked into the ground at the exact spot he'd just vacated. A third arrow sank into a tree trunk near Ellysetta's head.

Rain's eyes flamed at the sight of the poisonous black missile quivering in the tree so close to his *shei'tani*. Despite the howling protest of the *sel'dor* embedded in him, he sent Fire spinning from his outflung hand. It scorched several trees and ignited the three Elden bowmen who'd shot the arrows.

Ellysetta grabbed him and yanked him to his feet. Together, they raced up the final ridge, scrabbling over slick piles of fallen leaves and tumbled rocks. A storm of arrows erupted from the trees at their backs. Ellysetta flung a blast of Air to knock them off course.

At the bottom of the hill, a pair of yellow-robed apprentice Mages stood surrounded by archers and swordsmen. Magic crackled around them in a visible nimbus, and in their hands they coaxed deadly globes of blue-white flame to life.

One of the two Mages sent his ball of Mage Fire roaring towards them. Rain attempted a five-fold weave, but *sel'dor* howled through his flesh. His resulting weak, crippled weave only managed to deflect the Fire, not destroy it. The Fire plowed through another clump of trees, eradicating portions of them from time and space.

In a battle of magic today, even those two apprentice Mages would win.

"To the river, *shei'tani*. Hurry!"

Behind them, at the bottom of the hill, the second Mage released his fire. Rain looked back just in time to see it hurtling towards them. "Get down!" He flung himself at Ellysetta, knocking her to the earth and covering her body with his own as the enormous ball of blue fire roared over their prone bodies, close enough to singe Rain's skin with the burning ice.

A hail of arrows followed on the heels of the Mage Fire, and yet another volley of Mage Fire followed the arrows. Ellysetta deflected the arrows but Rain could not even slow the Mage Fire.

"Rain." Ellysetta gasped softly and grabbed his hand, squeezing tight.

A sudden blast of energy from the west ridge intercepted the hurtling balls of Mage Fire and destroyed them.

Their unlikely savior was a blue-robed Primage heading up a second troop of soldiers and archers. "Kill the Tairen Soul, if you must, idiots," the Primage shouted in Eld to the two apprentice Mages, "but harm the girl, and the High Mage will roast and eat your livers out of your still-living bodies."

Rain glanced behind them, to the Mages approaching from the west, north, and east, then looked down at the troops standing between them and the river. "That's our only chance," he said. "I don't see any Mages there."

Ellysetta raised her brows. "So what are we standing here for?"

He laughed, loving her. Then his expression went serious as he handed her two red Fey'cha.

She took the poison blades and searched his face.

"In case, I cannot save us," he admitted in a low voice.

Her gaze fell, and she nodded in solemn understanding. Their situation was grim. Rain would die before letting the Mages take her, and if he did, the Fey'cha would at least give her a way to avoid capture. She sheathed the poison blades carefully in the knife belt across her chest.

He touched her cheek. "Lend me your strength, *shei'tani?*"

"You need not ask."

"And give me one last kiss?"

She smiled and moved into his arms. "You need not ask for that either."

Her lips, so warm and soft, parted beneath his. She tasted of life and sweetness and all the dreams he'd ever dreamed as a boy. She tasted of hope and of a future he'd never allowed himself to want since he'd found his wings. Regret dimmed his pleasure. She was so young, her life so unfulfilled.

Ellysetta pulled away to look into his eyes. "No regrets, Rain. I have none."

Peace settled over him. He nodded, his throat too tight for words, and kissed her once more. *«Ver reisa ku'chae. Kem sera, shei'tani.»*

Her hands closed around his. The brightness that was Ellysetta flowed up his arms and filled him with peace and warm, rejuvenating strength. He gave her back the essence that was himself and watched her eyes flutter closed. She smiled, a secret, womanly smile. *"Ke vo san, shei'tan.* I always have. I always will."

Together they turned to face the advancing line of soldiers.

"There." Rain directed her attention to the spot where the line of soldiers was thinnest. He gathered his power. They would not have more than a few moments to make their escape. He would have to strike hard and fast, with only one or two concentrated weaves to open up a corridor between the advancing Eld.

She squared her shoulders. "Let's go."

They ran down the hill, magic blazing. Earth shuddered violently. The ground split open to the left and right, and dozens of soldiers toppled into the fissures. Fire and Air roared down the hillside, plowing through the remaining line of men and clearing a direct path to the Heras River.

Sel'dor screamed in Rain's flesh, amplified by the echo of Ellysetta's matching pain, but he roared his defiance of it and held his weaves until his very bones rebelled. They raced through the burning carnage as the remaining soldiers converged on them, swords drawn.

A badly burned soldier leapt from the smoking ruins of his fallen comrades to make a grab for Ellysetta. She slashed out with Rain's red Fey'cha. Blood spurted from the Eld's torn throat, splashing her face. She swiped her forearm across her face and kept running. Beside her, Rain swung his *seyani* sword in his left hand and fired off red Fey'cha with his right.

Behind them, the Mages had reached the crest of the ridge. A line of archers fired a volley of arrows. As they soared overhead, Rain saw the white stones attached to each arrow shaft already brightening. Rain grabbed Ellysetta's hand and put on a desperate burst of speed.

Too late. Portals opened like gaping black maws directly in their path. Mages and soldiers poured out, blocking their path to the river and cutting off their only hope of escape.

Cornered, breathing hard, Rain and Ellysetta turned to face the enemy.

The Fading Lands ~ Chatok

With the Baristanis healed and safely in tow, Kieran and Kiel led their small group back up and over the shattered mountain to the edge of the Faering Mists. Though Teleon and the Garreval now appeared completely clear of Eld, Kieran and Kiel took no chances. They traveled just inside the edge of the Mists, following that edge to the Garreval and emerging only to make a swift dash into the Mists-filled pass between the Rhakis and Silvermist mountains.

They stayed close to the *shei'dalins,* walking in the thinner mist that surrounded them, and the passage into the Fading Lands went without incident. Kieran held Lillis on his back, while Lorelle rode on Kiel, and the girls' kittens, who had also survived their ordeal, purred happily inside their slings on Kiel's and Kieran's chests.

Within a few bells of entering the Garreval, they emerged onto Taloth'Liera, the great, walled field that marked the boundary of the Fading Lands. Fey in full war armor stood atop the wall and flanked the mighty steel gates that led into the Fading Lands.

The warriors guarding the gate greeted Kieran and Kiel as if they'd risen from the dead. Which, Kieran supposed, they had.

"We're glad to see you alive and well," the captain of the gate said. "I'm sure Marissya-*falla* will make the Feyreisa's family feel right at home." *«Despite the current circumstances,»* he added on the Warrior's Path.

Kieran and Kiel shared a frown. *«What circumstances?»* Kieran asked.

The Forests of Eld

Eld surrounded Rain and Ellysetta on all sides, swords drawn, *sel'dor*-barbed arrows nocked and aimed. And with them were Mages. Scores of them. Yellow-robed Apprentices, red-robed Sulimages, and twelve of the most dangerous, the blue-robed Primages. The Mages' eyes were alight with the unholy red-sparked black of Azrahn, and each of them held globes of lethal Mage Fire at his fingertips.

"Throw down your weapons, Tairen Soul," one of the red-robed Sulimages ordered, "or we'll see how your mate likes dancing with our Fire."

Rain sneered at the threat. "Harm her, and the High Mage

will roast your liver and eat it from your still-living body," he reminded them in fluent, perfectly accented Elden.

To the right, the blue-robed Primage gave a wry laugh. "Very true," he acknowledged pleasantly in equally fluent Feyan. "You have good ears, and a wonderful command of our language." Suddenly, his eyes blazed black with red lights, and the line of Eld bowmen behind Ellysetta let their arrows fly.

Ellysetta cried out as half a dozen arrows plowed into her back and shoulders, dropping her to the ground and pinning her there. The red Fey'cha in her hands fell harmlessly to the dirt.

Rain let out a choked snarl of fury and reached for his own red Fey'cha, but five more bowmen shifted their stance to aim directly at Ellysetta.

"But," the Primage continued calmly, "there are degrees of harm. The High Mage wants her brought to him alive, but he won't mind a scratch or two. And I'm quite expert at knowing how to bring a Fey close to death while keeping her chained to life." All pretense of warmth left his voice, and his smile vanished. Eyes swirling with Azrahn threatened from the hard, cold face of an unforgiving enemy. "Now drop your weapons, or we'll see how much more *sel'dor* your mate can take before she cannot stop herself from screaming."

Rain dropped the sword and Fey'cha still clutched in his hands, then began to unbuckle the straps that held the rest of his weapons.

"*Nei,* Rain," Ellysetta moaned. Her face turned towards him, her eyes glazed with pain. "Don't do it!"

He shook his head. «*I have no choice, shei'tani, and they know it.*» He'd given her the red Fey'cha to take her own life if he was slain. But fighting would only ensure her torture and his certain death, and she would be left alone and vulnerable in the hands of the Eld.

When all his steel lay in the dirt at his feet, two soldiers and one of the apprentice Mages approached. Two of them gathered his weapons and retreated out of reach.

"Hold out your hands," the yellow-robed Mage ordered.

Rain extended his arms.

The Mage nodded, and the soldier beside him pulled a pair of black metal manacles from a large leather pouch. Long, sharp black spikes drove inward from the metal cuff, and thick, heavy metal chains joined the manacles together.

"We run across *dahl'reisen* from time to time," the apprentice Mage informed him, "so we've learned to always be prepared."

Rain shuddered and dropped to one knee as the Eld clapped the manacles over his wrists and drove the *sel'dor* spikes into his bones. The dark metal, poisonous to the Fey, burned where it touched him, making his skin redden and blister, short-circuiting his body's natural self-healing abilities. His wrists, like every burning wound where *sel'dor* shrapnel still lodged, would remain unhealed and in constant pain until the foul metal was removed.

The Eld stripped off his boots and drove a second set of spiked manacles into his ankles. The raw, searing pain left him breathless and dazed. Ellysetta wept openly, sobbing his name.

"What about her, Master Keldo?" the Apprentice Mage asked.

"Bind her hard," the Primage answered. "Wrists, ankles, and throat. Master Maur said this one is dangerous."

The apprentice Mage approached Ellysetta with heavy black manacles and chains.

"Leave her alone!" Rain ordered. He strained against his chains. "Do not dare to touch her."

"The bindings will cause no permanent injury," the Primage assured him. "But her magic will be contained." He issued a sharp command, and several soldiers rushed to hold Ellysetta down as the apprentice clapped the spiked manacles into place around her wrists and ankles.

Ellysetta screamed and began to struggle. Panic grabbed Rain by the throat. He lunged forward, trying to reach her, dragging the four Eld soldiers holding his chains off their feet. Someone cracked him hard over the back of his head, and he collapsed facedown on the ground.

The Fading Lands ~ Chatok

Kieran could scarcely believe the "circumstances" that the captain of the gate had been referring to. Once again, Orest was under attack. This time with dragons to combat the tairen. Once again Rain had called for every warrior in Dharsa to head for the Veil.

And once again, proving that his incalculable stupidity knew no bounds, Tenn v'En Eilan had countermanded that order just as he had countermanded Rain's order to defend Orest and the Garreval this summer.

To justify his command, Tenn had reminded the Fey that Rain was an outcast, a *dahl'reisen* stripped of his crown and banished for spinning Azrahn. He'd even gone so far as to warn that any Fey who chose to fight alongside their deposed king did so at his own peril and should expect no aid from the Fading Lands.

Kieran met Kiel's gaze in grim silence. *«That scorch-brained fool,»* he hissed to Kiel on a private weave. *«Teleon was destroyed, Orest nearly taken, and Tenn's still hiding behind the Mists, thinking that will save us? How can he think dividing us will make us stronger?»*

«We could head for Orest now,» Kiel suggested. *«The shei'dalins can take Master Baristani and the girls the rest of the way to Dharsa without us. If we hurry, we could make the Veil in a little over two days. From the sounds of it, the Fey at Orest need every blade they can get.»*

Kieran glanced at the girls standing alongside their father and the two *shei'dalins*. He wanted to head for Orest. His hands itched to hold his blades and feel the razor-sharp steel slice through Eld flesh and bone. He could almost hear the voices of his slain blade brothers at Teleon crying out for him to avenge their deaths.

He clenched his jaw and silenced them. *«Nei,»* he said. *«Nei, the Feyreisa entrusted her family's safety to us. I will not abandon that duty to another. We see them safe to Dharsa, and into my parents' care. And then we head for Orest.»*

«Agreed, but we need to move quickly. The sooner we reach Dharsa, the better.»

Kieran tugged at his lower lip. Where was a *ba'houda* steed when a Fey needed one? Celierians couldn't run even half the speed of a Fey for more than a few chimes, and they tired much too easily. Kieran and Kiel didn't have the strength to carry all three of them—and with a war on, the Garreval couldn't spare a single warrior to help them.

A gust of sandy wind whipped a long scarlet veil off one of the *shei'dalins*. Kieran watched it swirl and tumble through the air, with the *shei'dalin* running in pursuit, and his lips curved in a slow smile.

«I think I have an idea. Wait here.» Turning, Kieran jogged back into Chatok, returning a few chimes later with a pile of blankets he'd filched from the barracks. He set the blankets on the ground and summoned his Earth magic.

Lillis watched his weave with interest. "A carpet?"

Kieran gave her a grin. "Lillis, *kem'alia*, haven't you ever heard the story about the Feraz desert boy and his magic, flying carpet?"

Her eyes widened. "Oooh. We're going to fly?"

He laughed. "*Aiyah*, you are. Hop aboard. You, too, Master Baristani and Lorelle. *Kabei*. Now, hold on." Kiel and he combined their powers in an Air weave strong enough to lift the carpet several handspans above the sand. Another simple weave propelled the levitating carpet through the air. Soon, the flying carpet and its riders were racing across the sands towards Dharsa, with Kieran, Kiel, and the *shei'dalins* sprinting swiftly alongside.

Eld ~ North of the Heras

When Rain awoke, he was collared as well as manacled. The heavy metal yoke around his neck wasn't spiked like the manacles, but it blistered his skin, constricted his airway, and made breathing an effort. Even if he managed to break free of the Eld, there was no way he could run or fight with the collar limiting each breath to shallow, hard-won gasps.

Ellysetta lay beside him in the dirt, curled into a small, trembling ball. Her eyes were closed, her breathing shallow and labored. Both her wrists and ankles were bound in heavy *sel'dor* and a matching collar circled her neck, attached to a thick chain. Rain's gaze followed the length of hated black metal links to the Eld soldier holding the other end of the chain.

He couldn't have been out for very long. They were still in the forest. If much time had passed, he and Ellysetta would already be halfway to whatever foul den the High Mage called home.

Half a tairen length away, the Mages stood together, arguing over something. After a furtive but thorough look around, Rain estimated there were about five hundred Eld soldiers and bowmen gathered in the surrounding trees, weapons in hand but not aimed. Rain turned his attention back to the Mages, focusing on the blue-robed Primages. They were the greatest threat, the strongest source of enemy power. The other Mages were powerful—no Mage advanced beyond green robes without mastering the ability to wield dangerous levels of his own innate magic—but they were only apprentices to the darkest secrets of Azrahn.

The Primage called Keldo was the obvious leader. There was both arrogance and temper in the haughty arch of his blond brow and the unmistakable snap of command in his voice. A sash bedecked with sparkling jewels attested to his many victories, and rings of power gleamed on each of his fingers, including two thumb rings set with large black *selkahr* the size of Soul Quest crystals. Which Fey, Rain wondered, had died—or worse—so this Mage could wear those rings?

The Mages were still arguing. Keldo scowled and said something, but he kept his voice too low to carry far. Rain strained his ears to catch the tail end of what Keldo was saying.

". . . You think Primage Garok could ever have conceived—let alone carried out—the capture of the Tairen Soul and his mate? Don't be such fools. Master Maur is the greatest Mage in the history of Eld, and thanks to his vision and leadership, we stand on the eve of the greatest victory Eld has ever known." Keldo made a slashing gesture. "No. We deliver Master Maur's prize to Boura Fell, as ordered. If Garok believes he is the better Mage, let him issue challenge. I, for one, will never bet against Master Maur."

So . . . there was apparently dissension in the Eld ranks. Rain wished there was some way to put that knowledge to use, but once the High Mage had Ellysetta in his control, he'd be able to put his last Marks on her, and there would be nothing and no one with the power to defeat him.

He dragged himself closer to Ellysetta and reached out for her hand, but before his fingers could touch hers, the soldier holding Rain's chain gave his collar a vicious yank. Rain fell backward, choking and grabbing at the collar.

The Eld soldier smirked. "Not so almighty without your magic, are you, Tairen Soul?"

Rain narrowed his eyes. Even with all the *sel'dor* in him, he could still summon enough magic to weave the Air out of a pair of lungs.

The sight of the man's shocked, bulging eyes and sudden terror was worth the vicious beating Rain received as half a dozen soldiers leapt on him and bludgeoned him mercilessly until he released their comrade.

The choking soldier fell to his knees in the dirt, coughing and wheezing. Rain flung his hair out of his bruised and bloodied face and sneered. "Not so arrogant with no air in your lungs, are you, Eld *rultshart*?"

"Ah, you've awakened," the Primage observed in a cool voice. "And still full of defiance, though I'm sure the High Mage will rid you of that soon enough." His eyes went cold as he turned them on the still-wheezing Eld soldier. "Get up. You are a fool to taunt a Tairen Soul, even if he is *sel'dor*-pierced and bound. Unlike your friends I would not have intervened while he killed you. If you bait him again, I'll kill you myself, and I promise you, your death at my hands will be far more painful than mere suffocation."

The choking man blanched and lurched to his feet. "Understood, Primage Keldo." He saluted briskly and resumed his station, standing stiffly at attention.

"As for you," the Primage continued, piercing Rain with a cold stare, "bringing you back alive will add a substantial jewel to my sash, but your mate is the true prize. Cause me trouble, and I'll slit your throat without a second thought. Captain!" An Eld officer snapped to attention along with several of his men. "Prepare him." As the soldiers moved forward, the Mage told Rain, "These men are going to clean your wounds and pack them with *sel'dor* powder. We're all going to take a trip to the High Mage's palace, but in your current condition you'd never survive a journey through the Well of Souls. The smell of your blood would drive the demons mad with hunger."

Rain suffered the ungentle ministrations of the Eld as they doused him in water to wash away the blood, then rubbed his wounds with powdered *sel'dor* to soak up any fresh blood that might ooze from them. Keldo himself cleansed and packed Ellysetta's wounds, then stroked a hand over her cheek when he was done.

Rain's chains rattled. "Do not," he hissed.

The Primage arched a brow. For a moment, Rain thought he might dare some other, graver indecency, but apparently he remembered his own warning about baiting Tairen Souls. The Primage removed his hand, and Rain crawled over to pull Ellysetta into his arms. This time, the soldier holding his leash did not try to stop him.

At his touch, Ellysetta's trembling lessened. One arm crept up around his neck, and she turned her face into the hollow of his throat, flinching back when her skin touched his *sel'dor* collar, then settling against a spot on his chest instead.

His embrace seemed to draw her back from whatever nightmare had gripped her mind, and he felt her return to full consciousness. "Rain . . ."

"Shh. *Las, shei'tani.* I am here." He feathered a kiss on her pale brow, another in her bright hair, and kept his wary gaze on the enemy that surrounded them.

"Touching," the Primage sneered, but he made no move to separate the pair of them. Instead, he turned sharply to two of the yellow-robed apprentice Mages. "Gelvis, Harryl, open the portal."

"Yes, Master Keldo." The two apprentices raised their arms. The cuffs of their saffron robes fell back, and the air around their hands began to glow as they gathered their energies. Rain clutched Ellysetta close as the sickly sweet odor of Azrahn filled the air, and the temperature dropped several degrees.

He watched the patterns of the weave form, dark ropes of red-tinged black writhing like snakes, looping and intertwining, undulating, pulsing like blood through veins. The chill of Azrahn grew colder until Rain felt his skin tingle with false warmth. The weave outlined a wide rectangle and began to bleed inward upon itself, forming an impenetrable, pulsating darkness in the late-afternoon shadows of the forest. As the edges of the weave touched and the last light shining through was blotted out, Ellysetta began to moan. Her limbs trembled violently.

Bright shafts of white blazed out from the edges of the weave, and it fell inward, like a cloth falling down an abyss. Sheer, inky blackness loomed in the middle of the forest. A low, keening cry issued from deep within the darkness. Whispers, insidious, hungry, frightening, snuck into the world.

"Rain . . ." Ellysetta clutched at him, her skin gone clammy, her eyes open and unfocused.

"Interesting," the Primage observed. "She feels the Well open, just like a demon."

At last Rain's mind made the connection that had been eluding him for months. The wandering souls that occasionally sent shivers through Ellysetta and made her legs go weak. The whispering voices that had so terrified her when the tairen sang the Fire Song to cut the invisible bonds that tied Cahlah and Merdrahl to the earth and freed their souls to dance the stars. The pieces of the puzzle finally began to fall into place. When the Well of Souls opened, Ellysetta sensed it. The opening of the portal sapped her strength, leaving her weak and trembling. As if some part of her were being drawn back into the Well each time it opened.

Could the infant tairen whose soul had been stolen from the Well and tied to hers be trying to get back where it belonged? Or had whatever black magic the Mage had spun on her in the womb left her somehow uniquely connected to the things that dwelled in the Well?

"Rain . . ." she whispered. Her body went limp, and she slumped against him, unconscious.

Rough hands grabbed Rain's arms and hauled him to his feet. Ellysetta dangled from his arms, her head back, her curls spilling to the ground like a waterfall of flame. "Wait!" he snapped. "Something's wrong with her!"

Primage Keldo sneered. "Perhaps the fact that she's carrying her weight in *sel'dor*?" His expression hardened. "Pick her up and carry her, or we'll do it for you. The High Mage is expecting us, and he doesn't like delays. You two"—he jabbed a finger at two armored soldiers standing nearby, then jabbed again to the swords, Fey'cha, and weapons' belts piled a short distance away—"bring their weapons."

As the two soldiers rushed to gather the Fey steel, Rain lifted Ellysetta into his arms. The Primage nodded, and the soldiers standing behind Rain shoved him towards the gaping maw of the Well of Souls.

CHAPTER ELEVEN

Soul stained black by darkness
I've been banished to this half life.
All I have left is remembered honor
And for this I now must fight.
I'll protect those that I left behind
So they'll never feel this sorrow.
I'll hold the line day and night
So my Fey brethren will not follow.

> *Dahl'reisen's Lament,* by Varian vel Chera

The Forests of Eld ~ North of the Heras River

Before the sole of Rain's boot touched the ground in his third step towards the Well, the world went mad.

A shadowed blur whooshed past his ear. The expertly thrown red Fey'cha buried itself in the chest of one of the apprentice Mages holding open the gateway to the Well of Souls. Red blood blossomed. The Mage's mouth opened in a soundless scream.

Blackness came rushing out of the Well. *Demon!*

Rain tightened his grip on Ellysetta and shoved away from the Well, propelling them both backward as the formless dark mass enveloped the Mage. He caught a brief glimpse of the demon's snapping teeth and bloodred eyes. Then the air turned scarlet as the Mage's body shredded. Long strips of flesh peeled away from bones; blood sprayed in a fine mist that never made it to the ground, bones pulverized into powder. In an instant, he was gone—utterly consumed.

The red Fey'cha that had initiated the Mage's death fell to the forest floor only to disappear before it hit the ground.

A savage grin curled the edges of Rain's mouth. He didn't know how in the Seven Hells Bel had done it, but he'd somehow managed to reach them in record time. "Fey!" he cried, "*Ti'Feyreisa! Ti'Feyreisa!*"

The whistling whoosh sounded again, this time in force as scores of Fey'cha rained down upon the Eld. Half the Mages died before they had time to raise their shields. Demons howled and rushed out of the Well, driven to frenzy by the sudden rush of rich, red blood.

The Fey must have been using Gaelen's invisibility weave, because Rain didn't catch a single glimpse of black-clad warriors or even the slightest purple glow of a Spirit weave. But their steel flew with blinding speed and deadly accuracy, and that was all he cared about.

As swift and merciless as the demons that consumed the dead, the Fey rained down slaughter on the enemy. Eld screamed and scattered in fear as invisible foes ripped open Eld throats and chests, parted heads from shoulders, and cleaved mailed soldiers in two. Only the Fey'cha were visible, flying without cease, outpacing Eld arrows four to one.

Without the dead Mage's Azrahn to keep it open, one side of the Well doorway began to collapse. The apprentice Mage holding open on the other side gurgled as a red Fey'cha buried itself in his throat. He toppled over and was shredded and consumed before he could hit the ground. The doorway fell in upon itself, closing rapidly.

Primage Keldo leapt forward and channeled a concentrated burst of Azrahn to keep the Well open. Even as he did so, he flung a shield around himself and fired deadly globes of Mage Fire at the unseen attackers. "Get the girl into the Well!" he shouted. Fey'cha bounced harmlessly off his shields.

A dozen Eld converged on Rain and Ellysetta—and died. Their bodies dropped like autumn leaves.

Rain hauled Ellysetta into his arms and bolted away from the Well. Huge, furious balls of Mage Fire rolled past Rain on either side. He smelled the stench of seared flesh and heard the thud of ruined bodies falling to the ground as some of the Mage's shots hit the invisible rescuers. Rain kept running. His *seldor*-bound magic was useless, and Ellysetta's life was in danger. He had to trust the Fey to do their job. "*Fey, ti'Feyreisa!*" he shouted. "Fey, to the Feyreisa! Protect her! Shields up!"

A fiery hammerblow punched Rain in the back of one leg, sending him sprawling. The smell of scorched ozone filled his nostrils. He fell to his knees, and his elbows slammed so hard into the ground that his teeth rattled. He'd been struck by Mage Fire, and only the power of his golden war steel had saved him the loss of a leg. He released Ellysetta and rolled to his feet in time to see another of the Primages advancing on him, more Mage Fire blazing.

Half a dozen Fey materialized directly in the Primage's path. Another half dozen shimmered into visibility in a loose ring around Rain and Ellysetta. Mage Fire roared towards them. In the hands of the Fey, magic blazed to life, huge, powerful ropes of it forming a five-fold weave. Earth. Air. Water. Fire. Spirit.

A sixth, dark rope joined the rest.

Azrahn.

Rain's gut clenched. He spun instinctively towards Ellysetta, saw the six-fold weave surrounding her unconscious form, saw the scars on the faces of the Fey surrounding her.

It wasn't Bel who'd come to their rescue.

It was *dahl'reisen.*

His hand instinctively reached for his Fey'cha belts, but his steel still lay in a heap on the ground near the portal to the Well of Souls. Before he could make a move to recover his blades, a massive concussion shook the ground. Rain dropped to his knees as Mage Fire exploded harmlessly against one of the six-fold weaves.

More *dahl'reisen* added their weaves to the others. Power swelled until the very air crackled. Clouds boiled in the sky. Rain glanced back in time to see the Primage feed power into his shields in a desperate, doomed attempt to save himself as thirty-six *dahl'reisen* interwove their magic into a single, enormous rope of energy. It blasted through his shields like fire through paper, incinerating him in a single fiery flash.

The doorway to the Well of Souls collapsed. The feeding demons howled in fury as the closing door sucked them back into their world.

Abrupt silence fell over the Eld forest.

The *dahl'reisen* paused briefly to gauge the remaining number of enemy, then continued methodically exterminating the Eld. They made short work of those who fled and the few who remained to fight, and slit the throats of the still-groaning Eld wounded as they began dragging Eld bodies into a large pile and retrieving Fey'cha.

"Fire the bodies quickly." The order came from behind Rain's back. The speaker's voice was harsh and gravelly, and it held the unmistakable ring of command. "Jaren, you and your men send our fallen brothers back to the elements. Others will come. We must leave." The *dahl'reisen* obeyed without hesitation. The pile of Eld corpses burst into flames. The half dozen dead *dahl'reisen* who'd not been consumed by Mage Fire were gathered and laid out in a line. Six-fold weaves enveloped the bodies, then blazed bright. When the magic died down, the bodies of the slain *dahl'reisen* were gone.

Rain turned to the speaker, a tall dark-haired warrior with a thick scar that curved across his throat up to his left cheek. Rain did not recognize him, but that wasn't so surprising. Before the Wars, Fey had numbered in the hundreds of thousands.

"You will come with us," the *dahl'reisen* told Rain.

Rain glanced at the *dahl'reisen* still ringing around Ellysetta. Had these men who walked the Shadowed Path rescued them only to turn around and imprison them again?

"The woman and I are heading for Orest," Rain told him, then cursed himself for the useless attempt to hide Ellysetta's identity. He'd already shouted it to them all. *Fey, to the Feyreisa! Protect her!*

One of the *dahl'reisen's* dark brown brows lifted in a mocking gesture almost identical to the one Gaelen so enjoyed using. "Your sense of direction is somewhat lacking, Tairen Soul. This is Eld."

"We were . . . diverted."

"You are both wounded, and I imagine you would like to be rid of that Eld jewelry before continuing your journey." The *dahl'reisen's* nose wrinkled with distaste as he touched the *sel'dor* manacles welded in place around Rain's wrists.

Rain met his gaze steadily. "You know I cannot allow any of you to touch her."

The mocking brow arched again. "You believe you could stop us if we were determined to do so? *Sel'dor*-pierced and shackled?"

"I would die trying."

"Still so noble. Still so bloodthirsty. How many souls weigh on your own, Rainier vel'En Daris?"

"Millions," Rain answered flatly. "And you?"

"Not so many as that. But enough to leave me with this." He touched the scar on his neck and cheek. "Strange, is it not, that I should be the one banished."

"We suffer and survive our sufferings as the gods see fit."

"Ah, of course. The will of the gods." He tired of pricking Rain's honor. "You will tend your mate, Feyreisen. We who are the Brotherhood of Shadows do not touch Fey women. She will be safe enough, but with your permission we will weave Spirit upon her to keep her from waking. In her current condition, our proximity would be too harsh a torment for her to bear."

Knowing he had little chance, Rain agreed, and one of the

dahl'reisen spun a dense Spirit weave over Ellysetta. Rain watched closely to be sure there was nothing in the weave but patterns to make her sleep.

"Once we reach our village, we will remove your shackles," the *dahl'reisen* leader said as the other man finished the weave and stepped away. "There are women with healing talent who will see to you both. We will—" His voice broke off. He lifted his head with sudden alertness, his shadowed green eyes growing darker. "More Mages have arrived. Blue robes, by the feel of them—and many of them. We must cross the river quickly."

Only then did Rain scent Azrahn on the wind, so faint he might never have detected it without the *dahl'reisen's* drawing attention to it.

"The Eld are using the Well of Souls to travel," Rain told the *dahl'reisen* leader. "They've planted white stones throughout these woods to open portals to the Well at will."

"The *chemar*," the scarred warrior murmured. "*Aiyah*, they are a disturbing new development. The Eld only recently began using them, and they stink of witchcraft. We have destroyed all those between our position and the river. But we appreciate the warning."

Rain eyed the other man with speculation and an unsettling sense of confusion. *Dahl'reisen* walked the Shadowed Path. They were corrupt and untrustworthy . . . and yet there was something about this man . . . "Do you have a name?"

The *dahl'reisen's* eyes flickered with surprise. Fey did not ask *dahl'reisen* their names. *Dahl'reisen* were the dead— *nei,* worse than the dead, they were the dishonored.

"I am Farel."

Celieria ~ Orest

The sky over Orest was on fire. The screams of tairen and dragons rent the air. Great jets of searing flame and smoke boiled like demonic thunderclouds, turning the sky a sickly orange. Hundred-fold weaves kept the flames from burning most of the city, but the ramparts of lower Orest were scorched, parts of the stone walks littered with the seared rubble of bowcannon and the smoldering heaps of ash that had once been men. Two dozen bowcannon were still operational, surrounded by thickets of dense, protective weaves that the Fey opened to let the cannoneers fire, then sealed again once the shot was off.

The tairen darted in and out of the Faering Mists using the magical barrier for cover, soaring out to launch an attack and draw the fire of the dragons so the cannoneers could load and launch their ice shot, which exploded on the slick, superheated dragon scales like water dropped in a vat of hot grease. Three of the great beasts had fallen, their broken, bloody carcasses draped over the city's walls and rooftops, but the victory had not come cheaply.

"My Lord Teleos! Look!" One of the general's aides pointed to the east. An army was marching towards Orest, banners waving the familiar blue and gold of Celieria and an equally familiar gold gryphon on a field of red. "It's Lord Polwyr!"

Teleos fixed Fey eyes on the approaching army, and the tension in his gut didn't ease until he saw the familiar face of his neighbor and friend, Griffet Polwyr, heading up the column, riding his favorite white warhorse. "Thank the Bright Lord. He must have seen our signal fires. Quickly! Open the eastern gates and wave him in. Tell the cannoneers keep those dragons off him while his men cross the field."

Eld ~ The Heras River

A fog had moved in, blanketing the Heras in thick whiteness. Long black barges emerged from the mist as the *dahl'reisen* band approached the banks of the river. Dark sails snapped in an unnatural wind, and the shallow boats skimmed rapidly across the swirling current, steered by an unseen hand.

Along the Eld shores, *dahl'reisen* slipped like shadows

through the trees, their numbers—nearly five hundred strong—moving swift and silent.

Still holding Ellysetta, Rain struggled to keep up, and his steps fell heavily on the ground. With more Mages advancing rapidly on their heels, Farel had barely taken the time to strike the chains off the manacles clamped to Rain's ankles so he could run rather than hobble to the river's shore. His gait was awkward, the barbs from the *sel'dor* missiles shredding his flesh with every step. His body poured constant energy to heal the muscles even as they ripped against the barb's sharp edges, and the pain was so consuming, he'd had to separate his mind from his body.

As they hurried down the steep hillside to the water's edge, the black boats beached themselves on Eld soil. The *dahl'reisen* leapt aboard without pause and pushed off.

Rain had to admire the practiced economy of motion. These *dahl'reisen* moved like a swift, honed blade, each man acting as a seamless part of the whole. Even without their impressive invisibility weaves, they could no doubt strike without warning and disappear before anyone could summon a defense.

He clambered aboard the last boat and took the seat Farel indicated. Ellysetta's head lolled back against his arm, her bright hair spilling down to the boat bottom in a fall of wild spirals. Her lips were parted, her breath whispering through in shallow gasps. Around him, *dahl'reisen* cast furtive glances filled with curiosity and longing and envy. How long had it been since they'd seen a Fey woman? Since they'd stood even half a league from one?

He drew Ellysetta more closely against his chest. His flat gaze met the others, warning them off as the boat pushed away from the shore and turned, heading for the other side.

"You are the Brotherhood of Shadows," Rain said. "Did Gaelen vel Serranis send you to rescue us?" Of course, it had to be Gaelen. The reckless, rock-headed *lu'tan* would have done anything to save Ellysetta, even send *dahl'reisen* for whom coming within a mile of a Fey woman was an act punishable by death.

Farel's eyes flickered. "What do you know of Gaelen vel Serranis?"

"I know he leads a band of *dahl'reisen* he calls the Brotherhood of Shadows. He came to Celieria several months ago with reports of Mages returning to power and the Eld gathering an army."

"You cannot have captured him. You would have ordered his death for approaching his sister."

"Aiyah, I would have."

"Yet he still lives."

"He does." Rain was not about to tell the *dahl'reisen* that Ellysetta had restored Gaelen's soul. They might be Gaelen's comrades, they might have rescued Rain and Ellysetta from certain doom, but they were still *dahl'reisen,* Fey outcasts who had chosen life on the Shadowed Path over *sheisan'dahlein,* the honor death. They were what Gaelen had been before Ellysetta restored his soul, honor-lost warriors capable of committing the most heinous of all Fey crimes—even murdering a Fey woman. Rain had not forgotten that Gaelen had originally come to Celieria City to kill Ellysetta because he believed she was Vadim Maur's daughter. Instead, Ellysetta had restored Gaelen's soul, and he'd bloodsworn himself to her protection.

"You confuse me, Tairen Soul."

Not half so much as I confuse myself. Rain sighed and pressed his lips to Ellysetta's brow. She had entered his life and tilted all his certainties into questions.

"We would have saved her regardless of Gaelen's commands," Farel announced abruptly. "She is Fey. We may have lost our path, but we still own enough of our souls that we would not have allowed a *fellana* to fall into Eld hands."

Rain looked up. Farel was watching Ellysetta. There was no mistaking the helpless adoration, the naked longing. No Fey woman had ever claimed Farel's soul, yet still he could not help but love them. It was plain on his face that even now, even *dahl'reisen,* he remembered the dreams of every Fey boy and man for a truemate, he remembered the untarnished beauty and limitless love of Fey women. He might want to blame them for his banishment, but he could not.

"Beloved of us all," Rain said quietly.

"The gods have mercy upon us."

With another man, Rain would have laughed at the familiar rejoinder. But he could not laugh with a *dahl'reisen* whose only hope of mercy had perished long ago.

The boats reached Celierian shores under the protective blanket of mist, and the *dahl'reisen* disembarked as quickly as they had boarded. As the last man leapt to dry land, the boats dissolved and shrank, becoming the fallen trunks of trees littering Celierian shores.

"The Mages will likely follow us," Farel said. "And not necessarily by the river. We slay them where we can, but the Eld have thoroughly infiltrated the borders. The north belongs to Eld, and only now does Celieria begin to know it."

"So Gaelen warned us months ago, but few believed him."

Farel nodded, but this time silenced any bitter reply he might have made. "Gaelen told us to keep you safe until he arrived, so you'll be coming with us."

To one side, a *dahl'reisen* emerged from the mists leading a black *ba'houda* horse. "Can you ride, Tairen Soul? It's either this or we carry you and your mate on a pair of litters. We cannot afford to let you slow us down."

"I can ride," Rain said. Flamed if he would let some *dahl'reisen* cart him about like a decrepit mortal. It wounded his pride to allow Farel's men to lift him into the saddle, but better that than allow the *dahl'reisen* to touch Ellysetta. When the *ba'houda* actually moved, more than his pride hurt but he gritted his teeth and bore it, clasping Ellysetta tightly against him as they galloped through the Celierian hills.

Every so often, a small squad of *dahl'reisen* would peel

off from the main group and lope away in some different direction. Decoys, Rain presumed, sent to befuddle any followers and to erase the signs of passage of the main party. The *dahl'reisen* operated with impressive precision. Which wasn't all that surprising since all *dahl'reisen* were seasoned Fey veterans with many centuries of training and warfare beneath their belts. Once, they had been among the best warriors of the Fading Lands.

Rain was grateful for the *dahl'reisen* weave that kept Ellysetta unconscious. Between the *sel'dor* in her body, his own burning pain, and the presence of the *dahl'reisen,* she would have been screaming in torment. And with his arms around her—his body pressed against hers, their shared pain would have formed an agonizing harmonic.

Rolling farmland ended at the edge of a deep wood, and the *dahl'reisen* came to a halt. Rain's innate tairen sense of direction and long-forgotten memories pinpointed their location. This was Verlaine Forest, the deep, vast woods in northwest Celieria. Legally, the forest was part of King Dorian's family holdings, but in reality Verlaine Forest belonged to no one. During the Mage Wars, Fey, Celierians, and Elves alike had found refuge here amongst the trees, using the forest as a base from which to launch attacks against Eld. Dark, bitter battles had been fought all around the forest's edges, terrible magic released in and around its ancient borders, but the Eld had never conquered the dark Verlaine, nor penetrated its deepest interior.

Farel approached and laid a hand on the neck of Rain's mount. "You'll have to run from here. Not even *ba'houda* will enter this wood. Do you have the strength to carry your *shei'tani* and still keep up?"

Rain arched a brow. "You just lead us to safety. I'll find whatever strength I need to follow."

The corner of Farel's mouth lifted. "Then follow, Tairen Soul." He turned and plunged into the dense, dark forest of the Verlaine.

Rain adjusted Ellysetta in his arms, set his jaw, and ran.

Eld ~ Boura Fell

"Escaped? What do you mean my prizes have *escaped*?"

Primage Vargus stood before Vadim Maur, shaking like a leaf in a hard wind. "The *dahl'reisen* were using their invisibility weave—the one that renders them completely undetectable. They came in such numbers, with no warning, and they destroyed all the *chemar* in the area so we couldn't flank them. We searched for them, but found no sign of their tracks. We can only assume they've crossed the river and taken refuge in the Verlaine by now."

Vadim paced, the hem of his purple robes swirling around his feet with each brisk step and sharp pivot. He'd been waiting impatiently for the arrival of Ellysetta Baristani, and when she had not been delivered to him within one bell of her capture, he'd gone looking for an explanation—and found Vargus in the war room, sweating a river as he tried frantically to coordinate a doomed search for the missing captives.

"We did at least recover the Tairen Soul's blood, Most High."

Vadim stopped abruptly in a billow of purple velvet. "Did we?"

Vargus nodded. "Quite a lot of it. Enough for Primage Grule to ensure that the next time the Tairen Soul flies near Eld will be his last."

"See it done."

Vargus bowed and exited the room.

Vadim began to pace once more. The *dahl'reisen*. They'd been a thorn in his side for centuries, slaughtering his *umagi*, foiling the raids he sent to bring back the magical offspring from the breeders he'd released into Celieria in the hopes of creating a greater and more powerful pool of prospective breeders. He'd captured a number of the *dahl'reisen* over the years and added their gifts to the bloodlines he was creating. For that usefulness—and because he hadn't wanted to tip his hand to the Celierians—he'd never sent a large enough force into Celieria to kill them.

But now—incredibly—it seemed the *dahl'reisen* had joined forces with the Fey.

And that was an alliance he could not allow.

Vadim wrenched open the door to his office and barked a curt command to Zev.

"Summon the Mharog."

Melliandra leaned close to the bars of Lord Death's cell and spoke in a low voice. "Remember I once asked you if you could show me how to unravel a ward?"

Lord Death's head was bent over his bowl as he scooped hot stew into his mouth. At her question, his glowing green eyes looked up, pinning her. "I remember. I also remember telling you it takes magic to unweave magic."

"What if someone just recently discovered they have magic? Could you teach them how to use it?"

His eyes narrowed. "I used to be a *chatok* . . . a teacher. But learning magic takes time."

"What if you don't have much time?"

"That would be unfortunate. Instruction cannot be rushed."

She took a breath. She couldn't believe she was about to suggest this. "What if you didn't exactly instruct?" She swallowed, and forced herself to spit it out. "Mages control people. They make them do things, even magical things."

"Mages do many things Fey do not. Controlling others through magic is one of those."

"Yes, but could you if you had to?"

Lord Death's brows drew together. "What are you thinking, child? What are you asking me to do?"

"There's an important battle coming. The High Mage is planning to personally oversee it. He'll be leaving Boura Fell. It would be the perfect time to get your things."

The Fey set down his bowl and gripped the cage bars. "When?"

"In a few days. Like I said, there's not much time. That's why I need to know, if I can bring you someone with magic, and I show you the wards that need to be unraveled, can you—I don't know—spin a weave of some kind to control their magic so they can unravel the wards?"

"Who is this magic user? How do you know you can trust him?"

She bit her lip. Once her secret was shared, it could never be unshared. But then, she'd already shared other secrets with this Fey, ones that would be far more perilous to her if he ever revealed them.

"Her, not him. The magic user is a girl. And I know I can trust her, because she's me."

Celieria ~ Orest

"I am very glad to see you, my friend." Teleos clasped Griffet Polwyr's forearms. The neighboring Border Lord's men had been deployed in lower Orest, while the nobleman himself had been escorted to the command center in Upper Orest.

"And I you, my friend. I saw the signal and the fire in the sky"—he jerked his chin towards the tairen and dragon fighting claw and fang overhead—"and thought you could use a hand."

Despite the grim circumstances, Teleos laughed. "You thought right. I've never been happier to see your ugly face." He and Griffet had been friends since they were lads. Griff's second son bore Dev's name.

A sudden cry rang out over the Warrior's Path. *«Portal opening near the south gate! Fey to your posts! Sound the alarm!»*

The bells of Lower Orest began to ring. Teleos swore. A single portal had opened a mile east of Lower Orest, well out of cannon or weave range. A score of Eld soldiers emerged, racing north and south, and in their wake, dozens and dozens of other portals opened. Elden warriors and Mages poured out in a thick, black tide. Behind them, a second row of portals spewed batteries of bowcannon and siege weapons.

"Looks like they mean to take her this time," Dev said.

Griffet moved to Dev's side. "They do, my friend," he said softly. "I'm sorry, but they do."

"Griff?" Dev turned in time to see his friend's eyes turn to bloody black horror. The sickly sweet ice of Azrahn washed over him. "Ah, no." Dev's mournful whisper ended on a choked grunt. His breath fled his lungs in a sudden, agonized gasp and pain doubled him over as the blade in Griffet's hand slid under the scales of Dev's armor and sliced through his belly, driving up towards his heart.

Celieria ~ The Verlaine Forest

For most of the day, Rain and the *dahl'reisen* picked their way through the Verlaine's heavy underbrush and dense stands of trees, pausing only a few times for brief rests. Progress was slow until the daunting thicket of the outer forest gave way to an older, deeper wood where small, persistent saplings and evergreen molia bushes vied for survival alongside great, densely needled conifers and thick, gnarled oaks. Twilight descended, and the forest gloom became an impenetrable darkness. Rain's eyes adjusted automatically, his elongated Fey pupils opening wide to let in every hint of light. Where mortals would be blinded by darkness, Rain and the *dahl'reisen* had the clear vision of cats hunting in the night.

A loud scream rent the air. Rain jerked to attention.

"Lyrant," Farel said. "The forest is full of them . . . along with other vicious, Shadow-spawned creatures created and loosed upon it by the Mages."

They ran deeper into the forest, and Rain began to spot the shadows of *dahl'reisen* sentries perched high in the branches above. He knew there must be conversations flying over private Spirit weaves, but the *dahl'reisen* were too disciplined for him to detect the barest hint of it.

They approached a deep thicket draped with thorny, flowering sago vines. Except for the faintest glow of a privacy weave and the fact that the *dahl'reisen* sentries now allowed themselves to be visible, Rain would not have given the thicket a second thought.

"We're here," Farel said. The vines parted as Farel approached, and he ran through the resulting tunnel without slowing. The *dahl'reisen* guards watched silently, their faces inscrutable, as Rain and Ellysetta passed by them and followed Farel through the opening.

They emerged from the long tunnel at the edge of a village. A remarkable, unexpected, secret village—large enough it could nearly be called a city—hidden in the heart of the Verlaine.

Rain looked around with a mix of shock and admiration. He had not expected something so large, nor so impressive. *Dahl'reisen* Earth masters had done their work well. Cabins nestled amongst the trees, integrated with an almost Elvish flair so that they were scarcely distinguishable from the forest as they hugged the thick trunks and perched high in the heavy branches. Vine bridges draped from tree to tree. Rope ladders and hanging wooden stairs that could be raised or lowered at will granted access to the buildings overhead. Round, illuminated orbs hung from the tree branches, casting a golden glow upon the city in the trees and the forest floor below, where well-worn paths bordered carefully tended gardens.

Villagers rushed out to meet the returning raiders. Among them were several dozen more *dahl'reisen*—some in full leather and steel, others looking incongruously like Celierian townsmen in tunics and breeches—numerous mortal men and women, even elders with wrinkled skin and whitening hair. And there were children, scores of them, varying in age from the smallest babe still suckling at its mother's breast to tall, stripling youths on the cusp of adulthood. Rain stared at the children in wonder, seeing more than one Fey face among them. They all watched him with a mix of intense curiosity and deep-rooted wariness.

As the *dahl'reisen* entered, the villagers moved forward. Women opened welcoming arms and clasped suddenly weary-looking *dahl'reisen* to their breasts. Small children cried "*Gepa!*" Father! Several women gave choked cries and rushed to clasp the hands of the wounded, while others waited and stood in grief-stricken silence as Farel's warriors delivered unto them the steel and *sorreisu'kiyrs* of the fallen.

Watching them, Rain's throat grew tights. He remembered countless similar scenes from his own childhood. Happy homecomings when his father, Rajahl, had returned safely from battle. Bitter homecomings when Rain himself had brought the wounded and as many dead as he could carry back from a particularly bloody clash with the Mages.

He had never dreamed to find such warmth . . . such love . . . in a *dahl'reisen* village.

A tall woman in dark skirts approached Farel. She was young despite the wealth of startling white hair she wore tied back with a simple band. Her face was barely lined, her eyes large, clear pools of misty gray surrounded by thick black lashes. Rain estimated she had seen no more than thirty mortal years. She paused at Farel's side and clasped his hands, staring up into his eyes. Though they did not embrace or speak aloud, Rain guessed this was Farel's chosen companion.

The white-haired woman released Farel's hands and accompanied him back to Rain and Ellysetta.

"This is Sheyl," Farel said. "She will tend to you and your mate once we rid you both of the *sel'dor.*" He led Rain over to a smith's forge built in a small clearing off to one side of the village. Six *dahl'reisen* followed—to guard the villagers from the Tairen Soul, Rain supposed—but the others dispersed, moving as far from Ellysetta as they could, some even leaving the village altogether.

The smith was not *dahl'reisen,* but neither was he wholly mortal. His muscles were thick as a Celierian's, but his eyes were pure Fey, pale, crystalline blue and glowing with latent magic. He turned to Rain, a folded wad of leather in his large hand. "If you will allow me, Feyreisen, I'll remove that collar. You can lay your mate on that cot in the corner, then come sit on this bench."

Rain hesitated, searching the man's gaze for any hint of treachery. When he found only sincere compassion, he nodded and laid Ellysetta gently on the clean bedding. A blanket had been folded neatly at the end of the cot, and he draped it over her before returning to straddle the bench near the forge.

The smith tucked the wad of leather between the collar and Rain's neck, then slipped a small steel plate between the leather and the collar.

"Turn your head away."

Rain obeyed, and someone—he couldn't tell if it was the smith or the *dahl'reisen*—summoned a five-fold weave. The dominant thread in the weave was Fire. He could feel the concentrated heat of it. Cooling Water and brisk Air kept the heat from penetrating through the leather or spreading through the rest of the collar. The five-fold weave went suddenly ice-cold, and a sharp blow made Rain flinch. After repeating the process another five times, the despised collar fell away.

"Beylah vo," Rain said, rubbing at his throat. He took a deep breath and winced as the shrapnel still buried in his chest reminded him sharply of its presence.

"Sha vel'mei," the smith replied. And in perfect Feyan, he added, "Removing the manacles will be quite painful, I'm afraid. There's no way to break open the bonds without driving the spikes farther in, and they leave thorns we must then cut out."

"It can't hurt more than it already does, but see to my mate first," Rain ordered. Now that he knew what the removal procedure entailed, he would not allow Ellysetta to suffer her bonds a moment more than necessary.

"As you wish," the smith agreed, "but I'll need you to hold her. As I said, the procedure will not be pleasant."

Rain returned to Ellysetta and knelt at her side, gathering her against his chest as the smith first removed Ellysetta's collar then the manacles binding her wrists and ankles. Even with the weave keeping her unconscious, the pain of the procedure roused Ellysetta enough that she sobbed and fought Rain's grip until the smith had removed the last of her bonds.

Then it was Rain's turn again. He hissed through gritted teeth as the smith worked on the barbed shackles piercing his wrists. When the first shackle fell free and the sharp pain of the thorned spikes ripping out of his bone almost wrenched a cry from his throat, Ellysetta roused once more.

"Rain?" Her eyes fluttered opened, dazed and filled with empathetic pain. Now free of her *sel'dor* manacles, enough of her power must have returned that she was able to fight off the weave meant to keep her unconscious. She reached for him, groping blindly, and when her fingers grasped nothing but air, she pushed herself off the cot and crawled across the dirt floor to reach him. The *dahl'reisen* made no attempt to stop her. Instead, they carefully backed out of her way so that she could not accidentally touch them.

"Ellysetta, *nei.*" Rain tried to push her away when she grasped his hand. "Do not touch me while they are removing the shackles. You will feel it too clearly."

Though barely conscious, she would not be dissuaded. Instinct, pure and Fey, drove her. Her long fingers curled around his bleeding wrist. She murmured his name over and over, weeping, as a featherlight weave of healing Earth and soothing Spirit penetrated his abused flesh. He felt her pain as the despised *sel'dor* buried in her flesh rebelled against her use of magic, but she persevered, ignoring her own torment as she tended his.

"Stop," Rain pleaded, pulling away again. Even if she could ignore what she felt, he could not. "Enough, *shei'tani—*" The word he'd so carefully avoided using slipped from his lips. He glanced up in time to see Farel's eyes narrow.

"Leave her." The white-haired Sheyl stared at Ellysetta, her eyes sympathetic. "Can you not see she feels it anyway? Let her find what comfort she can in trying to heal you. Lian, finish quickly. She will try to bear the brunt of his pain for him."

Rain kicked up a leg, halting the smith. "*Nei,* do not."

Sheyl's pale eyes flashed with sudden fire. "You Fey are fools," she snapped. "Always trying to protect your women from their own nature. It hurts them more, do you not understand? Worse, you make them weak, when they need to be strong!"

The accusation took him aback as much as the woman's fearless attack.

"Don't scold him for what he does out of love." It was Ellysetta who spoke, surprising them all. Her eyes were closed, but her voice, though quiet, was lucid. "If it is my nature to ease his pain, it is his nature to protect me from it." Her lips curved in a wan smile. "He knows I am a coward at heart."

"That you are not," he denied. He drew her up into his arms and whispered his vulnerability for her ears alone. "My sun rises in your eyes, *shei'tani.* I cannot bear for you to be hurt."

Her eyes opened, and she lifted her hand to his face, stroking her fingers against his skin. "Then let me heal you."

Tears pricked his eyes. He kissed her once with great tenderness and released her. "Tend me if you must, Ellysetta, but do not try to take all the pain upon yourself."

Rain nodded his permission for the smith to continue. Ellysetta knelt at his side. She flinched when he did as the second wrist shackle fell free, and cried out with him when Lian pulled off the first of the manacles piercing his ankles. Despite his command, she absorbed the worst of his torments into herself and muted them. Her tears and fingers and soft lips brushed over the deep puncture wounds at his wrist and each ankle.

When the last despised manacle fell free, they were both exhausted and trembling. Rain gathered Ellysetta into his arms and simply held her, resting his head against hers, breathing when she breathed, clasping her hand and offering back what strength he had.

"It is true then," Farel murmured. "Rain Tairen Soul has found his truemate."

Rain looked at him. Farel and all of the other *dahl'reisen*, men who had long ago learned to bear suffering without emotion, stood there, their eyes reddened with the bottled tears *dahl'reisen* could not shed and their hands clenched tight. They stood witness to the love that would always be their deepest dream, and it still had the ability to touch them as nothing else could.

"It is true," Rain confirmed.

He saw the woman Sheyl meet Farel's gaze and saw the brief nod between them. *Gods, how could I be such a trusting fool?* He started to rise, reaching instinctively for his absent weapons' belts. The weave came crashing down upon him like a killing wave. Darkness descended with brutal abruptness.

CHAPTER TWELVE

The Fading Lands ~ Dharsa
7th day of Seledos

"Kieran!" Robed in green and white and shining like a star in Dharsa's fragrant night, Marissya v'En Solande raced down the steps of the gold-and-white palace of the Fey king. Her truemate, Dax, followed close on her heels. Together, they rushed across the courtyard and rounded the great, Fire-lit tairen fountain, to greet the approaching band of weary travelers.

"Mela." A smile broke across Kieran's face. He loped across the remaining distance and fell into his mother's outstretched arms, savoring her flurry of hugs and kisses, and submitting with good nature to the thorough maternal inspection that followed. "I am well and unharmed, *mela*," he assured her, lifting her hands to his mouth and kissing them before stepping into his father's fierce embrace. *"Gepa."*

"You worried your mother and me." Dax's eyes were suspiciously bright when they broke apart. He cleared his throat and gripped his son's forearms. "I wish I could ask you never to do so again."

Kieran ducked his head. His parents would never make such a request because he could never honor it. Worry was the burden of every Fey warrior's parent.

"Lillis, Lorelle. Master Baristani." Marissya stepped past Kieran to greet Ellysetta's family with calmer, but no less heartfelt, embraces. *"Meiveli ti'Dharsa.* Kiel." Her smile turned solemn. She hugged the blond warrior, kissed him on both cheeks, and held his hands tightly. *"Beylah vo, ajian.* Thank you for bringing Kieran home safely."

Marissya waved everyone towards the palace. "*Teska*, come inside. Master Baristani, I will show you and the girls to your rooms. I'm sure you must be weary."

They were, Kieran knew. The girls hadn't had the energy to do more than ooh and aah over the starlit beauty of Dharsa. Tomorrow, however, would be a different story. As soon as they were rested, they'd be bounding all over the city, getting into the Haven only knew what sorts of mischief. He grinned just thinking about it. Quiet, well-ordered Dharsa was about to get a much-overdue jolt of joyful chaos.

As his mother led the Baristanis into the palace, Kieran's brief humor turned solemn. He and Kiel followed Dax to one of the balconied terraces overlooking the city.

"We passed Eimar v'En Arran on our way here," Kieran said. After Tenn's latest refusal to support Rain, Eimar v'En Arran, Air master of the Massan, had gathered several thousand like-minded Fey and headed for the Garreval to join the war. Kieran watched his father closely. "Is there no hope Tenn will admit he was wrong and repair the breach between himself and Rain? Does he not understand the evil of the Eld?"

Dax sighed. "He understands, but he is convinced he's doing what's best for the Fading Lands."

"How? By tearing us apart? Dividing our people?"

"By keeping us safe. By holding to the Light and living with honor, in accordance with the Scroll of Law." Dax put his hands on the balustrade and leaned forward, watching the glowing lights of the fairy flies darting through the gardens and the Fire-lamps of the city flickering through the trees in the valley below and on the sides of the surrounding hills. "I've known Tenn a long time. I do not question his motives. I truly believe he's doing what he thinks is right."

"Do you think he's right, *Gepa*?"

"I think he is an honorable Fey." After a brief pause, Dax met his son's gaze, and added, "I also think there is a reason other than their link to the prides that our kings have always been Tairen Souls and not truemated Fey Lords."

Kieran nodded. Tairen Souls were born to defend the

Fading Lands. Every one of them expected to die in battle, and except for the occasional accident, every one of them did. A Tairen Soul also knew, before binding himself in *e'tanitsa*, that his duty to the Fading Lands came before his duty to his mate. But Tenn was a truemated Fey Lord, and his strongest instinct was to keep his mate safe.

"The girls are already asleep." Dax, Kieran, and Kiel turned as Marissya joined them on the terrace. "I never realized how dear they had become to me until we thought they were lost. It is good to have them back." Her expression turned somber. "They were asking for Ellysetta."

Kiel and Kieran shared an uncomfortable silence.

"We thought it best to not tell them that Rain and Ellysetta had been banished," Kiel admitted. "In fact, I think it's best if we tell them she and Rain are away fighting the war and will return when they can. It's true enough. If Rain and Ellysetta could return tomorrow, I'm sure they would."

"You haven't heard then?" Dax said.

"Heard what?" Kieran asked.

"Bel sent word on a private weave this morning. Rain and Ellysetta were shot down over Eld yesterday. No one's heard from them since."

Celieria ~ Dahl'reisen Village in the Verlaine Forest

The *dahl'reisen* carried the unconscious bodies of the Tairen Soul and his mate to a small cabin not far from the smithy. There, Sheyl scrubbed their wounds clean of *sel'dor* powder before slowly and painstakingly removing each ragged shred of the black Elden metal from their bodies.

She regretted the brutal but necessary weave that had robbed both Fey of their senses. She knew the Tairen Soul's hesitant trust in his *dahl'reisen* rescuers would be gone when he woke, but after witnessing how difficult it had been for him and his mate to suffer the removal of their manacles, she'd suspected the surgery to remove their *sel'dor* shrapnel would have been beyond their capacity to endure. The Mages had engineered *sel'dor* to block Fey magic, cause immense pain, and resist efforts to remove it. Not even powerful Fey healers could coax *sel'dor* out of flesh using magic, and there was no magic—regardless of how powerful—that could completely weave away the pain. Neither she nor Farel was willing to risk having their village destroyed by a Tairen Soul driven mad by his truemate's pain.

She worked on the Tairen Soul and his mate for bells, opening wounds with a razor-sharp black Fey'cha, digging about with long steel pincers to remove the *sel'dor* fragments, then probing with bare fingers to make certain she'd gotten it all before healing the damage both she and the Eld weapons had caused. Two other village women with healing talents assisted her.

By the time she was done, the small steel bowl beside the raised surgery cots was filled with bloody black metal ranging from small pea-size bits to long, dagger-length shards. Sheyl had seen more than her share of wounds filled with *sel'dor* shrapnel, and she was amazed that Rain Tairen Soul had even managed to survive, let alone retain his faculties, with that much of the poison metal in his body.

It was a testament to his strength and endurance—and to his mate's powerful magic. She'd probably been healing him from the moment he was first struck, though it was obvious neither of them was aware of it. Sheyl had seen it clearly the moment they rode into the village, the Light flowing from Ellysetta into her mate, the shadows of pain and death flowing out of him back into her. Without her, he would almost certainly have died.

Sheyl closed the last of the Tairen Soul's wounds and laid another weave upon the matepair to guarantee they would sleep the night. Ellysetta's Light was too dim for Sheyl's liking, and she needed uninterrupted rest to recuperate. Only then did Sheyl open the door and admit the other village women waiting outside.

The women bustled in and began the familiar task of making Sheyl's patients comfortable after their surgery.

They deftly stripped the remaining clothing from the unconscious Fey couple and washed them thoroughly with warm water and soap to cleanse away all traces of blood and grime.

"Sheyl." One of the women summoned her to Ellysetta's side. "Look."

The woman was standing over Ellysetta, holding a curling black spiral of Azrahn in her palm. On Ellysetta's left breast, just over her heart, four shadowy points lay like a ring of bruises against her pale, luminous flesh.

Sheyl recognized the Marks instantly. Memory—premonition—flashed. A cry of denial rose up in her heart, but her expression remained carefully blank.

"What are we going to do? Four Marks. Her presence puts us in terrible danger."

"Calm yourself. She's been unconscious almost the entire time. Even if the Mage was watching through her eyes, he couldn't have seen much."

"Farel will still want to know."

"And I will tell him," Sheyl assured her. "Now finish drying them, and have the men carry them to the top room. Tell Imrion and his brothers to spin a weave around the cabin to block what they can of the *dahl'reisen's* pain from the Feyreisa. Shutter the windows and post guards at the door. I will take their armor and leathers to be cleaned and mended." She gathered up the discarded pile of golden armor and studded red leather and let herself out of the cabin.

Farel was waiting for her across the yard. His face was as blank as hers. She wasn't ready to face him yet, so she turned away and carried the armor and leathers to a small cabin farther down the main village thoroughfare. She gave them to another of the village women and stayed to chat. He waited, patient as time itself, until she abandoned her attempt at procrastination and went to him.

When she reached his side, he held out his hand, uncurling his fingers to reveal a black Fey'cha.

"When we recovered the Tairen Soul's steel from the

Eld, Rythiel found this." In a swift, practiced motion, Farel flipped the blade to show her the Fey markings emblazoned in the pommel.

Sheyl recognized the name symbol instantly. "That's Gaelen's mark."

"I found it with several others, all bloodsworn. They are hers. The Tairen Soul allowed a *dahl'reisen*—and not just any *dahl'reisen* but Gaelen vel Serranis—to bloodswear to his truemate. How can that be, Sheyl?"

"Have you asked Gaelen?"

"He will not answer. I told him they were safe, that I had brought them here as he commanded. All he would say was that we must protect her from the Eld even if it costs the life of every man, woman, and child in this village."

Because of that, she almost didn't tell him about the Mage Marks on Ellysetta's chest. Though she had loved him all her life and told him more than she ever revealed to another living being, there were still many things she kept from him. Some things no person should have to know. But another woman had seen the Marks first, and Sheyl knew it would not remain secret for long.

"She bears Mage Marks."

Farel was rarely caught off guard, but this time his mouth almost fell open. "What?"

"Four of them."

His brows snapped together. "Then why would Gaelen command us to bring her here? Her mere presence endangers us all."

"I don't know."

Did the Tairen Soul know about his mate's Marks? Was that why he allowed a *dahl'reisen* to bloodswear himself to the Feyreisa? Did he perhaps think Gaelen, who was at least a fourth-level talent in Azrahn, could use his forbidden skills to help protect the Feyreisa from Eld Mages? Sheyl's mind whirled with questions and possibilities, but she cut them off quickly. If she allowed her mind to ask the questions, her second talent might provide the answer, and she could not do what she must in the coming days if the outcome would be in vain.

Her second talent was premonition. Unfortunately, she always saw true, and it was rarely something pleasant. The gods had not given her the vision of possibilities, only of unalterable destiny.

"At least she can't have seen much," Sheyl said to ease the guilt and recrimination she knew Farel was feeling for having brought such a danger into their village. "You told me she was unconscious most of the way."

"She was."

"Then I'm right. She can't have seen much—which means the Mages can't have either. I've put them in the top room, shuttered the windows, and posted guards. They will both sleep until dawn."

He began to pace, a sure sign of overwhelming agitation and distress. "They can't stay here."

"Nei," she agreed. "You must take them away tomorrow, at first light."

"We should kill them both now, while they sleep."

She shook her head. "Don't talk foolishness. Any *dahl'reisen* who killed her would become Mharog."

He whirled on her. A muscle ticked in his clenched jaw. "Then we get one of the mortals to do it—one of the old men—and we feed him to the *lyrant* when it's done so the Dark deed dies with him."

"Nei." Sheyl's voice was calm and even but as unyielding as stone. "You will not harm her. You will take her away in the morning. And you will grant her and the Tairen Soul safe passage out of the Verlaine."

"Sheyl—"

"Nei. Dahl'reisen you may be, but your soul remembers what it is to be Fey—even when it is inconvenient. She is a *shei'dalin,* and you are pledged to protect her from harm. And he is the last Tairen Soul. If you kill him, the Eld win, and you know it. Now, it is late, and I am tired. Come, take me to bed."

"Sheyl, every moment she spends in this village puts all our lives in danger. You think I can just forget that and go to bed?"

"Aiyah, you can. We are safe enough for now. They will leave tomorrow. You and the *dahl'reisen* will go with them. I want tonight." She took his hand and tugged him towards their cabin.

"The Tairen Soul is healed. He would never allow *dahl'reisen* to escort his *shei* —" He broke off, eyes narrowing slightly. "You've seen this? That they would leave, and I would accompany them?"

"Aiyah," she lied. He'd not been in her vision, and that meant there was a chance to save him. "Now come, Farel vel Torras. Your hearth witch needs your attention."

He allowed her to pull him towards their cabin. And when the doors closed behind them, her hands helped him to shed his weapons and leathers.

Eld ~ Boura Fell

Steel clattered outside the High Mage's library door, the sound reverberating in the stone chasm of his chambers. Vadim glanced up.

"Come in," he commanded. "And refrain from terrifying my soldiers."

Six tall, dark figures entered on booted feet that made no sound as they walked, and with them they brought an icy chill that prickled even the High Mage's flesh. Behind them, the Eld soldiers who had accompanied them were trembling so hard their armor rattled.

With a wave of his hand, Vadim dismissed the soldiers and turned his attention to the six creatures standing before him. They had been Fey once, then *dahl'reisen*. He had captured them centuries ago, and unlike so many of their brethren who had died in his untender care, they had crossed that final bridge, leaving the Shadowed Path and descending into total Darkness.

They were the Mharog, Fey who had given themselves utterly to evil. Immensely powerful. Utterly merciless. With skin as pale as snow and pure black eyes like bottomless chasms, they were frightening creatures, and even Vadim Maur, who owned their souls, harbored a carefully hidden terror of them.

"You summoned us to serve?" The tallest of the six asked the question. His voice was a whispered song of power, mesmerizing and deadly. Azurel he was called now, though once he'd claimed another name that had been celebrated in the Fading Lands.

"Your old friend Rain Tairen Soul has a truemate."

A dangerous light sparked in Azurel's black eyes. During the Mage Wars, he'd been sent by Rain Tairen Soul to fight in the desperate, bloody battle that had delivered him into Mage hands and ultimately drove him down the Dark Path. Over the centuries, Vadim had used that event to batter down the *dahl'reisen's* defenses and breed hatred in his heart for the Fey and for Rain Tairen Soul in particular.

"One of my Mages had captured them, but the *dahl'reisen* who've harried us for so many years along the borders rescued them. The *dahl'reisen* harbor them now." He'd never sent a force capable of defeating the *dahl'reisen* into Celieria before, afraid of tipping his hand, but the need for discretion was over. It was time to release the hunters and let them pursue their prey. "You will track them down, destroy the *dahl'reisen* village, and bring the girl and any survivors to me. The Tairen Soul is yours to kill."

He gestured to a shadowy corner of his office, where a hard-eyed Mage in rich blue robes stood in silence. A sash heavily laden with jewels of achievement circled his waist several times and hung down to the floor. "This is Primage Dur. He will accompany you, along with two hundred of my Mages and a garrison of my best men into Celieria."

"Your men will hinder us."

"Don't be a fool and don't take me for one," Vadim snapped. "Six Mharog, even ones as powerful as you, aren't strong enough to confront the Tairen Soul and hundreds of *dahl'reisen* on your own. Besides, the Feyreisen's mate is Fey born. Your touch would kill her. My men accompany you so that she will be returned to me alive. If she is not, rest assured you will continue your service to me in demon form."

Azurel hesitated long enough to make Vadim gather his power, then he gave a lingeringly insolent bow. "It will be as you command."

As silently as they had entered, the Mharog slipped away. Vadim sat as his desk for several long chimes, his fingers steepled.

Celieria ~ The Dahl'reisen Village
8ᵗʰ day of Seledos

Dawn broke over a beautiful land of lush forests. As the sun rose, pastel morning skies became vivid cerulean, bright and cloudless over a verdant countryside. Shining lakes and rivers teemed with fish. Flocks of birds soared above herds of pronghorns bounding through thick forests. Silver-horned Shadars thundered across open plains, while winged Aquilines danced over glassy mountain lakes, touching golden hooves and feathered wingtips lightly on the water's surface in a show of aerial mastery.

A familiar roar sounded, and Ellysetta turned to see a pride of tairen race across the sky, fur shining in the sunlight. Dozens of juveniles flew with the pride, some engaging in mock battles, while others tested their wings for the first time beneath the watchful eyes of their elders. Attentive adults flew below and behind the smallest of the kitlings, ready to break an infant's fall or snatch a weary kit from the sky.

The tairen flew north, towards the jagged volcanic peaks of the Feyls, where Ellysetta could see hundreds more tairen circling the updrafts around the smoking peaks and launch-

ing themselves into the sky from the labyrinth of caverns riddling the range.

She turned her eyes west, and there was Dharsa, a shining jewel of white stone and golden spires rising from the forested hills like a crown. Moored boats bobbed in the harbor, while others sailed up and down the River Faer. The city streets were busier than she'd ever seen them, thronged with thousands of Fey, Elves, and other races.

And there were children. Hundreds of children. Infants cradled in their mothers' arms. Toddlers playing in orchards and gardens overflowing with starry white Amarynth. Fey youths gathered in the Warrior's Academy and the walled courtyards of the Hall of Truth and Healing as robed elders instructed them in the ways of magic and Light.

The Feyreisen's palace rose from the city's central hill, and there in the courtyard outside the Hall of Tairen, stood Marissya and Dax and with them a tall warrior in black leathers who was idly scratching the ear of the brown tairen kitling at his side. Three other kitlings played in the Source-fed fountain while an adult tairen Ellysetta did not recognize perched on the golden roof overlooking the courtyard. As if sensing her presence, the young warrior looked up. Eyes like blue stars—whirling with the opalescent radiance of the tairen—met hers.

«Keralas,» she whispered, and the warrior—Marissya and Dax's as yet unborn Tairen Soul son—smiled.

The whirling radiance of his eyes flashed, a blue starburst that intensified to dazzling white light that blotted out her vision.

When she could see again, she was no longer in Dharsa. She was, instead, at Orest, and a Dark army stretched across the land like a blanket of death. Hundreds of thousands. Millions. Armed and armored, man and monster standing side by side, their eyes pitiless chasms of malice. At the head of the army stood the personal guard of the Dark Queen, thousands of once-Fey warriors, faces scarred, eyes *black and merciless, their once-shining skins now a lurid, corpse white, utterly devoid of the warm silvery Light that had once suffused them. They looked the perfect vision of the unspeakable evil they had become.*

The Dark Queen stood in the center of her guard, her scarlet hair piled high and threaded with ropes of black, selkahr jewels, her lips bloodred, her eyes death black, her skin white as milk. Her fell beauty dazzled the senses, an enthralling illusion that drew men to their deaths and masked the true horror of her Lightless soul. She was the Corrupter, the Light Eater, the Consumer of Souls, and in her wake red flowers bloomed like a trail of blood. Selgoroth, the flower of death, antithesis of the starry white Amarynth that bloomed in the steps of Fey women bearing young. Clusters of poison thorns hid amidst the Selgoroth's scarlet petals, and the flowers' black hearts exuded a noxious miasma of decay. Where Selgoroth bloomed, all other life withered and died.

Before the Dark Army, the last defenders of Light had assembled. Elves and Fey, shining silver and gold. With them stood the few mortals who still remained unenslaved—those who possessed enough immortal blood in their veins to resist the deadly pull of the Dark Queen's consuming power. The shimmering amber and green and silvery blue bodies of Danae forest and water sprites. Aquilines and Shadar. And the last pride of the tairen—Steli and Sybharukai, Corus, Fahreeta, and Torasul, even the kitlings, so young their pelts were still plump with the soft, fluffy down of their hatching-fur.

The Dark Queen raised her arms and shouted a command that boomed like thunder across the field. Her army gave an echoing cry, and the earth trembled as they began to march.

The Queen spread her arms wide and leapt into the sky, shifting into a cloud of boiling black mist from which emerged a nightmarish creature. A tairen, or rather what should have been a tairen—just as a darrokken should have been a wolf. Furless, scabrous skin the color of dried blood *stretched across the creature's massive form. Eyes of whirling flame glared over a snarling muzzle, and black acid dripped from its razor-sharp fangs.*

The monster screamed a challenge, and the tairen leapt into the sky to answer her.

«Elan, shei'tani. Ve leiliath.» Awaken, beloved. You are dreaming.

Ellysetta woke in a strange room, lying in a strange bed. The first gray light of dawn filtered in through a large skylight overhead. Linen sheets were draped over her bare skin, and a soft linen pillow stuffed with some fragrant herb cushioned her head.

Rain lay spooned against her back, one arm and one leg thrown possessively over her. His long, lean body radiated warmth, and one large hand cupped her breast. A broad, warm hand stroked down her side, smoothing over her arm, pulling her close. She turned her head to find Rain's eyes half-opened, the irises gleaming a soft lavender behind their thick veil of black lashes.

"Another nightmare?"

"Vision," she corrected. "I can't decide which is worse— seeing the terrible things I could become, or realizing the visions don't terrify me like they used to."

Magic hummed in his flesh, and as they lay there, skin to skin, body to body, she realized the faint vibration of her own magic had altered to match his, forming a subtle harmonic balance, a completeness she'd never noticed before. It was as if the energy of his magic flowed into hers, and hers flowed into his in a natural communion. Even their heartbeats and their breathing had settled into a synchronous rhythm.

As the haze of sleep faded, memories flooded in. The missiles that had shot Rain from the sky, their race for escape, the Mages with their *sel'dor,* death so near . . . She rolled over to face Rain and found him awake and watching her, no sign of injury on him.

"Rain, what happened to us? Your wounds . . ." She laid her palms on his chest, sending her senses inward, but if there was a single grain of *sel'dor* powder still left in his body, she could not find it.

His laid his hands over hers. "Gone, *shei'tani.* There is a hearth witch here with strong healing talents. She tended us both."

"Where is 'here'?"

"In the *dahl'reisen* village in the Verlaine. Do you not remember?"

"Vaguely." She recalled only snatches of last night, hazy images of scarred *dahl'reisen,* children, and a woman with white hair. "If we're in a *dahl'reisen* village, why don't I feel them?"

"There's a weave around this little house to shield you. A six-fold weave. They used Azrahn. They must have spun it when we were unconscious." That statement ended with a distinct rumble of unease.

"Are we prisoners?"

"I don't know. Their intentions are a mystery, but they claim Gaelen sent them to rescue us from the Eld."

"Have you tried to reach him to confirm that?"

"Of course, but the six-fold weave blocked me." He smoothed his hands over her hair. "Half of me wants to burn this village down about their ears. The other half wants to thank them. All the *sel'dor* is gone from both of us. Our steel is not here, but I could break through that six-fold weave without half trying. They have to know that. I don't think they mean us harm." He gave a short, humorless laugh. "And I can hardly believe I'm hearing myself say that. But why would they have rescued us from the Eld, removed the *sel'dor* in both of us, and healed us?"

"I don't know."

A knock sounded on the cabin door and Ellysetta barely had time to pull the linen sheet up around herself and Rain before the door opened to admit the white-haired woman Ellysetta remembered from last night.

She held Rain's armor and Ellysetta's leathers in her arms, and two other village women followed on her heels, carrying trays of food and drink. The women deposited the food on a table beside the door, sneaking furtive looks at Rain and Ellysetta before exiting the room and closing the door behind them.

The white-haired woman set the armor and leathers down. "My name is Sheyl. I am the healer who tended you last night." She inspected the two of them with a healer's critical eye. "You both appear recovered from your injuries. I hope you slept well." She looked at Ellysetta. "No remnant pain?"

Ellysetta shook her head. "None, thank you."

"Very good." Sheyl laced her fingers together and regarded them silently for a moment. She seemed to be fighting some silent debate within herself. After a moment, she drew a breath and forced a smile. "Your leathers and armor have been cleaned and mended. Your weapons will be returned to you when you leave the village. Farel is waiting for you now. I will give you time to eat and dress, then take you to him. "

She turned to leave, then stopped again with her hand on the door latch. "The *dahl'reisen* were once the Fading Lands' greatest warriors. Remember that." She lifted the latch and slipped out of the cabin.

"What was that about?" Ellysetta asked, frowning.

"I'm not certain, *shei'tani*." He rose from the bed and began to dress.

The Fading Lands ~ Dharsa

When the Massan entered the hall where they conducted their business, they found Kieran vel Solande waiting for them.

"Kieran," the Massan leader, Tenn v'En Eilan, greeted him as the *shei'dalin* and the other members of the Massan entered and took their seats. "Your mother told us you had emerged safely from your ordeal and were returning home.

We are glad to see you well. What can we do for you so early this morning?"

Kieran had been up half the night, using the new Warrior's Path his father had shown him so he could get news from Orest. The battle was going badly. As for Ellysetta and Rain, no one was certain as to their fates.

His hands clenched at his sides. He couldn't believe Tenn and the others were sitting around the table so calmly. "You can tell me what in the gods' names were you thinking when you banished the Feyreisen and delivered his truemate—a *shei'dalin* and a Tairen Soul—into the hands of the Eld?"

"Mind your tongue, young warrior," Tenn warned. "We did no such thing."

"Of course you did. What else did you think would happen when you declared her *dahl'reisen* and expelled her from the safety of the Fading Lands? You call yourselves warriors of honor?" He hawked and spat on the floor. "*That* for your honor."

"How dare you?" Venarra v'En Eilan, Tenn's *shei'tani*, who'd taken Marissya's place as the *Shei'dalin*, jumped to her feet. "How dare you insult the Massan in such a manner?"

"How dare you betray our king and put his mate at risk?" he shot back.

"*We* put *her* at risk?" Nurian v'En Soma, Spirit master of the Massan, gave a short laugh. "Fey, you don't know what you're talking about. It was *she* who put *us* at risk. Shei'Kess showed us the evil she would bring. Death, war, destruction, the Fading Lands overrun by Dark ones, *her* sitting on the ruins of the Tairen Throne."

"Venarra, Nurian, please." Tenn held up a hand. "Kieran is young and passionate, and he shares a bond of friendship with Rain vel'En Daris because of the years they spent together at the Academy. He doesn't understand what it takes to lead a country, the hard decisions we must make, all the consequences we must weigh when making those decisions."

"Hard decisions?" Kieran laughed.

"Yes, hard decisions," Tenn reiterated. "Contrary to whatever your parents or your friends may have led you to believe, we banished Rain and Ellysetta for one reason only: because they both willingly and deliberately wove the forbidden magic."

"Aiyah, my mother told me," Kieran said, unimpressed by the revelation.

"Look at him," Yulan, the Earth master of the Massan, said in tones of disbelief. "He knows what they did, and he doesn't care."

"I know they spun Azrahn to save the tairen."

"And you think that makes it all right." Tenn shook his head. "Show me, young Kieran, the passage in the Scroll of Law where it says spinning the forbidden magic is not forbidden so long as you do it to save the tairen." He waited a moment. "*Nei*, you can't, because no such passage exists. The law is clear. The punishment for weaving Azrahn is banishment—no matter the reason for the weave. We acted, because we had to act. We had no choice."

"Of course you had a choice. You could have done what was right!"

"We *did* do what was right."

"Nei," Kieran spat. "You did what you thought was safe. The vision in Shei'Kess frightened you, so you betrayed our king and his mate and forsook your oath to protect our women from harm. I was at Teleon. I saw the Eld murdering my friends. They weren't there to defend themselves against Fey aggression or whatever ridiculous notion you've invented to justify your treachery. The Eld were there to kill Fey, slaughter Celierians, and capture the Garreval. You've lost sight of who the true enemy is, Tenn."

"Oh, have I?" Tenn challenged. "The Eld left us in peace for a thousand years until Rain vel'En Daris went to Celieria and began stirring up ancient grievances and beating the drums of war."

"Did someone strike you a sharp blow to the head while I was gone?" Kieran exclaimed. "Of course the Eld left us in peace for the last thousand years! Rain scorched them off the face of Eloran! It takes time to recover from a blow like that."

Kieran thrust his hands through his hair and turned in an agitated circle. "I can't believe you can sit there with a straight face and try to portray the Eld as peace-loving innocents who just want to get along. The Eld hate us. They always have hated us. They want to conquer the world in the name of Seledorn and they know we're the only ones with the power and the will to stop them! Or, at least, we used to be!"

"Enough!" Tenn rose and held up a silencing hand. "It's clear you have strong feelings on the matter, young vel Solande, but the decision has been made. The Massan will not commit more precious Fey lives to Rain Tairen Soul's senseless war of aggression against the Eld."

Kieran stifled a scream of frustration. Tenn was as stubborn as an Earth master. He'd made his decision, dug in his heels, and the gods could lay waste everything around him before he'd change his position or admit he was wrong.

So be it. But Kieran had no intention of blindly following a council who refused to acknowledge obvious truths.

He turned to the Water master of the Massan, who had always been a level-headed Fey and a warrior his parents had long called friend. "Loris . . . I know you don't agree with this any more than Eimar did. The Eld attacked *us*. They're the ones who started this war, not Rain. You know Rain is right to confront them. You know the Fey were born to fight the Dark, not hide and hope it will go away. Honorable Fey don't abandon our friends when they need us most."

"I said enough," Tenn growled. The room grew warmer as the Fire master's temper flared. "Out of deference to your mother, we let you speak. And out of deference to her, I will not punish your youthful intemperance or demand restitution for the insults you have flung in our faces. But this council has work to do, and you have outstayed your welcome here. You will leave now and put a leash on that tongue of yours, or you will spend the next month in bound labor."

Kieran gave a bitter laugh. "You talk about considering

the consequences of your actions. But did it never occur to any of you, that by banishing a Mage-Marked Tairen Soul from the safety of the Fading Lands, you might actually be instrumental in ushering in the very doom you're so afraid of? *Nei?* Well, consider this. Rain and Ellysetta were shot down over Eld. They haven't been heard from since."

For the first time, he saw the Massan's rock-headed certainty waver. The first glimmer of genuine doubt—and fear—entered their eyes. *Nei,* they'd never thought beyond their own shortsighted desire for safety.

"You'd better pray the Eld don't capture Ellysetta and finish what they started," Kieran said. "Because if they do, and the Mages gain a Tairen Soul's power, not even the Mists will save you."

Celieria ~ Dahl'reisen Village

When Sheyl returned, she carried a blindfold in her hands. "I'm sorry, but I must ask you to put this on," she told Ellysetta. "We know of your mate's Marks," she said to forestall Rain's objections. "We check everyone who enters this village. The blindfold is a precaution to safeguard the location of our village. With our shields, even four Marks should not be enough for the Mage to use her eyes and ears, but we cannot take the risk."

"Of course," Ellysetta said, reaching for the strip of cloth. "*Nei,* Rain, it's all right." She laid a soothing hand on his wrist to calm his rising tension. He did not like the implication that Ellysetta's mere presence was a threat. "They are right to protect themselves. For all we know, it was my eyes that told the Mages where to open their portals yesterday."

"It was not."

"We don't know that for sure. For the villagers' sake, I will gladly cover my eyes. Here. Help me put this on." She lifted the folded cloth over her eyes and turned for Rain to tie the ends together at the back of her head.

"You will want to spin a weave around your mate, Tairen

Soul," Sheyl said when Ellysetta's blindfold was secure. "The cabin's weave is shielding her now, but she will lose that protection when she crosses the threshold. Most of the warriors have gone to a different part of the village to spare your mate what pain they can," Sheyl informed him, "but a goodly number remain. They do not trust you any more than you trust them."

I am wrong to allow this. Dahl'reisen should not stand within a mile of my shei'tani.

Ellysetta put out a searching hand and felt her way down Rain's arm to his wrist. He had not sent that thought in Spirit. It had escaped his mind of its own volition. *«Las, shei'tan. We owe them our lives—and this is their home. They have far more right to be here than we.»* She wove calm and peace upon him to accompany her words. *«Weave the shield, and let's go. Our friends in Orest need us.»*

Shamed by his lapse, Rain reinforced the barriers in his mind, then snapped the shield weave around Ellysetta with a burst of magic.

When they stepped across the cabin threshold, the *dahl'reisen's* presence struck Ellysetta, piercing through the powerful weave Rain had placed around her. Without the Azrahn, his shield was not half so effective as the *dahl'reisen* weave around the cabin had been, and he felt the pain hit her like a blow. He gathered her close and grasped her hand, feeding her his strength until she drew a deep breath and nodded.

Sheyl approached, her silvery eyes intent. "There are a few sensitives among us. Mostly they live outside the village, where they cannot feel the *dahl'reisen* so strongly. If you will permit me, I can summon a villager to add Azrahn to your weave, Feyreisen. It will help her block the pain."

"*Nei.*" Rain refused before Ellysetta could speak. Gaelen he trusted to weave Azrahn in Ellysetta's presence, but Gaelen was *dahl'reisen* no more. Then Rain glanced at her pale and trembling form, and shame filled him. "*Sieks'ta, shei'tani*. I should not refuse so hastily. Sheyl is right. You are in pain."

She gave a wan smile. "So long as you hold my hand, it is manageable."

"Tell me if it gets worse," Sheyl instructed. "If you will both follow me. Farel grows impatient when he's kept waiting."

Rain held Ellysetta's hand and guided her after the healer. He wished she was not blindfolded. The sight of this *dahl'reisen* village in the early-morning light would have filled her with delight. The cabins nestled high in the trees, vine bridges connecting one tree to another. It reminded him of Navahele. Everywhere were signs of not just functionality but artistic beauty. From the intricate, decorative curling of the vines on every bridge and stair to the graceful lines of the buildings, with their exquisitely carved doors and shutters and leaf-covered roofs.

The village seemed at most a part of the forest itself.

"Did the *dahl'reisen* build all this themselves?" he asked.

Sheyl nodded. "Many of them turn to gentler things to keep the darkness at bay. Some, like the *dahl'reisen* who fashioned these cabins, find peace working with Earth. Others prefer creating things without any magic at all."

A woven vine bridge linked the cabin to another larger cabin nestled in a nearby tree. Sheyl led the way across the gently swaying bridge, and Rain guided Ellysetta after her, sending commands in Spirit to guide her feet.

"We are a village of outcasts," Sheyl continued. "The mortals among us were either winded as children by the villages where we were born—or we are descendants of those who were."

"Winded?" Rain repeated. "That's a term I'm not familiar with."

Ellysetta answered. "It's a custom in many of the northern villages. When babies are born with deformities or dangerous magic, the villagers take them out to the woods and leave them for the winds to spirit away—which is just a pretty way of saying they abandon them to starve or be eaten by predators. Which is what Mama and Papa thought had happened to me when they found me abandoned in Greatwood as a child."

"Your mother was so afraid of magic. I'm surprised she would adopt a child she already suspected must have dangerous powers."

"Papa told me that when Mama was a little girl living in Dolan, her baby sister Bessinita was winded for having Fire magic. Bessie was only two when she was taken off to die. Papa said that was what made Mama take me in. When she looked at me, she saw her baby sister, and she couldn't leave me to die."

Rain noticed Sheyl frowning at Ellysetta. "Something is wrong?"

Sheyl's frown cleared and became a sheepish smile. "I'm sorry. I was just thinking of all the poor children lost to such an evil custom." She bent her head and continued walking at a brisker pace. "Your mate's explanation of winding is correct. The Mage Wars left many scars here in the north. The remnant magic still lives in the ground, seeps into our water, our food, our bodies. Most of us born in the north possess some sort of talent, but usually it's something small and unnoticeable—sensitivity to the emotions of others, a gift for growing things. In some of us, the magic is stronger, more pronounced. Or, the gift is something fearful. My mother had a vision in which she saw the death of a neighbor. She made the mistake of telling someone. When the neighbor died, my mother was blamed. She was seven months pregnant, but the villagers bound her arms and legs and left her in the forest to die. She was half-dead when Farel rescued her. She died in childbirth that same day."

Ellysetta stopped walking. "You remember her death. You weren't even born, but you remember it."

The color left Sheyl's cheeks. "Your gift is strong, Feyreisa. I'm usually much better at shielding my thoughts.

Yes, I remember. And I remember that the vision for which my mother was killed was mine. She saw it because I lived in her belly."

"Oh, Sheyl." Ellysetta reached out blindly to clasp the other woman's hands. "You believe you caused her death. How can you, a healer, still believe that? You were a baby, an innocent life."

Tears filled Sheyl's eyes and spilled over. She smiled and tried to pull her hands away. "I was right. Your gift is strong, but as I said, you should conserve your strength."

"She does not realize she's doing it," Rain said quietly. "To her, she is merely sharing the love in her heart, as she has all her life."

"Doing what?" Ellysetta asked. "What am I doing?"

"Healing, *shei'tani*. You are healing her. As instinctively as you read her thoughts a moment ago."

Ellysetta released the other woman. "I'm sorry. Again."

"I am not offended," Sheyl answered. "You should not apologize for being what you are. Which is quite remarkable, you know. I've never met such a strongly gifted sensitive who could bear to walk within half a mile of this village, even with our shields."

"Is that so surprising? You don't seem to have any trouble living here among the *dahl'reisen*, and you have strong magical talents."

"I'm not empathic. I sense disease and I see the flows of magic, but I cannot sense thoughts and emotions." They had reached a hanging stair that led down towards the forest floor below. Sheyl paused. "Before we go down to Farel, there is someone I would like you both to meet."

Moving past the stair, she led them through the trees and across two more vine bridges to a larger building circling the broad trunk of a massive oak. Entering a small, wedge-shaped room on the south side of the building, Sheyl indicated a set of empty rocking chairs in a cozy sitting area. "Please, have a seat." She went to the windows and pulled the curtains closed before walking to a small connecting door on the eastern wall. "Wait here. I'll only be a moment. The Feyreisa may remove her blindfold."

Sheyl slipped through the door and returned a few chimes later with another woman clad in a serviceable green woolen dress with a tan apron tied around her waist. The other woman was older, clearly mortal. Her curling brown hair was streaked with silver and tied back in an untidy bun, and her bright, inquisitive brown eyes were crinkled at the corners with deep laugh lines.

"Ellysetta Feyreisa . . . Rainier Feyreisen . . . this is the woman I wanted you to meet. She came to us forty years ago as a small child . . . winded near the village of Dolan for possessing the gift of Fire. We call her Bess . . . but the name her parents gave her was Bessinita."

CHAPTER THIRTEEN

Shadowed Path, soothing path,
Choice from pain and sadness.
Aching path, desperate path,
Escape from lonely madness.
Darkened path, forsaken path,
Hide from fear and sorrow.
Lonely path, empty path,
Save me from the 'morrow.

Dahl'reisen's Plea,
a song of prayer, by Varian vel Chera

Celieria ~ Dahl'reisen Village

Ellysetta stared with burning eyes at the sister Mama had loved and believed long dead. "I . . . I don't know what to say."

The woman named Bess clasped her hands before her waist. "Sheyl explained to me about your mother. Clearly, I must be that Bess your mother loved, but I don't remember anything from that life before."

"Of course, you don't. You were a baby . . . a precious baby who should never have been thrown away because of your gift." She remembered the sadness in Papa's eyes when he'd told her the story and told her how that one moment, that one loss, had changed Mama's life forever.

She gulped past the growing knot in her throat. "You should know that my mother found me in the forest of Great-wood," she told Bess. "My birth parents had put a glamour on me to make me look mortal. So when she found me, she assumed I'd been winded like you, for some dreadful, dangerous magic. She knew I was magic—she feared it more than she feared anything else in the world—but she took me in anyway and loved me in spite of her fear. She did that because of you . . . because she couldn't bear the thought of what had happened to you happening to another child." Ellysetta blinked back tears. "You don't remember her, but she never forgot you. She would want you to know that. She would want you to know she loved you very much."

"She must have been a very special woman," Bess said

"She was." Tears welled in her eyes as the memory of her mother's death and the horrible ache of her loss punched deep. The grief was still too fresh—never more than a memory away. "I loved her very much, and I miss her every day."

Bess's eyes softened with compassion. "I'm sorry for your loss. All of us here in the village know what it's like to lose someone you love."

"Thank you." Ellysetta wiped away her tears, but more just took their place. "I know she's just a stranger to you, but may I—may I . . . share her with you?" She held out her hands, palms up.

Bessinita hesitated, then placed her hands in Ellysetta's.

Ellysetta's mouth curved in a trembling smile. "Her name was Lauriana. She married a man named Sol Baristani—my papa—a woodcarver and a wonderful man whom she loved very much. They have two other daughters. Twins named Lillis and Lorelle . . ."

Through the touch of their joined hands, she gave Bess the memories of her mother and their family and the deep love they had shared. Little scenes of their life that Ellysetta treasured. Mama laughing over some silly joke. Mama holding Ellie close . . . kneeling beside her bed to say evening devotions. Mama delivering a stern lecture when the twins got into some sort of mischief, and Papa teasing her out of a mood with kisses and a pot of tea by the fire. Mama could be stern and fierce, but, like the tairen defending her kits, that fierceness was her way of protecting her young—of protecting Ellie and the twins the way she hadn't been able to protect her sister Bess.

When she was done, Bess had tears in her eyes as well, and a melancholy smile on her face. "*Beylah vo.* Thank you for giving me this gift."

"*Nei,* it's you who've given me the gift. Sometimes it's hard to remember all the good in the world in the face of so much bad." Ellysetta stepped back and reached for Rain's hand, squeezing tight and letting the vast comfort of his love wash away her remnant sorrow. All this time, Mama's sister had been alive . . . saved by the *dahl'reisen* . . . raised by them . . . *loved* by them. How could *dahl'reisen* walk the Shadowed Path yet still have wrought such obvious good?

The white-haired hearth witch cleared her throat. "There's something else I have to show you and a favor I must ask of you, before I take you to Farel. Would you both, please, come this way?" Sheyl walked to the door Bess had come through. "We are a private people. Our survival has depended on our discretion and our ability to keep our existence a secret, but the time for that has passed." Sheyl lifted the latch and pulled open the door to reveal a long, curving room that wound around the giant tree trunk.

The room was filled with children, at least sixty of them, ranging in age from tiny infants to five-year-olds. A dozen village women tended the tiniest of their charges, while the older children gathered in groups supervised by one or two adults. Noisy, childish chatter and the tiny cries of babies demanding maternal attention filled the air, muted from the outside world by a privacy weave tied to the room's floor, ceiling, and walls.

"These are our children. And this is our greatest secret."

"Oh, Rain . . ." Ellysetta reached for Rain's hand. *«So many children, shei'tan.»*

Rain stood frozen in the doorway and let the noise wash over him. He'd known there were children. He'd seen a number of them yesterday when he'd entered the village. But he hadn't realized the true enormity of what he'd seen. He forced himself to breathe as he scanned the room, seeing the bright glow of Fey magic shining from child after child. More than half of the children were Fey. Even before the Mage Wars had left the women of the Fading Lands barren, it was rare for thirty children to be born in a village this size in twenty years, let alone four or five.

A chill, too-sweet odor made his hands reach instinctively for his missing blades and he spun in the half crouch of a warrior, his eyes scanning the room for the person spinning the forbidden magic. A woman at the far end of the room held a spiral of Azrahn in her palm. At her feet, a semi-circle of children held their own, less organized spirals of the black magic.

Horror sapped all moisture from his mouth. "You teach them to weave the forbidden magic?"

Sheyl glanced back at the children in question, then returned her wary gaze to him. "Azrahn is not forbidden here. I know the Fey believe otherwise. You banish your strongest warriors if they dare to weave it." The corner of her mouth curled up. "Your customs aren't so different from the villagers who cast out their children and abandon them to die. You just wind your children at an older age."

Rain's head snapped back as if she'd slapped him. "The customs are nothing alike. Azrahn is the evil tool of the Mages." But even as said it, he remembered Ellysetta saving the tairen with Azrahn, himself saving her, the warriors and civilians who would have died without Gaelen's weaving Azrahn so Ellysetta could hold dying souls to life, the countless lives Gaelen had saved by detecting the Mage claimed hiding among the allies.

"Azrahn is just magic, a mystic like Spirit. Is Fire or Spirit evil? *Nei,* though, the manner of their use can be. It is no different with Azrahn. Which is why we teach our children from a very early age how to weave their magic—more importantly, how to control it. The ones with Mage Marks do not spin it, of course, but the rest of us do."

"Some of these children are Mage-claimed?" Rain asked

"Marked, not claimed. And, yes, some are. The *dahl'reisen* save the ones they can and bring them here, where we can protect them and give them some semblance of a free life, safe from the Eld.

"It is Azrahn that lets us offer them that haven," she added. "We spin it in our shield weaves to hide our presence from the Mages. We use it to detect Mage Marks and know who is a real danger to us, and who is not. Most of us here in the village possess at least some ability to spin the soul magic, and we are not evil." She gestured to the room at large. "These children are not evil."

"Why would Gaelen not tell us about you?" Ellysetta asked, her stunned gaze roving over all the little faces.

"All of us have sworn a blood-oath never to reveal information about our village and our children. The Eld would slaughter us. The Celierians would burn us out. The Fey would never accept *dahl'reisen* back within their borders, and none who live in this village would ever settle in a place where our men are not welcome. We are outcast, and keeping our secrets ensures our safety."

"Then why show us now?" Ellysetta asked.

Before Sheyl could answer, a childish laugh rang out, and a tiny voice cried, "Again! Again!" Ellysetta gasped and clutched Rain's hand in a tight grip. She stared in disbelief at the face of a child she'd loved dearly and never thought to see again. "Rain, that's Bannon!"

The son of her best friend, Selianne Pyerson, was dressed like a village child and playing with the other toddlers. She sent a frantic gaze towards the other end of the room, where the infants were, searching for another sweet face dominated by the big blue eyes so like Selianne's. "And Cerlissa!" Cerlissa, Selianne's baby, had grown so much in the last four months, but the chubby-cheeked infant, sitting on a rug, playing with blocks, was most definitely Selianne's daughter.

"You know Bannon and Cerlissa?" Sheyl asked.

"Their mother was my best friend. She died trying to protect me from the Mages." After Selianne's death, when the Fey found her husband murdered and her Elden mother hanging from a knotted cord, Gaelen had promised he would take Selianne's children to a safe place where they would be welcomed despite the Mage Mark set upon them by the Mages who'd killed their mother. "Gaelen said he would take them to a safe place, but he wouldn't tell us where."

"They were taken in by a couple who lost their own child to a *lyrant* last year."

Ellysetta bit her lip. The children were obviously happy and well tended, but— "Please, may I see them?"

"Of course." Sheyl signaled, and two of the village women collected the children and carried them across the room to Ellysetta.

"Bannon! Cerlissa! Oh, I'm so happy to see you both!" The baby Cerlissa chewed her fingers and laughed in delight. Bannon, however, regarded Ellysetta with no hint of recognition in his solemn blue eyes. But of course, she looked like a stranger to him. He'd only known Ellie, the woodcarver's daughter, never Ellysetta, the Fey *shei'dalin*.

She spun a quick Spirit weave, transforming in an instant to the plain mortal Ellie Baristani she'd been when they'd known her. "It's me, dearling," she told him. "It's Auntie Ellie." She knelt before him and held out her arms. "Auntie Ellie, Bannon. Don't you remember?"

When he still looked confused, she reached into the pocket of her apron where she'd always kept a little treat for him when she went to see Selianne. She pretended to gasp in surprise, "Oh! What do I have here in my pocket?" Another quick weave spun from her fingertips, and she pulled her hand out to brandish a tiny, painted wooden horse just like the ones she used to coax her father into carving for Bannon.

The little horse and the once-familiar custom of Auntie Ellie's magical pocket of treasures sparked a memory. A tiny smile curved the boy's lips, revealing a mouthful of pearly baby teeth. He reached for the horse and fell into her arms to give her a kiss, and say, "Thank you, Auntie Ellie," as he had so many times before.

Her arms closed around him, holding him tight, and she squeezed her eyes shut against the tears that welled up at the sound of his sweet voice. "Oh, Bannon." She cupped the back of his head in one palm and stroked her fingers through his baby-fine hair. Holding him again was almost like having Selianne back. She didn't want to let him go, and even when she set him down so she could take Cerlissa in her arms, she kept stroking Bannon's back and hair.

She wanted to keep them with her. She wanted to take them with her now. But they'd been taken in by a couple who'd lost their own child . . . and she and Rain were headed back to war—with no guarantee that either of them would survive it.

No matter how much she ached to keep Selianne's children with her forever, this was where they belonged. So she held them and smiled her brightest, despite the threat of burning tears, trying to squeeze months of love into a handful of chimes.

Watching her, Rain's heart swelled with a mix of love and sorrow. She would be an exceptional mother. Even in the guise of her mortal self, the joyous warmth of his *shei'tani's* deep capacity for love shone bright as a star. She deserved children—far more of them than even *shei'tanitsa* matepairs ever had. And once she forged the last thread of their bond to complete their *shei'tanitsa* union, he would do everything in his power to see that Amarynth bloomed eternally in her footsteps.

"Sheyl," he murmured, as his *shei'tani* cuddled her friend's children. "You said you had a favor to ask of us."

"I'm sure you've already guessed, Tairen Soul." Sheyl clasped her hand at her waist. "The world grows more dangerous every day. War has begun, and it will only get worse. The *dahl'reisen* will fight to defend the Fading Lands as they have these many past centuries, and our village will be left vulnerable. Will you grant safe harbor to our women and children while our men fight the Eld?"

"Aiyah." There was no hesitation, no other possible response. "You cannot weave Azrahn within our borders, of course. And the Mists will not permit the *dahl'reisen* to enter, but your women and children—even your men who are not *dahl'reisen*—will be welcomed with joy."

"And will you give me your Fey oath on that—and vow that we will all be free to leave again—even the children?"

"Of course."

"Then I have one last secret to show you."

Sheyl led the way to the back of the nursery and opened a door to a smaller adjoining room. Several young children were gathered round a short table, squishing lumps of clay into shapes with their small fingers.

"Muri," Sheyl called. "Come here, kitling. There are some people I want you to meet."

"Sheyl! Sheyl!" One of the children, a chubby toddler with bright blue eyes and masses of dark ringlets ran forward, her little arms extended.

A smile softened Sheyl's face, and she knelt to scoop up the child. "Hello, dearling."

"Look what Muri made." The girl held up a piece of dough shaped in a lumpy, four-legged mass. "Horsie!"

"That's lovely, kitling. Your mother will be so proud of you." Still holding the child, Sheyl turned to Ellysetta and Rain. "This is Murialisa."

"Oooh." The child stared at Ellysetta. "Bright, pretty lady."

"Yes, she is very bright, isn't she, kitling."

Rain stared at the little girl in shock. There was no mistaking the Fey glow in the child's eyes and the slender Fey delicacy just revealing itself in her childish features. "The father . . . cannot be *dahl'reisen*?" Girl children were not born outside the bonds of *shei'tanitsa*. And yet he was staring at a child, a girl, in whose veins ran not some mild form of magic but the shining light of strong Fey blood.

"No," Sheyl confirmed. "Muri's father was born in this village, but his father before him was *dahl'reisen*." She kissed Murialisa's round cheek and set her down. "Go back to your play, kitling." When the child was once again industriously molding clay dough into animal shapes, Sheyl murmured quietly, "Murialisa's grandfather was killed by the Mages seventy years ago. Her father truemated eight years ago with a village woman from the borders of Lord Barrial's lands."

Rain grasped Ellysetta's hand. "Truemated? The son of a *dahl'reisen* truemated with a Celierian?"

"She is not Celierian. Or rather, not as you mean it. She is not simply a hearth witch, infected by the magic of these lands. Powerful immortal blood runs in her veins. Fey, definitely, probably Elvish as well. She is very gifted, just like her *shei'tan*. Murialisa is their second child. They also have a seven-year-old son."

"A truemate lives in this village? Amongst the *dahl'reisen*?"

"She is a strong empath, but she has a natural ability to shield herself, just as the Feyreisa seems to have. She and her mate live at the edge of the village, where she feels the pain of the *dahl'reisen* the least. Murialisa has an even stronger shielding ability. The *dahl'reisen* are careful never to touch her, but she can be around them without any apparent difficulty."

"No wonder you protect your secret so vigilantly," Rain murmured, unable to tear his eyes from the small, luminescent girl who had returned to her play. "This child is a gift beyond price." He swallowed thickly and met Sheyl's eyes. "I will tell the warriors at the Garreval to expect you."

Celieria ~ Dahl'reisen Village

Mortals, half-bloods, and *dahl'reisen* stood silent as Sheyl guided Rain Tairen Soul and his blindfolded mate down the last of the hanging steps to the tended walkways and gardens on the forest floor. Farel and a small army of *dahl'reisen* clad in full war steel had gathered beneath the trees.

As Rain looked around the village in the soft gleam of morning's light, he saw what he'd been too weary and dazed by pain to notice last night—Amarynth, blooming in profusion along the walkways of the *dahl'reisen* village. Even knowing about the little Fey girl Murialisa born to true-mated parents, the sight of the undying flower still struck a deep and profound chord in his soul.

Life bloomed with defiant joy here in the shadow of lost souls.

Farel broke away from his companions to approach the Fey, halting half a tairen length from Ellysetta. A visible glow of Spirit and Azrahn surrounded him and the other *dahl'reisen*.

"We have shielded ourselves to protect the Feyreisa from our pain," he told Rain. "I apologize that we cannot make the shields stronger, but too much Azrahn will reveal our location to the Eld."

"I'm fine, thank you," Ellysetta said. *«Oh, Rain, they've shielded themselves and still there is so much pain. How can they bear it without going mad?»*

«Most do not, shei'tani. It is one of the reasons they must be banished from the Fading Lands. No matter what we've seen here today, do not think these men are like the rasa. They walk the Shadowed Path, and there is very little that keeps them from plunging into the abyss. As your mate, I should have sworn honor vengeance against them just for standing in your presence, but I accepted their help instead.

If I were not already cast out, the Massan would be within their rights to banish me just for that.»

«But they aren't evil yet,» Ellysetta protested. *«You know they aren't. And we owe them our lives.»*

«I know.» His gaze strayed again to the starry white blooms. Nothing about these *dahl'reisen* fit what he'd been raised to believe about them. And nothing made sense.

The warriors of the Fading Lands had clung to their honor with fierce devotion, yet their bonded mates were barren. These *dahl'reisen* wore the marks of their dishonor on their faces and spun the forbidden magic without apology . . . yet their unbonded mates bore Fey children capable of truemating, and Amarynth bloomed in their village in abundance.

Everything about this village defied the most ancient and deeply held Fey beliefs and turned the most unshakable pillars of their civilization completely on their heads. He didn't know what to think. It was as if the whole Fey world was going just as mad as he was.

"Sheyl assures me you and your mate are healed and rested well enough to travel. My men and I will escort you out of the forest."

The sound of Farel's voice snapped Rain back to attention. "I appreciate your offer," he answered, "but I am healed enough to Change."

"That would not be wise. Nothing flies over the Verlaine. The top of every tree is set with poison darts and a motion-sensing spell that targets anything above it. The allies set up the defense during the Wars to keep the Eld from spying, and we improved upon it. You wouldn't get a half man length above the canopy before you'd be filled with enough *lyrant* venom to bring down the entire Fey'Bahren pride." Farel's stony expression softened just slightly. "You were headed for Orest. Gaelen told me to bring you to him at the northwest corner of the Verlaine, and so I shall."

Rain glanced back at Ellysetta. *«It shames me to ask it of you, shei'tani, but can you bear their presence for another day?»*

She didn't hesitate. *«Of course.»*

«I'm not sure how well they can hold their shields all that time,» he warned.

She lifted her chin. *«I'll survive whatever I must.»*

He turned back to Farel. "Agreed. But your men must keep their distance. I mean no insult, but I don't want them within two tairen lengths of the Feyreisa."

Farel nodded. "*Kabei.* Sheyl will bring your steel." He started to turn away, then stopped to add in a low voice, "And thank you, Rainier vel'En Daris, for allowing us to serve the Fading Lands with honor once again." He held Rain's gaze steadily. "I know accepting our aid goes against everything you were ever taught. Truthfully, were I you, I'm not sure I could have done it. But I give you my oath, sworn on the soul of the mother I loved, that we will see you and your mate safely out of the Verlaine and that we will do you no harm." He did not wait for acknowledgment, but pivoted on his heel and strode away, straight and proud as any Fey.

Rain thought of Gaelen, who had come to Celieria fully expecting to be slain for approaching his sister but nonetheless determined to warn the Fey of the Eld army massing near the Fading Lands and protect his sister from the growing threat of Eld. *Dahl'reisen,* the soul lost, were supposed to be beyond Fey honor, men well on the path to evil, but he was having trouble reconciling that image with what he had seen of these *dahl'reisen* who called themselves the Brotherhood of Shadows.

Sheyl and another woman brought Rain's and Ellysetta's weapons, and as Rain donned his steel, the women helped Ellysetta into hers.

Still blindfolded, Ellysetta put a hand over one of the Tairen's Eye crystals set in her hip belt and summoned a weave of Earth to detach the crystal and reset it in a pendant hanging from a gold chain. "It is an ancient custom of the Fey to leave behind a gift in thanks for kindness rendered. I would like you to have this, Sheyl, as a token of my thanks."

"Nei," Sheyl demurred. "I know a Soul Quest crystal when I see one, and I know how precious they are. I cannot accept such a gift. It is too much."

"I want you to have it. The crystal belonged to a warrior named Dajan vel Rhiadi, who sacrificed his life trying to save me from a demon sent by the Eld. Please, take it. May Dajan's *sorreisu'kiyr* offer you the same protection its owner once offered me."

Sheyl looked to Rain for help. "I am the unbonded mate of a *dahl'reisen*. Such a gift is not proper."

"You are the woman who healed us after your mate saved our lives," Rain corrected. "Dajan died in Ellysetta's service. His *sorreisu'kiyr* is hers to bestow. It is a fitting gift for the service you and the Brotherhood of Shadows have done us."

Sheyl glanced uncertainly at Farel, who looked equally as perplexed. Finally, she took the pendant from Ellysetta's outstretched hands and placed it around her neck. The crystal settled between her breasts, close to her heart. "Thank you. You do me a great honor."

Ellysetta held out her hands to embrace the other woman. "Blessings and peace upon you, Sheyl. May the Light always shine upon your path and keep you from harm. Tell Bess I look forward to seeing her again soon, and would you please give this to Bannon and Cerlissa's adoptive parents for me?" She spun Earth to form a small glass globe into which she wove her fondest memories of Selianne. "When they feel the time is right, I'd like Bannon and Cerlissa to have this . . . so they won't forget their mother or how much she loved them."

"Of course." Sheyl took the globe.

"We should go," Farel interrupted. "We have a hard day's travel ahead of us, and no time to tarry if we're to meet Gaelen at the rendezvous point on schedule."

Rain waved an arm. "Lead the way."

Farel's gaze flicked to the gathered *dahl'reisen*. A dozen squads of six warriors each immediately broke into a run and jogged through the thicket tunnel. "Our spotters," he said. "They will travel ahead of us to make sure the way is clear. Come. Your mate can lose her blindfold once we're a few miles away from the village." He turned and jogged towards the tunnel himself, leaving Rain and Ellysetta to follow.

Rain took Ellysetta's hand and wove Spirit to guide her steps. The remaining *dahl'reisen* followed after them. Stoic women stood beside their children, eyes dry and faces pale as they watched their *dahl'reisen* loved ones depart.

When the warriors were gone, Sheyl turned to the remaining villagers. "The Tairen Soul has offered us shelter in the Fading Lands until this war is over. We leave in three bells. Hurry! And pack only what you can carry without hardship. It's a long walk to the Garreval."

The Fading Lands ~ Dharsa

"Why do you have to go, Kieran? We just got here." Lillis pouted at Kieran, who had joined her for a late breakfast on the most beautiful terrace she'd ever seen to tell her that he and Kiel were leaving and that she and Lorelle should be very good and stay out of trouble while they were gone. Her excitement over being in the magical city of the Fey was completely gone now. All she could think was that Kieran was going away again—and she'd only just got him back!

"Ellysetta and Rain need all the help they can get, so Kiel and I are going to go help them. You want us to help them, right?"

She scowled at the breakfast plate filled with delicious fruits and delicate pastries that almost tasted better than comfits. Her shoe scuffed on the terrace stone beneath her chair. "Yes," she admitted.

"That's why we have to go, *ajiana*. I'm sorry. I know this isn't what you wanted. But I am a warrior of the Fey, and Rain is my king, and we have to stop the bad people from hurting others the way they hurt the people of Teleon."

She picked up a small, slender-tined fork and pushed a pile of chilled berries around on her plate. "But I'll be afraid when you're gone." She jabbed her fork into a plump strawberry.

The admission pierced Kieran's heart as surely as the sharp tines of her fork skewered the berry. He leaned over to press a kiss on the top of her head and closed his eyes against a sting of tears. She'd told him about her time in the Mists, how he hadn't been there in the "village" and how worried she'd been that something had happened to him. And then she'd woken, broken and in pain, and terrified. And he hadn't been there again.

And now he was leaving her.

He pulled up a chair and sat beside her, leaning over to take her hand. "Lillis . . . *ajiana* . . . this is the safest place in the world for you to be right now. If it weren't, I promise I wouldn't leave you for any reason."

Lillis stuck the berry in her mouth and chewed, refusing to look at him.

He sighed and glanced over towards the far corner of the terrace, where Kiel was receiving an equally chilly response from Lorelle. *«Time to go, kem'jeto,»* he spun on a private weave.

Pushing away from the table, Kieran stood and walked over to the open archway that led out to the terrace. Sol Baristani was standing by the marble column, smoking his pipe and talking to Kieran's parents while the children ate breakfast.

"They're not happy with us," Kieran admitted. "I wish we could stay—at least until they got settled in—but Orest is under siege, and the allies are outnumbered."

"They'll be all right once their mad wears off," Sol assured him. "You two go do what you must. And take care of yourselves."

Kieran nodded. "Be well, Master Baristani. *Mela. Gepa.*" He hugged his parents. His mother was no more pleased than Lillis to be losing her son again so soon, but she understood. He was a warrior of the Fey. His place was with his king, defending the Fading Lands from harm.

At least he and Kiel wouldn't be going alone. After Kieran's altercation with the Massan, Loris v'En Mahr, the Water master, had followed Eimar's example and resigned his seat, declaring his intention to travel with Kieran and Kiel to Orest in support of Rain and the allies. He'd put out the word announcing his decision and inviting all who shared his concerns to join them. Three thousand more Fey and more than forty *shei'dalins* had done so.

Celieria ~ Verlaine Forest

The Mharog Azurel stood at the northern edge of the Verlaine Forest, draped in a long, hooded, black shroud to keep the mud-morning sunlight from falling upon his skin. He and the others who'd once been Champions of Light were creatures of Darkness now, and sunlight scorched their flesh like fire.

Pale lids descended over nightmarish eyes, and he turned his head slowly in a half circle to scan the forest for his prey. Put a *shei'dalin* within a hundred miles of a Mharog, and he could find her. A *shei'dalin's* Light—the same Light that in his previous Fey existence had offered the promise of profound love and joy—shone to his Mharog eyes like a garish sun. And *her* Light blazed so bright it set the horizon aflame. To his surprise, smaller Lights—many of them—lay in a cluster to the east of the Tairen Soul's mate.

Hatred and loathing consumed him. Watching Rain Tairen Soul scream and rend his own flesh when she died would be a pleasure he'd savor for centuries.

His eyes snapped open. A hiss rattled from his throat. "The village is there," he told his companions. He pointed to the south, where he'd seen the cluster of smaller Lights. "The Tairen Soul and his mate are there."

"If Tairen Soul and his mate have left the village, why

hasn't he just Changed and flown away?" Rachuss, one of the Mharog, asked.

"This wood is filthy with traps," Primage Dur answered. "Poison darts shoot down anything that flies. If the Tairen Soul tried to take wing, he'd be dead before he cleared the top of the trees."

"Then they're trapped," Angramar, another Mharog growled. "Can we use the Well to reach them?"

Dur shook his head. "We've not been successful keeping *chemar* in this region," he said. "The *dahl'reisen* destroy them as quickly as we put them in place."

"We will run them down on foot, then," Azurel said. "You Mages, take the soldiers and head for the village. Chernos"— he nodded his cowled head at another robed Mharog—"will accompany you so you don't lose your way. The rest of us will follow the Tairen Soul and his mate."

"You know what the High Mage commanded," the Primage objected. "You are not to approach the woman alone."

"The High Mage commanded me to bring the woman to him alive, and I will do so," Azurel countered, his voice as smooth as iced silk. "But you and your soldiers slow us down."

Dur stood his ground. "You go nowhere without us, Mharog."

Hidden by his robe's long sleeves, Azurel's hands clenched into fists, his long, black fingernails digging into his flesh. He'd spent a lifetime hating the Mages. Embracing Darkness hadn't changed that. It only meant he didn't kill them as often.

"Very well, then. We split up. Send half your Mages and soldiers with Chernos. The rest of you, follow us. And keep up."

Farel slowed and jogged back towards Rain and Ellysetta. "The Eld have breached the Verlaine."

"Mages?" Rain asked.

"Scores of them, all blue-robes. They lead a garrison of

soldiers . . . They have a Mharog with them. They're heading for the village."

Ellysetta's cheeks drained of color. "Because of me?" she asked with dread. She'd removed her blindfold a bell ago. "Did the Mage use me to find the village?"

"I don't know. We've kept you well shielded and we blindfolded you. Everything I know about Mage Marks tells me that should have been enough to protect against four Marks . . ."

"But?" Rain prompted.

Farel gave him a shuttered look, the kind warriors gave one another when the news was grim. "But there's a second Eld party heading on an intercept course with us . . . and they have five Mharog leading them."

"We've got to go back," Ellysetta exclaimed. "We've got to help Sheyl and the others."

"*Nei*. Getting you to safety comes first. Sheyl understands that."

"But the children! Cerlissa and Bannon!" Rain caught her when she lunged towards the *dahl'reisen* leader.

"And if the Eld *are* somehow tracking you, going back would lead them straight to the women and children. Right now, the Eld forces are split. It's best for all of us if they stay that way." Softening his voice, Farel added, "Besides, Sheyl has already begun the evacuation of the village, and I've summoned reinforcements to guard their retreat. They will be as safe as I can make them."

"But—"

Rain squeezed her shoulders. "Farel's right, Ellysetta." «*Shei'tani, their women and children are the only Lights left in these warriors' lives. If dahl'reisen still retain any part of their Fey hearts—and gods save them, I'm beginning to believe these do—staying with us, trying to get you to safety, when their women and children are in danger must be almost more torment than they can bear. Do not berate them for it.*» He met the *dahl'reisen's* gaze. "Can we make it out of the Verlaine before the Eld can cut us off?"

"We need to change course. Head due west . . . maybe southwest . . . force them to come around the northwest corner. That will buy us a few bells."

"A few bells are better than none. Lead the way."

Farel started to turn, then hesitated. "Sheyl told me you offered our women and children sanctuary in the Fading Lands. Was that at her urging?"

"Aiyah," Rain admitted softly. "She showed us your nursery this morning . . . and the child Murialisa. How could I refuse her?"

"That's why she showed you." Farel's shoulders sagged. "She saw this attack coming. She kept it from me because she wanted to be sure I was away." He took a deep breath, and when he looked up again, his features had once more settled into a stony expression devoid of all emotion. "What she sees comes true—always—so I am where I'm supposed to be, as is she. Let's get you to Gaelen—and we need to pick up the pace."

Farel spun a command to the lines of *dahl'reisen* bringing up the rear. *«Brothers, circle the Feyreisa! Ring of Protection!»*

The *dahl'reisen* burst into action, parting into two columns to circle around Ellysetta, careful to keep their distance. They ran as graceful as pronghorns, leaping fallen trees and dodging low-hung branches with astonishing speed. Rain and Ellysetta were clumsy tanglefoots by comparison and had clearly been slowing them down.

Farel glanced back over his shoulder. "What are you waiting for, Tairen Soul? Let's run."

The last of the villagers hurried out through the thicket tunnel, beneath the watchful eyes of the remaining *dahl'reisen*, while Sheyl ran door to door, checking every room, nook, and stair in the *dahl'reisen* village to make sure no one had been forgotten.

Urgency beat at her, accompanied by the sensation of a heavy weight pressing down upon her. It was like that sometimes with her second gift. Not a clear vision, but simply a driving need that hounded her until she heeded its call.

Now was such a time.

She couldn't shake the feeling that someone was still here. Someone had not left with the others.

«Sheyl, we must go.»

«A few more chimes. I'm almost done.» She raced across a vine bridge leading to the last cluster of tree homes in the village, the ones that hugged the farthest perimeter of the compound. These were the houses the sensitives occupied . . . the homes of Murialisa's parents and other couples like them.

The pounding in her veins grew stronger, the weight pressing on her chest heavier so that her breath came in shallow gasps. She opened the door of Muri's house and ran room to room. The bedrooms were filled with signs of frantic packing: clothes strewn in haphazard piles across the bed, drawers and wardrobes open, their contents in disarray. But there were no people, nothing that couldn't be lost to the Eld. The true treasures of the house, Muri and her parents, were gone.

Sheyl ran out the back door and checked three more homes on the same level of the cluster before bounding down the hanging stair, making the treads rock wildly. She leapt to the platform beneath and opened the first door she came to. That house was empty, as were the second and third after that.

The fourth house, however . . .

She burst through the front door, shouting, "Is anyone here?" Before the echoes of her call died out, she heard the choked cry, and then she knew.

She headed straight for the bedroom and flung open the door. Carina, whose man had been among those who had not returned last night from rescuing the Feyreisa, lay in a muddled pile of sheets that were soaked with sweat, maternal waters, and blood. Her jaw was clenched, her hands gripped around the tight, rippling mound of her unborn child. The child was coming . . . and it was early by three months.

Sheyl drew a deep breath and let it out. The urgency and

the crushing weight of fate fell away, replaced with imperturbable calm and a detached, faintly melancholy sense of acceptance.

So this was how her death was to be written.

More warriors were on the way. From every corner of the Verlaine, all blades not manning a scout post were racing to hold off the Eld invaders and buy time for the villagers to escape. But they would not come in time to save Sheyl.

She crossed the room to the bedside and took the frightened, laboring woman's hand in hers. "Carina." With a smile, she caressed the woman's flushed brow. "Don't worry, dearling. I'm here. I won't leave you."

Throughout the morning and well into afternoon, the *dahl'reisen* kept up a punishing pace. Light, lithe, they sped across the densely wooded terrain the creatures of the forest they had become, their feet barely touching the ground as they skimmed over mossy rock and tree and burbling stream, each step finding the perfect purchase. Most Fey warriors—even at their fastest pace—rested fifteen chimes out of each bell. The *dahl'reisen* only rested ten.

When at last Farel called a half bell rest, Rain and Ellysetta collapsed onto the ground, out of breath and energy. Around them, some *dahl'reisen* found a mossy stump or fallen tree to sit on. Others simply folded their legs and sat where they stood.

Rain and Ellysetta took a seat at the base of a large oak tree. Farel unclipped a flask from his hip belt and tossed it to them.

"Water from the Heras," he told them. "It's the closest thing to pure *faerilas* in Celieria. It should help you both."

Rain thanked him and uncapped the flask, taking the first, experimental sip before handing the flask to Ellysetta to drink her fill.

As Rain leaned back against the oak and let his gaze wander, he noted the *dahl'reisen* nearby pouring a stream of the *faerilas*-infused water on their hands before drinking.

"What are they doing?" he asked, nodding a chin in their direction.

Farel glanced over his shoulder. "Testing themselves. The waters of the Heras burn like acid on the skin of any creature of the Dark. We require all warriors in the Brotherhood to pour the water on their hands before witnesses at least once a day and after every battle. It's how we know who has fallen too far into Shadow."

"What do you do if they have?" Ellysetta asked.

Farel eyed her steadily. "We let the forest have them."

The scream of a *lyrant* broke the quiet. Ellysetta swallowed and looked away.

Farel stood. "It's time to go."

Eyes closed, Azurel checked the position of the Feyreisa's Light. "We're losing them," he said. "I knew you'd slow us down. They'll be free of the forest before we can reach them." Once they were out of the Verlaine, Rain Tairen Soul could Change, and all hope of capturing him and his mate would be lost.

"What can we do?" Dur asked.

Azurel considered the options quickly and gauged the distance to the two targets. "How many *chemar* do you have?"

The Primage's brows drew together in a suspicious frown. "Why?"

"How many?" A low rattle, like a *porgil's* warning before it struck, vibrated in the Mharog's throat.

Dur's composure slipped, revealing a flash of fear before he caught himself. "Three dozen."

One pale, imperious hand extended from the cuff of the black robe. "Give ten of them to me."

The Primage hesitated . . . then, with obvious reluctance, surrendered his pouch of *chemar* stones. Azurel spilled a dozen of the stones on the ground, near a pile of fallen leaves and twigs. He closed his eyes, drawing an image in his mind. Green Earth gathered at his call. The leaves fluttered, then began to spin.

"What are you doing?" Dur demanded.

Twigs rose up in the air. Their thin ends split, and the frayed ends curled around the spilled *chemar* like tiny claws. Brown, dead leaves knit together, fluttering like feathers in the weave's swirling breeze.

"Shortening our trip."

Farel pushed them hard until sunset. He called a few bell's rest for evening meal, which consisted of cold journey cakes, *faerilas*, and a few chimes of sleep. As their brothers rested, *dahl'reisen* quintets scouted several miles in every direction.

"Listen." One of the warriors in the quintet scouting the rear flank lifted his head. "Do you hear that?"

His brothers cocked their heads and listened for half a chime before shaking their heads. "Hear what?" the *dahl'reisen* asked.

Then the breeze shifted, blowing towards them, and the currents of air carried with them a tiny, almost imperceptible sound. Little pops of sound in a continuous series. Pop. Pop. Pop.

"That."

The sound grew louder, coming closer.

"I hear it now," one of the *dahl'reisen* said. "Almost like the sound of an elf's fingerbow firing, only hundreds of them together. But what is—" His voice broke off. His eyes widened. He turned to the *dahl'reisen* sitting next to him, an Air master. "Lirn, get up there." He pointed towards the treetops overhead. "Hurry. Tell us what you see."

Silvery white Air gathered in a powerful burst and launched the *dahl'reisen* skyward. Lirn landed on a thick branch high in a nearby tree, then leapt again, moving with effortless speed until he reached the topmost branches.

The popping sound was much more noticeable up there, and Lirn turned his head towards the sound . . . and by the light of the setting sun saw the dark smudges of a distant flock of dark birds winging towards him, no more than a tairen length above the forest canopy.

Shock froze him in place for a stunned few moments. They couldn't be birds. Nothing flew over the Verlaine and lived—and he knew the forest defenses were working. That's what the popping sounds were . . . the constant streams of poison darts firing at the flock of birds.

Yet the birds continued to fly.

He narrowed his eyes, bringing the distant creatures into closer focus, and saw the dead leaves flapping like wings, prickled with so many darts the thing looked more like a flying quillspine than a bird. No wonder the darts had no effect. Poison couldn't kill a thing already dead.

Lirn's focus moved lower. Tiny stick legs dangled beneath the pumping wings of the birdlike creatures . . . and clutched in each twiglike claw was a gleaming white stone.

CHAPTER FOURTEEN

"We've got to go. The Eld have found a way to send *chemar* into the forest." Farel's grim pronouncement brought Rain and Ellysetta to their feet. He explained quickly about the birdlike creatures. "They're still twenty miles out, but closing fast. The scouts are going to try to destroy them."

"Can we outrun them?" Rain asked.

"Nei. Even in an open field at our top speed, we'd still run slower than these creatures fly. They'll be upon us within the bell. I've already asked for thirty-six volunteers to build a Wall of Steel. That should buy us at least some time."

"Even thirty-six won't be enough against five Mharog and scores of Mages."

"I know, but when the first Wall falls, we build another, and another. As many as it takes until you're clear of the Verlaine and able to Change."

"What's a Wall of Steel?" Ellysetta asked.

Rain supplied the answer. "It is a line of warriors who will stand and fight to the death before allowing a single enemy to pass. Once they make their Wall, the only way they'll leave it is through victory or death."

"What?" Ellie couldn't believe she'd heard right. "But that's suicide!"

"It is the only option." Farel didn't meet Ellysetta's horrified gaze but instead kept his eyes fixed steadily on Rain's. "I've called more *dahl'reisen* from the borders, but the closest are still three bells out."

"No!" Ellysetta stepped directly in front of Farel, forcing him to look at her. "I will not allow it. Do you hear me? We all go, or we all stay. But none of you will be left behind to die. I will not permit it." Her furious voice rang out, bringing scores of *dahl'reisen* heads around in surprise.

Farel bowed. "Your concern is appreciated, *kem'falla*, but we who are the Brotherhood of Shadows no longer live within the glory of the Fading Lands nor answer to her laws. Though we serve her still, we rule ourselves."

"Rain . . ."

"Nei, shei'tani. He is correct. No duty or oath binds him to your command, nor even mine. Besides, this is an honorable death." He met Farel's gaze. "Choose your men."

"This is senseless!" she protested. "Let's at least try to outrun the Mharog before condemning thirty-six men to death!"

But Farel was already walking away, calling his warriors together to ask for volunteers.

Ellysetta spun to confront her mate. "The Fey cannot afford to keep losing its warriors, Rain."

"These men are already lost, *shei'tani,* but this is a chance for some of them to regain their honor."

"Scorch honor! Rain, they can bear children—Fey children. They can bring life back to the Fading Lands."

"Aiyah, they can bear children, and that is blessing from the gods. But it is you, *shei'tani*—not these *dahl'reisen*—who are the true hope of the Fading Lands." When she made a face and started to turn away, he caught her shoulders in a firm grip and gave her a small shake. "Listen to me. *You* are the one the Eye of Truth sent me to find. *You* saved the tairen and brought fertility back to the Fey. Gaelen was right to tell them to protect your life even if it cost the lives of every man, woman, and child in their village. And they are right to abide by his command."

Ellysetta scowled and pulled free to stalk away. All her life she'd read about the glorious history of the Fey, and she'd wept over histories that detailed the courageous deaths of noble Fey heroes who'd given their lives to hold back the Dark. But it didn't feel the same when it was her they were dying for.

She knew she couldn't stop them. When Fey warriors were honor-bound on a course of action, they let nothing stand in their way. Noble, rock-headed idiots. If she didn't love them so much for their valor, she'd be tempted to kill them herself for their stubbornness.

She spun back to glower at Rain, jaw set, arms crossed. *«So be it. But if they can die for me, then I can bless them before they go.»*

Rain couldn't have looked more surprised if she'd slammed a fist in his face. *«Ellysetta, nei. You know you cannot touch them.»*

Her lips tightened. *«They live with their pain day in and day out, for centuries. Surely I can bear it for a few moments.»*

«You have no concept of how terrible their true pain is. They've been shielding you all this time. You've only sensed a fraction of it.»

«You forget I touched Gaelen.»

«And nearly killed us both,» he reminded her grimly. *«The hurt they carry is too great for any Fey woman to bear»*

She almost faltered then. She remembered the shattering torment of Gaelen's lost soul. But then she glanced at the stoic faces of the *dahl'reisen* who had suffered so much, who had been reviled and outcast by the very people they'd lost their souls to protect yet still, nobly, strove to protect them, and determination bloomed anew. *«Then help me bear it. Give me your strength.»*

«Shei'tani, I am so close to madness, I doubt I could withstand you healing a single rasa right now.»

She bit her lip. She remembered what healing the *rasa* had done to Rain, how close he'd come to shredding his mental barriers—and he'd not been in the grip of bond madness then. She couldn't do that to him again. But she couldn't let the *dahl'reisen* just walk towards their deaths and do nothing, either.

«Then I will bless them without laying hands upon them. Because, one way or another, I will do this. We owe them that much.»

* * *

Many more than thirty-six *dahl'reisen* came forward to offer their lives for her. So many more that Ellysetta nearly wept to see it. They looked at her with such determination and pride. Despite Rain's assurances, it did not seem right that so many immortal lives should be sacrificed for hers.

She made no further attempt to dissuade them except to refuse the service of any *dahl'reisen* with a living mate or child. "No woman will be widowed, no child orphaned, on my behalf," she declared. Something in her voice, or perhaps the light of battle in her eyes, must have convinced them to heed her word, because two dozen of the volunteers bowed their heads and stepped back, withdrawing as she requested.

From those remaining, Farel selected thirty-six tall, fierce men, all of whom seemed to grow taller and fiercer when Farel chose them. They ringed around him as he gave them their final commands and farewells. When he was finished, each *dahl'reisen* removed his Soul Quest crystal from around his neck and handed it to Farel. The gesture pierced Ellysetta's heart. She knew, without asking, why they did it: Warriors heading for certain death would not give the Eld more Tairen's Eye to pervert into *selkahr*.

"Wait," she commanded when the thirty-six would have departed. "Is it not customary for *shei'dalins* to bless Fey warriors before they head into battle?"

Shock rippled across the *dahl'reisens'* faces, and when she approached them, they fell back, casting alarmed looks at Farel first, then Rain. Ellysetta halted. She would not chase these men around like a girl threatening boys with kisses in a schoolyard. "Rain, tell them."

With a face carved of pure stone, Rain said, "The Feyreisa will bless you before you leave."

The *dahl'reisen* stopped in their tracks. Around them, their brethren murmured amongst themselves with a mixture of shock, awe, and disapproval.

"Come here, to me," she ordered.

The warriors shared uncertain glances, then reluctantly

approached her, stopping a man length away and dropping to one knee.

With Rain at her side, she approached the first warrior. "For my *shei'tan's* sake, I cannot touch you," she said. "But I ask that you drop your shields."

The *dahl'reisen* lurched back in horror. "*Teska, kem'falla,*" he pleaded, "I bear shame enough for choosing the Shadowed Path instead of the honor of *sheisan'dahlein.* Do not blacken my soul further by forcing me to share the evil in my heart with you. Just speaking the words of the blessing is enough—and more than I deserve."

Anger blossomed in her heart. It was an abomination to her that this man was about to die on her behalf, yet still he thought himself evil and unworthy of a simple kindness. "What is your name?"

The *dahl'reisen* looked up. His eyes were lavender, almost the same shade as Rain's. "Varian, *kem'falla.*"

"Varian, if there were evil in your heart, you would not be trying so hard to spare me from it." She lifted her chin and glared at them all, her eyes hot with righteous anger. "You are worthy. All of you are worthy. Never doubt it."

Fierce anger burned inside her at the thought of these proud, brave men fighting and suffering for their people, only to receive banishment and a life of torment as their reward. And even then they continued to defend the very people who had rejected them.

She would not reject them. She would not allow them to flinch from her in shame. She could not stop them from their course, but she would not allow them to face their deaths believing themselves unloved and unworthy.

Ellie reached out and placed her hands on either side of Varian's face. She did not touch him, but even so his pain and despair screamed up her nerves, radiating from his un-shielded body in palpable waves. She gave a choked cry. The agony of his soul was intense, like putting her hand on a hot griddle and willing it to stay there as the flesh seared away. But when Varian started to raise his shields again, she barked "Do not!" and spun a fierce web of Spirit to stop him. She had fought and won the battle to save the tairen kitlings. She would fight and win this battle, too.

Rain's hands gripped her shoulders. Love and strength poured into her. *«Weave your blessing, shei'tani. I am with you.»*

At his touch, peace settled over her raging emotions and muted the *dahl'reisen's* despair. She closed her eyes, gathering her emotions and summoning the shining golden magic of her *shei'dalin's* love. Fierce love. Unwavering acceptance. Belonging. Family. Ellysetta wove those emotions and memories into her thoughts and sent them arrowing into the mind of the warrior whose face she held between her hovering palms.

"You honor me, Varian. May the gods watch over you and keep you safe. Go with my blessing and my love, and come back to me if you can." Instead of delivering the traditional *shei'dalin's* kiss to his brow, she poured upon him a small, radiant burst of her essence, absorbing his terrible sorrow and returning love in its stead.

When she released him, he bent his head and clumsily re-formed his shields. Though his *dahl'reisen* eyes, incapable of tears, remained dry, his shoulders quaked with the force of his emotions. He fumbled with his Fey'cha belts, pulling free one of the many black-handled daggers. Both his hands and his voice shook as he sliced his palm and let six drops of blood fall upon the small blade and spoke the vow of blood-swearing. "I know a *dahl'reisen* has no right to this honor," he declared, staring up at Rain, "but I do ask that this pledge be witnessed."

"Witnessed," Rain agreed. He glanced at Farel. "The bond requires a second."

"I do not understand you at all, Tairen Soul," the *dahl'reisen* general muttered, his expression wavering between disapproval and disbelief. Then he turned to Varian and barked, "Witnessed. And may the gods have mercy on all our blighted souls."

Varian's blade flashed briefly, sealing the bond, and he held it out to Ellysetta, hilt first.

She took the Fey'cha and Rain spun a quick Earth weave to add Varian's steel alongside the other *lu'tan* steel woven into her studded scarlet leathers. "Do you have family in the Fading Lands, Varian?"

Startled, the *dahl'reisen* looked to Rain as if for guidance before answering, "*Aiyah, kem'falla.* I have two younger brothers—at least I did when the Wars ended."

"And your parents?"

"They died in the Wars."

"What are you brothers' names?"

"I am *dahl'reisen.* I do not speak their names."

"Then weave them to me in Spirit. Your brothers should know that *dahl'reisen* or not, you remain, in your heart, a warrior of honor and a champion of Light. I want their names so that I may tell them."

After a final, brief hesitation, Varian gave her the names on a wispy thread of Spirit, whispering them as if he feared dread repercussions for speaking them even in his mind. *«They are Silvannis and Moren vel Chera, of Lissilin.»*

«Beylah vo, Varian vel Chera.»

Rain's hand touched the small of her back. *«Well done, shei'tani.»*

She took a deep breath and exhaled the remnant pain from standing so close to an unshielded *dahl'reisen.* *«You were right about his pain. I don't think I could have borne it without you.»*

With Rain at her side, Ellysetta repeated her blessing for each of the remaining warriors. One by one, they hunched over, sobbing as her *shei'dalin's* love tore through the numb, emotionless barrier that blanketed their *dahl'reisen* souls. One by one, they bloodswore themselves to her and gave her the names of any family who'd still been living when they left the Fading Lands.

And when they rose to their feet, one by one they retrieved

their Soul Quest crystals from Farel and presented them to Ellysetta.

She did not immediately accept the proffered crystals. All she could think of was the Fey custom of giving a *shei'dalin* the crystals of the warriors who died on her behalf. Though she had blessed them, though she knew she could not stop them, she was still horrified that they would sacrifice themselves to save her.

«Ellysetta,» Rain's Spirit voice whispered in her mind. *«Look in their faces. Look in their eyes. You have given them back their honor and their hope. This is not a sacrifice to them. This is their salvation.»*

Ellysetta looked at her newest *lu'tan* and realized that Rain was right. The *dahl'reisens'* eyes—normally so shadowed and grim—seemed lighter, all but glittering with eagerness. These were not innocent boys, rushing off to their first battle with false expectations of glory and heroism. These were battle-hardened warriors who knew the bitter truth about what they were about to face. And still they embraced their fate willingly, even joyfully.

She held out her hand and accepted their *sorreisu'kiyr.* "I will hold these for you until your return."

The *lu'tan* stepped back. One of them wove Earth, and their leathers changed colors from black to vivid flame, the chest blazoned with a golden tairen rampant whose green eyes glowed with a magical light.

As one, they cried, *"Miora felah ti'Feyreisa!"*

Before the last echoes of their cheer faded, a familiar, icy tingle ran up Ellysetta's spine. Her knees went weak, and she had to clutch Rain's arm to keep from falling. "Rain—" Her voice broke off on a groan as a blanket of agonizing foulness engulfed her.

"What's wrong?" Farel asked.

Rain turned a grim gaze in his direction. "Not all the *chemar* were destroyed. The Well is open. The Mharog are here." *«Shei'tani, can you run?»*

She inhaled, trying to breathe through the sick agony

twisting in her belly. The *dahl'reisen* were shielded. The Mharog were not, and the cloying horror of them was worse than anything she'd ever felt before. "I'll manage," she rasped. "Let's go."

Farel gestured, and the *dahl'reisen* began to run.

The thirty-six who had volunteered for death ran in the opposite direction, the joy in their eyes replaced by lethal determination.

"What's this?" Primage Dur squinted at the glow of magic in the forest before them. Twelve shining warriors in red leather stood interspaced between a line of gnarled trees, blocking the advance of the Eld. "Who are they?"

"Dahl'reisen," Azurel hissed.

"Are they . . . singing?"

"It is a Fey warriors' song called 'Ten Thousand Swords.' " The Mharog spat on the ground. "No *dahl'reisen* sings that song."

But singing they were. What had the Feyreisen's mate done that *dahl'reisen* would sing with all the fierce pride and joy of the Fey?

They continued to sing even as the glow of their magic began to coalesce into thick, powerful ropes. Fire, Earth, Air, Water, Spirit . . . and then Azrahn. "They use Azrahn freely." Even at this distance, the sweet chill of the forbidden mystic made the back of his teeth ache and his own power rise in response. "One of them, at least, is a master of it. Or close enough so it makes little difference."

"Foolish, foolish Fey. Do they not learn?" The Primage sneered, closed his eyes, and sent a whip of Azrahn arrowing across the distance to Mark the fools who wove Azrahn in the presence of a Mage. A moment later, his sneer faded. His brow furrowed. His Mark had found no target. "What's this?" The Mage spun Azrahn again, and again the *dahl'reisen* eluded his claiming. "They've somehow shielded themselves against my Marks."

"Just as well." Azurel closed his fists around hilts of the

long, black-bladed knives at his waist that had replaced the curved *meicha* scimitars he'd once worn. He smiled with eager bloodlust. "I prefer to wet my blades in a fight."

Beside him, the other Mharog growled deep in their throat, and Azurel could sense they were as eager as he to spill the blood of these *dahl'reisen* who sang as if they were still Fey. The song, once so beloved, seemed a symbol of all that the Mharog had lost, all that they now reviled.

Without warning, the Eld soldiers behind them gave choked gasps and crumpled. Even as they fell, a red Fey'cha glanced off Azurel's own, ever-present shields and sliced the unprotected hand of the Eld captain standing beside him. The captain's eyes widened in horror at the sight of his bleeding hand. His fingers spasmed. Then his arm began to shake as the tairen venom spread rapidly through his veins. Within moments he was gasping for air and clutching at his throat as a white froth bubbled at the corners of his mouth. The poison reached his brain, and he dropped to the ground, stone dead, eyes staring.

Azurel nudged the body aside with one foot and scanned the trees around them. Another barrage of Fey'cha ricocheted off the Mages' hastily erected shields, followed by a concussive blast as a twelve-fold weave from the first group of *dahl'reisen* slammed into the forward shields.

"These twelve are not alone. Have your archers clear our flanks." Azurel directed the attention of the Mages to the dense forest on either side of them. He could sense nothing, but *dahl'reisen* weren't fools enough to send a mere twelve blades against five Mharog and so many Mages.

Dur snapped the command on a whip of Azrahn. *«Archers, fire. Rain sel'dor on our flanks!»*

The air turned black with flying arrows. Azurel watched closely, looking for the telltale energy flares of *sel'dor* hitting Fey shields. He would be very surprised if the *dahl'reisen's* admittedly impressive invisibility weaves could completely hide shields strong enough to block *sel'dor.*

«One in the large fireoak there, another near that tumble of rocks. Two more in the trees to our left. Earth, on my command. Shake them out of the trees. Now!»

Green Earth arced outward from two of the Mharog, with Azurel directing rippling flows of it both to his left and his right. The ground bucked and heaved. The tumbled pile of boulders shuddered, massive rocks shifting and falling, and the *dahl'reisen* taking cover there gave a sharp cry, quickly silenced. Nearby, the large oak that sheltered the second *dahl'reisen* shook wildly from the force of the powerful quake. With a mighty groan, the tree toppled, and as the *dahl'reisen* in the branches tumbled to the ground, two of the Mharog broke his shields with a six-fold weave, and Dur followed with a blast of Mage Fire that sliced the warrior in half.

The line of trees to the right shivered but stood firm beneath the attack of the two Mharog as a masterful counteractive weave of Earth dispelled the rippling force. The Eld bowmen released another hail of barbed arrows while Mages peppered the woods with globes of blue-white Mage Fire. Beneath the Mharogs' feet, the earth gave a sudden, heaving lurch that knocked them off-balance.

A shout rose from the back of the infantry formation, and Azurel turned to see the Eld soldiers falling upon themselves, teeth bared in feral snarls as they sliced and hacked at one another. A heavy black-and-lavender weave lay over the Eld like a shroud. He tracked the weave back to its source—more *dahl'reisen* hidden by their admittedly impressive invisibility weaves—and flung a blistering combination of Fire, Air, and Azrahn at them, but that blast exploded harmlessly against another six-fold shield.

From the front, another brutal, twelve-fold hammer cracked the forward shields. An intense Spirit and Azrahn weave shot through the breech, plowing into two Mages, who suddenly turned and began to throw Mage Fire at their own brothers—incinerating half a dozen Mages and enough of Azurel's shields to crisp his hair and singe the side of his face before his own red Fey'cha dispatched them.

Azurel touched his scorched flesh. His eyes narrowed.

"Time for you Mages to earn your jewels, Dur," Azurel snarled to the Mage. "Take out the Spirit masters before all your soldiers slaughter themselves and your weak-minded Mages kill the rest of us. And send something with a kick, not your easily diverted little fireballs. The ones spinning Spirit are directing most of their energy into the illusion weaves, but the others are shielding them. The Mharog will take care of the blades in front."

Dur nodded grimly. "Mages!" Blue-white Mage Fire gathered in Mage hands, a glowing ball that grew larger and brighter, illuminating the concentration and strain on the Mage's face as he fed power into it. The massive fireballs shot out of the Mages' hands straight at the Spirit master. The Mharog spun a four-fold weave to box in the Spirit master so he couldn't leap clear of the Mage Fire's path.

Trapped, the *dahl'reisen* dropped his invisibility weave. He faced, unflinching, the approaching fire and screamed defiance into its consuming maw, *"Miora felah ti'Feyreisa!"*

The Mage Fire plowed into him and flared with a thunderous boom. When it dissipated, the *dahl'reisen* Spirit master was gone. Without his energy to sustain it, his weave dissolved, and the Eld soldiers under its control came to their senses, shaking themselves and looking about in shock.

Dur took out the other Spirit masters in the same manner, and after that the air filled with flying Fey'cha, Mage Fire, arrows, and magic. The remaining *dahl'reisen* fell after a brief but intense battle.

The last to die was a lavender-eyed *dahl'reisen*. He lay mortally wounded, the lower half of his body in ruins. As Azurel approached, the fallen man gave a bloody, triumphant smile and plunged a red Fey'cha into his own chest.

"Miora felah ti'Feyreisa," he whispered as his body spasmed. A moment later, his eyes went blank, and his head

lolled to one side. The smile remained on his face even in death.

Azurel knelt beside the corpse. Azrahn came to his call, whirling in his palm as he tried to summon the dead man's soul.

But for the first time in his five hundred years of being Mharog, something blocked him.

Frowning, he fed more energy into his Azrahn weave, trying to force the *dahl'reisen's* soul to answer his call.

Still, it did not come.

Instead, a great blinding light rushed up at him. Furious, defiant love, so hot it made the ice of his soul crack and shudder. In sudden, breathless terror, he ripped apart his Azrahn weave and threw himself back away from the *dahl'reisen's* corpse.

"What's the matter?" Dur asked.

Azurel bit back a sharp curse and rose to his feet. "His soul is bound. It cannot be summoned."

"What do you mean 'bound'? Bound to what?"

"To her, you idiot. His soul is bound to her. Bloodsworn."

Azurel stalked to the next closest *dahl'reisen* corpse. Steeling himself to confront the white light, he tried to summon the second *dahl'reisen's* soul. It, too, defied his call. As did the next, and the next, and the next. "They're all bloodsworn. Every scorching one of them. That's why you could not Mark them when they wove Azrahn." Azurel's fists clenched, and his teeth ground together. "Never would I have believed Rainier vel'En Daris would allow *dahl'reisen* to bloodswear themselves to his truemate."

Dur eyed him skeptically. "The Mages bind the souls of all their followers, but those souls can still be summoned after death."

"Bloodswearing is different. It is more like *shei'tanitsa* than your soul-binding. They have willingly tied their souls to hers, dedicated themselves to serve only her in life and in death. It is a compact that cannot be broken or perverted."

Through a combination of Magecraft, Feraz black magic, and Merellian demon sorcery, the High Mage had managed to tie a tairen's soul to Shannisorran v'En Celay's but never had he succeeded in calling v'En Celay's soul to his service. Nor had he ever have been able to claim a bloodsworn soul.

"Step aside and let me try."

Azurel's eyes narrowed, but he stepped back and allowed the prideful Primage to approach the *dahl'reisen's* corpse. He watched as Dur summoned Azrahn and called to the dead man's soul, watched him feed more power into his summons, and almost smiled as the Mage swore and threw himself away from the body.

"What was that?" Dur gasped.

"That was Rain Tairen Soul's mate—or rather, the power of her bloodsworn bond. It defends the souls in her keeping."

"It felt like . . . love."

Azurel's lips curled. "Of course. Love is the greatest power of a *shei'dalin*. With it, she could break you completely. Every evil you have ever worked, she could force you to relive through the eyes of those who loved your victims. You would shred your own flesh from your bones in self-loathing."

"I never believed the stories were true."

"Now you know differently." Few of the Mages who'd earned their blue robes after the Wars had ever seen a *shei'dalin* at work. Most had only ever known those broken creatures captured by the Mages, bound with *sel'dor*, and tortured to insanity. And so they thought *shei'dalins* were weak and insignificant. They forgot that the truemate bond did not form between uneven halves. The truemate of a powerful Fey Lord would have her own power, vastly different but nonetheless equal in strength to her mate's.

Azurel called Fire to incinerate the *dahl'reisen* dead. "There were only thirty-six *dahl'reisen*. This ambush was not meant to stop us, only slow us down." He held out a hand. "Give me more *chemar*."

This time, Dur didn't hesitate before handing over another ten stones. Azurel dumped them on the ground. A chime later, another flock of deadwood birds winged skyward, *chemar* clutched in their talons.

Tears blinded Ellysetta, but she ran without slowing.

The ones who'd gone to hold back the Mharog were dead. She'd felt each one of them as they perished, Varian the last. They'd died not in fear, but in joy.

She'd felt that, too.

Rain ran close at her side. His soul sang to hers with love and pride, and he wrapped her in supporting weaves, feeding her his strength as they ran.

The bloodsworn *dahl'reisen* had slain scores of Eld soldiers, more than a dozen of the Mages, and even one Mharog. Still, she wept. They had been strangers to her until today, yet each had willingly died to prevent her from falling into Mage hands. She wept because somewhere—either in this world or the next—there were mothers and fathers and sisters and brothers who had loved them. She wept because those men had not died as strangers but as her friends. In giving her blessing and accepting their oaths in return, she had taken a little bit of each warrior into herself, and it lived there still. It always would.

The *dahl'reisen* around her sang a warrior's lament on weaves of Spirit.

She answered with her own, an elegy Celierian women sang when their men returned from war not in glory but in caskets. She wept as she sang. It was a song meant for weeping.

«Enough, shei'tani,» Rain said, when the last note died away. *«You will have us all on our knees if you do not stop.»*

Surprised by Rain's remark, she wiped her eyes and turned to find tears streaming down his own face. The *dahl'reisen* ringed closest around them were white-faced, their eyes dark with the torment of tears they could not shed.

«You wove your sorrow as you sang.»

«Sieks'ta.»

«Nei, do not apologize. It is good to mourn them. They died with honor, as Fey should die.»

«I would mourn them even if they did not.»

«Aiyah, but it is better that they are deserving of your tears. And it will ease their families' sorrow to know they died with honor. If we survive this war and are allowed to return to the Fading Lands, I will accompany you to visit the families of the ones who died today.»

She nodded. *«Do you think Varian and the others bought us enough time?»*

Rain met her gaze, his eyes bleak. He shook his head.

Celieria ~ Dahl'reisen Village
8th day of Seledos

Outside the bedroom window of the *dahl'reisen* house perched high in the treetops, the skies over the Verlaine had lightened with the first blush of the coming dawn.

Sheyl smoothed a damp cloth over Carina's forehead, brushing back tangles of sweat-darkened hair and weaving what relief she could to ease the woman's pain. She'd tried for bells yesterday to keep the child from coming, but the birth would not be stopped. Sheyl wasn't sure she was a powerful enough healer to keep either mother or child alive—the child was coming months too soon, and the labor was not an easy one. Throughout the night, she'd spun healing weaves on the child in the womb, hoping to mature its lungs and heart enough that it could breathe on its own after birth. Sheyl knew her own death would come today, but she hoped to spare Carina and her child.

"Arin . . ." Carina whimpered, calling once more for the dead father of her child. "I want Arin . . ."

"I know, dearling. I know. Shh. Save your strength for yourself and your baby. That's what he would want." She moved down to the foot of the bed to check the baby's progress. "The child is coming. I can see the baby's head. Push now, Carina."

The woman's teeth clenched, a strangled cry rising in her throat as she strained to push the child from her womb. A few chimes later, Carina's son greeted the world with his first, weak squall. Sheyl handed the child into his mother's arms then swiftly went to work delivering the afterbirth and spinning a healing weave to seal off ruptured blood vessels that threatened to hemorrhage Carina's life away.

The door to the chamber opened. One of the warriors who'd stayed behind to guard Sheyl and Carina poked his head in. "The Eld are here. We've got to go."

"She still too weak. She'll die if we move her."

"She'll die if we don't." He pushed into the room and bent to scoop Carina up from the blood-soaked sheets. "I'll carry her. You run. Now."

The barked command left Sheyl little desire to argue. She ran.

Outside the bedroom, away from the privacy weave the *dahl'reisen* had spun to silence Carina's labor cries, the cacophony of war was deafening. Mage Fire had shattered the village shields and now bombarded the village without pause. Felled trees toppled like slain giants, crashing down upon one another. Fire burned all around, its orange flames devouring the autumn bracken on the forest floor, licking hungrily at the trunks of trees, climbing the vine ladders and hanging stairs with ferocious speed.

This was her vision—the death and destruction she'd seen. The world seemed to slow as she turned her head to the left, looking for the death strike she knew was coming. She saw the Mage archers break through the thicket wall, arrows nocked, bowstrings taut. She saw the gloved fingers release, and the black, barbed arrows fly like deadly, soaring birds. One of the *dahl'reisen* shouted and spun a fiery wind to intercept the arrows' flight, but he was too late.

The arrow slammed into her breast with enough force

to propel her backward. She lay on the ground, staring up, breathless and dazed, as the top of a nearby tree crashed down upon her.

The Fading Lands ~ Dharsa

"Why did Kieran and Kiel have to leave again? I'm worried, Lorelle. I've got a bad feeling. Like maybe we'll never see them again."

Lillis frowned as she rolled the small jingle ball across the beautifully woven carpet in the center of the even-more-beautiful bedroom she and Lorelle had been assigned in the Fey palace. The twin golden bells tied to the pretty white stone at the center of the mesh ball chimed merrily as the ball rolled. The same man who had given Lillis and Lorelle their kittens had also given them the jingle balls. Though most had been crushed by their fall on the mountain, this one had miraculously survived.

Snowfoot, her kitten, pounced on the ball and batted it between his small paws with pure, kittenish delight, and while normally that would make Lillis laugh and want to cuddle her adorable pet, at the moment she barely even noticed the kitten's antics. Her mind was somewhere else. Somewhere troubling.

Lorelle scowled. "Honestly, Lillis, what's wrong with you? We're here in a beautiful, Fey-tale palace, in a beautiful, Fey-tale room. Papa's here, and happier than I've seen him in ages—did you see that workshop Lord Dax had set up for him? When this war is over, Ellie and Rain and Kieran and Kiel and Bel and everybody are going to come home, and we'll all be happier than ever."

"I'm just worried, that's all."

Lorelle jumped up. "Well, don't be! Kiel and Kieran are going to be fine. They are!" She stamped a foot for emphasis. She stalked over to the arched doorway leading to the balcony outside their room and stood beside the sheer drape billowing gently in the breeze. Her arms crossed over her thin chest. "We're all going to be fine," she insisted again, as if to convince herself as much as Lillis.

A knock on the door made them both turn.

"Come in," Lillis called.

The crystal doorknob turned, and the door pushed inward. A beautiful Fey lady—was there any other kind?—stood on the threshold. She had lovely long, black hair hanging in ringlets down her back, and the prettiest eyes Lillis had ever seen, deep blue-green and as bright as gems. She looked like she'd stepped from the pages of a Fey tale, clad in a gown of flowing green fabric embroidered with tiny golden leaves, flowers, and birds.

"Hello," Lillis greeted. "Who are you?"

"My name is Tealah. I was—am—a friend of your sister, the Feyreisa."

With a spurt of sudden eagerness, Lillis clambered to her feet. "You know Ellie?"

"Ellie." For a moment Tealah looked confused. "Ah, you mean Ellysetta Feyreisa. *Aiyah.* We spent many bells together when she was here. I am the Keeper of the Hall of Scrolls, and she liked to read very much." Slender black brows arched in inquiry. "Do you girls like to read, too?"

"I do." Lillis cast a despairing glance over her shoulder at her twin. "Lorelle prefers to play Pirates and Damsels."

"That's not true." Lorelle uncrossed her arms to put her hands on her hips. "I like to read. I just don't like to read all those mushy lovey-lovey stories you like."

"She likes reading about sword fights," Lillis said with a sigh. "And about all the battles in the Mage Wars. As long as there's blood and violence, and someone dies, she's happy."

"I see." With a smile that suddenly looked a little nervous, Tealah said, "Well, I thought perhaps you might like to spend some time with me today at the Hall of Scrolls. I'm sure we can find something to . . . ah . . . entertain both of you."

Lillis snatched up Snowfoot, and a flailing paw sent the jingle-ball rolling. "Can we bring our kittens?"

Tealah looked from Lillis to Lorelle, who had bent to pick

up Pounce. The twins both smiled as sweet and innocent as young Lightmaidens and made their eyes very large and pleading.

"I . . . I suppose so." Tealah nodded. "*Aiyah,* why not?"

Twin smiles beamed bright as the Great Sun. Clutching their kittens to their chests, the girls skipped out of their bedroom, out of the palace, and down the hillside as Tealah led the way to the Hall of Scrolls.

In their bedroom, the small jingle ball with its white stone came to rest out of sight beneath a large chest of drawers.

Celieria ~ Verlaine Forest

"We're surrounded." Farel delivered the news without a hint of emotion. They'd been on the run all night and into the morning. Several more Walls of Steel had stood—and perished—but the Mages and Mharog kept coming.

Rain's arms tightened around Ellysetta. She'd sensed the opening of the Well half a bell ago, and Farel's scouts had traced the sickly sweet odor of Azrahn back to four portals ringing their current position. "So we make our stand here," Rain said.

"*Nei.* We're only thirty miles from the forest's edge. The reinforcements I sent for are attempting to flank the Eld blocking our path. Our best hope is to push forward." His fingers closed around the hilts of his *meicha* in a tight grip. "*Sieks'ta.* I thought traveling through the Verlaine was the safest route, but it seems I've only endangered your lives by slowing our escape."

"You owe us no apology," Ellysetta said. "If not for you, we'd already either be dead or prisoners of the High Mage."

"I spoke with the reinforcements I sent to the village. The Eld beat them there by half a bell, but the Brotherhood was able to rout them. The Mharog and a dozen Mages escaped—I expect they'll join the others here shortly—but the rest perished. The *dahl'reisen* have already Fired the village and gone to escort the women and children safely to the Garreval."

Something about Farel's expression made her stomach clench with dread. "But everyone got out safely before the Eld arrived . . . didn't they?"

"Almost everyone. A woman and her newborn son perished, along with ten of the *dahl'reisen* who stayed behind to protect her while she gave birth. Sheyl was wounded."

"Is she going to be all right?"

"*Aiyah*. The warriors found her unconscious and trapped beneath a fallen tree, but once they were able to free her and revive her, she was able to heal herself. She's running with them now to catch the others up."

Ellysetta watched him closely. "You don't look happy at the news."

"I'm happy she's alive—especially as that gives me the chance to wring her neck when I see her again." His lips compressed in a thin line, and a hint of anger lit his eyes. "She admitted to me she'd seen her death. The night you came to our village, she told me she'd had a vision of me escorting you both out of the Verlaine, but that was a lie. The only vision she saw was of her own death, and she sent me away with you because she didn't want me to die trying to protect her from a death she knew couldn't be stopped."

"But she's alive," Ellysetta pointed out. "So clearly her vision was wrong."

"Her visions are never wrong. She was supposed to die, just as she saw." Farel straightened and met her gaze full on. "But you changed that. You gave her a gift—a *sorreisu'kiyr* pendant. It stopped the arrow meant for her heart. You changed her fate, Feyreisa. You saved her life, in a way no one but the gods could have done, and for that I owe you a debt I can never repay."

"I will not hear any more talk of debts owed," Ellysetta said. "You saved our lives. Any possible debt has already been paid in kind."

"Nei, we rescued you from Eld for Gaelen, for all the times he sacrificed for us. My debt to you still stands." He shifted his gaze to Rain. "I have spoken with the *dahl'reisen* and told them how your mate saved Sheyl. Many of them have been thinking about Varian and the others. About how like Fey they looked when they left. They died with joy—and with more honor than a *dahl'reisen* has a right to expect."

"They died with the honor of a *lu'tan,*" Rain corrected. "No matter what Dark choices they may have made in the past, today they chose *sheisan'dahlein.*"

Farel's fingers plucked one of his Fey'cha from its sheath, and he bent his head to polish a nonexistent spot on the gleaming steel. "We are also prepared to die for the Feyreisa today, but we want . . ." He broke off, cleared his throat, and rephrased. "That is to say, my brothers and I would humbly ask . . ."

Rain cut him off. "You wish to bloodswear yourselves to Ellysetta."

The *dahl'reisen* leader looked up, making a visible effort to meet and hold Rain's gaze. "I know that you have no reason to offer us a salvation we do not deserve . . . and in all honesty, I must tell you we intend to weave Azrahn in her defense."

"Aiyah."

Farel continued in a rush. "Six-fold weaves are much more effective than five, and we could do more to defend her with them if we were free to weave Azrahn without fear of Mage Marks."

"Aiyah."

"Bloodsworn to a *shei'dalin* as bright as the Feyreisa, we might even—" Farel broke off, blinking in shock at Rain's swift, unequivocal assent. *"Aiyah?* You mean . . . you agree?"

"Aiyah." Rain covered Ellysetta's hand with his and threaded his fingers through hers. "I agree it is the best solution."

"I—" Farel's mouth opened and closed. "Just like that?"

Rain gave a weary smile. "Just like that."

The last few bells, with the torment of the *dahl'reisen* and the foul presence of the Mharog beating at Ellysetta, forcing her to divert more of her energy to shield herself, he'd begun to feel the effects of the bond madness more strongly. His thoughts were becoming cloudy and confused. Rage simmered just below the paper-thin surface of his control, and he knew that open battle with Mages and Mharog would quickly shred what semblance of sanity he still retained. When that happened, Ellysetta would need as many protectors as she could get—including ones willing and able to slay him.

Even if he did survive this battle, he had no illusions about surviving the war. Without him, all hope of erasing Ellysetta's Mage Marks through *shei'tanitsa* would be lost, and the Massan would never let her return to the Fading Lands. These *dahl'reisen,* so unafraid of spinning Azrahn, were no strangers to protecting those Marked by the Mages. Perhaps, after his death, they would be able to find a way to free her of her Marks as he had not.

It was a risk. A scorching triple tairen-sized risk. If Ellysetta did fall to the Dark, a bloodsworn army of *dahl'reisen* would make her even more dangerous. But, then, Hawksheart had already said if Ellysetta fell to the Dark, all Light in the world would fall with her. Whether she went with the *dahl'reisen* at her side or without them, the end result would be the same.

"Gather your men. She will not bless them—I don't think either of us could survive her blessing four hundred *dahl'reisen*—but they can swear their bonds, and I will stand witness."

"I—" Farel closed his gaping mouth and snapped into a deep bow. "*Beylah vo, Feyreisen.* For my men and I, I thank you." Farel started to leave, then turned back. "I almost forgot. Sheyl gave me a message for you, Feyreisa. She had another vision while she lay trapped beneath that tree. A vision about you. She said to tell you that when all seems lost, let love, not fear, be your guide."

Ellysetta looked surprised. "Hawksheart said almost the exact same thing to me when we were leaving Navahele."

"I would say it was coincidence," Rain answered, frowning, "but when it comes to Elves and their portents, there's no such thing."

"At least the message sounds more hopeful than ominous," Farel said. "I hope it serves you well." And with that, he gave a final bow and strode away to gather his men.

The bloodswearing went quickly. With the enemy approaching, there was no time for pomp or ceremony. The *dahl'reisen* knelt in groups, and in unison each group of warriors swore on their life's blood and black Fey'cha steel to protect and defend Ellysetta Feyreisa in this life and the death that followed. Farel was among the last to pledge his bond.

When they were done, the pile of steel at Ellysetta's feet was too large to even contemplate weaving into her leathers. Instead, *dahl'reisen* Earth masters gathered and spun her leathers and bloodsworn blades into a gleaming, more feminine steel replica of Rain's golden armor, complete with its own full complement of blades and a scarlet-plumed helm.

The *dahl'reisen* formed a circular Wall of Steel twelve *dahl'reisen* deep around Rain and Ellysetta. Earth magic pulsed with sudden energy, and black leathers flashed to vivid scarlet, emblazoned with a golden tairen rampant with green eyes. The shout rang up from hundreds of *dahl'reisen* throats, a joyful, defiant cry: *"Miora felah ti'Feyreisa!"*

And they began to sing.

CHAPTER FIFTEEN

What will emerge from this paused emptiness?
What emotions will spark? Which hopes ignite
And burst like fire weaves from nothingness
A fierce blooming in the desperate night.
Quick bursting light, souls reaching in the dark
Where love can take form, unfurl wings, be born
And burn like the stars, silver, spare and stark
Or fail to fly, crash, lie bloody and torn

Lie broken, forlorn, or take wing, fly free
Explode in to life, with Tairen roar
Rending the air. Rending her. Rending me.
To leave us gasping, stunned, searching for more
Forged, anvilled, hammered, tempered, together,
True mated. Loved. Forever. Forever.

   Shei'tanitsa Sonnet, by Ellysetta Feyreisa

Two bells and twenty hard-won miles later, the *dahl'reisen* were no longer singing. The grim battle for survival left little breath for anything beyond shallow gasps to fill straining lungs as magic and blades filled the air, and the forest Verlaine ripped apart at its roots.

The Wall of Steel had lost many of its men, and the Brotherhood used the bodies of the fallen as cover for the living. The *dahl'reisen* forming the Wall rotated continuously. Every few chimes, the outer layer of warriors moved back to the center of the ring to rest while the next row of brothers took their places on the outer line. As *dahl'reisen* died, the ring wall shrank in upon itself, always keeping twelve warriors deep.

At the center of the Wall of Steel, protected by a dome formed from multiple dense, impenetrable thirty-six-fold weaves, Ellysetta healed what wounds she could with each rotation of the Wall. At her side, Rain performed all tasks that required laying hands on the *dahl'reisen*—digging shrapnel from wounds, setting bones, holding flesh together—leaving Ellysetta to spin her healing weaves. The pain of so many *dahl'reisen,* crowded so close, coupled with the bludgeoning evil of the Mharog, had long since overloaded Ellysetta's senses. She was operating now in a numb fog. Healing whatever wound the *dahl'reisen* put before her, moving when they told her to move, collapsing to her knees when they told her to stop.

Mage Fire pounded the dome with relentless fury until the sky overhead was a blue-white storm, but still—miraculously—those shields held.

Eld ~ Boura Fell

"Orest is taken, Most High. The generals await your command." Primage Vargus bowed low.

Vadim barely heard him. His attention was focused intently on the glowing map of Celieria where the myriad tiny white lights indicating clusters of *chemar* shone moved through the Verlaine Forest. He zoomed in, tracing the progress of Dur and the Mharog as they pursued the Tairen Soul and his mate. Regrettably, the attack on the *dahl'reisen* village had been routed several bells ago.

"Master Maur?" Vargus prompted.

The High Mage held up a hand for silence as he scrolled

the view north, illuminating the bright collection of light now sparkling in the Celierian city of Orest, and farther north to Crystal Lake and the abandoned Fey city of Dunelan, where a few bright dots were slowly making their way around the lake. Finally, he scrolled the map west, across the dark, unlit countryside of northern Fading Lands, the Feyls, and the southern reaches of the Pale, where another four pinpoints of light had nearly reached the thinnest stretch of the Feyls due north of Dharsa.

Everything would soon be in place. He waved, and the glowing tracker map winked out.

"Tell them to secure the city and prepare for the next phase of our attack."

Celieria ~ Verlaine Forest

"Enough with this . . . siege," Azurel hissed to the Primage Dur. "We're no closer to capturing the Tairen Soul's mate than we were two bells ago. Time for new tactics."

Dur scowled. "And just what do you propose? We've tried everything we can to get through those shields. Nothing has worked!"

"There is a saying in the Fading Lands . . . sometimes it's better to send a mouse than a tairen."

Dur rolled his eyes. "In plain Elden, if you please."

"We don't need to get through their shields. Only this does." He held up a *sel'dor*-tipped arrow that he'd modified to hold a *chemar* in its shaft. "Surely we can weaken their shields enough to get a single arrow through."

Dur arched a brow. "How good is your aim?"

Within a few chimes, the Primages ramped up their bombardment of the Fey shields, pummeling them mercilessly, while six of the Mages combined their powers and focused a bombardment of highly concentrated Mage Fire on a single handspan of the Fey shield.

It took a while, but the small area thinned. And when it did, Azurel and his companions let fly.

One of the arrows broke upon the already-regenerating shields, but two of the *sel'dor*-tipped missiles sliced through, into the center of the protective dome.

Ellysetta's legs went weak as the all-too-familiar sensation of ice spiders shuddered up her spine.

"Rain!" she cried, falling to one knee. "Portal!"

Rain spun, red Fey'cha in his hands. His eyes flamed tairen-bright, pupils disappearing as his beast rose in response to the threat to his mate. Three Mharog leapt out of the portal and dove towards Rain.

"Fey! Ti'Feyreisa! Ti'Feyreisen!"

In desperation, Ellysetta tore one of the bloodsworn blades from her belts, slicing her palm deep. Blood welled in a swift, scarlet flow, and she smeared it over the shining surface of her bloodsworn-steel-forged armor to summon her *lu'tan*.

"Kem'lu'tan! Ku'vallar! Ku'vallar!" Help me!

A second portal opened behind her. She only had the briefest warning before an icy hand closed around her wrist.

"Neiiii!" The shriek of terror and denial ripped from her throat as a Mharog's black blade with its red Fey'cha hilt slammed into the side of Rain's neck.

Rain's vision clouded, and his red Fey'cha fell from abruptly nerveless fingers as the combination of tairen venom and the corruption of the Mharog's poison blade spread through him. His legs folded, and he dropped heavily to his knees. One hand reached for the hilt of the blade protruding from his neck, then fell away as he toppled to the ground.

He lay on his side, struggling for breath and watching helplessly as Ellysetta shrieked in a Primage's grip and fought his efforts to drag her into the Well. Rough hands grabbed him by the neck and clawed fingers closed around his jaw, squeezing hard. The foul decay of a rotting soul poured into Rain's mind. Festering memories of a once bright Fey life, destroyed by the deliberate betrayal of an unfeeling commander. Destroyed by *him*—by Rain.

"She will die in torment, Tairen Soul," an icy voice hissed. "Think of that as you burn forever in the Seventh Hell, and know that Maron vel Dunne has had his vengeance."

Rain looked into the hate-maddened eyes of the Mharog without the slightest flicker of recognition. His mouth formed the soundless question.

Who?

The Mharog's face contorted and he gave a high-pitched shriek. Dark steel flashed as he yanked his *meicha* from its sheath and held it over Rain's head like an executioner's axe.

Before the blade could descend, a Fey warrior surrounded entirely by a glow of golden light reached Ellysetta's side. He slashed at the Mage with blades that gleamed like sunlight. The Primage staggered back away from Ellysetta, a look of shock on his face, bloody stumps where his hands had been and a ribbon of red slashed across his throat. Demons howled out of the Well, surrounding the Mage in a cyclone of shrieking shadow.

Freed, Ellysetta lunged, Fey'cha drawn, towards the Mharog standing over Rain.

Nei . . . nei, shei'tani. Do not! Rain tried to shout the warning, but none of the muscles in his throat were working. He couldn't speak.

Sensing Ellysetta's presence, the Mharog turned, swift as a snake, but too late to save himself. Her blade plunged into the Mharog's heart just as another blade, this one blazing like the sun, took off the creature's head. The Mharog's decapitated body remained standing for several, long moments, showering Ellysetta and Rain with a fountain of icy black blood. Then the legs collapsed, and the body toppled to the ground. Ellysetta crumpled, too.

She was screaming as if her body were burning from the inside out, as if her skin was being ripped from her bones.

The other two Mharog gave shocked grunts and crumpled to the ground. Someone knelt over Rain, bathing him in warm, golden light. A hand turned him on his side, reaching for the pouch at the back of his hip belt where he kept the

cloth-wrapped Shadar horn gifted to him by Galad Hawksheart.

"You must live, Feyreisen," a voice commanded.

As Rain's vision dimmed, and his breath strangled in his
throat, he wanted to tell them not to bother. Ellysetta's face
was frozen in a rictus of pain, her eyes as dark as dead stars.
The sight shattered his heart, leaving hope a dead thing in
his breast.

Shei'tani . . . shei'tani . . . nei . . .

Death wasn't peaceful.

It was full of shouts and clanging steel, the roars of tairen,
and searing heat like the fire of the gods . . . images flashing
for barest instants before his eyes, lights, shadows, familiar
faces, a whirl of trees and stars overhead . . . smells, like the
aroma of a campfire burning in a chilly winter night and the
odor of something noxious that made him gag and retch.

Hands held him down. Pinned him as he fought and Raged
against them. He shouted obscenities, epithets, cursed them
and their offspring to eternity burning in the Seventh Hell.

Then silence fell over him like a heavy blanket, and death
became a still, black sea into which he sank with an exhausted sigh.

Celieria City ~ The Royal Palace

As he had every night since receiving news of Prince
Dorian's demise, Kolis Manza slipped into the king's bedchamber by way of the servant stairs that opened to the
king's dressing room.

Master Maur was growing impatient to have Celieria
firmly under Mage control. He'd sent a special envoy with an
offer to end all hostilities if Annoura agreed to terminate the
Fey-Celierian alliance and send what was left of her armies
against the *dahl'reisen*, who had been hiding in the Verlaine Forest and using it as a base to attack Eld and murder
Celierians along the border who opposed them. Despite a

firm push or two from Kolis, Annoura had as yet refused to agree, and it now fell to Kolis to ensure she woke in a more malleable frame of mind.

He stood in the darkened dressing chamber until he heard Annoura settle into bed, then waited for her breathing to assume the steady rhythm of sleep before he slipped into the room and padded silently across the floor to her side.

He blew a puff of *somulus* powder in her face even though he doubted it was necessary. Annoura wanted to believe. She wanted to think Dorian had really returned to her, that it was truly he holding her in his arms each night, making love to her.

He began to spin the Spirit weave of Dorian, returning to his love, but as he reached for the tie of her nightgown and sent the first, faint pulse of masked Azrahn into her body, he froze. His nostrils flared, and in a sudden motion, he snatched the wavy-edged *sel'dor* dagger from the sheath at his waist and plunged it into Annoura's chest.

The queen's expression didn't change, and her breathing continued uninterrupted. But the area of her chest around Kolis's dagger spat small showers of lavender sparks.

"I told you a Spirit weave wouldn't fool him for long."

The voice came from an empty part of the room. Kolis leapt to his feet, Mage Fire blooming in his hands just as five-fold weaves and several red Fey'cha flew from the empty room around him. His Mage Fire dissolved, and he staggered as the blades sank into his chest.

Five Fey and a mortal materialized inside the room.

"You!" he exclaimed, staring in disbelief at the mortal's face. "But you're . . ." His words slurred as the tairen venom raced through his body. His eyes rolled back and his body collapsed.

Prince Dorian—the new King Dorian XI—eyed the twitching corpse coldly. "Dead?" he finished. "So they tell me." He flicked a glance at the Fey. "Get this piece of *krekk* out of my palace."

Leaving the Fey to dispose of the body, Dorian exited

his father's bedchamber and strode down the hallway to a warded room where Gaspare Fellows and the *dahl'reisen* sent by Dorian's father were watching over his unconscious mother, the queen.

The *dahl'reisen* looked up when he entered. The spiral of shadowy Azrahn in his palm winked out, and he nodded. "It worked, Your Majesty. The Marks are gone."

Dorian closed his eyes and bowed his head in weary relief and murmured a brief prayer of thanks that at least he'd been able to save one person he loved. He sat on the edge of the bed beside his mother and took her hand as the *dahl'reisen* removed the weave keeping her unconscious.

His mother's lashes fluttered, then slowly lifted. Her delicate silver brows drew together in hazy confusion when she saw him. "Dori?"

Tears sprang to his eyes. "Yes." He pressed a kiss to her hand. "It's me."

"You're alive!" She sat up, flinging her arms around him. "Thank the gods. They said your ship went down."

"It did, Mama. The Danae saved me. The Tairen Soul's trip to Elvia brought us the allies we needed to defeat the enemy at Great Bay."

"Oh, Dori!" Abruptly, tears filled Annoura's eyes, and her features twisted with a mix of elation and grief. "Dori . . . oh, Dori, he's gone. He's gone."

"I know, Mama." Dorian put his face against his mother's neck as he hadn't done since childhood. They both wept, mourning the loss of the husband and father who'd been the center of their lives.

Eld ~ Boura Fell
9th day of Seledos

Damn them! Damn them! Damn them for their incompetence!

Vadim Maur snatched the silverglass mirror off his bedchamber wall and smashed it against the stone. It exploded with a satisfying crash, sending shards and splinters of glass flying in all directions. He grabbed the carved chaise in the corner of the room and slammed it into the wall until it broke into kindling. The small private desk and chair suffered a similar fate a few chimes later.

Vadim stood in the center of the wreckage, panting with exertion and trembling with rage.

Did he have to do everything by himself?

Kolis Manza was dead. Prince Dorian—the new king—was not. Annoura and the unborn child who were to have been Vadim's power in Celieria were lost to him. And working in league with the *dahl'reisen*, the new King Dorian had instantly begun a purge of not only his court but the entire city. Centuries of planning and careful cultivation were unraveling with increasing speed.

And to top it all off, Ellysetta Baristani had escaped capture. Again.

Of all the bitter disappointments—of all the gross ineptitudes—that was the worst.

His Mages had failed him. All of them. Nour had failed. Manza had failed. Keldo had failed. Dur and the Mharog had failed. Every Primage and Sulimage he'd entrusted to bring his great plan to fruition had failed.

"Damn them!" If they weren't already dead, he'd kill them himself for their bungling.

Throughout history, High Mages of Eld had held their Dark throne through a combination of strength, cunning, and ruthlessness. But no amount of cunning or strength could disguise the string of failures that had dogged his footsteps from the moment he'd fixed his eye upon Ellysetta Baristani. Or keep the whispers already circulating in the Mage Halls from gaining strength and credence. Primages who had been waiting for him to falter would seize upon the survival of Prince Dorian, the loss of Celieria's throne, and not one but two failed attempts to capture the Tairen Soul and his mate as proof that Vadim Maur no longer enjoyed Seledorn's Dark favor.

He needed a decisive victory—fast. And this time he had no intention of sending a lesser Mage to bungle the job. He would oversee the next stage of this battle himself.

Vadim released the privacy wards sealing his room and summoned a trusted *umagi* to clean up the mess while he returned to the war room. Vargus and the other Primages were still there, several of them talking in quiet whispers. They fell silent when he entered. Vargus watched him with trepidation, the others with carefully constructed blankness.

"Vargus, pack your bags. You and I will be heading to Boura Dor tomorrow to oversee the next phase of our attack from there. And Garok?" Vadim turned to the Primage he suspected of leading the rumblings against him in the Mage Council. "You, Fursk, and Mahl are coming too." He named the other two Primages who were most loyal to Garok. "I have an important job in need of your great talents."

To his credit, Primage Garok's expression never changed. "Of course, Most High." He executed a smooth bow. "It is our honor to serve."

Vadim hid his satisfaction behind a cold mask. When he achieved his great victory, he would be on hand to take the credit. His greatest detractors, unfortunately, would either perish as heroes supporting their Mage or die as incompetent fools, depending on the outcome of their battles.

When cunning and strength were not enough for a High Mage to hold his throne, it was time for ruthlessness. In particular, the swift and decisive elimination of all who opposed him.

Celieria City ~ The Royal Palace

Annoura, Dowager Queen of Celieria, sat alone on a stone bench in the private palace garden that had been Dorian's favorite. Winter had come, and the trees had all lost their leaves weeks ago. It seemed fitting, somehow, to be here now, alone in a barren winter garden.

A sealed letter lay in her lap. Her name was written on the front in a familiar script. Dorian had sent the letter to Dori, in Great Bay, before his death. The ink was a bit smudged from seawater. When Dori's ship went down, the letter was tucked in an oilskin pouch strapped to his waist. Her son had come very close to dying. If not for the Danae water spirits who had rescued him from his sinking ship, he would have drowned at the bottom of Great Bay.

The Danae had saved him, and he had returned to Celieria City with Gaspare Fellows, a *dahl'reisen* from Cannevar Barrial's land, and the Fey, to save her. After all she'd done, after all her hatred and accusations, the Fey and a *dahl'reisen* had still come to save her. That was a humbling realization. But not nearly so humbling as the realization that her Favorite, Ser Vale, had been a Mage, one who'd nearly claimed her soul.

She had harbored, in her innermost circle, an Elden Mage who had planned the execution of her entire family in order to claim her soul and rule Celieria through her and the royal son she carried in her womb.

She ran the pads of her fingers across the folded parchment of Dorian's last letter to her. She was afraid to crack the seal, afraid what harsh truths might lie inside, but eventually, she mustered the courage. The blue wax broke in two. She unfolded the parchment and began to read.

My Dearest Annoura,

I hope this letter finds you well. The battle has not yet begun. We wait in growing tension and dread, which I suspect is the enemy's intent. But the waiting is a boon as well, for it has left me with much time to think.

There is a saying here along the borders: A man never sees more clearly than when he looks death in the eye. As I sit here in this cold, dark castle, on yet another cold, dark night, waiting for war, I know it is true, for I see more clearly than I have in a long time.

I have thought a great deal about the difficulties that have beset our kingdom, and this war that has sprung upon us with so little warning. I have my suspicions, which I have written in a letter to our son and asked him to share with you. I will not dwell on those suspicions here. This is not a communication from a king to his queen, but a letter from a man to his wife.

When a Fey warrior meets the woman who completes him, his soul's truemate, he knows in an instant. And in that instant, whether she will have him or no, he binds himself to her, heart and soul with the words "Ver reisa ku'chae. Kem surah, shei'tani," which means "Your soul calls out. Mine answers, beloved." And he spends the days of their courtship—the rest of his life, if necessary—proving himself worthy of the magnificent gift of her love.

I know how those Fey feel, my darling. That was how I felt the first moment I met you. How I still feel, today.

I pray the gods will see me safely through the coming war, but should I perish, I do not want my last words to you to be those bitter sounds we exchanged at the North Gate. I would, instead, leave you with the truth I discovered that day in Capellas so many years ago. The truth that even now gives me courage to face whatever comes. That truth is this . . .

I love you, Annoura. I will love you forever, my good and valiant queen, my beloved wife, my soul's eternal and truest mate. Ver reisa ku'chae. Kem surah, shei'tani.

> *Yours eternally,*
> *Dorian*

The parchment fluttered to the dead winter grass. Dorian's wife pulled her knees up close to her chest like a child, covered her face with her hands, and let the harsh, broken sobs of loss and despair shake through her body.

Celieria ~ Edge of Verlaine Forest
9th day of Seledos

Rain woke to find himself lying on a cot beneath the fabric dome of a tent whose walls billowed gently in the winter wind. His head was on fire. Every muscle and bone in his body ached. He lifted his left arm and frowned at the sight of the spiraling Shadar horn strapped to his forearm, its pointed tip buried in the vein at his elbow.

What the flames? He reached for the ties cinching the horn to his arm.

"Don't touch that." The familiar voice rang with cool command.

Rain turned his head to frown at the white-haired Sheyl, who was standing beside a table on the far side of the tent.

"It's the only thing holding you to sanity."

He blinked at her in confusion. "What do you mean? And what are you doing here?"

"I am here because Farel called me when you were struck by a Mharog blade. We used the Shadar horn to draw the poison from your blood, but when we tried to remove the horn, you nearly killed the *dahl'reisen* helping me tend you. Farel says the bond madness is upon you—and that it hasn't just begun."

His mind was still so fuzzy, her words only half registered. "It began over a month ago. Not long after the first battle for Orest." He put a hand to his head and massaged the ache at his temples. "Ellysetta has been helping me keep my barriers strong."

Ellysetta.

He sat up so quickly his head spun. *«Shei'tani!»* He sent the call along their bond threads, but received no answer. She was still alive—he wouldn't be if she weren't—but something was preventing him from reaching her. His imagination flooded with all number of horrifying possibilities.

"Where is Ellysetta? What happened to her?"

Sheyl regarded him with a mix of compassion and regret. "She slew the Mharog. But in doing so, she took his poison—his Darkness—into herself and nearly extinguished her Light in the process. We had you together at first, but even unconscious, she kept trying to weave all her strength to you. We had to separate you in order to keep her alive."

Rain flung the coverlet aside and swung his legs over the edge of the cot. "I must go to her."

Sheyl started towards him. "Wait. You're still not in any shape to—"

His head snapped around, and he shot her a glare so fierce she clamped her mouth shut and didn't say another word as he pushed himself to his feet.

As he rose, the bulky horn knocked against his body, shifting in its straps, and the tip started to pull out of his arm. Instantly, voices in his head began to scream and the heat of unfettered Rage rose so fast he thought the top of his head would explode. He shoved the horn back deep into his arm and drew a shuddering breath when the madness faded.

"Let me do that." Sheyl crossed the remaining distance between them and strapped the Shadar horn securely back in place. "There's no need to rush to her side. The *shei'dalins* are with her. They've been working through the night to hold her to the Light."

His head reared back. "*Shei'dalins?* There are *shei'dalins* here—near the *dahl'reisen*?"

"They came through the Garreval with warriors of the Fey. But do not fear. Once the Fey drew near, Farel and the *dahl'reisen* headed north to set up a separate camp to avoid causing trouble. They shielded their camp, and so far, the *shei'dalins* have shown no sign of sensing their presence."

"Help me get dressed, then take me to Ellysetta."

Sheyl sighed but acceded to his demands. Since there was no possibility of fitting his war armor over the Shadar horn, she helped him into a pair of black leather breeches and pulled a soft, loose-fitting, linen tunic over his head.

When she was done, Sheyl walked to the entrance of the tent and held the flaps open. "Come on, then. I'll take you to your mate." Her lips twisted in wry grimace. "Now that I think about it, you'll probably do more with one touch to bring her back to us than a full day of *shei'dalin* healing has managed."

Outside, a small city of tents had sprung up in what appeared to be a large clearing in the Verlaine Forest. The ground and the perimeter of the trees were black with char. A light drizzle fell from a dark, overcast sky, and the smell of scorched wood and earth hung heavy in the damp air. Skinned deer and small game were roasting over campfires.

"How long was I out?" Rain asked as they walked.

"All night and most of the day."

A loud, roar rumbled across the sky, and Rain looked up. "The tairen are here?"

"Three of them," Sheyl confirmed. "They came with the Fey from Kreppes and burned a path through the forest to reach you. Farel says they arrived only a chime or two after you fell. They burned out the rest of the Eld. No one wanted to risk moving you or the Feyreisa, so the *dahl'reisen* and your Fey just set up camp around you."

His Fey. He could just imagine how well things must have gone when Bel, Tajik, and Gil set eyes on a small army of *dahl'reisen*. Clearly, the Brotherhood's service to Ellysetta had prevented—or at least delayed—the usual lethal vengeance Fey law demanded for any *dahl'reisen* who came within a mile of a *shei'dalin*, but Rain wasn't looking forward to the justifiable tongue-lashing he was sure Bel, Tajik, and the others had in store for him, especially when they found out he'd let the *dahl'reisen* bloodswear themselves to Ellysetta.

The hearth witch led him through a maze of Fey tents to the far side of the encampment.

"She is there." Sheyl pointed.

Even without the glow of powerful shields around it, a single glance would have told him which tent held Ellysetta, because stretched out on her belly, wings tucked against her sides, Steli-*chakai* had her whole body curled around the tent like a mother tairen protecting her nest of unhatched kits. Her tail had completed the circle around the tent, and the tip of it rose and fell in a rhythmic motion near Steli's shoulder.

"I will take my leave of you here," Sheyl said. "There are *dahl'reisen* in need of healing and I promised Farel I would come as soon as you woke. When your mate is recovered, Farel would like you to meet with him at the *dahl'reisen* camp. There are others who wish to serve, if you will allow it."

The driving need to reach Ellysetta pounded at him like hammers, but Rain paused long enough to nod his assent. "I will meet with him, and thank you both for all that you have done to help us. Ellysetta and I are in your debt."

"You offered sanctuary to our families. All debts are already paid in full." Sheyl laid a hand on his arm. "Go to your mate. May the gods hold you both to the Light."

"*Beylah vo*," Rain said, and bolted for the tent without a single backward glance.

The great white tairen had ripped the stakes from the ground on one side of the tent and poked her head beneath the heavy fabric walls to keep a concerned maternal eye on Ellysetta. A mournful, crooning tairen song hummed in her throat.

As Rain neared, Steli's crooning stopped, and her tail stilled. The white tairen withdrew her head from beneath the tent flap and great blue, pupilless eyes turned upon him, whirling with distress.

«Ellysetta-kitling does not wake. Steli sings, but she does not hear.»

Rain laid a hand on the tairen's furred cheek. *«I will sing, too, Steli-chakai. Perhaps, between the two of us, we can rouse her.»*

The white tairen rumbled her assent and lifted her head so Rain could enter.

Inside the tent, six *shei'dalins* and the five warriors of Ellysetta's primary quintet stood huddled around a table in the center of the space. They parted as Rain approached, revealing Ellysetta's motionless form.

The sight of her stopped him in his tracks. He'd never seen her so close to death. Her natural, Fey luminescence had drained away, leaving her skin a pallid gray-white. Against it, her wealth of flame-colored curls seemed lurid, almost garishly bright. Dark rings shadowed the skin beneath her eyes, and her lips had taken on a bloodless blue tinge.

"Shei'tani," he whispered, and he moved without conscious thought, crossing the remaining distance between them to take her hand in his. Her fingers lay cold and limp in his palm. He pressed them to his face, his lips, as if mere contact and desperate love could breathe warmth back into her flesh. On the threads of their bond, sent with a warming wave of his own essence, he called, *«Ke sha taris, Ellysetta. Ke sha eva vo.»* I am here. I am with you.

Ellysetta gave no response.

He glanced up at the *shei'dalins* and Fey crowded around. "She is alive." He said it almost as a challenge, as if daring them to contradict him.

"Barely, I'm afraid. And only because we will not let her go." The *shei'dalin* closest to him threw back her veil.

Rain found himself staring into the sympathetic face of Jisera v'En Arran, the dainty but indomitable truemate of the Massan's Air master, Eimar v'En Arran. "Jisera *falla*, you should not be here," he chided. "What is your *shei'tan* thinking?"

Jisera arched a slender blue-black brow. "What every right-minded Fey in the Fading Lands should be thinking, *kem'Feyreisen*. That if we lose this war, there's no hope for any of us. So it's best to go out fighting for what we know is right." Her dark brown eyes were usually soft as a doe's, but at the moment, they glittered like polished stones. As tiny and slight as she was, and despite her deeply empathic nature, like that of all the strongest *shei'dalins*, Jisera v'En Arran had a spine of steel.

As quickly as possible, she caught him up. "More *shei'dalins* will be coming—they stayed behind to see those villagers you sent to the Garreval safely through the Mists. Those children . . . so many children. . . ." Her throat moved on a convulsive swallow. "Some of them looked Fey. There was a little girl . . ." Her eyes grew moist, and she blinked rapidly. "I commanded the warriors at Chatok and Chakai to let them through and told them if Tenn objected he could just come to Orest and discuss it."

Rain bowed his head, humbled by her bravery and unswerving support. "*Beylah vo, kem'falla*, and thank you for everything you've done for my *shei'tani*."

"*Aiyah*, well, don't thank me for that until she comes back to us."

The mere suggestion of any other outcome sparked an instant, involuntary swell of fear and Rage. The Shadar horn went hot against his arm, and as the horn released is potent Elvish magic, he could swear he felt Ellysetta's fingers twitch in his palm.

"Call to her, Rain," Jisera urged. "You share the strongest bond. Perhaps she will respond better to you than she has to the rest of us."

Rain nodded and leaned closer to Ellysetta. Closing his eyes, he began to call to her along the threads of their bond. Behind him, her head once more poking in under the side of the tent, her blue eyes whirling and glowing like stars, Steli added her voice to his.

Three bells later, Rain's hope was beginning to falter. In addition to the calls of a *shei'tan* to his mate, the calls of Ellysetta's *lu'tah*, and the calls of the *shei'dalin*, he and Steli had tried every tairen song they could think of. Rain's song. Steli's song. Pride song, kin song, mate song, mother song. Nothing had worked. Nothing had roused even the slightest response.

"Do not lose hope," Jisera said. "The Feyreisa is stronger than any *shei'dalin* I've ever known. To kill a Mharog." She shook her head. The top layer of her hair was plaited in a net of tiny black braids, joined together with tiny gold and crystal beads that shimmered in the candlelight. "No other *shei'dalin* could have survived it."

"She is a Tairen Soul," Rain said, his eyes closed, his head resting on Ellysetta's hip.

"With a heart as bright and as strong as the sun," Tajik added in low voice. "In that respect, she is much like my—" His voice broke off abruptly, and Rain opened his eyes in time to see him glance at Gil, who casually shifted to take the heel of his boot off Tajik's toe.

The seven of them—Ellysetta, Rain, and all five warriors of her primary quintet—had sworn a Fey oath to Galad Hawksheart not to reveal the truths they'd discovered in Elvia. And though they would each willingly have foresworn their oaths and broken their honor in order to rally the Fey and rescue Shan and Elfeya, the urgency of this war had stopped them. Hawksheart's secret remained unspoken, and their Fey oaths remained intact.

"Like your what, Tajik?" Jisera asked.

Tajik cast a defiant glower at Gil and completed his remark, "Like my sister. The Feyreisa's courage and strength remind me of my sister, Elfeya."

Rain saw Gil's tense shoulder relax. Tajik both told the truth and yet honored his oath to Hawksheart. Fey loved passionately, and mourned deeply, even centuries after the loss of a loved one, so Jisera would not think it odd in the least that Tajik's sister remained in his thoughts.

She reached out to grasp Tajik's hand. Golden light glowed about their clasped hands and her eyes took on an amber glow as she wove peace on Tajik. "I never knew Elfeya-*falla*, but if she was anything like the Feyreisa, then she was very special indeed."

More special than Jisera knew. More special than any of them had suspected before Hawksheart's revelations.

Rain wondered bitterly what Tenn v'En Eilan, the leader of the Massan, would do when he found out that Ellysetta, the woman Tenn had reviled and cast out of the protection of the Fading Lands, was the daughter of the greatest warrior and most renowned *shei'dalin* born in the last fifty thousand years—perhaps longer. Rain's Rage flared at the memory of Tenn's betrayal and the way he'd intentionally laid a trap to catch Ellysetta weaving Azrahn so he could banish her. He'd known about her Mage Marks, known what terrible danger she'd be in outside the safety of the Faering Mists. And still, Tenn had done it.

The Shadar horn burned as it drained the heat from Rain's veins and dulled the sharp edge of his Rage.

In his hand, Ellysetta's fingers twitched again.

Rain stared at the slender fingers with sudden suspicion. Her hand was motionless once more, but he had not imagined the small flinch.

"The Shadar horn consumed the poison of the Mharog blade that struck me, correct?" he asked.

"*Aiyah*," Jisera confirmed. "So the hearth witch, Sheyl, informed me."

"Then is it not possible the horn's magic could cure what ails Ellysetta as well?"

Jisera frowned at him. It didn't take a Spirit weave to know what he was thinking—or to see how those thoughts alarmed her. "The horn is the only thing keeping you from madness."

"So cut it in half. Use half for me, half for Ellysetta."

"We don't know that half a horn is any use at all."

"We don't know that it isn't," he countered. "Hawksheart gave the Shadar horn to me for a reason. I doubt that reason was so I could live to go mad when Ellysetta dies. If Ellysetta doesn't recover, I'm dead anyway. This, at least, gives us a chance."

Jisera crossed her arms. Slight and sweet though she appeared, she was also stubborn as a rock. And she'd never been one to take unnecessary risks—especially when it came to the safety of the lives in her care. "It's too dangerous, Rain."

He sighed and ran his good hand through his hair. "Jisera, war is here, and I'm the Tairen Soul. If I don't fight, the Eld will win. I can't fight with this strapped to my arm." Rain gestured to the bulky horn strapped to his arm. "And I can't fight with my mate hovering on the cusp of death. You're going to have to graft the Shadar horn to my bones anyways. So why not start by grafting just half and giving the rest to Ellysetta?"

"Even if we tried that, there's no guarantee the horn will help her."

"It better, because we've tried everything else."

Jisera set her jaw. Then after a look at the other *shei'dalins*—and, Rain suspected, a private word with them—Eimar's mate gave a curt nod. "*Bas'ka.* We'll need a table. And you'll need to agree to be strapped down and rendered unconscious. I don't want you Raging on us while we're trying to do this."

"Agreed," Rain accepted. He signaled to Ellysetta's quintet. Rijonn wove a second table, complete with metal restraining straps. When he was done, Rain got on, lay down, and let Bel and the others strap him in. "*Beylah vo,*" he said as Jisera and the *shei'dalins* gathered around him.

"Don't thank me unless this works." Her eyes turned amber and began to glow.

Ellysetta lay trapped in a sea of black ice. She couldn't move, couldn't feel, couldn't speak, and yet every part of her being was writhing in agony, burning from a fire she could not quench, screaming until her throat was raw and her ears were ringing.

Rain was dead. She'd seen the red Fey'cha pierce his throat. She'd plunged her own blade into the rotting heart of the Mharog in wild fury. Only she hadn't died as she'd expected. Instead, the undiluted evil of the Mharog had seized her and pumped its foul corruption into her soul. The howling torment of every life destroyed by the Mharog bombarded her senses, as did the Mharog's fiendish pleasure each time he'd drained a soul of its Light.

Hatred, malevolence, the unquenchable lust for pain and destruction: the Dark emotions feasted on her Light. They ate away at her *shei'dalin* mercy, her compassion and gentleness, her hope, dissolving layer after layer of civility and restraint until they reached the dangerous, equally Dark monster that lived at the core of Ellysetta's soul.

And when the foul malignancy of the Mharog touched that, the beast roared to life. A vast, Raging Darkness that dwarfed the Mharog's by magnitudes. *Her* Darkness. Every bit as powerful and potently evil as her Light was good.

In terror, she'd done the only thing she could. She raised barriers around her mind and fortified them with a containing weave that mimicked the binding spell Galad Hawksheart had once used on her. The weave used the beast's magic against it, so that the more it Raged, the stronger its bonds became.

And there Ellysetta lay in torment, locked inside her mind with the horror that lived in her soul.

Ellysetta. A voice called her name—Rain's voice, infused with the vibrant notes of tairen song. The sound sliced through the deafening roars of the beast and her own endless screams.

In the icy darkness of her self-imposed prison, the notes of his song didn't just glimmer—they blazed bright as the Great Sun.

Come back to me, shei'tani.

Shei'tani. Her battered mind latched onto the word like a talisman. *Rain? Is that you?* Hesitant, afraid this might be some trick of the Mharog, she reached for his Light . . . then wept as it enveloped her in fierce, familiar flows of heat and strength.

Ke sha taris, kem'reisa. Ke sha eva vo.

His Light burned through the layers of dark ice and fanned the dim, nearly extinguished flickers of her own Light back to fiery brightness. With a roar of cold rage, the beast retreated into his lair, and the powerful weaves of her self-imposed prison faded.

Ellysetta's eyes opened, and Rain was there, his face pale, his expression taut with worry, but whole and unharmed. *Alive.* Before she could even open her mouth to speak, he dragged her into his arms, kissed her soundly, then clutched her so tightly to his chest she could hardly move.

"*Beylah sallan*," he whispered against her skin. "I thought I'd lost you when you stabbed that Mharog, *shei'tani*. Don't ever scare me like that again." Fine tremors shivered through his entire body and the hands stroking her hair were trembling.

"I thought *I'd* lost *you*," she told him in a broken voice.

"You nearly did."

"I don't understand." She squirmed in his arms, needing to see his face, touch him to ensure he was real. "You died. I saw that Mharog kill you. He drove his red Fey'cha into your throat." For a moment she wondered if she'd dreamed that, but when she reached up to touch the spot where the Mharog blade had pierced his throat, she discovered that Rain's previously unblemished Fey skin now bore a faint, vertical scar, proof of his near-death encounter with the Mharog. "How is this possible?"

"*Aiyah*, well . . ." Rain grimaced. "Much as I hate to admit it, I'm in Hawksheart's debt. That Shadar horn he gave me saved my life—and yours."

Ellysetta pressed her lips against the faint scar and whispered a prayer of thanks. "Bright Lord bless him."

Someone cleared a throat. Ellysetta glanced around and

blushed to discover she and Rain were not alone. They were lying on a raised table in the center of a tent. Her quintet and six veiled *shei'dalins* were gathered around them. "My friends . . . thank you. Gaelen . . ." She reached for his hands. «*You and your dahl'reisen friends saved our lives, kem'maresk. There aren't words enough to thank you.*»

Another throat cleared—well, rumbled impatiently was more like it—and Ellysetta's attention shifted to the side of the tent, where one entire fabric wall had been ripped free of its mooring stakes. The unmoored side of the tent lay draped like a rumpled scarf across a very large white tairen head.

"Steli!" Ellysetta swung her legs over the edge of the table, ignoring the protesting voices that told her she was too weak and needed to rest. She *was* weak. Her knees started to give way as soon as she stood. But Rain was there to catch her, and with his arm around her waist to hold her steady, she crossed the floor to Steli. She leaned against the strong, furred jaw, closing her eyes against a sudden swell of tears.

"I am so glad to see you, my pride-mother," she whispered in a choked voice.

«*Steli's heart sings to see you safe, kitling. Steli was . . .*» Steli gave up Fey words for tairen speech with which she spun an image of a tairen mother, crying mournfully over the body of a listless kitling. «*Ellysetta-kitling must not give Steli such sadness again.*»

"I promise I will try not to."

Steli nudged Ellysetta back a step, gave her a maternal lick, then scolded, «*Ellysetta-kitling must not set fang or claw on Mharog. Mharog not good prey. Good only for burning.*»

She gave a rueful laugh. "I've learned my lesson, Steli-*chakai*. Believe me."

"All right, that's enough now," Jisera pronounced. "The Feyreisa and Feyreisen both just woke up. I need to do some tests before I can be sure everything went as well as planned. That means the rest of you need to clear off. Now, please."

The tiny Fey woman gave everyone, including Steli, a stern look. The quintet quickly decided they could guard Ellysetta from outside the tent as well as from within. Steli, however, lifted the edge of one lip and growled irritably.

«It's all right, Steli-chakai,» Ellysetta soothed. *«I'll be fine.»*

Steli sniffed and declared, *«Steli-chakai will go hunt. Bring back tasty meat for Ellysetta-kitling.»* With one more growling glare for Jisera, Steli yanked her head out of the tent and flounced off.

For the next full bell, Jisera ran both Rain and Ellysetta through a battery of tests, checking their physical recovery, their bodies' reactions to the Shadar horn, their ability to call and weave magic, Rain's ability to control his bond madness. By the time Jisera pronounced them well enough to leave *shei'dalin* care, night had fallen and the slivered crescents of Eloran's two moons were high in the sky.

Four of Ellysetta's quintet gathered round Ellysetta as she and Rain walked the now-barren campground. Gaelen, however, was nowhere to be seen.

«I'm here,» Gaelen announced on the quintet's private Spirit weave when Ellysetta asked where he was. *«Just invisible. None of the dahl'reisen know that Ellysetta restored my soul, and if they see me, the secret will be out.»*

«I thought you trusted your Brotherhood friends,» Bel said, frowning.

«I trusted them to save Rain and Ellysetta because I had no choice. But I wouldn't have turned to them at all if they'd known she could restore their souls.»

Rain started to remind Gaelen that Farel was bloodsworn and was therefore incapable of harming Ellysetta, but he swallowed the words before they left his mouth. He hadn't yet revealed that he'd let *dahl'reisen* swear their *lute'asheiva* bonds to his truemate.

"We received some good news from Dharsa."

Rain arched a brow. He couldn't think what it could be, unless Tenn v'En Eilan had suddenly come to his senses. "Let's hear it. I could use some good news."

"Kieran and Kiel are alive, as are the Feyreisa's family and two of the *shei'dalins* we feared lost at Teleon. Kieran and Kiel escorted them all safely to Dharsa before heading to Sohta and the Veil with Loris and another three thousand Fey."

Ellysetta stopped walking. "They're alive? They're safe? All of them?"

"*Aiyah*," Bel confirmed. "All of them. Lillis, Lorelle, and your father."

Her chin trembled. She turned quickly, pressing her face into Rain's throat and wrapping her arms around his waist.

He felt her whispering an inaudible prayer of thanks, and tightened his own arms around her waist before grinning at Bel. "That isn't just good news, *kem'maresk*. That's the best news we've had in months."

"I thought you would be pleased." Bel smiled fondly at Ellysetta. "We also received word from Celieria City. It seems Hawksheart kept his word to speak with the Danae and convince them to help us. Dorian's ship went down, but the Danae's *nyatheri*, the Water spirits, saved him from drowning and helped sink the enemy ships."

"That's something at least."

"Unfortunately, the news gets less pleasant after that. Prince Dorian—King Dorian—returned to Celieria City last night to catch a Mage in the act of Marking Queen Annoura."

Ellysetta lifted her head. Her fingers clenched around Rain's. "Is she all right?"

"She's safe and so is her baby. The Marks disappeared when the Mage was killed trying to escape."

"Who was it?" Rain asked.

"The Queen's Favorite, Ser Vale, but it seems he wasn't the only one. The old King Dorian apparently sent some of Lord Barrial's *dahl'reisen* down to Great Bay to help his son. And the new King Dorian ordered those *dahl'reisen* to check everyone in the palace. Dorian's Spirit master tells me they've already found at least fifty Mage-claimed among the courtiers and palace servants, and that doesn't include any of the Mage-claimed who lost their Marks when Vale died. Now the entire city is on lock-down. No one gets in or out until they've been checked for Mage Marks by Lord Barrial's *dahl'reisen*." Bel regarded his friend and king. "You were right, Rain. The entire city had been infiltrated, and gods only know how long it's been going on."

Rain nodded in weary acceptance. He should have been glad for both the vindication of his suspicions and the unmasking of Eld's servants in Celieria, but he wished he'd been wrong. Not for the sake of the greedy fools who sold their souls in exchange for wealth and power, but for the ones, like Ellysetta and her friend Selianne, who'd been Marked against their will.

"And Orest?" he asked. "What news from our friends there?"

"Not good."

Bel's expression went grim. "Orest fell last night. Lord Teleos was nearly slain, but the Fey got him through the Veil and to the *shei'dalins* in time for healing. The Fey managed to evacuate the upper city and part of Maiden's Gate, but the rest . . ." He shook his head. "All told, we lost at least two thousand Fey and another five thousand Celierians—along with two of the tairen."

"And the Eld?"

"Six of the dragons went down. We estimate we took out two companies of Elden soldiers and about two hundred Mages."

"Four thousand men and two hundred Mages. And we lost seven thousand?"

Bel nodded. "Polwyr and his men opened portals all over the city. The *fezaros* came riding through with that potion of theirs again, and the Fey were so busy fending off demons, Mages, and *darrokken* and evacuating everyone they could through the Veil, they didn't realize what was happening until it was too late."

Seven thousand lost. Seven *thousand*. When the allies didn't have two thousand to spare.

Farel's four hundred bloodsworn *dahl'reisen* had just become even more valuable to Rain than before. To him and the Fey.

He shared a troubled gaze with Ellysetta. He wasn't sure how well her quintet would take the news about the *dahl'reisen lu'tan*—especially Gil and Tajik. He didn't even want to think about the reaction of the other Fey. The ones who'd broken with Tenn and the Massan to support him might well reconsider their decision when they found out what he'd done.

«*You know we have to tell them about Farel and his men,*» Ellysetta said on a private weave.

«*I know, and we will,*» Rain replied. Just as soon as he could muster the courage to do so.

The conversation was not going to be a pleasant one.

"You let *dahl'reisen* bloodswear themselves to your *shei'tani*? Have you lost your mind?"

Rain and Ellysetta both winced at Eimar v'En Arran's outrage. He was taking the news much worse than Ellysetta's quintet had done earlier.

Once the *lu'tan* got past their initial shock, they had appreciated the benefit of ensuring that the *dahl'reisen* would not harm Ellysetta and could not fall farther into Shadow. Just to be sure, however, Rain had sent Gaelen and the rest of Ellysetta's primary quintet on ahead, to meet with Farel and determine if the *lute'ashieva* bonds would indeed hold strong against the temptation of a restored soul.

"The *dahl'reisen* saved our lives," Ellysetta told Eimar. "Many of them sacrificed themselves so Rain and I could escape the Eld. They aren't the honorless *rultsharts* you believe them to be."

"They walk the Shadowed Path!" Eimar exclaimed. "They chose it!"

"They didn't choose it!" Ellysetta retorted. "At least not the way you mean. They simply chose not to die. They suffered so much in defense of the Fading Lands, they lost the ability to feel anything but pain and anguish. And even then, they chose to stay alive, to suffer unimaginable torment so they could defend the very people who reviled them."

"Bah!" Eimar shook his head, making the crystal bells in his hair chime. "They had an honorable choice—*sheisan'dahlein*—and they did not take it."

"Rain and I had a choice as well—to weave Azrahn or let the tairen die. Did *we* choose wrong, too?"

The Air master scowled. "That was different."

"Not according to Tenn and the rest of the Massan," she reminded him.

"Those villagers you met on your way from the Garreval—those are the families of these *dahl'reisen*," Rain said. "Among them is a Celierian-born woman who truemated the son of a *dahl'reisen*. Truemated, Eimar. And they have children—including a daughter who possesses Fey gifts."

The first appearance of doubt eclipsed the outrage on Eimar's face. "That's impossible."

"So I always believed, but I was wrong. We Fey have clung to our honor, and our women are barren. These *dahl'reisen* have clung to their lives, despite their dishonor, and their women bear young—even young capable of truemating. We need to know why, Eimar."

"You don't need to let them bloodswear to the Feyreisa to figure that out."

"*Nei*, I don't," Rain agreed. "But we're also in a war, and we're short on blades. The *dahl'reisen* leader, Farel, has asked to meet with me and Ellysetta this afternoon. With the *shei'dalins* and the other Fey here, Farel and his men aren't sure how best to honor their *lute'asheiva* bonds. They will not come near the other *fellanas*, but they cannot go far from

Ellysetta. Farel also tells me there are other *dahl'reisen* who wish to bloodswear themselves to Ellysetta and fight openly for the Fading Lands once more."

Eimar spread his hands. "What do you want from me?"

"I sent Ellysetta's quintet on ahead to meet with Farel and observe the other *dahl'reisen* who wish to bloodswear to my mate. If, after their evaluation, her *chakor* has no objections, Ellysetta and I will travel to the *dahl'reisen* camp to accept the other bonds. I want you to come with us. I want you to see these *dahl'reisen* for yourself, then tell me whether or not you can fight alongside them."

Celieria ~ Dahl'reisen Camp

Stiff wariness infused the warriors of Ellysetta's primary quintet as six *dahl'reisen* stepped out of the forest and into the open fields of Celieria. Bel, Tajik, Rijonn, and Gil watched the scarred Fey with undisguised distrust, while the *dahl'reisen* returned their gazes with defiance mingled with faint hints of shame.

"Which one of you is Farel?" Bel asked.

"I am," said the *dahl'reisen* with dark brown hair and a scar that curved across his neck and up his cheek.

Gaelen had shown Bel an image of Farel before they left camp. The *dahl'reisen* who had stepped forward was indeed the one shown in Gaelen's weave. "I am Belliard vel Jelani, Chatokkai of the Fading Lands."

"I know who you are, Belliard vel Jelani."

Bel's brows arched. "We have met?"

"Nei. A friend showed me your image once."

"I didn't know *dahl'reisen* had friends," Gil said in a cold voice.

Farel gave a bark of humorless laughter. "And here I thought, as bloodsworn defenders of the Feyreisa, we might meet in peace."

"This *is* peace," Tajik said in a cold voice. "You're standing before us, and we're letting you live."

"A mercy most apprecia . . ." Farel's sardonic reply hung in midword as Gaelen released his invisibility weave and appeared at Bel's side. " . . . ted." The last syllable of the word dropped from Farel's mouth into a stunned silence. Farel swallowed. "General."

"I've asked you repeatedly to call me Gaelen."

Farel's face went blank as he looked at Gaelen surrounded by the other Fey. "You are . . . *with* them? But you are—" His voice broke off.

Bel saw the *dahl'reisen's* eyes narrow as he scanned Gaelen's face, then saw those same eyes go wide in sudden, shocked understanding.

"Your scar . . . it's gone!"

"Aiyah," Gaelen confirmed.

"And . . . the rest?"

"Gone as well. My sister Marissya says my soul is an unsullied as an infant's."

Farel's throat moved on another heavy swallow. "But how is such a thing possi—" He looked up, his eyes filled with certainty. "The Feyreisa."

"Aiyah," Gaelen answered. "Which is why, my friend, I must ask if there are any of you—either those who have already sworn their bonds, or those who wish to—who might break it if they discovered she can do this?" He pointed to his unscarred face.

With Steli and the other two tairen flying overhead, Rain, Ellysetta, Eimar, and the Fey *lu'tan* ran north along the edge of the Verlaine towards the *dahl'reisen* camp.

Bel and Gaelen had sent word of their findings earlier in the *dahl'reisen* camp. There had been a handful of questionable *dahl'reisen* among Farel's assemblage, but Gaelen assured Rain they had been dealt with. Rain didn't ask how, and Gaelen didn't volunteer any more information, except to say there was no chance they might harm Ellysetta or the Fey, now or in the future.

A mile before they reached the camp, Xisanna and Perhal

flew ahead to make certain all was well, while Steli landed and stalked protectively behind her adopted kitling, ready to scorch the first threat that reared its head.

Farel and Ellysetta's primary quintet were waiting to greet them at the curve of the last hill. The moment the Fey rounded the last hill and stepped foot on the field where the *dahl'reisen* had gathered, they froze in their tracks.

"I don't believe it," Eimar whispered.

"I had no idea there could be so many," Ellysetta breathed.

"Nor did I," Rain said in a hoarse voice. He swallowed to moisten his dry throat and gazed across the vale with stunned eyes. Stretched out before them, more than a mile in every direction, were row after row of tents. An entire army—a very, very *large* army—was camped at the edge of the Verlaine Forest.

Not just a few hundred. Not even the few thousand Rain had suspected there were.

Tens of thousands.

"So tell me, Farel," he rasped, "exactly how many blades do you count in the Brotherhood of Shadows?"

Beside him, Farel smiled. It was the first genuine smile Rain had ever seen on the *dahl'reisen's* face. The warrior cast a proud gaze over his assembled brothers. "*Dahl'reisen*? Thirty thousand. Sons of *dahl'reisen*? Another forty."

Rain almost choked on his own tongue. Gods save him. Seventy thousand.

Seventy thousand.

Twice the number of all the Fey still living.

Rain's stunned gaze traveled across the seemingly endless sea of warriors, the outcast sons of his homeland. And he saw the pride on their scarred faces, the renewed light of hope shining from eyes that had been dark with shadow for centuries.

"They all wish to serve the Fading Lands," Bel said. "All thirty thousand *dahl'reisen* have asked to bloodswear themselves to Ellysetta, and fight on her behalf to regain some part of their honor as you allowed Farel and his men to do. Their sons have offered their bonds as well."

"I will accept *dahl'reisen* bonds," Ellysetta said, "but not the bond of any Fey who still has a chance to find his true-mate."

"Some might argue that sons of *dahl'reisen* are not Fey, Ellysetta."

"They're Fey enough."

Bel smiled. "As I was saying, even the young ones are good fighters. The *dahl'reisen* have taught them well."

Eimar couldn't believe what he was hearing. "Bel? You truly approve of this? You trust these *dahl'reisen*?"

Bel shrugged. "Two nights ago, I would have called Rain a fool for allowing *dahl'reisen* to bloodswear to the Feyreisa. But today . . . well, today, he and the Feyreisa are alive because of them . . . and I"—he lifted his hands in a dazed gesture—"I learned that I have a nephew. My brother Ben, didn't die in the Wars as I thought. He joined the Brotherhood of Shadows and mated a Celierian woman. They had a son before he died fighting the Mages."

Bel turned his head towards the *dahl'reisen* horde, where a young, unscarred warrior stood talking with his brothers. As if sensing Bel's gaze, the warrior glanced up. Apart from a brief, darting glance from Rain to Bel and back, no expression crossed the young warrior's face, but he put a hand over his chest and bowed slightly in a Fey gesture of welcome and acknowledgment.

"His name is Beren." A faint, melancholy smile curved the corner of Bel's mouth. "He has Ben's eyes."

"Bel . . . *kem'jeto*." Rain was at a loss for words. He remembered Benevar vel Jelani, Bel's older brother, and how Bel had idolized him. The pain of his loss had honed Bel to a razor-sharp blade, and he'd become a deadly terror on the battlefields throughout the remaining months of the Mage Wars. "My sorrows for your brother, but *mioralas* for his son." Rain clapped a hand on Bel's shoulder. "With joy, I celebrate this new warrior of the Jelani line."

"*Beylah vo.*" A brief silence fell between them, then Bel admitted in a low voice, "You know, Rain, if I'd known Ben was still alive . . . I think perhaps I would have traded my own honor to be with him . . . to spend the years with him."

"Perhaps that's why he never let you know."

Bel, the most honorable Fey Rain knew, nodded sadly. "I wish he had though, Rain." He met his best friend's gaze. "I really wish he had."

Rain looked out across the seemingly endless sea of warriors, the outcast sons of his homeland. Many of them banished for weaving Azrahn—the same crime for which he and Ellysetta had been banished, a crime he was beginning to think wasn't half so evil as he'd been raised to believe. And instead of looking upon them with revulsion and dread—instead of seeing their scars and reviling them for their dishonor and the threat of Shadow that hovered over their bleak lives—he saw Fey. Warriors, brothers, friends. Fey whom someone like Bel had once known and loved.

And for the first time, he accepted the possibility that here, in the most unlikely place and from the most unlikely quarter, he had just found the allies he'd been looking for.

CHAPTER SIXTEEN

Celieria ~ Dahl'reisen Encampment

Ellysetta thought bloodswearing thirty thousand souls would have taken much longer than it did, but Farel and her quintet had already decided how to handle it. They divided the *dahl'reisen* into blocks of five hundred and each block swore their oaths simultaneously. Ellysetta's existing *lu'tan* stood amongst the groups to ensure that every *dahl'reisen* made a proper and complete oath.

What to do with the massive pile of thirty thousand bloodsworn Fey'cha became a subject of heated debate, but in the end, both Fey and *dahl'reisen lu'tan* agreed to weave a new suit of armor for Ellysetta, this time using only a small button of metal from each bloodsworn blade. The remaining, unused portions of the Fey'chas were buried in the Verlaine, under a thirty-six fold protective weave, to be retrieved and taken to a place of honor and safekeeping after the threat of war had passed.

To say that Ellysetta and her quintet were happy with the decision to bloodswear the *dahl'reisen* was stretching the truth, but as Tajik said with a sigh as they prepared to leave, "War is a strange thing, *kem'jitanessa*. I've seen bitter enemies fighting side by side, because they hate the thing they're fighting more than they hate each other. Sometimes, you have to take your allies where you find them and hope for the best."

She laid a hand on his arm. She knew how difficult it was for him to overcome a lifetime of revulsion for the warriors who walked the Shadowed Path, but he had not been among them. He had not spent time with them as she had, nor seen the love and vulnerability in their eyes when they were safe in the circle of their families, nor felt their shame at having fallen from the honorable path of the Fey warrior.

"They saved my life, *kem'melajeto*," she told him gently. "They saved Rain's life too." She looked at the assembly of *dahl'reisen*, the scarred faces filled with purpose and determination rather than shame, and at the larger gathering of their sons and grandsons, fine, fierce young warriors who'd never learned that they were suppose to revile the scarred, soul-shadowed Fey instead of love and honor them. "I think they may just save us all."

Watching her, Tajik shook his head, a peculiar half-smile on his face.

"What is it?" she asked.

"You just looked very Elvish just then. And very like your mother." He glanced back at the *dahl'reisen* camp. "I hope you're right, Ellysetta. I hope they do save us. But I'll settle for just knowing this wasn't the biggest mistake we've ever made."

Celieria ~ Allied Encampment by the Verlaine

With fifteen bells of hard travel lying between the Fey army and Orest, Rain and his generals had agreed to spend one final night camped beside the Verlaine and set out before sunrise.

As he and Ellysetta retired to their magic-warded tent for the night, Rain shed his steel and spun his war armor to the stand in the corner. His bones warmed as the Shadar horn added its power to his weave.

The tiny boost to the magic made Rain go still.

He closed his eyes, fingers curling in loose fists. Earlier this evening, he'd spun that same weave without the Shadar horn supplementing his control. His condition was deteriorating—and much more rapidly than he'd hoped. How long did he have? Days? Bells? Did he even want to know when there was nothing he could do about it?

He blew out the candle lamp. His elongated pupils reacted to the loss of light instantly, lengthening and widening, adapting like a cat's to the tent's dark interior. That much of him, at least, still worked as it should.

Naked, his skin glowing silver in the dark, he glided on silent feet towards the sleeping pallet. Ellysetta pulled back the coverlet and when he crawled in beside her and lay down, she scooted closer, snuggling against him and putting a hand over his heart. The instant her skin touched his, the tension in his body began to fade. Her love and concern washed over him, enveloping him in a haven of peace and comfort. With just her touch, she calmed the crying madness in his soul and filled the cold, empty places inside him with light and warmth.

His arms closed around her, holding her tight. "I was afraid I'd lost you," he confessed in a low voice. "When I saw you slay that Mharog." Even the memory of it made him shudder.

She pressed her face against his throat. "I thought I'd lost you, too. It didn't matter what happened to me then." Her voice became nearly inaudible as she added, "Or so I thought."

He brushed her soft, curling hair back off her forehead, stroking the smooth satiny skin. "What do you mean?"

Her teeth worried her lower lip in a moment of indecision. "I never really knew what true Darkness was until I stabbed that Mharog. As vile and depraved and malevolent as the Mage is, comparing him to the Mharog is like comparing a deep Shadow to a world utterly without the smallest glimmer of light. I've never felt anything so unrelentingly, consumingly evil."

She pulled back to look up at him, and her eyes were bleak with remembered horror. "I felt his soul, Rain—or rather the void that exists where his soul once did. It's a bottomless, Light-eating abyss. His only pleasure comes extinguishing the Light of others in the most brutal ways possible, because Light, in all its forms, has become anathema to him."

Skin to skin, he could feel her distress as if it were his own. She was genuinely terrified. "Put it from your mind, *shei'tani*."

"I can't, Rain. That's the problem." Her brows drew together. "For the first time, I truly understand what will happen if I fall to Darkness. I won't become the Mage. I'll become Mharog . . . and I'll consume every last spark of Light in this world. That's what Lord Galad was trying to tell us."

"Nei, shei'tani, you won't. I won't let that happen." He took her shoulders in a firm grip and stared into her eyes as if his own, fervent insistence had the power to convince her. "I promise you, so long as I live, I will not let you fall."

Her arms twined about his neck, and her slender body surged against his, seeking shelter. He knew she didn't believe him—if the gods willed she should fall, she would—but for both their sakes, she was as willing to pretend that hope was enough. That together, they could hold the Darkness at bay, no matter how powerful its call.

When the bright sweetness of her essence began flowing into him, he caught her hand in his. *"Nei,"* he said, though he savored the stirring pleasure of her selfless gift. "Keep your strength for yourself, *shei'tani*."

"But you are weary." She pressed kisses against his throat, and where her lips touched, more bright golden warmth flooded his skin.

"I will be fine."

"Aiyah, you will." She agreed in a throaty voice. Her lips curved against his neck. "I will see to it." Another heady rush of sweetness shot through his veins.

He should have refused her. She'd already given him more strength than she had to spare. But if tomorrow's dawn was to be their last together, he wanted sweet memories to take with him beyond the Veil.

His hands stroked the soft coils of her fiery hair then down her satiny skin to cup one small, perfect breast. *"Fellana,* I am yours. Do with me what you will." And he surrendered to her lips, her hands, her love, letting her pour herself into him as he poured himself into her. The richness of his tairen song rose in his throat and he sang the shining, wordless notes on weaves of Spirit, wrapping them in wild beauty as she wrapped them both in the vast, deep power of her love.

Later, much later, when she slept in boneless exhaustion by his side, he lay awake, staring at the ceiling of their tent as it rippled in the breeze off the mountains.

He'd never been a Fey who spent much time in prayer. Before the Wars, he'd never truly appreciated the many blessings of his life, and afterwards, he'd held a bitter grudge against the gods and their whims. But now, on the eve of a battle that, despite his encouraging words, promised almost certain death for them all, Rain closed his eyes and, before he let sleep claim him, sent up a simple, but fervent prayer.

Please, gods, grant me time enough to finish this. Time enough to make her safe.

Eld ~ Boura Dor

"Master Maur!" Primage Kron, commander of Boura Dor, rushed to greet the purple-robed High Mage of Eld. "Welcome to Boura Dor, Most High. It is an honor beyond measure to have you join us."

Vadim threw back his hood and cast a cold silver gaze around the central command room deep in the heart of the subterranean fortress.

"Yes, well, some tasks are too important to leave to underlings. Vargus," he turned to the elderly Primage who had accompanied him from Boura Fell. "Set up the tracker."

"Most High." Primage Vargus bowed and moved towards the central table to weave the spell that would allow the Mages to track and activate the *chemar*.

"Kron, has your team reached Crystal Lake?"

"A few bells ago, Most High. There were scouts in Dunelan, but the *dahl'reisen* helped us eliminate them. Quietly, of course, though I doubt it will be long before their brothers raise the alarm."

"Good. Order them to begin. And send reinforcements with bowcannon. Once the Fey realize what we've done, they'll send Earth and Water masters to repair the damage, possibly escorted by tairen. Then I'd appreciate the use of your spell room."

The Primage hesitated only a brief instant before he bent at the waist in a low bow. "Of course, Most High." He turned to one of his own Primages. "Ogran, send the command to our Mages at Crystal Lake. Tell them to begin, and to report back when it's done." Turning back to Vadim, Kron gestured towards the door. "If you will follow me, Most High, I will escort you personally to my spell room and release the wards so you may make use of it."

The Rhakis Mountains ~ Crystal Lake

Standing alone in the center of a clearing on the side of the mountain peak, a blue-robed Primage opened his Azrahn-blackened eyes. He turned and picked his way down a narrow, rocky mountain path, to the group of two hundred Sulimages waiting below.

"We have our orders. It's time to begin."

The red-robed journeyman Mages turned to face the soaring mountain that formed the western shore of Crystal Lake. Blue-white Mage Fire gathered in their palms. One after another, in a deliberate, rhythmic pattern, they began bombarding the mountainside. Rock and stone disappeared, eradicated from time and space by the fiery globes of Elden magic.

Beginning on the western slope of the mountain and working quickly towards the east, they carved a deep channel into the rock, creating a chasm where none had existed before.

As the Mage-made gorge neared the shores of Crystal Lake, and the remaining earth and stone holding back the lake grew thin, water began to seep out. The moisture increased to flowing rivulets, then spurting leaks as rock and stone shifted, then cracked beneath the strain.

A final blast of Mage Fire finished it off. Chill and crisp, the water of the high mountain lake burst through the compromised rock and gushed into the newly-formed gorge. White and foaming and moving rapidly, a new river rushed away towards the west, emptying Crystal Lake with impressive speed.

As the surface of the lake dropped, the flow of Sourcefed waterfalls that fed the Heras River slowed to a trickle. Within a bell, they had dried up altogether.

Eld ~ Boura Fell

When Melliandra learned that Vadim Maur had left Boura Fell to prosecute his war, she knew her time had come. She hurried down to the *umagi* dens to retrieve the length of knotted rope and the black canvas bag she'd stolen from the guard halls and hidden in a rock-covered cubby hole in the rat tunnels. She stripped off her ragged tunic and tied the canvas bag to her torso, securing it by winding the length of rope repeatedly around her body. Once that was done, she slipped the tunic back over her head and pocketed a small, sharpened knife and the ring of keys she'd painstakingly carved from discarded bits of metal.

Her heart was pounding in her chest as she slipped back into the *umagi* den and made her way up a series of stairways until she reached the corridor directly above the High Mage's private apartments. There, she made her way to the door to the refuse shaft and ducked into the closest abandoned room to unwind her rope and canvas bag. She tied a looped knot on one end of the rope, tightened it as best she could, slung the canvas bag over her back, the coiled rope over her arm, and cracked open the door to peer out into the hallway.

When the coast was clear, she darted out of the room, opened the refuse shaft door, and clambered inside. She hooked the looped end of her rope on the *sel'dor* stake she'd driven into the rock last week, then took a breath, grabbed the rope, and began lowering herself down the slimy, muck-coated walls of the refuse shaft. Her bare toes slipped on the ooze-covered rock. Only her tight grip on the knotted rope kept her from tumbling helplessly down the deep, dark shaft to the *darrokken* pit below.

Overhead, light streamed in as someone two floors above opened the doors covering the refuse shaft. Melliandra flattened herself against the wall just as a stream of garbage and the Dark Lord knew what else came raining down. A rotting lump of something landed on her shoulder, gagging her with its foul stench.

Her skin broke out in a clammy sweat. She turned her head abruptly as her stomach threatened to erupt and breathed rapidly through her mouth. Shadow take her! Whatever the putrid lump was, it *reeked!* Worse, she could feel the wriggle of maggots and rotworms moving inside the gelatinous blob.

She gave her shoulder a violent twitch and felt the lump dislodge and roll down her back. The refuse doors overhead closed again, and the shaft fell into darkness once more.

A soft, blindly seeking mouth nudged the skin near her ear.

With a choked cry, Melliandra lost her battle with her stomach and nearly lost her hold on the rope. Only quick thinking and desperation saved her. She twisted one arm and one leg around the rope and dangled there, retching helplessly while her free hand slapped at the tiny maggots and rotworms writhing in her hair.

So much for bravado. It seemed this *umagi* was little braver than any other squeamish squeal of a girl when it came to some things.

When her stomach had emptied and she was as sure as she could be that no other crawlies remained in her hair, she put both hands back on the rope and continued inching her way down the refuse shaft to the door that led to Vadim Maur's private incinerator and spell room.

Upon reaching the door, she muttered a brief curse. She'd been hoping the Mage would forget to ward the refuse-shaft door before he left, but no such luck. He might be inhabiting a less powerful body now, but Vadim Maur was too careful a Mage to leave even something as insignificant as a refuse chute unprotected against intrusion.

Ah, well. She'd hoped to be in a less precarious position for her first attempt to weave magic, but since when had the gods ever done her a kindness? If this was where she had to prove herself, so be it.

Carefully, using a combination of the detailed instructions Lord Death had so painstakingly planted in her mind and the sensations she'd gleaned from the High Mage's mind, she summoned her magic. She'd intended to call only the smallest tendril, but instead her power came in a rush, flooding her body with sudden, electric sensation. Cool and sweet, intensely pleasurable. She closed her eyes on a wave of euphoria so great she nearly lost her balance and toppled from the slippery ledge.

The wards around the refuse-shaft door lit up, bright as flame in the darkness. Startled both by the brightness and her own intense power, she released her magic and crouched there, trembling, waiting for any hint that Vadim Maur had detected her activity.

One long moment passed, then another and another. A full chime she waited, but nothing happened. She wasn't sure if Vadim Maur was still in the Well of Souls, if his distance from Boura Fell blinded him, or if her ability to hide her thoughts had become so strong she could now hide her magic as well, but whatever the reason, she couldn't sense him. The usual weight of his dark omniscience was absent. There was no prying invasion of her mind, no evil snap of his hated voice jabbing into her brain demanding to know what she was about. There was only silence and solitude, the comforting aloneness of her mind.

She drew a deep breath and tried to calm her racing heart. If the High Mage had not sensed that unchecked flare of power, she might just be able to pull this off, after all.

"You can do this, Melliandra. You *must* do this."

She fixed a picture of Shia in her mind, focused on the ice blue eyes, rimmed in dark cobalt. Shia's eyes stayed bright and steady as Shia's face faded, replaced by a younger, more masculine version of Shia. A child's face. A boy. Shia's son. Watching Melliandra with unblinking intensity. He was depending on her.

She summoned her magic once more.

This time, she braced herself for the rush of pleasure, clinging to her rope and panting as sensation crashed over her in waves. Was this what the Mages felt when they worked their spells? No wonder magic was everything to them!

The wards on the refuse door went bright again. She stared hard at the pattern, matching it thread by thread to the same one she'd seen through Vadim Maur's eyes the last time he'd released the ward on the refuse shaft door. Nothing had changed, thank the Dark Lord.

Whispering, "You'd better not have betrayed me, Fey," she closed her eyes and released the first of the weaves Lord Death had planted inside her mind. Magic swelled. Swallowing her fear and distrust, she surrendered control of her body—and her magic—to the Fey's implanted instruction.

Her eyes flew open. She watched with intense concentration as the magic inside her rose, shaped itself, merged with the glowing threads of the ward and began to unravel it. She examined every sensation in minutest detail, every muscle that tensed, every nerve that tingled, every thought and breath and tiniest movement. And she painstakingly filed those observations away in the secret compartment in her mind so that she could take them out later for study.

Once she escaped Boura Fell, there would be no Lord Death to teach her magic; so until that day of freedom dawned, she was determined to learn all she could from every possible source, Mage or Fey. Shia's son possessed powerful magic, and she would not let him face the world as defenseless as she had been all her life.

At last, the threads of the ward fell apart and disintegrated. She reached into her pocket for the dull knife she'd stolen from the kitchen. With a little maneuvering, she slipped it through the tiny crack between door and stone wall and released the latch.

The hallway leading to Vadim Maur's spell room was pitch-black, but as Melliandra set her feet (carefully wiped clean of the muck from the refuse-pit walls) upon the stone floor and took her first step, the hall sconces sparked to life. She gasped and leapt back into the opening to the refuse shaft, fearing discovery, only to frown as the sconces dimmed almost instantly.

She waited a few moments, then cautiously lowered herself back into the hall. The sconces relit. She jumped again, instinctively, but soon realized the lights must be spelled to activate based on motion in the tiny space. She took a few cautious steps, ears straining for possible signs of discovery. When none came, relief loosened the tension in her shoulders, and she began to move with more confidence, examining her surroundings with swift, searching eyes.

A curling stair led up into the darkness of Vadim Maur's personal chambers. Using the directions she'd gathered from eavesdropping in Vadim Maur's mind, she made her way to the warded treasure rooms where he kept his most valuable magical implements. The next of Lord Death's unwarding weaves opened the treasure-room door, and chamber's ceiling sconces lit up as Melliandra slipped inside.

The walls were covered from floor to ceiling with shelves and drawers, all filled to the brim. Chests and cases were piled high against the far wall and stacked around and beneath a table in the center of the room. Her mind boggled at the sight of so many weapons, jewels, books and scrolls, cauldrons, chalices, and crystal flagons filled with who knew what.

Melliandra took another breath and stepped forward. Time to get to work.

Eld ~ Boura Dor

Vadim Maur stood in the doorway of Primage Kron's personal spell room and looked around in approval at the small, tidy space. The spotless mosaic tiles lining the floor, ceiling, and walls gleamed in the candlelight. A beaten copper basin rested on the central spell altar, and fresh water poured into a small stone basin against one wall. The distinctive, cleansing scents of lemonroot and shadowsage perfumed the air of the closed space. Like all serious students of magic, Kron took extraordinary care in tending to his spell room.

"This will do," Vadim said. He glanced at the Primage. "Leave me."

Kron bowed and backed out of the room. "If you require anything at all, the bell outside the spell room will summon my most trusted *umagi*."

Vadim waited for the spell-room door to close before he allowed the sneer to lift the corner of his lip. As if the High Mage of Eld would ever be foolish enough to use an *umagi* loyal to another Mage to assist him with a spell. Kron knew that of course, which meant the offer had been more courtesy than genuine.

Vadim picked up the copper basin, filled it with fresh water from the wall fountain, then reached into his robe pocket to retrieve a small, chilled vial of blood. He shook the vial vigorously before uncapping it and pouring half the contents into the basin.

As the blood mingled with the water, Vadim thrust his hands, each finger covered with rings of power, into the mixture. His eyes closed and he invoked his seeking spell to amplify the power of his call. In his old body, he could have reached his target without aid, but he hadn't been in this body long enough to know the full extent of its capabilities and its limitations. He had no intention of spending a critical bell or two trying to locate his distant contact only to discover he couldn't manage it without an amplifying spell.

The power of the spell enveloped him, and he focused his mind into a single, sharp arrow of concentration. The rest of the world fell away. His consciousness shot up on waves of Azrahn, spiraling up through the spell room's exhaust pipe into the world above, then racing west towards the Lysande Ocean.

Eld ~ Boura Fell

Locating Lord Death's things was simpler than Melliandra had expected. Between the blood call she'd gleaned from the High Mage and the weave Lord Shan provided, she could feel the presence of his belongings tugging at her, as if they were lodestones and she were steel. Accessing them, however, proved more difficult than she'd hoped.

She'd known the High Mage warded his greatest treasures with multiple wards. What she hadn't anticipated was that no two objects in his treasure room could be accessed exactly the same way. Each chest, each case, had its own special combination of warding spells, several layers deep.

It took her a full bell of painstakingly trying to piece together the proper combination of unraveling weaves before she managed to open the large trunk containing Lord Death's blades and leather weapons belts. She stuffed the blades and harnesses in her canvas bag, along with two daggers the length of her forearm for herself—after all, who knew what dangers lurked in the world above?

When it came to unlocking the case containing what she hoped was Lord Death's crystal, however, she ran into trouble. The first six wards she managed to identify from her memories and unravel using Lord Death's Spirit-weave commands. The seventh set her back on her heels. She'd never seen this particular pattern before. And that meant, Lord Death had given her no spell to unweave it.

"Dark Lord take it!" she hissed. The High Mage must have changed the final ward before leaving Boura Fell. The threads before her were more complex, more tightly woven, than any she'd encountered yet. She had no idea where to even begin taking this one apart, and, according to Lord Death, one wrong move would kill her.

These wards are deadly. If you unweave them incorrectly, the magic will turn upon you and you'll die an agonizing death.

Melliandra glared at the glowing threads of confounding

magic. She hadn't come this far to fail. Without that crystal, Lord Death said he couldn't defeat the High Mage. She wasn't entirely sure she believed him, but she couldn't take the risk.

She needed that crystal *now*.

If she left without it, there was no guarantee she'd ever have a second chance to get it. Worse, the Mage Halls were rife with rumors about the new fortress being constructed above ground and the speculation that the High Mage intended to make that his new palace. If he moved, he would no doubt also move his most prized prisoners and the most promising offspring of his breeding program as well. Both Lord Death and Shia's son would be taken away to a place she could not go.

She would lose everything. Her chance to kill the Mage. Her chance to save Shia's son. Her one chance at freedom.

Melliandra gripped the table so hard her knuckles turned white. No. No, she would not fail. She would get Lord Death's crystal, or she would die trying.

All wards can be undone. All it takes is patience, magic, and enough time to map out the solution and implement it.

Lord Shan's words echoed in her mind as she cleared a spot on the table, sat down, and began to examine the seventh and final deadly ward keeping her from the key to her freedom. She'd paid very close attention as Lord Death's Spirit weaves had guided her through the releasing of all the previous wards. She'd especially noted how her body felt as the Spirit weave commanded her to summon and wield her magic. If she could figure out this pattern, she might—just might—be able to unravel this one on her own.

The Pale ~ North Slopes of the Feyls

Pale, thin, windburned, three of the soldiers of Eld who had set out last autumn on a mission assigned by the High Mage of Eld trudged through the deep snow blanketing the northern slopes of the volcanic Feyls mountains. Only three of the original party of twenty remained. Four had been buried under an avalanche of snow only a few days past. One had fallen while climbing a cliff face. Two more had fallen ill and been left behind. Three had been separated from the rest and died in a snowstorm. The rest had died in a series of unfortunate accidents. Neither the frozen ice wastes of the Pale nor the northern slopes of the Feyls were hospitable to outsiders.

But three had nearly reached their destination, and for what Master Maur required, even one survivor was enough.

The three stood halfway up the mountain at the base of the shifting, iridescent radiance of the Faering Mists. Snow covered the ground, and their breath made clouds of mist that coated their bearded faces with fine layers of ice crystals.

One of the three knelt to build and light a fire in a small, rocky hollow that offered at least some protection from the wind howling through the tall peaks. As he did so, a dark, pervasive consciousness pressed down upon him. His muscles froze. His lungs contracted, forcing him to breathe in short pants.

The paralysis lasted for only a moment, but that was long enough for his mind to be ripped open and thoroughly plundered. His head lifted of its own volition, turned slowly to scan his surroundings. He caught sight of his two companions and realized the same commanding power had gripped them.

«Your location will do. Set the chemar in a secure place where the portal can open without interference. The first Mages will arrive in four bells.»

The crouching Elden soldier acknowledged the order. *«Understood, Master Maur. It will be as you command.»*

Eld ~ Boura Fell

The air in the treasure room had grown stifling. Sweat trickled down the sides of Melliandra's face as with painstaking care, she slipped that last threads of the seventh magic ward free.

Relief overwhelmed her, and she buried her face in her hands. Shaky breaths shuddered in and out of her lungs as a series of fine tremors shuddered through the muscles she'd kept locked into place for who knew how many bells while she unraveled the weave.

When her body stopped shaking and her racing heart slowed back to a normal beat, she reached for the brass latch on the case. Half expecting poison darts to shoot out the moment she pressed the release catch, she moved to one side and held her breath again until the catch popped open with nothing more dire than a *snick* of sound.

The case opened, revealing drawer after velvet-lined drawer of jewels. Rings. Pendants. Jewelled cuffs and armbands. Torques and ropes of shining crystals.

She had no concept of riches. No *umagi* born and raised in a Boura did. But the gleam and sparkle of the chest's contents dazzled her eyes, and the hum of power that rose up from the jewels roused a spark of avarice in her heart. These glittering baubles were, if not the source of Vadim Maur's power, at least the tools he used to amplify it. Her fingers itched to gather them up, to take them all with her. Surely something so powerful would come in handy one day.

She reached for a large, faceted blue crystal that she could almost swear was calling her name, but before she could touch the glittering gem, the memory of Lord Death's stern lecture sounded in her mind. *You do not know what you will find in this room. There will be objects of great power, including many objects of terrible Darkness, things that can consume the souls of the unwary. Touch nothing except what you know belongs to me.*

She'd already broken her word by taking the two daggers for herself. But those blades had not vibrated with magical energy as these jewels did. They had not called to her in seductive voices, begging her to take them.

Her hands curled into fists, tucking her wayward fingers tight against her palms.

Get the crystal you came for, Melliandra, then close the chest, she told herself sternly. *Quickly before you do something stupid.*

The scold helped. She tried her best to ignore the call of the blue crystal while she peered through the drawers, looking for the stone Lord Death had drawn in her mind. She found it and many more like it in the third drawer. Dark red cabochon crystals, most gleaming with rainbowed lights.

To verify which stone belonged to Lord Death, she invoked a final Spirit weave, one that filled the air with a song of intense, exotic beauty. One of the largest of the crystals in the drawer suddenly flared with a whirling burst of brightness deep in its center. That was it. That was the one she'd come for.

She snatched Lord Death's crystal from the velvet, then shoved the all the drawers back into place and slammed the chest doors closed. She didn't even breathe until the latch clicked back into place and the seductive call of what lay inside the case fell silent. As swiftly as possible, reversing the actions she'd taken to unravel Vadim Maur's protective weaves, she restored the wards around the case. Then, and only then, did she let herself cup the gleaming crystal in her palms, release the song weave once more to make the lights inside the stone shine and dance, and crow in silent victory.

She'd done it. She'd *done it!*

Eld ~ Boura Dor

With his communications in the spell room complete, Vadim Maur returned to Boura Dor's command center. The three adversaries he'd brought with him from Boura Fell were gathered in the corner, talking quietly amongst themselves. He called them over.

"Primage Rutan has gathered an assembly of Mages by the Well of Souls. I want you three to go with them. I have decided that you, Garok, should take command, with Rutan reporting to you. This mission is vital and should be led by the most experienced and powerful Primages available. Rutan will give you the details when you join him."

The Primages bowed and murmured. "As you command, Most High."

Vadim watched them depart with satisfaction. Once Garok learned what the mission was, he his cronies would pursue victory with every bit of might and determination they possessed, because a triumphant return from where they were headed would earn each of them the greatest jewels they'd ever fastened to their sashes—and a standing in the Mage Council that would catapult them into direct line for Eld's Dark throne. Unfortunately for them, Rutan and a score of his most trusted Mages—all of whom Vadim had personally raised to the blue—had orders to ensure that Primages Garok, Fursk, and Mahl did not return from this mission alive.

Almost smiling, Vadim turned back to the table in the center of the room. "Ah, Vargus, you've got that tracker up. Excellent."

The tracker was on a wide view, showing the Feyls, the Rhakis, and more than half of the Fading Lands. A pinpoint of light in the center of what should have been total darkness made his brows snap together. He lunged for the tracker, spinning the command to zoom in on that small flicker of light. When it did, he nearly screamed in triumph.

His hand closed around Vargus's neck, and he bent low to hiss his commands in the startled Primage's ear. "Contact Boura Fell. Get me every *dahl'reisen* in our service, all of my Black Guard, and every available Primage from Fell, Maur, Gorin, Kovis, and Loc. I want two thousand at least."

Vargus cleared his throat. "Most of the Primages are already here, Master Maur, as you commanded them to be. There aren't two thousand Primages left in the Bouras."

"Then get me all you can. I'll take Primages and Sulimages—even yellow-robes if that's all there is. Pull every Mage off the Heras from Odol to Kovis. This is more important than protecting against anything that might come up the river. And get me that Celierian brute of mine . . . Brodson. I want them all here before twelve bells tomorrow, armed and ready for battle."

He straightened and spun on his heel. "Kron, I'll need that spell room of yours again."

A bell later, Vadim's consciousness was once more soaring through the night on threads of Azrahn, only this time it headed south, into Celieria.

Celieria ~ Allied Encampment

Ellysetta dreamed again of a ruined building and a secret, windowless room housing the dark mirror that began to glow silver-blue like Lord Hawksheart's mirror pool in Elvia when she approached. As the phosphorescent surface began to swirl, the face of the stranger who somehow seemed so familiar appeared in the mirror's depths. Blond hair billowed gently around the stern, Fey-beautiful masculine face.

She lifted her hands. Magic swirled around her fingertips in a bright glow, threads of gold and black weaving in a pattern she'd never seen before. The eyes of the man in the mirror went bright. He began to speak, but she couldn't hear the words.

Suddenly, a dark shadow enveloped her and the world went dark. When she could see again, the scenes from vivid and familiar nightmares raced before her eyes. Herself, bound by heavy chains and clad in a green, boat-necked gown, standing beside a cowled Mage. Her sisters, Lillis and Lorelle, trapped in a pit and screaming for her to help them as a pack of snarling darrokken closed in for the kill.

And then, the most terrifying scene ever to haunt her nightmares: Rain, chained to a wall, as a knife drove deep into his chest. Rain, his dying eyes fixed upon her, as a sword severed his head. Lillis and Lorelle, their eyes black as night, dancing in the shower of his blood.

Ellysetta's eyes flew open, and she came awake with a gasp. She sat up and lifted her hands, expecting to see them covered in Rain's blood. Instead, she saw the spotless white linen of her nightgown with its soft lace cuffs. With a shuddering gasp, she buried her face in her hands. She wasn't in some dark Mage fortress. Her sisters weren't Mage-claimed and Rain wasn't dead.

A dream, she told herself. *It was only a dream.*

But when she reached for Rain, needing to verify his safety, her searching hand encountered only cold, empty space.

Alarmed, she spun a swift Fire weave to light a candle lamp. The soft glow of light blossomed, revealing the rumpled pile of furs where Rain had been sleeping and the barren rack where he kept his steel at night. His war armor was missing—and so was he. «*Rain? Where are you?*»

Even before she finished the worried call, the tent flaps parted and he ducked inside, glowing silver and gold in his war steel. "Forgive me, *shei'tani*," he apologized. "I didn't mean to alarm you. I was just outside, trying to let you sleep as long as I could."

Relief that he was here, and unharmed, left her drained. "It's time?"

"*Aiyah.* The rest of the camp is already packed."

Ellysetta ruthlessly banished the remnant terror from her nightmare. They were riding to war. She wouldn't add her fears on Rain's already overburdened shoulders. She rose without hesitation and spun her own armor and steel into place. "Then let's go, *shei'tan*."

In less than a handful of chimes, her *lu'tan* spun the bulk of the tent and its furnishings back to the elements, and condensed the rest into small, lightweight parcels for easy transport.

And then the Fey army began its march towards Orest and war.

CHAPTER SEVENTEEN

Tairen roar a battle call
As warriors gather one and all.
Face the foe that now steps forward
With Fey'cha red and glinting sword.
To save the magic Fey of lore
Answer now the call to war.
    Call to War, by Tevan Fire Eyes, Tairen Soul

Celieria ~ One hundred miles south of Orest
10th day of Seledos

At midday, as the Fey army halted to rest and eat, Rain and the commanders of allied forces gathered in a magic-warded tent several miles east of the main militia. Fearful of the Mage using her eyes to spy upon the allies, Ellysetta remained behind with the other *shei'dalins*.

When Rain introduced Farel and his men to the other commanders, the air in the tent became decidedly chilly. The cool reception was not unexpected. Deeply ingrained Fey beliefs would not change in the blink of an eye, and thanks to the Mages' relentless subversions and the *dahl'reisen's* own murderous actions along the borders, the Celierians were no more eager to welcome *dahl'reisen* among their ranks than their immortal neighbors.

"I understand your reluctance to trust the *dahl'reisen*," Rain told them. "A week ago, I shared it. But I have since learned that the *dahl'reisen* who form the Brotherhood of Shadows are not so honorless, nor so irredeemably soul-lost, as I have always believed their kind to be. They saved El-lysetta and me not once, but twice, without any thought for their own safety or even their own survival."

He swept a hard gaze across the gathered commanders. "That is not, however, the reason I have welcomed them. Simply put, we need them. Our numbers are few while our enemy's are great. We cannot win this fight without them." He turned to Bel. "Bel, show them what we are up against."

Lavender Spirit sparked in Bel's eyes, setting them aglow as he raised his hands and began to weave. The Fey scouts dispatched earlier in the day from the allied camp had sent back images of Orest and its surroundings, and Bel had pieced the images together to create a large, three-dimensional map of Orest.

The city was crawling with Eld, Feraz, and what looked like Sorrelian and Imrhi mercenaries. Hundreds of thousands of them. Throughout Upper and Lower Orest, and lining the north shore of the Heras, batteries of bowcannon were trained on the Faering Mists and the surrounding areas, their barbed missiles glinting evilly in the sunlight.

As the faces of the commanders grew grim, Rain continued, "These last few days have taught me that as much as I value Fey honor and customs, there is something I value more. That something is the safety and survival of the people I love. If protecting my kingdom, my people, and my mate from Elden evil means I must accept aid from unconventional quarters, then so I shall. Farel and his warriors have bloodsworn themselves to Ellysetta. They wish to fight in defense of the Fading Lands and its allies like the Fey warriors they once were, and I shall allow it. And should they perish in that fight, I shall honor their sacrifice no less than I honor the sacrifice of any other warrior of this alliance."

He gave them a moment for that to sink in, then said, "If there are those among you who do not feel as I do—if you cannot, for whatever reason, allow yourself to fight in the same army that welcomes these *dahl'reisen*—then you may leave now. Return to whatever place it is you call home and go with my blessing and my thanks for your service. And I will pray to the gods that you spend the rest of your days in peace and that the evil those of us who remain are about to face will never find its way to your doorstep."

He looked from one grim face to the next, hoping to impress upon them both the depth of his sincerity and his belief that this was not just the right course to take, but the only course. "The *dahl'reisen* and I will excuse ourselves for ten chimes so that you may discuss your concerns openly amongst yourself and make your decision. If you choose to leave, do so before we return. Those who remain, I expect your full commitment and support to all members of this alliance, regardless of what personal feelings you may harbor."

Rain made his way to the tent entrance and held the flap aside for Farel and his lieutenants to pass through. With a last nod to the Fey and Celierian commanders, he ducked through the opening and let the tent flaps fall back into place.

When Rain returned, he was pleased to see everyone had chosen to stay, though he suspected Bel and Lord Barrial may have had some hand in convincing the others.

"The army is large, by anyone's estimation," Rain said as the commanders examined Bel's three-dimensional weave of Orest, "but with the *dahl'reisen* joining us, the Eld are not as insurmountable a force as they would otherwise have been."

Cann Barrial arched a brow. "No, they just outnumber us at least ten-to-one and have the advantage of holding both high ground and fortified defenses."

"*Mei sorro.*" Rain gave a wan smile in acknowledgement of the verbal hit. "But before the *dahl'reisen* joined us, we were expecting the odds to be forty-to-one or higher, so ten-to-one is actually good news." He turned to the map. "We still have our work cut out for us. They've bulked up the bowcannon batteries here and here and here." He pointed to the cliffs circling Upper Orest, the city walls of Lower Orest, and Maiden's Gate, the fortified series of battlements that stairstepped up the mountainside from Lower to Upper Orest. "These are tairen killers and they need to go."

"Do we really need to waste lives storming a well-defended city?" Commander Bonn asked. "They can't go west into the Mists, and the spray from Kiyera's Veil is poison to them. Why not just pen them in and wait."

Farel shook his head. "Penning them in won't work. The Mages can use the Well to come and go at will. And as for Kiyera's Veil, the Mages have already dammed the Source that feeds it to take the Heras out of play. The northern falls are dry and the river levels have been dropping all day."

Guilt stabbed Rain. He was the one who'd made the call not to send warriors to Dunelan. "*Sha vel'mei*. I should have sent troops to protect the Source before leaving for Elvia, but I thought we could dispatch warriors from Orest if there was trouble."

Bel shook his head. "Don't berate yourself, Rain. It was the right decision at the time. We thought the Army of Darkness would strike at Kreppes. Any of us would have done the same."

"Speaking of the Army of Darkness, is anyone besides me still waiting to see it?" Gaelen looked up from the table, where he'd been scanning the three-dimensional Spirit weave with intensity. "I mean, clearly this isn't it." He gestured to the Spirit weave of Orest.

"I wouldn't exactly call it a ragged band," Eimar replied with an arched brow. "There's easily half a million blades in the city."

"*Aiyah*," Gaelen agreed, "but this Mage spent decades—possibly centuries—planning for this war, laying the groundwork, infiltrating the north, doing everything possible to drive a wedge between Celieria and the Fading Lands. Do you honestly believe half a million troops was the most he could come up with? We cobbled together close to a hundred thousand in just a few months."

"Maybe there is no Army of Darkness," Cann suggested. "Maybe it was just deliberate misinformation leaked to divide our forces and scatter our armies across the continent and make us easier to defeat. If this Mage truly does command such overwhelming numbers, why would he not have unleashed them at Kreppes or Great Bay? It would have ensured an Elden victory. With the King's Army destroyed, they could have swept through the whole of Celieria in a matter of months."

"I agree," Gaelen said.

"One thing my centuries in the Brotherhood taught me was never to underestimate this Mage. He plays to win. He doesn't bluff and he always has backups for his backups. It would be a mistake for us to believe his Army of Darkness doesn't exist just because we haven't seen it yet."

"I think Kreppes and Great Bay were the diversions, and the Fading Lands has been the target all along," Rain said. "Think about it. We were holding Orest and keeping the Eld at bay until we captured that Mage and learned about this supposed Army of Darkness. Once we were lured into leaving Orest and dividing our forces, King Dorian was murdered by Sebourne. Prince Dorian nearly drowned when his ship went down in Great Bay. Our forces were winnowed. The Eld took Orest. And Annoura was left surrounded by Mage-claimed courtiers, and would have been claimed herself by the Mage masquerading as her Favorite." Rain spread his hands. "My guess is the Eld never intended to take Celieria by force. They've always intended to conquer it from within, then use it as a base to launch on the Fading Lands."

"What about Mists?" Eimar interjected. "No invader who ever went into the Mists has ever come out again."

Rain shrugged. "Maybe they've found a way through it using the Well. Maybe they've learned how to circumvent its magic. Maybe they have some weapon or magic we haven't seen yet." He'd already contacted Sybharukai and asked her to recall half a dozen of the tairen from Orest and have them scout the perimeters of the Faering Mists for any suspicious activity. "All I know is, if they want Orest this badly, we can't let them keep it."

"Which brings us back to where we started," Bel said.

"Aiyah. And our first priority is to take out those bowcannon batteries. Both here on the wall"—Rain pointed to the image of Maiden's Gate—"and here across the river in Eld."

"The *dahl'reisen* will take the cannon across the river." Farel grinned with dark humor. "We're used to raiding beneath Mage noses."

"Bas'ka. Then, Cann and Commander Bonn, I'll need you and your best cannoneers and siege masters marching with the Fey here and here. The Fey will give you cover, while you give the Eld hell."

"With pleasure," Cann said.

"What about siege weapons?" Bonn asked. "We left everything behind."

"Rijonn and the Earth masters will weave them for us like they did at Kreppes."

"And if there really is an Army of Darkness?" Gaelen asked.

Rain fixed a grim look upon him. *"Dai tabor, Fey, bas desrali lor bas tirei."* Then, Fey, we die where we stand.

Celieria ~ Orest

The Great Sun was just beginning to set, turning the Faering Mists into a sea of flame, as the armies of Light crested the last hill overlooking Orest and the Heras River valley. Steli, Xisanna, and Perahl, who had been running with the allies rather than flying above them to avoid giving away their position, drew to a halt behind Rain and Ellysetta and crouched there, growling low in their chests at the sight laid out before them.

As Rain and his generals had seen earlier today in Bel's

weaves, the city was overrun. Instead of the bright colors of
Celieria and House Teleon, the purple flags and pennants of
Eld now snapped in the breeze from the battered ramparts
of Lower and Upper Orest. Instead of the colored tabards
and shining silver armor of Fey and Celierian defenders,
black armored Eld swarmed the city like a colony of ants.
Smoke billowed up from the charred remnants of buildings
throughout the city. Fey and Celierian corpses, impaled on
pikes, surrounded the walls of Lower Orest, serving both
as a macabre victory boast and a grim warning to would-be
patriots who might think to recapture the city for Celieria.

But it was on the gatherings of great, gleaming black
dragons that Rain's gaze became fixed. Like flocks of colossal vultures, they perched on the half-eaten bodies of fallen
tairen, toothy snouts ripped the remaining chunks of flesh
and hide from bloody bones with ravening savagery. Wings
flapped and hisses, roars, and blasts of flame erupted as the
dragons fought over their terrible feast.

Ellysetta reached for Rain's hand. Her fingers curled
around his, squeezing tight. "Who?"

"Barsul and Storus. They were the youngest of Cahlah's
kits before this last hatching."

She gave a fanning waving and murmured a prayer for the
tairens' souls. "We will avenge them, *shei'tan*."

"May the gods will it should be so. I have marked their
locations. After this battle, the tairen will take what is left
of their remains back to Fey'Bahren for their Fire Song, so
their songs will not be entirely lost to the pride."

Rain dragged his gaze from the tairen remains and
scanned the lines of the allied troops. The *dahl'reisen* had
circled around to the east, leaving the Fey and Celierians
to advance from the south. As they had for the battle of
Kreppes, hundreds of Earth masters had spent all afternoon
constructing trebuchets, siege towers, and bowcannon of
their own to aid in the reconquest of Orest.

As Farel had pointed out earlier, normal siege tactics of

blockading the city and waiting for starvation and thirst and the Mists to take their toll would not work. The best hope of victory was to drive the enemy troops out of the city walls and onto the field. While Mages might be able to protect themselves against Fey attacks, on an open field, the rest of their army would find even ten-to-one odds against an army of Fey swordsmasters to be a statistical disadvantage.

Unfortunately, it wasn't going to be easy to convince the Eld they should surrender their fortified mountain stronghold and confront the Fey on an open field. The only way Rain knew how to do it was to make Orest more hazard than haven—starting with taking out those bowcannon batteries and the dragons so the tairen could have free reign of the sky.

"He's here."

"Who?" Rain frowned at Ellysetta. A strange stillness had settled over her, and her shadowed gaze was fixed on a point north of Orest.

"The Mage." She clasped her arms across her chest. "I can feel him. He's come to witness his victory."

The Shadar horn in Rain's veins went hot as Rage rose, swift and violent. Instinct moved him closer to her side, blocking her body protectively with his as he followed her gaze north. His eyes narrowed and he adjusted their focus to bring the distant shores of Eld into closer view. A purple canopy had been erected behind the lines of bowcannon, and dozens of blue-robed Primages were milling about beneath it, but if the High Mage was among them, Rain could not see him.

"It will not be his victory, but ours," he assured Ellysetta.

With visible effort, she turned away from Eld. "May the gods will it should be so."

His heart ached at how pale she looked beneath her forced calm. She was so afraid, but so determined not to show it, so determined to be brave for his sake. He lifted a hand, brushing back the wayward curls from her face in what he hoped would not be the last of their small intimacies. "I love you, Ellysetta Baristani."

Her mouth trembled, and her beautiful eyes glimmered

with a sudden sheen of tears. She blinked them back quickly. "And I love you, Rain." The tears she would not shed made her voice sound low and throaty so that it purred across his skin like velvet. "I always have. I always will."

"Rain." Bel gave an apologetic look as he interrupted. "Forgive me, but the troops are in position."

Rain nodded. He threaded his fingers through Ellysetta's and lifted her hands for a kiss. "I have to go now, *shei'tani*."

"I know." They had said their good-byes before, during their last few chimes of rest before the final push to the battlefield, but even so, she caught his face in her hands and pulled him down for a last kiss farewell. *«Come back safe to me, shei'tan.»*

He caught her tight against him and poured his heart, his soul, his life's essence into that kiss. Trembling, aching, he whispered, *"Ver reisa ku'chae. Kem surah, shei'tani."* He held out an arm to Bel and the rest of Ellysetta's quintet. "Guard her well, *kem'jetos*." The quintet and three hundred of her *lu'tan* would stay behind to guard Ellysetta and the other *shei'dalins* in the healing tents.

Then, regretfully but purposefully, the Fey who was Rain, the *shei'tan* of Ellysetta, folded back into the privacy of his soul. And it was Rainier vel'En Daris, Feyreisen, King of the Fading Lands, Defender of the Fey, who stepped forward to stand before the assembled army of Light and called them one last time to war.

Aloud and on weaves of powerful Spirit which he spun and flung out upon the whole the assembled armies, he called, "My friends . . . today, we are not Fey, Celierian, or *dahl'reisen*, but brothers, united and strong, each of us honorable and worthy warriors of Light. We are the steel no enemy can shatter. We are the magic no Dark power can defeat. We are the rock upon which evil breaks like waves. We are warriors of honor, champions of Light." He pulled one of his *seyani* swords from its scabbard and raised the blade high, letting sunlight gleam on the long blade of golden steel.

"To victory my brothers!" he cried. "And to life!"

"To victory and life!" came their answering cry.

Rain raised his golden war horn and blew the call to battle. Across the fields of Orest, other horns, Fey, Celierian, and *dahl'reisen* alike, blew answering blasts, and the army of Light began to march.

Remembering the speed and distance of the bowcannon that had shot him down over Eld, Rain ordered Steli, Xisanna, and Perahl to stay behind near the healing tents.

"When it is time, pride-kin, you will strike, but you cannot fly against Orest now—not with so many bowcannon trained on the sky. The danger will be great enough when I call upon you." Grumbling, the tairen acquiesced.

With only Rain flying overhead, the armies of Light advanced upon occupied Orest. He flew back and forth, scorching the field before them to destroy any *chemar* scattered upon the ground. Their advance was slow, but unhindered, which made him nervous. He expected the dragons to attack. The allies' own bowcannon were aimed skyward, ready to fire, for just such an event, but instead, the great, scaled creatures retreated from the field, winging away to perch like reptilian vultures on the walls of Orest. No doubt their masters preferred to draw the tairen closer to Orest and the batteries of deadly bowcannon perched on the ramparts before they struck.

The allies were halfway across the field when the first of the black Shadows appeared amongst them.

"Demons!" someone cried.

Fey magic burst forth in powerful, five-fold weaves, shielding the Celierians and plunging into the dark shades of the dead. There were hundreds of them. Thousands. Orest had been conquered, and more than one night had fallen upon the bodies of the Mage-slain, giving the Mages ample time to call and bind the souls of the corpses left littering the field. They appeared amidst the allies, demons of Celierians and Fey, whose slightest touch would drain all Light and life from their victims.

Rain wheeled and dove towards the army, preparing to Change, when the first of the dragons leapt from the ramparts of Orest and headed his way. Six others followed on its tail. So that was the plan. Distract his own cannoneers with demons, then attack Rain undeterred by allied cannon fire.

It was a good plan, but neither Fey nor Tairen Souls were so easy to outwit. Rain soared back up, skyward, spewing flame and roaring a challenge.

«Cannoneers!» he cried. *«Look to the skies. Fey, protect the cannons. Air masters! Give those beasts a taste of trouble!»*

Howling winds swept across the skies, buffeting the dragons and slinging them across the sky. Rain gave a grim, chuffing laugh and dove after the first of the scaled monsters. The beast saw him coming and trumpeted a challenge, spewing its green-tinged, acid flame. Rain dissolved into the Change, letting both flame and dragon pass through him, then re-formed behind the beast and ripped its back raw with razored claws and breathed tairen fire into the unprotected flesh. As the dragon shrieked and plummeted from the sky, Rain roared in victory and dove after the next.

Standing aboveground, shielded from the sun's glare by a purple canopy, Vadim Maur had come to watch his great victory unfold with his own eyes. When the Fey had advanced across the field, he'd ordered the dragons back to Orest to draw them closer before releasing the demons and a handful of dragons to thin their ranks.

Now it was time to make them earn each man-length of progress.

"Vargus, tell the Mages to counter the winds! Kron, are the cannoneers ready with Grule's special bolts?"

"Ready, Master Maur!"

"Then fire at will, Kron. Take the Tairen Soul out of the sky."

* * *

«Rain! Watch your flank! Incoming from the west and north!»

Rain saw the shadows in the sky, streaking towards him. Bowcannon bolts, six of them, flying much faster than a bowcannon bolt should—just as they had when they'd shot him from the sky. But the Eld didn't have the element of surprise this time. He pumped his wings and soared high into the sky, well above the bolts' trajectories.

«Beware, Feyreisen! The scorching things are following you!»

What? He glanced back over his shoulder, and sure enough, the six bolts had changed their flight to mirror his and were still coming strong—straight at him. Rain rolled left, putting on a burst of magic-powered speed. The bolts rolled after him, still gaining. He dove for the battlefield. The bolts dove too. With each passing moment, the distance between then decreased. Left, right, up, down, Rain zigged and zagged across the sky, trying to shake the flaming things off his tail, but they would not be shaken.

He tried burning them out of the sky, wheeling around to face them, flaming them as they raced towards him, then Changing at the last possible instant. The bolts raced through his mist, unharmed by his flame, but the instant he re-formed, they looped back around to come after him.

Krekk. The Eld must have warded the missiles to make them resistant to his flame. He spied a dragon swooping down upon the Fey, and his tairen mouth curled up, baring fangs. *Time for a little game of dodge-tairen.*

He dove for one of the dragons, spewing fire. Two of its brethren saw his attack and dove after him, coming at him from two sides. Fangs and claws ripped and shredded, wings tangled. Acid fire and tairen flame spewed in fiery maelstrom. And then, as the five bowcannon bolts zoomed close, Rain Changed. The bolts passed harmlessly through his mist and slammed into the three dragons, driving them out of the sky and pinning them to the ground. Rain landed in

Fey form beside them, drained of magic and breathing hard. He finished the three dragons off with red Fey'cha.

«Rain!» Ellysetta's warning shriek sounded in his mind.

He looked up to see the sixth dragon diving in for the kill.

"I'm all right. I'm fine." Rain caught Ellysetta's hands in his. Though the sixth dragon had given him a good scorching, Steli had swooped in to snatch him from harm's way. She'd jabbed the reptile in the eye with her tail spike in passing, and left his twitching body for Xisanna and Perahl to finish off. Thanks to a bell of intensive healing by Ellysetta, he was fit enough to fight and determined to return to battle. "I have to get back."

With the help of Air masters and a few well-timed barrages of Fey bowcannon fire, the allies had kept the remaining dragons at bay. The demons were gone and the allied army was once more on the move, but as they drew closer to the walls of Orest, they would need him in the air, providing what defense he could.

Ellysetta closed her eyes. He felt her struggle against her *shei'tanitsa* need to keep him safe. He knew what it cost her to say, "I know, *kem'san*," and let him go. She was strong. Much stronger than most truemated *fellanas*. Much stronger, and far more courageous, than she ever gave herself credit. It was much easier to fly into danger yourself than to watch the one you love do so.

"Rain. Ellysetta." Bel rushed into the healing tent. "Come quick. You'll both want to see this."

Curious, they both followed him out of the tent, only to stop in surprise as Bel gestured to the south. There, just cresting the next line of hills to the south, a large army approached. Rain estimated at least thirty thousand troops, all with gleaming bows and quivers across their backs. Their armor shone with rich copper hues in the morning light, and a lustrous golden glow enveloped them, as if they carried sunlight in their skin.

That glow—and their distinctive cavalry, some winged

and others graced with a single spiraling horn—identified the newcomers even before Rain discerned the distinctive leaf-shaped scales of their armor and the delicate, tapering points of their even-more-distinctive ears.

Despite Galad Hawksheart's numerous refusals, the Elves had come at last to join the war.

"Welcome," Rain said when the leaders of the Elvian army halted before him. "I am glad beyond words that Lord Hawksheart changed his mind after all."

The Elvian commander, a tall, broad-shouldered Elf with waist-length hair the color of sunset and rich sapphire eyes regarded Rain with the disconcerting intensity of his kind. "We do not come at Lord Galad's bidding," he replied in a low, lyrical voice. "The Lord of Valorian commands the Elves of Deep Woods. We answer to the Lady."

"You are from Silverwood," Ellysetta said.

The commander's bright gaze fixed instantly on her, and the power of his gaze made the breath leave her lungs. "And you are Ellysetta Erimea. I have heard tales of your brightness, but they do you no justice." To her surprise, the Elf commander clasped a fist to his breastplate and dropped to one knee before her. "Blessings of the day upon you, Ellysetta Erimea. It is our honor to serve the Winter Star." He bowed low, over his knee, murmuring something in Elvish that she did not understand, but the thousands of Elves behind him suddenly followed his lead, each dropping to a knee and bowing low before her.

"It is I who am honored, my lord commander." The welcome of these Elves shocked her, and the near reverence with which they regarded her left her unsettled and embarrassed. "Please, rise, and be welcome."

"I am called Tamsin Greywing, my lady," the Elf said as he stood, "general of the armies of west Elvia." He turned to the two elves beside him, one a broad-shouldered, chestnut-haired male with the unflinching yellow eyes of a wolf, the other a stunningly beautiful Elf maiden. "This is my second in command, Gavin Fenwolf, and this is—" He glanced back at Ellysetta and his voice trailed off.

"You may call me Commander Silverleaf," the Elf maiden finished for him. Her voice was pure music, sweet as a song played by crystalline bells, but her face, with its piercing silver-grey eyes, possessed a composed, almost stern quality despite her great beauty. Masses of pale gold hair hung down her back in a multi-ply plait as thick as Ellysetta's arm. "I lead the Aquiline riders."

"We bring you greetings from our queen, Illona Bright-hand," General Greywing continued. "The Elves of Sil-verwood extend our hand of friendship and offer you our strength in this battle against the enemies of Light."

Across the river, on the shores of Eld, Vadim Maur noted the arrival of the Elvish army. His lips compressed in a hard line.

So, the Feraz hadn't been keeping Hawksheart occupied after all. He would have a word or two for Fezai Madia the next time he saw the arrogant witch.

Turning to Vargus, he barked his next command. "Release the revenants."

Sound rumbled across the scorched plains outside Lower Orest. The ground beneath the allies' feet began to shake. Ellysetta looked down in surprise. "Is it an earthquake, 'Jonn?"

The giant Earth master's dark eyes glowed green as he sent his great magic plunging into the ground below. A moment later, he shook his head. "*Nei*, not the earth. Something inside it."

"Something like what?" Rain asked

Before Rijonn could answer, a cry sounded down the line. "Look!"

Rain and Ellysetta turned. Something was pouring out of

the ground near the south gate of Lower Orest. From a distance, it looked almost like a swarm of termites bubbling up from a disturbed nest.

"What is that?" Ellysetta asked.

Beside her, the Elf commanders muttered something in their native tongue.

Rain's expression went grim. "Revenants? What the Seven Hells are revenants?"

General Greywing's eyes went dark. "Black magic. Very old, very deadly black magic. The world hasn't seen their like in at least ninety thousand years." He glanced at Commander Silverleaf and said, "The knowledge was lost. How did this Mage find the spell?"

"It doesn't matter, Tam." She turned piercing gray eyes on Rain. "Get your people out of there, Feyreisen. This is not an enemy Celierians can kill, and Fey will find it difficult." Authority snapped in her voice. "Swords are useless—worse than useless—as is most magic."

Rain gave the command without question, then scowled at Silverleaf. "If swords and magic are useless, how the Hells are we supposed to kill them?"

"Elvish Light arrows. Tairen fire. Hundred-fold weaves—though more than hundred-fold is better. Other weaves have little effect. Whatever you do, don't slice off even the smallest bit of the revenants' flesh. They multiply when split."

"Lovely," Gaelen muttered.

Beside him, Bel's eyes went hazy as he spun the warnings to the allies. Dozens more holes in the ground had opened up, and revenants were pouring out into the sunlight. The Celierians were running for their lives back to the allied encampment, while the Fey brought up the rear and spun shields to slow the revenants' advance.

"*Bas'ka*, you heard her," Rain commanded. "Swords and magic are useless. *Kaiven chakor*, get Ellysetta and the *shei'dalins* to safety."

"*Bayas*," Commander Silverleaf countermanded. "That

you must not do, Tairen Soul. The Feyreisa must fight at your side."

Rain's brows slammed together. "What? Are you mad?" He glanced from Greywing to Commander Silverleaf. "Who the scorching Hells are you, Elf? And don't give me that 'You may call me, Silverleaf' *krekk*. Obviously you are not Greywing's subordinate."

"I am a seer of the Elves, Tairen Soul, and I have come to advise you on behalf of Elvia's queen, Illona Brighthand. If you send the Feyreisa away, you will perish and she will fall to Darkness. Your only hope to survive this battle is to stay together and fight as one. You hold each other to the Light."

"Are you saying if we fight together, we will survive this battle?"

The Elf hesitated. "*Bayas.* I cannot say that. There is risk. But if you send her from you, risk becomes certainty. You will die; she will fall."

Rain stared hard at the Elf commander, trying to read those impenetrable gray eyes, but as with most Elves, looking into her eyes was like staring down a bottomless well. They gave away nothing.

"Rain, let's go." Ellysetta's hand brushed his. "You heard her. Tairen fire is one of the few weapons we have against this army." «*It's time for trust, not doubt, shei'tan. The Elves are right. We're stronger together than apart. You know it as well as I.*»

He wanted to refuse. The danger to them both was very real. He'd just almost died himself. But already, the entire field around Lower Orest was blanketed with foul, maggot-colored monsters. There were easily two hundred thousand of them, and thousands more scrambled out of their boreholes with each passing chime. Behind the allied lines, the earth shifted and bulged upward as a new line of holes erupted and began spewing revenants to cut off the allies' retreat.

Rain spun to face Ellysetta's primary quintet. "You five

organize the hundred-fold weaves. Let's kill as many of those creatures as we can, starting with those." He jerked a hand towards the line of revenants threatening the allies' rear flank.

"The Aquiline riders will assist you," Commander Silverleaf said.

"I'm counting on it." Rain leapt into the sky and Changed. Ellysetta's quintet flung her skyward on a weave of Air, and she slid effortlessly into the saddle strapped to the back of Rain's neck, her *dahl'reisen*-forged armor shining in the sunlight.

As Rain wheeled around to head back towards the field of revenants and prepared to fire, he heard Greywing cry, "Elves! Take aim!"

The Elvian general didn't look up to watch Rain's approach, but just before Rain flew past, he cried, "Fire!" The Elves loosed their Light arrows, and the sky before Rain and Ellysetta lit up with blinding brightness.

Rain, the tairen, and the Aquiline riders flew through the wake of the Light storm. They burst from the brightness with tairen fire and arrows blazing to incinerate the monsters threatening the allies' retreat.

Fire consumed long tracts of revenants in red-orange flame. As they burned, they emitted a grating, high-pitched screech that rattled Ellysetta's bones. She shielded her ears against the noise but kept her eyes open and scanning the sky.

Bowcannon bolts turned the sky dark, flying from Orest and across the river. She spun whirling cyclones of Air and Fire to stop them, but the missiles were too plentiful for her weaves alone.

«Gil!» she cried. *«You and the Air masters keep those bowcannon bolts off of us.»* Instantly two dozen cyclones sprang up around the tairen and Aquilines, catching the bolts midair and leaving the tairen and Elves free to rain fire and Light arrows down upon the revenant masses.

The Mages clearly didn't like that much, because the rest of the dragon flock took wing from the peaks surrounding Upper Orest. They screamed, the sound like great trumpets blaring. Long, serpentine necks ended in wedge-shaped heads with snouts filled with sharp, curved teeth. They flapped their massive wings and soared over the fields of Orest on a direct course with the tairen and the Aquiline riders. With them was a female dragon nearly twice the size of the rest. Clearly, she was the pack's queen, for when she bugled a command, the others obeyed.

«Dragons, Rain. Coming from our left, off the Rhakis.»

«I see them. Silverleaf, you deal with the revenants. The tairen will take the dragons.»

Commander Silverleaf raised her bow in acknowledgement, and the Aquiline riders spiraled down. Elvish bows sang and Light arrows zipped towards the ground in streamers of golden light, as if the sky were raining sunshine. Each revenant pierced by the golden arrows went bright and exploded in a cloud of black dust.

Above the fray, Rain's wings spread wide and pumped to gain loft. Steli, Xisanna, and Perahl raced ahead in a V formation as, with a deafening roar, four more tairen burst from the Faering Mists south of the healing tents. Fahreeta, Torasul, and two younger pride mates sped north across open Celierian land to join their pride-kin above the battlefield.

The dragons rocketed towards the pride, fangs bared, razor sharp claws extended. Great cats and dragons slammed into one another in the sky, fangs and claws slashing, tails whipping as they tumbled through the air. As the ground zoomed up to meet them, they broke apart. Both tairen and dragons were soaked with their own blood, still neither gave quarter. They simply flew back to a higher altitude and reengaged.

The tairen belched boiling clouds of flame, but the dragon queen heeled back and flapped her great wings. Magic swirled in the air, and a brutal gust of wind blew the tairen's fire back upon them. The monster dove below the pride and rolled onto her back beneath them. The dragon queen opened her own venomous maw and spewed searing jets of green, concentrated acid-flame.

On Rain's back, Ellysetta cried out in horror as the monster's corrosive spew sliced through the tairen like Mage Fire, scything limbs from bodies. Maimed and mortally wounded, Fahreeta and the two younger tairen fell from the sky in a shower of blood and smoking gore.

The queen screamed in victory and shot out on a burst of speed only to circle around for a second pass. Fire boiled from Torasul's muzzle in a searing orange cloud as he dove to the aid of his fallen mate.

Steli roared and burst through the concealing cloud of smoke above. With her white ears laid back against her skull, razored claws extended, she stooped towards the dragon queen. The foul beast glanced up too late to dodge Steli's attack, and the pair clashed in midair, claws and fangs ripping and rending, wings and tails tangling in a savage battle for survival and supremacy. They plummeted towards the earth, roaring and screaming as each fought to rip out the other's throat and claw open the other's belly.

They crashed into the ground with the force of a meteor. Debris exploded upward into the sky, then showered down in a hail of dirt and shattered rock, radiating out from the great crater where the two creatures lay in a limp tangle of limbs.

Steli had taken the brunt of the fall. Wings and back broken, she lay in the pit, struggling for breath. The dragon queen hadn't fared much better, but she could still move. She dragged the heavy weight of her body towards Steli and lifted herself up on trembling forelegs over the white tairen's shattered form. The monster opened her maw, yellowed fangs dripping green poison as she prepared to deliver the death-bite. Steli's pupilless blue eyes, their fierce glow dimmed with pain, gazed up, unflinching, defiance mixed with the grim acceptance of defeat.

"Get away from her, you monstrous *petchka*!"

Ellysetta's furious shout heralded a searing jet of tairen flame that enveloped the dragon's head just before she struck.

The queen reared back, roaring. Ellysetta leapt from Rain's back, riding a column of Air down to Steli's side and peppering the dragon queen's head and neck with Fey'cha as she went.

Rain's curved tairen claws sank into the tough, super-heated hide of the dragon queen's back, and with a mighty pump of his powerful wings, he hauled the foul creature into the air. Curving tairen fangs snapped at the dragon's neck but the long, serpentine neck writhed and twisted, eluding him. The dragon hissed and struggled, spewing acid flame. He rocketed skyward in a rapid, magic-powered ascent, carrying the queen far above the earth, to a part of the sky where the air grew thin and so cold a drop of water would freeze in an instant.

The abrupt change in altitude and temperature acted like ice shot on the dragon's hide. Steaming scales cracked, ripping fissures down into the vulnerable flesh beneath. The queen shrieked in agony as the icy cold of the high atmosphere seared her.

At last, Rain managed to sink his fangs into the dragon's long neck. The touch blistered his muzzle and tongue, but he held on with grim determination and pumped venom into her veins until the creature went limp.

With a roar, he released her.

The dragon plummeted earthward. Limbs limp, dead wings fluttered like pennants tied to a falling rock as down the body of the great beast fell. She landed on the battlements of Orest with a mighty crash, shearing the whole of Maiden's Gate off the side of the mountain and taking four full batteries of bowcannon and thousands of Eld troops with it.

With a scream of triumph and vengeance, Rain followed close behind her, tairen fire boiling from his muzzle to scorch the remaining bowcannons.

* * *

Ellysetta laid a hand on Steli's broken body and flooded her with a wave of healing and strength to ease the great cat's labored breathing. From beneath half-closed lids, the cat's dimming eyes regarded Ellysetta with mute suffering. The dragon had struck a mortal blow. Steli's body was shattered and losing blood rapidly. What wasn't pouring out through the gaping holes ripped into her hide was flooding her lungs and chest cavity. Steli was dying.

Howling, shrieking with savage bloodlust, the revenants were closing in. They had already reached the edges of the crater. Ellysetta stared up in horror at their round maws, filled with row upon row of needle-sharp teeth, that gnashed and bubbled with frothy green slime. They moved with shocking speed, their clawed hands and feet gouging into rock and dirt for traction. The monsters would be upon them before she managed to do more than stop the worst of Steli's internal bleeding.

«Rain!» she cried. *«Help us.»* "Hang on, Steli," she begged. She'd cut her fingers throwing Fey'cha at the dragon queen, and she wiped the blood off on her armored leg before holding her hands over Steli and summoning her healing magic. *Please, gods, please,* she prayed in silence as she sent her consciousness and healing Light into her beloved pride-mother.

A golden light gleamed at the corner of her eye. Ellysetta turned, expecting to find one of the Elves, only to gasp at the sight of a Fey warrior, gleaming bright as the sun. But it was the sight of the warrior's radiant, unearthly beautiful face that left Ellysetta stunned.

"Varian?" It was him. The *dahl'reisen*—one of the first thirty-six who'd sacrificed his life for her in the Verlaine. She'd felt him die, heard the song in his soul as he passed through the Veil. And yet, here he stood, impossibly beautiful, unscarred, unburdened by the shame that had weighed so heavy upon him. His skin shone like the sun, and eyes were filled with such boundless love and serenity she wanted to weep with joy.

"I don't understand," she whispered. "How can you be here?"

"None shall harm you while in life or death I have power to prevent it," he said, and his voice tolled like a great bell, resonant and pure. "This I did swear with my own life's blood, in Fire and Air and Earth and Water, in Spirit and in Azrahn." He drew his sword. The blade blazed with a radiance so bright Ellysetta had to cover her eyes. "Summon the others, *kem'falla*. Touch your blood to the bloodsworn steel. Quickly."

Rising to her feet, Ellysetta pulled a Fey'cha from the harness across her chest and sliced her palm deep. Pain stung for a brief, sharp instant, then blood welled, bright red and plentiful. She coated both hands and smeared them across her armor's shining steel.

All around her, bubbles of strange mist appeared like clouds of sunlight, golden bright and radiant. The clouds expanded until they became a ring of light surrounding Ellysetta and Steli that coalesced into the forms of a hundred shining Fey warriors, former *rasa* and *dahl'reisen lu'tan*, standing side by side, each clad in golden armor that gleamed like the sun.

"Heal her, *kem'falla*," he urged. "We will keep you safe." Varian raised his sword high overhead. "For love and for Light!" he cried. *"Miora felah ti'Feyreisa!"*

The ring of Light Warriors echoed his cry, and together, they plunged towards the oncoming revenants. Their swords sliced through the unholy throng, and unlike steel which merely split the hideous creatures and left them to regenerate into twice the threat, the Light Warriors' swords, like the arrows of the Elves, turned the revenants to clouds of harmless black dust.

Steli gave a panting whimper of pain, and Ellysetta tore her gaze from the Light Warriors and set to work healing her pride-mother. Rain arrived a few chimes later, heralded by clouds of boiling flame that incinerated the revenants around the crater's rim.

«Beylah sallan, shei'tani,» he sang. *«I was worried I wouldn't reach you before the revenants did.»*

"You almost didn't," she told him. "Varian and the others kept them at bay."

«Varian who? What others?»

She looked up from her healing. There was no one in the crater but herself, Rain, and Steli. Varian and the Light Warriors were gone.

After healing Steli's shattered bones and organs, Rain flew Ellysetta to tend the other injured tairen. The dragons were dead, but the two youngest tairen had perished with them, and Fahreeta had lost a wing to the dragon queen's flame. The rest of the pride managed to lift her wounded body and fly it to safety. With his mate wounded, Torasul's fierce, protective instincts were on full display. He would let none of the Fey or *shei'dalins* approach Fahreeta, leaving Ellysetta to weave a new wing for Fahreeta on her own. With Rain's help, she managed, but when she was done, they were both near-staggering from exhaustion.

As she and he paused to eat and regain their strength, Ellysetta sliced her hand and rubbed it against her armored thigh and tried to summon Varian again. An army of Light Warriors would be a huge asset to the allies. But none of the Light Warriors answered her call, though to her embarrassment, several of her *lu'tan* came running.

"Sieks'ta," she apologized. "I didn't mean to call you. I was trying to reach someone else."

Commander Silverleaf, who had taken a brief respite from the sky to rest her Aquiline and heal the wounds that marred his white hide, watched Ellysetta. "They do not come because you are not in peril," she said.

Ellysetta looked up in surprise. "I beg your pardon?"

"The spirits of your *lu'tan*. The ones who have passed

beyond the Veil. They are not your army, to fight on your command. They bound themselves to you in love, by their own free will, not to kill for you, but to defend you from harm."

"So they won't come when I call, but if I walked out into a pack of revenants, they would?"

"If you put yourself in peril, they would come, and they would extinguish their own Light to defend yours." The Elf woman's eyes were steady and unwavering, giving away nothing. "Is that what you will do?"

"That would be a perversion of their gift, wouldn't it? To force them to fight, when all they swore was to defend?"

Silverleaf remained silent, and that seemed answer enough.

"I will not abuse the great gift they entrusted to me."

The Elf neither commended Ellysetta nor condemned her. She simply turned and walked back to her Aquiline, but Ellysetta had the feeling she had just passed a very important test.

Rain and Ellysetta took to the skies once more, and the battle continued well into the night.

To the north, the *dahl'reisen's* attempts to take out the bowcannon across the river were unsuccessful. The Eld had strewn the ground around them with *sel'dor* dust, which sparked like mad against the *dahl'reisen* invisibility weaves, making them instantly detectable. Between demons, Mages, and *darrokken*, the warriors were slaughtered in a few brutal, bloody chimes of battle.

Earth masters tried to seal the boreholes by turning soil to stone, but the corrosive flesh of the revenants still ate through. The bodies of Elf, Fey, *dahl'reisen*, Aquilines. Shadar, and tairen littered the field, coated in thick layers of black dust from the destroyed revenants.

The allies were exhausted. Bells of nonstop battle, with little rest or food, and no *faerilas* to rejuvenate flagging magical energies, had beaten them down.

And still, the revenants came.

The Pale ~ North Slopes of the Feyls

The slivered crescents of the Mother and Daughter moons rode low in the night sky over the Feyls. Moonrise had brought with it a surge in power for the Mages who had been bombarding the Faering Mists with Mage Fire since their arrival the previous night, and as the night deepened, that surge increased.

Three thousand Mages now stood on the peaks of the Feyls, oblivious to the ice and snow around them. Great, blazing blue-white globes, some the size of tairen, flew through the air, exploding with concussive force against the shifting rainbowed radiance of the Mists. With each blow, the Mists flared bright.

"Keep firing!" Primage Garok shouted over the roar of exploding magic.

Around him, the other Mages continued the barrage, each drawing deep upon his well of magic. Several pooled their power to amass larger globes and send them flying into the Mists.

The magical curtain shuddered beneath the assault, its clouds undulating in frantic waves, bending inward where the concentrated barrage hit hardest.

"Mahl! Rutan! Concentrate!" He spun to address a group of Mages working together to combine their flows of magic into a single, enormous globe of Mage Fire. "Fursk! Keep those Mages channeling power! Make that Fire as big as you can!"

Pale faces strained. Sweat broke out on pallid brows and trickled down the sides of ashen faces. The globe of Mage Fire centered between the thirty-six Primages expanded, growing larger and larger, until they could barely hold it aloft. Shouting with exertion, they heaved the massive sphere towards the Mists, straight into the center of the barrage.

Magic exploded, bolts of searing blue-white light shooting out like cracks of lightning.

For one, shocking, shuddering instant, the Mists thinned, and a small hole appeared at the center of the thinned area. Primage Garok had a clear view straight through the Mists to the snow-capped Feyls on the other side. The edges of the hole fluttered like a tattered sail pierced by a great sword. Then sparks of magic sputtered, and cloudy, rainbow-lit wisps of mist surged inward to fill the empty space, the tendrils reaching for each other like desperate hands reaching across a chasm. The tiny hole in the Mists sealed.

But it had existed.

"It's working!" Garok crowed. "We need more power. Mahl, Rutan, you and your Mages add your Fire to Fursk's!"

Seventy-two more Mages joined the circle. The globe of Fire trebled in size. Garok called more Mages to join the others. The ring of magic wielders expanded to one hundred eight, one hundred forty-four, one-eighty. Then at last, the magic number, twelve hundred ninety-six. Thirty-six groups of thirty-six.

The globe of Mage Fire at their center was like nothing Garok had ever seen—or ever even read about in his centuries of existence. As big as a mountain, and nearly as large, hovering over the thirteen hundred Mages like some great, glowing god-sphere.

"Now!" he cried. "Now! Let it fly!"

The Mages bellowed a communal roar and heaved the massive sphere towards the Faering Mists. The Mage Fire sailed up the mountain towards the shimmering curtain. Brilliant, enormous, deadly, the Fire skimmed across the ground, catching the remnants of already battered trees and winking them from existence, leaving a trail of barrenness in its wake.

The massive globe of Fire plowed into the Faering Mists. Energy erupted like an exploding star. The flash of blinding light made Mages scream and cover their eyes. Then came the boom, a roaring wave of sound like the thunder of the gods, and just behind it, a blasting jet of air and magic and pulverized dirt that knocked the Mages to the ground and sent half a score of them flying to their deaths off the side of the mountain, their dwindling shrieks muted by the deafening roar as the Faering Mists rippled and shook, and split in two.

Celieria ~ Orest

A flash of light illuminated the western horizon. All heads turned on the battlefield of Orest as the clouds of Mist riding the top of the Rhakis Mountains suddenly flared with wild, riotous jets of color.

"What's happening?" someone cried.

The mountain shivered. Celierians closest to the steep slopes screamed and ran for cover as rocks and debris tumbled down towards Upper Orest.

Then the unthinkable happened.

With one last blinding blaze of light, the magical, rainbow-lit clouds that hugged the mountaintops collapsed inward upon themselves.

The great and magical barrier of the Faering Mists fell.

"The Mists are down!" someone shouted. "Gods save us, they've brought down the Mists!"

For the first time in one thousand years, the Fading Lands lay open and vulnerable to the outside world.

CHAPTER EIGHTEEN

The Pale ~ North Slopes of the Feyls

Garok hadn't been certain what to expect, but the complete destruction of the Mists was more than he'd dreamed possible. Triumph filled him with exultation.

"They're down!" one of the other Primages whispered. The whisper grew quickly to a racous, celebratory hurrah. "The Mists are down!"

Garok wasn't a Mage to waste time on self-congratulation. Getting through the Mists was only the first step. Reaching Dharsa, the core of the hated Fey homeland, was his goal. He'd been suspicious when Maur assigned him this mission, but he intended to make the most of it. When he returned to Eld in triumph as the Mage who'd brought down the Faering Mists and conquered Dharsa, even those Primages still hesitant to turn from Maur would look at him with new eyes.

"Archers to the fore!" he commanded. He paced across the rubble-strewn ground as the archers hurried to step forward. "Take aim! Fire!"

Bowstrings twanged in unison. Mages summoned the wind as a dark rain of *sel'dor* arrows, each modified to hold a *chemar* in the shaft, soared up the mountainside and across the now unprotected peak, disappearing on the opposite side.

Before the last arrow disappeared from view, Garok opened the Well of Souls and the Eld leapt in. The portal closed quickly on the heels of the last man. Within the darkness a fresh array of glowing blue lights lit the Well—the dozens of *chemar* that had found their targets lay before them, mere steps away.

"Primages, you know what to do." The Eld split into a dozen groups, each racing for a different spot of blue light inside the Well. They opened the portals using the *chemar*, and the instant the portals opened, archers fired more arrows through, while the Mages spun magic to carry the missiles much farther and faster than bowstring alone could have managed.

And so it went. Portals opened. Archers fired. On to the next portal. As they crossed the last line of the snowy volcanic peaks, a roar greeted one of the opening portals and a jet of flame lit up the interior of the Well, burning an entire company of Mages to ash.

The tairen had come to defend their territory. But the *chemar* were too many and the tairen too few. The Eld advanced with swift purpose towards the heart of the Fading Lands, the shining city on the hills.

Dharsa.

The Fading Lands ~ Dharsa

"The Mists are down! The Mages are coming." Marissya clutched the slight swell of her unborn child as she delivered the news to the Massan. "Sybharukai says they are using the Well to move across the Plains of Corunn. She doesn't know their numbers, but they're moving too fast, in too many directions. There aren't enough of the tairen to stop them. We must ward the city, quickly before it's too late."

"Down?" Yulan regarded her in disbelief. "The Mists can't be down!"

To his credit, Tenn didn't waste time doubting her word or hesitating in indecision. *«Fey, to arms! Defend the city! The Eld have broken through the Mists.»* To Marissya, he said, "You and Dax take the *fellanas* and the truemates to the Hall of Truth and Healing. Prepare to defend yourselves in case the Eld break through."

"What about you and Venarra and the rest of the Massan?"

Tenn's expression turned grim. "When we banished Rain, his duties fell to us. That includes the duty of defending the Fading Lands. Go. Quickly. Venarra, gather the *shei'dalins*. Nuri, Yulan, come with me."

The Fading Lands ~ Pass of Revan Oreth

"They did it." Kieran stared at the jagged, snow-capped peaks of the Rhakis mountains, visible now for the first time in a millennium. "Those scorching Elden *rultsharts* did it, Kiel. They brought down the Mists."

«Fey!» The cry rang out across the new Warrior's Path. *«Into the pass! Defend the Fading Lands!»*

Stone-faced and fire-eyed, Fey warriors shouted, *"Miora felah ti'Feyreisen! Miora felah ti'Feyreisa!"* and ran into the narrow, rocky pass of Revan Oreth. Kiel and Kieran ran with them.

The pass was many miles long, but as the Fey approached the last third of the trail through the mountains they heard the sound of rocks and pebbles tumbling down the mountainside, accompanied by a strange, clattering that echoed in the canyon, like the hard mandibles of millions of stone-shell beetles clicking madly.

«Fey! Weaves at the ready! Steel is useless. Hundred-fold weaves, or straight Earth and Fire only. Cutting them in half only grows two of them, so have a care. Light be with you, my brothers!»

The clattering noise grew louder, until it was nearly deafening. The Fey rounded a sharp curve in the pass, and the sight that awaited them made Kieran's blood freeze in his veins.

Coming towards them at an astonishing pace and in numbers the likes of which he'd never seen, were creatures. Thousands upon tens of thousands of creatures with grayish-white bodies and bald, eyeless heads. They looked vaguely and grotesquely manlike, and entirely terrifying.

As they neared, he could see the wet shine of their sluglike skins, the round, needle-filled holes of their green foaming mouths, the razor-sharp spines of their grasping, clawed hands and feet.

That was the clicking noise. The sounds of those clawed hands and feet scrabbling across rock with their darting speed. Some ran upright along the narrow path, but most raced on the sides of the mountain, covering the sheer cliff faces of the gorge like a monstrous swarm of beetles.

The first lines of Fey tried to stand their ground, spinning hundredfold weaves, filling the pass with blazing magic. But the revenants were too many. For each one they destroyed, ten more were there to take its place. The revenants reached the Fey lines and began leaping off the mountainside into the thick of the Fey.

Screams broke out as needle-filled mouths and acid skin ripped and dissolved shining Fey flesh.

"Earth masters! Bring down the mountains!"

Earth masters combined their weaves, tearing the sides of the mountain down and sending avalanches into the pass, burying the revenants beneath countless tons of broken rock.

For a chime, the Fey began to breathe easier. But then came the sound of shifting rock. The rubble moved. Clawed hands reached up from the shattered stone into the open air.

"Fey! Retreat! Retreat!"

Celieria ~ Orest

Rain soared across the sky, banking rapidly from left to right, soaring and diving. Another of those scorching Rain-seeking bowcannon bolts was on his tail. How many of the flaming things did the Eld have?

Below him, Fey dead littered a battlefield crawling with revenants.

«Shei'tani, how's your aim with a Fey'cha?»

«Getting better by the chime.»

He curled back his lip and gave a growling chuff of tairen

laughter. *«That's what I wanted to hear. If I fly low enough, do you think you can grab some of those Fey'cha harnesses with a weave?»*

«I know one way to find out.»

He chuffed again and blew smoke. Flying with her in battle had shown him an entirely different side of his *shei'tani*. Gone was the frightened, nightmare-stricken girl, gone too was the strong and powerful *shei'dalin* healer. In their place was a fierce Fey warrior—one with a good eye for strategy, unhesitating courage, and a deadpan sense of humor that would put Gillandaris vel Jendahr to shame.

«Then let's find out. And weave a shield around your hands in case the red Fey'cha slip their sheaths. There may be Shadar horn in your bones now, but I don't want to put it to the test.»

He felt the brief burst of magic.

«Done,» she said. *«Let's go.»*

He dove. Behind him, the bowcannon bolt followed suit. His wings spread wide and they soared low over the revenants. Fire boiled from his muzzle, incinerating a wide swath of the hideous creatures. Bright, blazing weaves shot out to his left and right, aiming just beyond the perimeter of his fire, and a collection of Fey'cha harnesses lifted up into the air.

«Got them.»

«All right. Then here's what we're going to do.» He sang her the images of what he had in mind in tairen speech. *«Can you manage that?»*

«I think so. Let's give it a try.»

Rain put on a burst of speed and soared up, heading straight for Orest. A frenzy of bowcannon bolts launched from the ramparts, but he flamed the incoming, rolled and dived to avoid those that survived his flame and kept to his heading. On his back, Ellysetta flung out spinning weaves of Air and Fire to clear a path. As they crossed the walls of Lower Orest, Rain veered sharply left then wheeled around back to the right and came in nearly parallel to the mountains.

On the ramparts of Upper Orest, the bowcannon were loaded, bowstrings cranked into firing position. Just before the sheer mountain cliff gave way to the stone ramparts of the upper city, Rain put on a burst of speed and said, *«Now, shei'tani.»*

Ellysetta launched from his back in an Air-powered leap. She shot up into the air, her own forward motion and magic carrying her over the tops of the cannoneers and Mages gathered on the ramparts. Red Fey'cha spit from her fingertips in a hail of death. Below her, Rain engulfed the battery in a boiling jet of tairen flame, consuming cannon and cannoneers alike. He Changed into Mist at the last chime so the bolt that had been following him plowed into the open portal to the Well of Souls, taking half a dozen screaming Mages and Eld with it. He changed back into tairen form in time for Ellysetta to land securely in the saddle. His wings angled sharply and they shot up in a near vertical climb, soaring past the falls of Orest, leaving smoldering fires and corpses in their wake.

They burst into the open sky over the Rhakis. In the distance, no longer hidden by the Mists, he could see the pass of Revan Oreth, where hundreds of thousands of revenants covered the canyon walls like insects.

The Eld hadn't brought bowcannon to the pass yet, so Rain took a few chimes to send a sea of boiling flame racing through the canyon. High pitched shrieks from burning revenants filled the air. Beyond the fire, Fey warriors cheered and raised their blades into the air. The echoing cries of *"Miora felah, ti'Feyreisen! Miora felah, ti'Feyreisa!"* followed him and Ellysetta as they banked around the column of steam rising from the first volcano of the Feyls and returned to the battlefield of Orest.

They burst from the pass over Upper Orest and dove back into the missile-filled skies.

«Rijonn, Tajik,» Rain called as he swooped down for another strafing run. *«Gather the Earth and Fire masters. I have a plan.»*

The Fading Lands ~ Dharsa

The sound of running and alarmed voices woke Lillis. That and a strange, icy cold that made shivers race down her spine. She sat up in bed, suddenly frightened. "Lorelle?"

"Lorelle's not here anymore."

A shadow lunged at her from the darkness. She opened her mouth to scream, but something stung her chest. Her head went dizzy and the world went black.

Den Brodson threw Lillis over one thick shoulder and headed into the Well, following the Black Guard who was already carrying Lorelle back to Boura Fell.

Behind him, before the portal to Lillis and Lorelle's room closed, the first screams broke the peaceful silence of the night as the others who'd come with Den to Dharsa opened more portals and an army of Mages, *dahl'reisen*, and Eld rushed into the Shining City.

Celieria ~ Orest

Bel snarled and hammered the revenants with powerful weaves of magic, all the while wishing he were slicing them to oozy green bits instead. Fey were used to fighting without magic. The Eld's fondness for *sel'dor* made certain of that. Warriors were far less accustomed to fighting without their steel. And despite the Elves' warning, he had to struggle to keep from reaching for his.

The foul stench of the revenants filled the air, making his eyes water and his stomach heave with each gagging breath. He was a master of all magics save Earth, which he could not weave at all, but his strength in all the other branches was exceptional. Even though his most powerful branch of magic, Spirit, was useless against these creatures, Bel was not.

He reached deep into the source of his power, drew it up into his body until his cells burned and light crackled around him in a glowing nimbus. He wove the vibrant threads into thick, sizzling ropes of power—Spirit, Fire, Air, Water—

and fed those ropes into massive hundred-twenty-five-fold weaves that he and his brothers slammed into the endless wall of revenants.

The monstrous creatures shrieked their ear-splitting wails. Many of them dissolved, but more still came.

«*Well done, kem'jeto,*» Gaelen complimented after a particularly fierce assault. Gil and Gaelen fought nearby, along with a grim-eyed Lord Barrial, who had enough Elf-blood in him to make use of the Light arrows he'd retrieved from fallen Elves, and enough Fey blood to spin a decent weave or two of his own.

Tamsin Greywing was mounted on the back of a Shadar and firing Light arrows as fast as he could. No matter how many he fired, his quiver never ran dry. As Bel watched, a revenant leaped toward Greywing, but the Elf cried something in Elvish and his mount reared up to impale the flying revenant on its spiraling silver horn. The creature exploded, enveloping Greywing and the Shadar in a foul, but harmless cloud of black dust. The Elf coughed and spat, patted the Shadar's shining neck in approval, then began firing off Light arrows again.

To the northeast of Bel's position, Azrahn surrounded Farel and his *dahl'reisen* in a shadowy cloud that glowed dark red in the night. Instead of twenty-five quintets spinning hundred-twenty-five fold weaves, thirty-six *chamas*—groups of six *dahl'reisen* spinning six-fold weaves—combined their power into massive two-hundred-sixteen fold weaves that pounded the revenants like steely fists.

Where the Fey's weave took out a dozen revenants in a single blow, the *dahl'reisen's* weave dusted a full score. But even that was not enough. For each revenant they destroyed, four more erupted from the ground to take its place.

Fey weaves and Elvish arrows set the air over the battlefield aglow, yet still the revenants advanced, pushing the allies back handspan by handspan.

Bel swore as more boreholes burst open and even greater numbers of the revenants boiled out of the earth. The supply of the thrice-scorched things was *jaffing* limitless. In unison, as if directed by some inaudible voice, the back lines of the creatures scrambled over the front and began leaping through the air to land in the midst of the allied lines. Where they landed, screams erupted as razor-sharp claws sliced skin down to bone and acid slime dissolved flesh on contact.

«Retreat!» Bel cried. *«Retreat!»*

They scrambled back, dragging the wounded with them. Bel slammed vortexes of Air and Fire at the creatures to buy his brothers time, and sent a private spirit weave arrowing across the battlefield. *«If you're going to do something, Rain, now's the time!»*

«Damn it, 'Jonn, Taj, are you ready yet?» Rain snapped the question across a private weave to the two warriors of Ellysetta's quintet. *«We're getting slaughtered here! I don't know how much longer we'll be able to hold out.»*

«Ready, Rain!» came the dual responses.

«Then tell them to go! Now!»

«Order given, Feyreisen.»

The ground began to shake and rumble. In Upper Orest, rocks broke off the surrounding peaks and tumbled down into the city. Rain saw buildings sway, and Eld Mages stagger as the ground beneath their feet became unstable.

The earth cracked. Steam vents opened in Upper Orest. Mages fell back in fear and began to flee as the rumbling of the earth grew more violent and the steam erupting from the vents grew hotter. With a sudden, deafening roar, the entire city of Upper Orest exploded into the sky. Black clouds of smoke and ash billowed upward and fountains of glowing orange molten rock shot into the air and began pouring down the mountainside into Lower Orest.

How do you get an enemy out of a fortified mountain haven?

You had Earth and Fire masters turn the mountain into an active volcano.

«They did it!» Ellysetta cried. *«They really did it!»*

His triumph and hers didn't last long. Barely a chime later, the cries rang out on the Warrior's Path.

«Dharsa is under attack! They're in the city! Fey! To arms! Dharsa is under attack! They're in the palace!»

«Rain!» Shocked into sudden sobriety, Ellysetta dug her fingers into the fur at the back of his neck. *«My family.»*

Rain instantly sent a Spirit weave racing across the distance to Dharsa. *«Marissya . . . Dax . . . get Ellysetta's family to safety.»*

And then, several long chimes later, Rain's wings faltered and she felt sorrow and concern well up inside him. Even before he spoke, she knew he'd received a private weave, and she knew the news wasn't good. Inside her chest, Ellysetta's heart turned to stone.

«Shei'tani . . . » Rain hesitated. *«I'm sorry, beloved. Your father is safe, but your sisters are gone. Dax says a portal was opened in their room. They've been taken.»*

"No." She said. Her lips felt numb. Her whole body had lost all feeling. All she could think of was the dream, that horrible, hateful dream of Lillis and Lorelle, their eyes black as pitch, dancing in a shower of blood. And she knew, just as Sheyl knew when she had a vision, that her dream would come true

«Ellysetta.» Rain turned his head as he flew.

"No." She said again, louder.

«Ellysetta, we will get them back. I promise you, shei'tani. As soon as this is over, as soon as we've defeated this army, we'll find out where he's taken them and we'll get them back.»

"NO!" This time she screamed it. The sound ripped from her throat like a tairen's roar. Rage blasted up from that place deep inside, the cold, Lightless place where the beast lived. Ice enveloped her. Hatred consumed her. She wanted these Eld and their foul creatures dead. She wanted this battle to stop.

She wanted her family back.

Now.

Her body began to shake.

On the battlefield, *lu'tan* and Fey cried out as their magic spun out of their control. One moment, they were spinning fierce weaves to hold back the revenants, the next moment the shining flows of their magic headed skyward, sucked away by a power greater than their own.

Standing between the retreating forces and the revenant hordes, Bel, Gaelen, and Gil all looked up towards the sky, knowing instantly what was happening.

"Ellysetta," Bel whispered.

Half a tairen-length away, Gaelen saw in shock that even the flows of Elvish and Elden magic were pouring into her.

"Bel, Gaelen," Gil called, "we have no magic and those revenants are still coming. I suggest we run, *kem'jetos*."

Dragging their gazes away from Ellysetta, they ran.

Hissing, the revenants followed.

The magic didn't burn inside Ellysetta, it froze. Her whole body felt encased in a block of ice.

«Shei'tani?» She heard Rain's call, but it came as if from a great distance.

These Mages liked death? Murder? Destruction? Well she would give them a taste of their own evil ways.

Her hands shot out, fingers splayed. Concentrated magic roared down her arms, setting her palms ablaze. She knew the weave. She'd seen it often enough. Fled from it often enough.

Power coalesced, blazing blue-white between her palms. She poured it forth, not in a great globe of power like the Mages did, but in a continuous, boiling jet, like tairen fire.

Mage Fire spewed from Ellysetta's hands, and spilled

across the battlefield from the walls of Orest to the allied lines in the east. It consumed revenants and the enemy forces fleeing the lava-ribboned volcano that had been Orest and gouged deep furrows into the earth.

«Shei'tani, nei.»

The tairen beneath her tried to bank, to turn her away, but she seized him with her power and forced him to her will. He flew where she bid him.

A voice was screaming in her head. Whether hers or his, she didn't know, and she didn't care. She wrapped herself in a weave of silence and kept pouring her wrathful river of Mage Fire upon the Elden army.

Vadim Maur watched the blazing, blue-white fire consuming everything in its path. Even the mass destruction of his great army couldn't stop the pride and savage satisfaction that surged through him at the sight.

"You wonderful, magnificent girl," he breathed. And with a crow of delight, using the bonds that already connected their souls as a conduit to keep her from absorbing his magic, he sent a concentrated weave of Azrahn stabbing into her soul.

He expected her to scream and flinch back as she had every time before, but instead a great force like nothing he'd ever felt suddenly fixed its gaze upon him. Power ripped through him. *Her* power. Purest Azrahn of a magnitude he never knew could exist. It plundered him, assaulted him, peeled him down to the smallest particle of a single cell, then put him back together again in the blink of an eye.

And even as his weave forged its fifth Mark upon her soul, her own weave stabbed him through to his core and seared every layer of his body and soul, leaving not just a Mark, but a smoldering brand.

His knees went weak. His bowels turned to water. She had Marked him. *She* had Marked *him*.

Vadim Maur grabbed the tent pole for support. Her power ripped from him the way a female tairen might retract her tail spike from the still-twitching body of her prey, but he knew she wasn't done. He could still feel her eye upon him, dread and merciless. He felt her gather her power for another strike and for the first time in centuries, he whispered, "Gods, help me."

His savior came from as unlikely a source as the one he'd called upon.

An Elf streaked across the sky on a white Aquiline charger. Light blazed from the Elf's upraised hand, and the beam fell upon Ellysetta Baristani like a shaft of concentrated sunlight. Now Ellysetta reared back in the way she hadn't done when Vadim Marked her, and the terrible force of her power turned away from the Mage, freeing him to sink helplessly to his knees.

"Master Maur! Master Maur, look!"

He lifted his head, gasping weakly for breath, and muttered a curse at the sight that greeted him. Sailing up the Heras, with *nyatheri* leaping through the black waters like silver-blue mermaids, came an Elvian armada, dozens of ships, silver sails filled with the air of a self-propelling wind, carrying thousands more Elves to join the battle. The trees on both shores bowed and danced in the ships' wakes as the *dryatheri*, the Danae tree spirits, aboard the Elvish vessels awakened the forests to their call.

Screams rose from the Elden shores as tree branches wound around Eld like serpents, crushing bones to powder, and large tree trunks opened up to swallow men whole. Soldiers drowned where they stood as seductive sirens rose from river's edge, enveloped them in an entrancing embrace, and took their lips in a kiss that filled their lungs with water. Others mindlessly followed the beckoning calls of beautiful mermaids and plunged into the Heras where *nyatheri* wrapped them in water vines and dragged them to the bottom of the river.

Vadim wanted to scream with rage. How could the day of his long-planned triumph have gone so horribly wrong? Two-thirds of his magnificent army was destroyed. The dragons were dead. Orest was an active volcano. The Elves and Danae had arrived in force. And Vadim's Mage-Marked future vessel had just made him soil himself.

But even as he gnashed his teeth in fury, cool reason was already taking over.

No Eld became High Mage without the courage to take a risk. But neither did he stay High Mage without learning to differentiate between risk and foolishness. And this High Mage knew the value of a strategic retreat.

All was not lost. Ellysetta Baristani still bore his Marks, he now had her sisters as well as her parents. When she came for them, he would be waiting. She only needed one more Mark. Just one, and then she and all her magnificent, unprecedented power would be his. And the world would tremble before his immortal greatness.

"Kron, sound the alarm. Evacuate Boura Dor. Everyone into the Well. We're retreating to Boura Fell."

Behind the Fey lines, protected by warriors who could call their magic once more, Rain knelt on the ground, holding Ellysetta in his arms.

The Elvian Commander who had called herself Silverleaf knelt beside him. The palm of her right hand no longer blazed sun-bright with the magic she had poured into Ellysetta, but Rain now knew who she was. A Seer of Elvia, just as she'd claimed. Elves truly didn't lie, after all. But she was also Elvia's queen, Illona Brighthand, the Lady of Silvermist, sister to Galad Hawksheart.

"Why would you hide who you were?" he asked.

Illona glanced up. "Does it matter?"

He grimaced. Why did Elves do half the things they did? "I suppose not. But will you at least tell me what happened back there, with Ellysetta?"

The Elf made a soft, regretful sound. "Your mate just faced a truth many of us are lucky never to know. She found out just what she was capable of."

His hackles rose immediately. "You will not tell me she is

evil," he interrupted. Even though she had seized his body and controlled him like a puppet on strings, he would not—could not—think the worst. "She is not. She is bright and shining."

"Very bright," the Elf agreed. "But as capable as she is of good, if she falls to Darkness, she will be equally capable of evil. You do her no favor by refusing to acknowledge that. Especially after today, when she had a glimpse of what she could become."

Ellysetta stirred in Rain's arms. Her eyes were still closed as she murmured, "I told you there was evil in me. I told you it was winning."

"Bayas, it is not unless you will it so." Illona laid her namesake hand on Ellysetta's hair. "Look at me, Ellysetta Erimea." When Ellysetta opened her eyes, the Elf continued, her voice brisk and stern, "I came here—I brought my Elves to your aid—because I did not want to see you fall. Was my faith in you misplaced? Will you give in so easily?"

"Easily?" Rain jumped to her defense. "You don't know what she's been through."

"I do know," Illona corrected in a sharp voice. "I am Elf-kind, and I have watched, just as my brother has done. I know exactly what she has suffered and for how long. But the Dark cannot claim what Light does not surrender."

"She has surrendered nothing. She has fought more bravely than most, suffered torments few can even imagine, and still her heart is kind, her soul bright and shining." Rain bent his head and pressed his lips against Ellysetta's hair. "We are together, Ellysetta. We are unharmed. No matter what happened today, we are still together. We still hold to the Light, and we always will."

"Will we?" Ellysetta's hand curled around his wrist. "I Marked the High Mage."

His mouth went dry. "You what?"

"After he Marked me, I Marked him back. It's a bit like forging a truemate bond, except with none of the love." She looked up at him, and there was such weary acceptance in her eyes, such increasing despair, it made him want to weep.

"Apparently, I'm not just a *shei'dalin* and a Tairen Soul, I'm also a Mage."

Rain moistened his lips and looked up at the Elf queen. "Is she? A Mage?" He couldn't believe he was practically begging an Elf for answers, but when it came to helping and protecting Ellysetta, he was discovering there wasn't a whole lot he wouldn't do.

"If she chooses to be, *anio*. She has the power to become one. But just because you *can* wield magic like a Mage, Ellysetta, that doesn't mean you must." The Elf queen sat back on her heels. "That is the other reason I came to you—to give you a truth my brother was unwilling to share. He has tried for many years to deny it, but the fact is that no one— not even Galad, with all his skill and power—can See with certainty the outcome of your Song. He cannot because you are a force rarely born to a world, something we Elves call *leinah thaniel*, the Song that sings all Songs, the Mirror that shows all Mirrors, the Change that changes everything."

"What does that mean?" Rain was so tired of Elvish mysticism. He just wanted answers, plain and simple.

"It means your mate holds within herself a divine spark, the power to do the unexpected, to change her Song and the Songs of others, just as she has already done many times." The Elf turned her gaze upon Ellysetta. "It means there is no 'meant to be' for you. There is only 'choose to be.' So choose wisely, Ellysetta Erimea. Much depends on it."

Illona Brighthand stood. "You know, in your heart, what is right. You proved that to me earlier today when you would not force the spirits of your *lu'tan* to your service. Trust in yourself—and know that the right path is rarely the easiest." She looked west and her eyes took on a deep, mysterious shimmer. "You both should go. The Fey need you in Dharsa."

"What about Orest?" Rain asked.

"The Eld are retreating. Your mate killed most of the revenants and my brother's Elves have arrived with the Danae. We will help your friends here to end this battle. Dharsa is where you are now needed most."

The Fading Lands ~ Dharsa
11th day of Seledos

Spurred by Illona, Rain and Ellysetta flew as fast as wings and magic could carry them. With the Mists down, they soared, unimpeded, over the Rhakis mountains, flying over the pass of Revan Oreth and giving the remaining revenants there a good scorching before continuing onward across the eastern desert and the Plains of Corunn.

They arrived with the dawn at the Shining City of the Fey. But instead of the raging battle they were expecting, they found the aftermath of one.

The jewel of the Fading Lands lay in ruins. Dharsa's buildings were shattered and smoking, their pristine white stones charred black. Scorched, leafless orchards dotted burned hillsides. Instead of jasmine and honeyblossom, the city smelled of smoke and death.

As they flew towards the palace, they could see Fey dragging the bodies of the dead invaders into a pile while six tairen took turns flaming the corpses to harmless ash. Elsewhere, other Fey carried their fallen brothers and sisters to the gardens, where quintets had gathered to send the bodies back to the elements.

"I don't understand," Ellysetta said as she and Rain landed in the tairen's courtyard near the Hall of Tairen and he Changed back into Fey form. "I thought the Elf queen said we were needed here."

"You *are* needed here." Marissya and Dax stepped into the courtyard. Sol Baristani and, to Ellysetta's surprise, the Elf Fanor Farsight followed close on their heels. "The Fading Lands will always need its Tairen Souls. And with the Mists down, we need you now more than ever."

"Papa." Bypassing the others, Ellysetta headed straight for her father and melted in his arms. She breathed the beloved aroma of his pipe smoke and was instantly transported back to the days of her childhood, when she lived surrounded by her family and secure in the warmth of her parents' love.

Tears gathered and she let them fall. "We will get them back, Papa. I promise you. Rain and I will find a way."

"I know you will." His hands patted her back. "For now, I'm just glad to see you safe, Ellie-girl." He pulled back and smiled through his own teary eyes.

With an arm around her father's waist, Ellysetta turned to watch Rain greet Fanor Farsight, the Deep Woods Elf.

"Farsight. I did not expect to see you here after Hawksheart said he could not help us."

One of Fanor's brows arched slightly. "Lord Galad said he could not join your battle against the High Mage. He never said he would not aid the Fey in Dharsa."

"They arrived in time to help the tairen rout the Mages," Dax said. "Unfortunately, the city had already been breached. *Dahl'reisen*, Black Guard, and a host of Mages got through. We lost hundreds, but it would have been thousands without the warriors who stayed behind as Tenn commanded. They kept the Eld at bay until the tairen and Elves arrived. Nurian and Yulan were killed in the fighting, and their mates passed into the Veil with them. Tenn nearly perished as well, but Marissya and Venarra managed to keep him alive. He's in the Hall of Truth and Healing now, helping his mate look after the wounded."

"He knew we were coming?" Rain asked.

"Aiyah."

"And he did not call for armed Fey to defend the Fading Lands against its *dahl'reisen* king?"

"You are *dahl'reisen* no longer. Sybharukai spoke to him herself. She told him the Fey'Bahren pride had chosen the next leader of the Fading Lands and that it was not him. She also told him that his brother, Johr Feyreisen, had already singled you out to be trained for leadership so that you might one day ascend the throne."

"I never knew that." Rain shook his head in wonder. "So that convinced him? Learning that his brother had been considering me for the throne?"

Dax snorted. "I think the kicker was when Sybharukai

told him that the tairen would drive from the Fading Lands any people who reviled or threatened you or Ellysetta."

His brows shot up. "She said that?"

"Ai-*yah*," Dax confirmed with grinning emphasis. "You should have seen Tenn's face when she bared her fangs and growled, 'Tairen defend the pride.' I swear, he near wet himself."

"Dax," Marissya chided, "you should not take such delight in that. Tenn has served this kingdom well for centuries."

"I agree that he did—right up until he decided to banish its king and queen, at which time, in my opinion, he earned himself a hard beating with a dull blade. Sybharukai let him off easy."

"I must thank her for coming to our defense," Rain said. "But it is time to repair the damage this war has wrought—both on the city and among ourselves. There is much to be mended, on all sides."

They spent all day doing just that, mending buildings and mending bridges with the Fey. Their first stop was the Hall of Truth and Healing, where Rain and Ellysetta met with Tenn and Venarra. The meeting was stiff and formal, but it passed without bloodshed or name calling. For a first step, that was enough.

They worked throughout the day, but with every wall they reconstructed, every weeping Fey they consoled, every stiff, cold-eyed warrior whose suspicions they allayed, Ellysetta realized that simply rescuing her sisters and parents from Eld wasn't going to be enough. This Mage had to be stopped, and according to the Elves, she was the only one who could. Even if it cost her life.

Perhaps that was the real reason Illona Brighthand had sent them here. Not because Dharsa needed them, but because she needed Dharsa and the reminder that even though the war was over, her own battle was not yet done. Because Ellysetta needed a day without war to remember why it was necessary . . . and what she was fighting for.

"You said that when we defeated the Army of Darkness, we would go to Eld to save my parents," Ellysetta reminded Rain as the afternoon drew to a close and the sun began to set. "That time has come. I don't want my sisters, or my parents, to spend one more night than necessary in Eld hands. And I'm going with you."

"*Shei'tani*. . . . You know I would give you the stars from the heavens if you asked it of me, but this . . ." Shadows turned lavender eyes to brooding violet. "Our bond is not complete. You bear five Mage Marks."

"If we don't find a way to defeat him, I may someday bear six." She framed his face in her hands. "I have to do this, Rain. It's what I was born for." The chime she said the words aloud, she knew they were true. "We are Tairen Souls, *shei'tan*, you and I both. We are Defenders not just of the Fey but of the Light, including the Light that shines in good people everywhere—in my sisters and my parents, in Celierians . . . in the poor people of Eld who never had a choice for any life but servitude and Darkness. This High Mage must be stopped. Not just defeated and left in peace to grow strong again, but vanquished. That is our purpose. That is why we were born."

"We should consult *Shei'Kess*. Perhaps it will—"

"*Nei*." She shook her head and gave a sad smile. "The Eye can show us nothing we don't already know. It's what we feel here—" she tapped first her chest, then his, "—that matters. You heard the Elf queen. I am *leinah thaniel*. There are no fates I cannot change, but this fate is one I cannot change without you. You are my strength, Rain. You are the courage I've always lacked."

He gave a choked laugh, and tears glittered in his eyes. "If I am your courage, then why does this idea of yours leave me so frightened?"

Her heart contracted, and she smiled at him, softly, through brimming eyes. "Because it *is* frightening, *kem'san*. Because it's dangerous, risky, the odds so stacked against us it's unlikely anyone could do this thing and live. And that's why a Tairen Soul was born to do it—why we were born to do this." She pressed her lips to his. "When a *feyreisen* finds his wings, he knows he was born to die protecting others. That is why we must go."

He drew her closer, nestling her in his arms and leaning his head against hers. "When did you get so wise, Ellysetta *kem'reisa*?"

Celieria ~ Orest
12ᵗʰ day of Seledos

Rain and Ellysetta spent half the night in Dharsa, the other half in Fey'Bahren with the pride and the kitlings, who had grown a great deal in the last two months. In the morning, they flew back to Orest to meet with the *lu'tan* and devise a plan to rescue Ellysetta's family and kill the High Mage of Eld.

Farel's men had captured a wounded Mage and a handful of Eld soldiers, all of whom they held in a bubble of thirty-six fold weaves. A little Truthspeaking and the threat of being eaten alive by a tairen had encouraged the soldiers to talk. They told their captors about Vadim Maur's main fortress where all magic-gifted prisoners were taken after their capture, and about how each Boura—each underground fortress of the Eld—contained a gateway to the Well of Souls that was kept open all the time.

The plan was to have one of the *dahl'reisen* open a portal and bring one of the Eld soldiers along to lead the Fey through the Well to wherever Ellysetta's parents and sisters were being held. They would invade the Boura using the *dahl'reisen* invisibility weaves, free all the prisoners, and use Ellysetta's connection to the High Mage to locate and kill him while they were there.

The "plan" had holes large enough to fly a tairen through—*nei*, an entire pride of tairen—but Rain couldn't come up with anything better. So with a bit of instruction from the captured Mage, Farel successfully opened the portal to the

Well of Souls. And into the Well, they went: Rain, Ellysetta,
her quintet, a hundred *lu'tan*, and the Elden soldier as their
guide.

The inside of the Well was an unpleasant place, dark and
cold, full of whispers and distant shrieks and swirling pools
of shadowy mist that the Eld advised them to avoid if they
valued their lives. How he knew where to go, Ellysetta didn't
know, but later, it would occur to her that was a question she
should have asked and gotten answered.

Because when they reached the gateway into Boura Fell,
which appeared as a glowing red circle within the Well, their
arrival did not come as the surprise they had intended. No
sooner had they donned their invisibility weaves and slipped
through the gateway into a large room, than the gateway
closed behind them. A barrage of tiny darts and a burst of
pale blue gas filled the air.

Ellysetta's vision blurred, and the world tilted crazily. She
and all the Fey fell, unconscious, to the stone floor.

Eld ~ Boura Fell

Ellysetta woke to the sickly sweet smell of rotting fruit and
the taste of misery in her mouth. Her bones ached. Her flesh
throbbed.

She could hear the moans of tortured creatures, feel the
despair sapping her soul. This was a place without hope,
without Light, and she knew she'd fallen into one of the
Seven Hells.

Her muscles clenched, shuddering as the sting of a thousand icy knives stabbed into her soul.

She swallowed, then coughed.

Sel'dor cloaked her in bitter, burning pain. A collar of
enslavement about her neck, manacles about her wrists and
ankles.

Her lashes fluttered as she forced her eyes open. Expecting
darkness, she was surprised to find herself in the center of
a well-appointed room. Beautifully furnished—deceptively

so, because beneath the silken surface, she could feel the acid burn of *sel'dor*.

She turned her head, her gaze moving instinctively towards the corner of the room where a shrouded figure stood in the shadows. As the figure approached her, the formless shroud became rich purple Mage robes draped around a tall frame.

The Mage threw back his cowl, and Ellysetta frowned in confusion at the stranger standing by her bedside. She had expected the High Mage, the architect of her nightmares, with his cloud of white hair framing a face that seemed both ancient and ageless. But this Mage was young and fit and . . . handsome. That seemed so wrong. Evil shouldn't wear a pleasing face.

Only the cold, silver eyes seemed familiar. That and the cruelty curled at the corner of his mouth.

Then he spoke, and though the sound of the voice was as unfamiliar as his face, the smug, conscienceless evil that resonated in every word was all too familiar. Whatever face he wore, whatever voice he used, this *was* the High Mage of Eld, the dark evil presence that had pursued and tormented her all her life.

"Welcome, my dear, to Boura Fell."

CHAPTER NINETEEN

"You've led me quite a chase for many years, but all that is at an end. You shall not escape me again." The Mage's expression was cool, his tone almost pleasant, but there was no mistaking the Darkness that shadowed his every word.

Ellysetta sat up with effort. The weight of her *sel'dor* bindings was so heavy she could barely move. She lifted her hands to the collar and brushed the backs of her fingers against the dozens of burning rings that pierced the lobes of her ears. Another half dozen armbands, lined with hundreds of sharp teeth, circled both arms with ropes of pain, and around her ankles, heavy manacles clamped tight, their sharp spikes driving into her bones.

The Mage watched her with cold eyes. "I don't usually take such precautions with my female guests, but experience has taught me not to underestimate you."

She licked her dry lips. "I know what you want. You will not have it. I'll die before I surrender my soul to you."

The edge of his mouth lifted in a sneer. "Such brave words. The Fey are always brave at first. But even the greatest among them has a weakness, and you, my dear, have many." He snapped his fingers, and two burly guards stepped forward. They hauled her unceremoniously up, releasing her manacles from the chains that had bound her to the bed and setting her on her feet.

«Rain!» She tried to call him on their private path, but her body suddenly convulsed in agony. A scream ripped from her throat, and she dropped to the ground. She lay there,

shuddering and gasping for breath as she waited for the pain to recede.

"They all try that, too," the Mage informed her. "I don't advise it. I've bound you in more *sel'dor* than any other guest of mine has ever borne."

When the worst of the pain had passed, and she could move again, Ellysetta lifted her head and glared at him. "What have you done with Rain?" He wasn't dead. He couldn't be dead. She'd know if he were—wouldn't she?

"Oh, he's here, never fear. And you shall see him, I promise. In fact, I'm rather looking forward to it. But first things first." He glanced at the guards and all pretense of civility— gloating or otherwise—dropped away. Silver eyes glittered with cold command. "Bring her."

The guards hauled Ellysetta to her feet by her chains and shoved her after the High Mage of Eld.

When the news first reached the *umagi* dens about the Fey captured trying to invade Boura Fell, a communal groan went up. The *skrants* knew what new prisoners meant: more mouths to feed, more bodies to dispose of, more torture chambers to scrub clean of blood, vomit, and the various other by-products of the Mage's favorite pastime.

Only recently released from the punishment detail she'd earned for missing two whole work shifts while stealing Lord Death's weapons and crystal, Melliandra had a different reaction: a gut-churning mix of excitement and terror.

Her time had come.

Unfortunately, the circumstances of that time were riskier than she'd ever imagined they could be. The same gossip who brought them the rumors about invaders also brought news that Lord Death and his mate had been moved to the observation chambers for the High Mage's entertainment. He would be under heavy guard, and he would be constantly tortured, then healed, then tortured again. If she thought for one moment that she would get another chance to kill the High Mage, she wouldn't even think about approaching

Lord Death now. She would have waited until Lord Shan was
back in his cell, manacled but otherwise unrestrained in his
barbed cage.

Time, however, was a luxury she didn't have. The other
whispers in the Mage Halls were too rampant to be disbe-
lieved. Among Vadim Maur's new guests were the Tairen
Soul and his mate. If Vadim Maur managed to claim a
Tairen Soul's power, nothing and no one would ever be able
to defeat him again.

That meant she needed to free Lord Shan without delay.
No matter how high the risk.

As the Mage led Ellysetta down the corridor, they passed
a large, dark mirror hanging on one wall. The sight of her
reflection made Ellysetta stumble. Everything about the reflection shining in the mirror's dark surface came straight
from one of her nightmares: herself, garbed in a boat-necked
green gown, hair unbound and spilling about her shoulders,
sel'dor bands clamped around throat, wrists, and ankles,
walking in the company of a purple-robed Mage.

Fresh dread curled in her belly. She remembered the
dream. Remembered what had happened in it.

Lillis and Lorelle.

She almost tried to reach for them, but the shredding
agony of the *sel'dor* bonds reacting to her magic was too
fresh in her mind.

The corridor wound around, and they reached a set of
carved stone steps that curled downward into the bowels of
the earth. The guards pushed her after the High Mage, and
together, the four of them descended several flights, passing two sconce-lit landings that led off to other levels of the
subterranean fortress.

They exited the stairs on the third level and walked down
another series of corridors to an observation room. She
could see different cells through the windows on either side
of the room. Through the murky glass on the right, she saw a
dark-haired Fey warrior being strapped down to a table. For

an instant, she feared the warrior might be Rain, but when the Fey was pushed down onto his back for the final bindings, she saw his face.

Not Rain's face, but not unfamiliar either. A face from her dreams. Her hands splayed instinctively against the glass in a gesture of horror and concern.

"I see you recognize my longtime guest." The Mage took pleasure in her torment.

She wanted to say she'd never seen him before, but the lie stuck in her throat. She clamped her lips together and glared.

"The great Shannisorran v'En Celay, Lord Death. A legendary warrior of the Fey. Your father."

Despite her effort to show no emotion, her chin trembled.

"And here." The Mage walked to the opposite wall, where another viewing window looked into a different cell. A redhaired woman, her body covered in cuts and bruises and healing burns, was bound to a table just like the one in the other room. "Your mother, the beauteous Elfeya, though as you can see, she recently displeased me and was punished for it."

Ellysetta clenched her jaw and closed her fingers into tight fists to hide the trembling of her hands. She knew what was coming. Her stomach churned with nausea at the prospect.

She turned away from the Fey parents she'd never known. They were, in most respects, utter strangers to her, but they'd suffered unspeakable torments to keep her from sharing their fate.

And she, in her desperation and misguided belief that she could outwit a master manipulator, had walked straight into Vadim Maur's trap.

"A thousand years you've held them," she told him bitterly. "A thousand years, you've tortured them without mercy. But they never gave in. Do you think I don't know that? Do you think I don't know they'd rather die than see me surrender my soul to save them?"

"Die?" Vadim Maur exclaimed. "Oh, they won't die. Not yet, at least. Not for a very, very long time." Several large, burly men entered the rooms where Shan and Elfeya lay waiting. "As I've learned over these last thousand years, Lord Death and his mate are quite strong. What I haven't yet learned is how strong *you* are." He leaned forward and spoke into a pipe that fed into both rooms. "You may begin."

Moments later, the screams began.

Melliandra hauled her black canvas bag out of its hiding spot, using the rope that held it suspended along the interior wall of the refuse pit. The days in the pit had not been kind, and the canvas had absorbed a rank collection of smells and stains. She tossed the bag into her cart and, at the first empty chamber she found, she snatched the bag and ducked inside. Quickly, she emptied Lord Shan's belongings from the black bag. The two long straps of daggers, she strung across her shoulders, and she tied the empty sword sheaths to her chest. The swords themselves, she transferred to a clean, canvas laundry sack and tucked behind a crate in the corner of the room. Using sheaths she'd stolen from the Mage Halls, she strapped the two daggers she'd stolen for herself to her legs—one on her right calf, the other on the opposite thigh—and strapped two sheathed red Fey'cha to her forearms, with their hilts just reaching her wrists. The oversized sleeves of the tunic she'd filched from the laundry specifically for this purpose draped down over her hands and hid the Fey'cha and Lord Shan's weapons nicely.

Done, she tossed the empty black bag back in the refuse cart. After finishing emptying all the remaining refuse bins on the level, she emptied the cart and returned it to its closet, then stepped into the pulley-driven kitchen lift.

She rode the lift down to the kitchens. No one noticed her in the flurry of activity.

"I'm impressed by your ability to remain such an uninvolved observer in the face of such agony." Genuine appreciation colored the Mage's voice. "No other *shei'dalin* has ever witnessed such torment without begging for it to stop."

Ellysetta spat a mouthful of blood. She'd wanted to beg. She'd wanted it so bad, she'd bit a hole through the inside of her cheek to keep from it. The screams of her parents still echoed in her head. They'd known she was there. And even as their guts were being ripped from their bodies, they were shouting for her not to give in, to be strong.

Telling *her* to be strong. *Her.* When she was the reason they were being tortured.

When she was the one upon whom the Mage had yet to lay the first unkind finger.

"I think there must be more Darkness in you than you want to admit," Maur continued. "It's doubtless one of the gifts you gained when I engineered your birth. You should thank me, Ellysetta, because without that gift, you'd be just another of those useless Fey females, as helpless as a rose without thorns. Instead, you're strong, powerful. More like me than you care to admit."

She gave him a baleful glare and remained silent. She wanted to tell him he was a liar, but she couldn't. No matter how vile his claims, they contained at least a grain of truth. She *was* different from other Fey women. She could kill without destroying herself. Not only that, she could *enjoy* it. She remembered Kreppes, and the grim satisfaction, the barbarous thrill, of gutting her enemy, hearing his scream, feeling the hot spew of his blood upon her flesh. There had to be something in her, some hardness, some Darkness, some bit of evil that spawned such a dreadful trait and such macabre joy.

One thing was certain. That core of Darkness hiding inside her must never be released—not for her parents' sake. Not for anyone else's sake either.

"If you think your stoicism has saved them even a moment of pain, think again," Maur said, misinterpreting her continued silence. "They will suffer for a long, long time for their part in keeping you away from me all these years." He leaned back to the pipe leading to both rooms, and said, "Summon the healer. When she's done, begin again."

He nodded to the guards holding Ellysetta's chains and turned towards the exit. A hard shove from behind sent Ellysetta stumbling after him. They went down four more levels, until they reached the bottom of Boura Fell. A long, dark corridor, narrower than the ones above, stretched into the shadows in both directions. Vadim Maur turned right and led the way to the very end of the corridor. There, next to a shuttered opening that reeked of refuse, a dark, narrow tunnel curved off to the left. The Mage took a torch from a stand bolted to the wall and lit it on one of the sconce lights.

As he led Ellysetta and her guards into the tunnel, the damp, narrow, black walls closed in around them. A terrible rotting smell made her shudder. The place smelled like death.

"Perhaps for ancient Fey you've never known, who long ago accepted their fate, you can stay strong," the High Mage said as they walked. The tunnel twisted back around to the right, and the awful stench grew stronger. "But what about someone you love more dearly? Someone more fragile, more helpless? I think you will find it much more difficult to let them suffer."

The tunnel opened up to a gaping black maw of a chamber. A black stone promontory, railed with twisting vines of *sel'dor,* extended out over the abyss. The air was cold and dank, thick with the odor of putrefaction.

The Mage raised his torch to a shallow gutter overhead. Light flared as whatever the gutter contained caught fire, and flame raced along the gutter's path, into the blackness. The gaping maw was a dark pit, and even before the fire concluded its circuit and fully illuminated the floor of the pit half a tairen length below, Ellysetta knew what was coming. She'd seen it before, in her nightmares.

She gripped the *sel'dor* railing, uncaring of the hot burn of the hated metal on her flesh. Her sisters sat huddled together in the midst of the dark, stinking pit, tethered by chains in the center of a nest of bones and other rotting scraps. The sudden brightness of the flames made them look up, shielding their eyes with their hands.

She wanted to scream the twins' names. She wanted to throw herself on her knees and beg the High Mage for mercy, just as she had in her dream. She dared do neither. She knew why he'd brought her, knew that no matter what she did, Lillis and Lorelle were doomed. If she refused to accept a sixth Mark, Lillis and Lorelle would die. If she did accept the Mark, Vadim Maur would own her soul; and he would use her to enslave her sisters. They would become those Azrahn-eyed imps of Darkness from her nightmares, their souls bound to evil.

Oh, gods, gods. Why have you done this? They are innocent. They are children!

She didn't think she had the strength to stand firm. Her sisters were the children she'd loved and cared for all her life, twin beacons of Light in a life full of fear and self-doubt.

"Will you not call to them, Ellysetta?" the Mage prodded. "Will you not tell them everything will be all right? I know you feel their fear."

She closed her eyes, trying to shut him out. *Aiyah,* she sensed their fear. It burned worse than the *sel'dor* that pierced her flesh. She could not even spin a simple Spirit weave to whisper of her love and beg their forgiveness for bringing them into such danger.

"You were so brave, watching your parents suffer so nobly on your behalf. But will you be so brave now, watching your sisters eaten alive? Hearing their shrieks of pain and terror?"

Ellysetta's head whipped around, her jaw going lax. *Eaten alive?*

The Mage leaned over the railing and raised his voice. "Your sister Ellysetta is here, little ones. Beg her to save you. She can, you know. All she has to do is give me what I want, and you will be released from the pit."

The rumbling screech of metal echoed in the pit as unseen gates opened.

Then came the scrabble of claws against stone . . . and the bloodcurdling howls of the *darrokken*.

"The High Mage sent me with food for the prisoner." Melliandra clutched the handle of the food cart in both hands.

The guard standing beside the door examined her with cold eyes. "I received no such order," he declared, and his meaty fingers tightened around the spiked staff in his grip. "The healer just left, but the High Mage usually saves food until the prisoners are returned to their cells."

Melliandra kept her expression blank and unemotional. "The High Mage is entertaining a special guest. He wants these two strong enough to survive a long time." When the guard still showed no sign of stepping aside, she added, "Or I can return to the kitchens and inform my mistress that you kept me from fulfilling the Great One's commands. I'm sure he will understand why his orders were overridden."

As she expected, just the hint of an ill report to the High Mage was enough to give the guard pause. His brows furrowed and he poked the tip of his staff in the direction of her cart.

"Lift the cloth on that tray."

Melliandra obeyed, revealing two bowls of fatted porridge, a pitcher of water, and a hammered-metal goblet. Simple fare. Nothing out of the ordinary for a prisoner.

After a brief inspection, the guard grunted and stepped aside. "Go on then, but be quick about it."

She murmured an assent and pushed the cart through the doorway.

Lord Shan, silent and still as the dead, lay strapped to the table at the center of the room. Pools of blood glistened on the dark stone floor and still dripped from the table, but Melliandra could see no obvious wounds. The healer had done her job well.

Vadim Maur's new torture master stood beside a table set with a variety of knives, hooks, and vises. Tools of the torturer's trade. He was sharpening his curved disemboweling knife. At the sight of Melliandra, he scowled. "What do you want? The healer has come and gone. Get out."

"Master Maur commanded me to feed the prisoner," she said. "He wants him kept strong, to make him last longer."

After some grumbling about interruptions, the new torture master set down his implements and moved aside.

Melliandra pushed her cart towards the table. She flicked a quick, searching glance around the room, noting the three guards who stood in the corners of the stone chamber, barbed *sel'dor* pikestaffs in hand. Four armed men. Worse than she'd hoped for.

"He can't eat like that." She gestured to the *sel'dor* straps that kept the Fey immobilized on the table. "He needs his hands to feed himself."

The torture master snorted. "I know what happened to Goram, and I've heard all the tales about how Lord Death can gut a man with his little finger. Feed him yourself. Because he stays where he lies, bound and strapped."

Melliandra ground her teeth. There was no way even Lord Death could defeat four armed men while restrained so securely he could barely move a finger.

"I'm not putting my fingers in his mouth. He'd bite them off for sure! Just one hand," she pressed. "Surely between the four of you, you could skewer him if he so much as twitches." When they still didn't budge, she offered a bribe few *umagi* could resist. "I'll bring you all hot stew from the Mage Hall kitchens for a week."

That did the trick. With a muttered oath, the torture master unhooked a ring of keys from his belt and tossed them to one of the guards. "Left arm only. The rest of you, look sharp. If he moves, spit him like a roast pig." He narrowed his eyes at Melliandra. "I like extra meat in my stew. Don't forget."

"Won't," she vowed.

Two of the guards held the barbed points of their pikes pressed against the Fey's throat while the third unlocked the restraining straps at his left wrist and elbow and jumped back. Melliandra watched their twitchy nervousness with a curious mix of satisfaction and trepidation. They feared him so much. She only hoped Lord Death's abilities lived up to his reputation.

The Fey flexed his arm with slow deliberation, curling and uncurling his fingers to return circulation, rotating his wrist, elbow, and shoulder. All the while, his slitted green gaze made careful note of the guards' reactions and the shifts in their location.

"Enough," the torture master declared. "Feed him and be done with it."

With a curt bob of her head, Melliandra took one of the bowls and approached the table. She held the congealing porridge close enough that he could scoop it into his mouth with his fingers. She knew the moment he touched the crystal she'd put at the bottom of the bowl. With casual deliberation, his eyes met hers. She glanced down at her right arm, where the cuff of her ragged sleeve gaped beneath her skinny wrist, and lifted her hand just enough to show him the red-handled blade sheathed at her wrist. His breath caught for an instant, the response so faint she only noticed because she was looking for a reaction. He'd seen the distinctive name mark etched into the pommel. His crystal, his blades. He'd nearly killed the High Mage last time, even without them. This time, she prayed whatever extra power his own weapons provided would give him the edge he needed to succeed.

Lord Shan stuffed the last of his porridge in his mouth, then pretended to cough, as if he'd swallowed some of the food the wrong way.

Torn between suspicion and alarm—the High Mage would definitely not be pleased if his prized prisoner escaped him by choking to death—the torture master took a step towards him.

Lord Shan moved so fast his hand was a blur. One moment

he was gasping for breath, the next, a red-handled dagger quivered in the torture master's chest, one guard collapsed across Lord Shan's body, his mouth working soundlessly as blood gushed from the gaping hole in his throat, and the pike he'd been pointing at Lord Shan was buried in the eyeball of the second guard. The third guard died on the point of a second red-handled dagger gripped in Melliandra's fist.

The thud of falling bodies and the clatter of the pikes against the stone floor brought the guard outside the door running in to investigate. He died before he took his second step into the room, the dagger from the torture master's chest buried hilt deep in the newcomer's throat.

Melliandra leapt across the room to drag the fallen guard inside and close the door. "Well, I guess you really can gut a man with your little finger."

He flashed her a look so flat and cold and full of death, she knew he'd earned every awed and terrified word ever spoken about him.

"That is the least of what I can do."

"Lillis! Lorelle!" Ellysetta's magic gathered, twisted into agony as it battered helplessly against *sel'dor* bonds. The scream ripped from her throat. "Noooo!"

The twins' terror beat at her. "Ellie! Ellie, help us!"

"Stop it! Please, stop this!"

The High Mage stood unmoved by her tearful plea. "You know how to stop it. The choice is entirely yours."

Her fingers clutched the railing, yanking at it with enough force to rattle the metal bars in their anchor holds. Another magic rose. Cold and sweet, untouched by the painful bane of *sel'dor*. She dared not grasp it, not even to save her sisters. To save them now, with that magic, was to doom them to a worse fate than death.

But as the sounds of the *darrokken* grew closer and the screams of her sisters more frantic, Ellysetta knew she could not just stand there and let them die either. She was not some helpless victim. She was a Tairen Soul, a champion of Light, a defender of the innocent. She was the daughter of Shannisorran v'En Celay, Lord Death, the greatest Fey warrior ever born. What would her father do? What would Rain do?

They would fight.

And if they couldn't fight with magic, they would find some other way.

In a move so fast she shocked even herself, Ellysetta lunged backward and struck out with both hands, using her *sel'dor* manacles to deliver crushing blows to the windpipes of the guards holding her chains. They doubled over in pain, gasping for air, and dropped her chains. She caught the trailing ends with a quick flip of her arms and spun towards the High Mage.

His hands were raised. Something stung her on the chest and neck. She managed two more rushing steps in his direction before the world went black.

Using the keys to the table restraints Melliandra found on the body of the dead torture master, she freed Lord Shan from his bonds. Once she was done, he took his dark red crystal in one hand and clenched his jaw briefly as green magic glowed around his fist. When he opened his hand, his crystal was set in a silvery chain, which he fastened around his neck.

"My mate? Elfeya?"

"In the next room. To the right of this one. Here." She tugged the tunic over her head to reveal the cache of gleaming Fey steel daggers set in their leather sheaths and harness straps slung across her chest. "You'll want these." Quickly, she pulled the belts free and handed them over.

He was off the table, reaching for the weapons. "My swords?"

"I had to leave them hidden. They were too bulky. But I brought you the sheaths. Wait!" She grabbed the blue robes she'd stolen from the Mage Halls, but he was already out the door, dagger belts slung crisscrossed over his naked chest, sword belts in hand.

She ran after him and nearly tripped over the body of a guard who must have come from the adjacent room to investigate. Melliandra muttered a curse, dragged the dead guard inside the torture chamber with the others, and thanked the Dark Lord that this part of Boura Fell wasn't frequented as much as others. The idiot Fey was going to ruin everything if he left a trail of corpses in his wake. The alarm would sound, and he'd never get near the High Mage.

She ran into the other chamber, intending to upbraid him for his carelessness, only to stop in her tracks. Lord Death had slaughtered the remaining Eld with an impressively tidy finesse. Three bodies lay crumpled on the ground, a single, neat little wound in each guard's chest or throat the only sign of violence. That wasn't what robbed her limbs of the ability to move. It was the sight of Lord Death and his mate—or, rather, it was the look on Lord Death's face as he helped his mate from the restraining table and ran shaking hands over her hair, and the radiant glow on her face as she gazed up at him . . . as if simply standing in each other's presence had flung open the gates of some unimaginable paradise and enveloped them both in a world of warmth and joy. That look struck Melliandra like a hard blow, and her eyes began to burn like they had the time the flue in the *umagi* den got blocked and filled the room with smoke.

She averted her eyes and cleared her throat to ease its aching tightness.

"You promised you would kill the High Mage." She interrupted in a raspy voice, as much to break them apart as to remind Lord Death of his vow. "You agreed that if I freed you, you would kill him."

Lord Death lifted his mate's hands to his mouth, but when he turned to Melliandra she was relieved to see that his expression was once more cold and dangerous. "So I did."

Releasing his hand, Lord Death's mate went to the nearby table laid out with the torturer's implements. She took a pair of stubby metal clippers the torture masters used to cut through fingers and toes and began snipping away the *sel'dor* hoops piercing her ears. Metal clinked against stone as she pulled each hoop free and tossed it to the ground.

"Well? Will you honor your promise?" Melliandra insisted.

"I honor all my oaths." Lord Death knelt beside one of the fallen guards and laid a hand on his leather armor. Green light began to glow around his hands and spun out to encompass the fallen guard. The guard's armor disappeared and re-formed on Lord Death's body as sleek, dark leather the color of spilled blood. He spoke a word and the swords she'd left hidden in that empty room materialized in their sheaths. His crystal gleamed like a dark prism on his chest. He rose to his full height—looking every bit the deadly Fey warrior of legend—and went to his mate, who had finished with the hoops at her ears and was slowly peeling back the metal bands around her upper arms, freeing herself from the hundreds of sharp, needlelike teeth sunk into her flesh. His hands gripped her bare shoulders, and he touched his mouth to her temple. Her eyes closed, and she leaned back against him but only for a moment. When her eyes opened again, her expression was as cold and resolute as his.

"Vadim Maur has our daughter," Lord Death said. He met Melliandra's eyes. "He dies today, or we do."

When Ellysetta woke again, she was lying on a stone floor. Her head was pounding, and just opening her eyes seemed too monumental a task. She shifted, trying to lift a hand to her head. Chains rattled and dragged across stone.

"That did not go at all the way you dreamed, did it?"

Despite the effort involved, Ellysetta forced her eyes open. She was lying in a dark room. A single lamp, suspended over her head, cast a circle of light around her. Vadim Maur sat on a stool at the perimeter of the light's circle, watching her with his cold silver eyes.

"It seemed like such a perfect plan. The dream was so vivid and you feared it so greatly, I thought you actually might succumb." He shook his head. "This next part, however, might still do the trick. Lorelle, my pet, give us a little light, will you?"

"What?" Ellysetta sat up straight.

Confusion and dawning horror her as a sweet, voice replied, "Yes, Master Maur," and a flicker of Fire lit a pair of candle lamps held in the hands of Lillis and Lorelle.

The twins stood behind Vadim Maur, dressed neatly in black velvet gowns, their curls brushed and tied back in black bows. Their eyes were pure black to match, and sparkling with dark red lights.

"Nei," Ellysetta choked. Oh, gods! Not this. Not her sweet, beautiful, innocent sisters. "Lillis. Lorelle. *Nei.*"

"You know," the Mage said conversationally, "it came as quite a surprise to discover that your Celierian sisters both possess strong magical gifts, including quite a significant talent in Azrahn. It certainly made them easier to claim—once my new torture master persuaded them to accept the first Mark. Of course, their magic doesn't hold a candle to yours, but they'll be quite useful, nonetheless." His cold silver eyes watched her closely. "Gifted female breeders are not as easy to come by as you might think."

She lunged for him, teeth bared, no thought in her mind but to rip him into bloody bits with her bare hands. Her chains were no longer held by guards. They were bolted to the stone floor, with no give. The collar around her throat ran out of slack first. Momentum made her fly off her feet. She landed hard on her back, choking for breath and tugging to loosen the collar around her neck that threatened to strangle her.

"There isn't a Hell hot enough for you," she snarled when she could speak. "You'd best kill me now, because if you don't, I swear by all the gods you will die by my hand."

He laughed with genuine humor. "I worked centuries creating you and expended countless resources getting you back. Are you really so foolish as to think I would throw all that away by *killing* you?" He shook his head. "No, I won't kill you, Ellysetta." He gestured to the guard behind her, who immediately grabbed her head in a viselike grip. The Mage stepped closer, ran a hand down one side of her face in a disturbingly gentle caress. "You know what I want. You can surrender now, without pain, or you and everyone you love will suffer until you do. And when I say suffer, I mean you and your loved ones will crawl on your knees and beg me for death. But I won't give it to you, Ellysetta. I intend to keep you alive for a very, very long time."

She jerked her head back to avoid the poison of his touch and tried to snap at him with her teeth, but the guards held her too tight. In the end, words were her only weapon. "My parents survived a thousand years of your torture. All I have to do is to survive long enough for you to make a mistake. And when you do, I will destroy you."

"You forget one thing, my dear." He ran a thumb across her lower lip. "For every one of those thousand years, your parents had each other. You, however, are all alone. Or soon will be." On that cryptic note, he turned, and said politely, "Lorelle, my sweet, give us more light."

Lorelle's Fire magic spun out, and half a dozen sconces along the walls flared to light.

Ellysetta's heart slammed against her chest.

On the other side of the room, his naked body heavily manacled and chained to the wall, was Rain. A stocky brute of a fellow stood beside him, next to a table loaded with torturers' implements, and as the brute stepped into the light, Ellysetta's jaw dropped.

"Den Brodson?"

"Hello, Ellie."

Ellysetta stared in disbelief at Den Brodson, the son of a Celierian butcher who had, at one time, been Ellysetta's (wholly despised) betrothed. The months had not treated him kindly. He was a young man, but his hair, greasy and unkempt, was now liberally streaked with gray, and there were deep grooves along the sides of his mouth and bags under his blue eyes. His ruddy complexion had faded to a sickly olive gray. His stocky build had softened to doughy fleshiness.

"Oh, Den . . . what have you done?" There was only one reason he would be here. He had sold his soul to the Mages. She shook her head in horror. As much as she'd always despised him, Ellysetta wouldn't wish Mage-claiming on her worst enemy.

"Young Brodson has been surprisingly useful for a mortal peasant," the High Mage informed her. "If not for him, my *chemar* might never have found their way to Teleon—and on to Dharsa. And he was quite adept at finding your sisters in Dharsa and bringing them back to me."

"You monstrous *bogrot*," she breathed. He'd always been a hateful bullyboy, but she'd never realized he could be such a fiend.

"You were supposed to be mine, Ellie Baristani!" he spat. "You bore my Mark! Your family signed the papers! You were mine!"

"I was never yours, Den," she shot back, "and I never would have been! How could you think I would ever give the smallest part of myself to a foul Shadow snake like you?"

Blue eyes, surrounded by stubby black lashes, narrowed with sudden, glittering malice. "Well, you won't be the Tairen Soul's either, Ellie Baristani. At least not for much longer." He looked to the High Mage. "Master?"

Vadim Maur nodded. "You may begin, *umagi.*"

"Wait," Melliandra said as Lord Shan started for the door. "You've been here a thousand years, but you don't know Boura Fell. If you stumble around blindly, you'll just get yourself killed or captured again."

"Do you know where he's got our daughter?"

"I know where he's got the Tairen Soul—I heard rumors in the kitchens. If he's still there, your daughter will most likely be nearby. If she's not, I know of a few other places to check."

"Then tell me quickly," Shan said.

Melliandra started to tell him but then stopped. There was too much he needed to know—and he needed all of it to ensure his best chances of success.

"That will take too long. It's better if I show you." It took a lot for her to make that offer. All her life, she'd lived in a body that was not her own, possessed a mind that was invaded at will. She'd been abused, both physically and mentally, again and again. As one who had spent her life powerless, she never willingly gave of herself without expecting some personal benefit in return. And she *definitely* never deliberately made herself vulnerable—not to anyone. Until now.

She lifted his hands to her face and opened her mind, offering him access to the part of her mind not even Vadim Maur could enter. "The information you need is here in my mind. Take it." When he didn't immediately take her up on her offer, she snapped, "Quickly, before I change my mind."

He gave her a deep, searching glance, then nodded and said, "*Beylah vo, ajiana.*" The way he said it felt almost like a kiss pressed against her cheek. "And forgive me, this may be uncomfortable."

She gasped softly as Lord Death dove into her mind.

She suspected he was being as gentle as he could, but she could feel him inside her head, briskly rifling through her thoughts, siphoning off the information he needed. Her heart thumped painfully in her chest, and her breathing turned ragged, fearing that he would look beyond the thoughts she'd pushed to the front of her mind to the other thoughts . . . the thoughts of Shia and her son. But he did not trespass. He took only what he needed and no more. Then her mind was her own once more.

"This will do," he said. "This will more than do. You have a good eye."

The compliment made her flush with pleasure. "Go," she ordered brusquely, to hide her reaction. "You don't have much time."

"Then come with us," Shan said. "We'll see you to safety once we kill the Mage."

"I can't. I've got things of my own to tend to."

Shan nodded in understanding. "Good luck, *kaidina*," he said. "I know you think the Fey would kill you, but you will always find welcome in the House of Celay."

The woman, his mate, reached for Melliandra's hands. "*Miora felah, ajiana.* Blessings of the Fey upon you, child, and may the gods grant you more joy than you ever thought possible."

The soft words were accompanied by a rush of warmth so strong, and a feeling of such . . . such . . . Melliandra had no words to describe it. The closest she could compare it to was the dizzying pleasure when she'd called her magic that time in the refuse shaft. It was like freedom and Shia's smile and sunlight and blue skies all wrapped up in a single moment that made her want to laugh and cry all at once. She closed her eyes and wrapped her arms around herself to hold the feeling to her for as long as she could.

When she opened her eyes again, Lord Death and his mate were gone.

Chained to the walls of a lightless cell in the bowels of Boura Fell, Bel, Gaelen, and the rest of Ellysetta's quintet awaited their turn in the torture masters' untender care. Since waking from their drugged sleep, gods knew how many bells ago, the screams of their blade brothers had not stopped. Those screams had been growing steadily louder, as the torture masters of Eld worked their way down the line of new prisoners.

A few chimes ago, however, the screams had fallen mysteriously silent.

"Do you think the torture masters have tired themselves out?" Gaelen pondered with black humor.

"More likely, we're next, and they've just gone to sharpen their blades," Tajik said.

Locked up in the room with them, Farel gave a grunting laugh of amusement. "Could be. They've been using them enough."

"You know," Gil announced, "as rescues go, I have to say, this one pretty much scorches *rultshart* turds."

About a man length from the source of Gil's voice came Rijonn's rumbling agreement. "Tairen turds."

"I told you," Gaelen said, "I had backups. I don't know what happened to them."

A metallic scraping sound came from the direction of the door, and they all fell silent. The scraping sound was followed by the distinctive click of the latch lifting free. The door swung inward, and a sliver of light—the first in bells—spilled into the cell, widening rapidly as the door opened more fully. Two armored silhouettes stood in the doorway.

"Well, aren't you a sorry sight," a familiar Fey voice drawled.

"Kieran?" Gaelen sat up straight. There wasn't much in life that could surprise him, but the appearance of Kieran vel Solande in the heart of Boura Fell definitely did. "What are you doing here?"

"Apparently, uncle, I'm saving you from a very nasty demise, though gods know, I'm sure it won't take me long to regret it."

Gaelen grinned, too pleased to take offense at his nephew's cheek.

"Well, it took you long enough," Bel groused, holding up his hands as Kiel ran over with a key to unlock his *sel'dor* manacles. "I was starting to get worried."

Gaelen turned on Bel in disbelief. "You knew they were coming?"

Bel arched a brow. "You think the High Mage is the only one who plans backups for his backups?"

Rijonn laughed, slow and deep.

Bel jumped to his feet, rubbing his wrists where the *sel'dor* piercings had chafed. "All right, *kem'jetos*. First we save Rain and Ellysetta, then we kick some Elden ass."

* * *

«This way, shei'tani.»

Shrouded in blue Primage robes and guided by the information Shan had retrieved from the *umagi* girl's mind, Shan and Elfeya made their way as quickly as they dared through the dark maze of Boura Fell. From the observation chambers, they had ascended several levels and crossed a wide common area filled with scores of Mages in green, red, and Primage blue. Though it cost Shan a great deal to keep his steel sheathed, they navigated that *lyrant* nest without incident and slipped down a hallway to the more private area they were in now. As they approached the intersection of two wide corridors, their steps slowed.

«The girl's map says there will be guards up ahead,» Shan said. *«At least six of them.»*

The plucky little *umagi* girl had given Shan more than a simple map of the fortress and the path to the place Vadim Maur was holding their daughter. She'd given him all the details about all the rooms and wards and guard postings along the way, and identified spots where they would have to exercise extreme caution to avoid being caught.

«Let me check,» Elfeya replied, and with a skill unaltered by centuries of confinement, she sent her empathic senses whispering out ahead of them. The tendrils of awareness curved around the blind corners and streamed, undetected, down the hallways, pale threads of invisible golden light, imperceptible to all but the strongest of senses. Swiftly, she verified the location and number of the guards.

«Four to the left, two to the right,» she confirmed.

«I'll have to take them all,» he replied grimly. *«If even one of them raises the alarm, we won't make it.»* Their path lay to the left, up a flight of stairs to a heavily guarded, private level of the fortress restricted solely to Vadim Maur and a select few Primages.

A flash of awareness made Elfeya's senses tingle. *«Someone's coming!»* The tingle darkened to discomfort, then outright pain. Her breath seized in her throat as she recognized the feeling. *«Dahl'reisen, Shan.»*

«Quickly,» he said, *«into this room.»* He turned abruptly towards a door on the left and reached for the *sel'dor* handle. The door was locked but unwarded. Ignoring the sear of pain, Shan sent his senses into the keyhole, examined the locking mechanism, then pulled a black Fey'cha from his harness. A quick weave of Earth drew the Fey'cha's tip into a shape that would release the lock.

He thrust the key-blade into the lock and turned just as Elfeya cried, *«He's here.»*

The door opened. He thrust Elfeya inside and glanced over his shoulder as he followed her inside. The corridor was empty. But Elfeya's pain was real. Shan had long ago learned to trust his mate's senses, even above his own. The *dahl'reisen* was there. Fey eyes could not see him, but he was there.

As the door swung closed, Shan's own warrior senses flared to abrupt life, as certain and infallible as Elfeya's empathy. He dodged left just as a red Fey'cha whirred past the spot his head had been.

The door shut. Another blade thunked deep into the *sel'dor*-braced wood. The first red blade, which had sunk into the far wall of the room, disappeared as the *dahl'reisen* spoke his return word.

«Scorch it. We must have given ourselves away.» Shan shed his Primage robes and reached for his black Fey'cha as he scanned the room for a position of safety and attack. There was a table in the center of the room. Elfeya was already racing to take shelter behind it before he spun the weave to flip it on its side.

Shan went high, racing up the wall and launching across the ceiling on an Air-powered leap, just as the door opened. His senses merged with Elfeya's, and he used her empathy to pinpoint the enemy he could not see. Black Fey'cha flew with unerring aim and blurring speed. The *dahl'reisen* grunted. Shan dropped to the floor, as magic spun from Elfeya's fingertips, wrapping the still-invisible *dahl'reisen* tight in bands of power.

Shan thrust his hands into the center of Elfeya's net, and sparks flew where his *sel'dor* bands touched the *dahl'reisen's* invisibility weave. He caught a brief glimpse of a pale scarred face and a mouth opening—no doubt to shout the alarm. His fingers closed around the *dahl'reisen's* throat, squeezing tight and cutting off his cry.

"I can't kill you, *dahl'reisen rultshart*," he hissed, "but I can make you wish I would."

"That would be a shame, *kem'chatok,* since he came to save you."

Shan's spine went straight as a board, and he spun around, Fey'cha flying from their sheaths into his hands. "Vel Serranis," he snarled, and he let fly his blades.

CHAPTER TWENTY

Come fly with me my love
Spread your wings with glee
Into the skies above
Together we will fly free

Come fly with me my mate
The one that fills my heart
Together passion we will sate
And never will we part

Flight of the Tairen Lovers,
a poem by Rainier v'En Daris, Tairen Soul

Shan's most infamous *chadin* dodged and deflected with a skill that would do any *chatok* proud, but he still didn't manage to escape all of Shan's blades. One Fey'cha caught him in the shoulder and one in the back of the right thigh as he spun away, before a cry on the vel Celay family path brought Shan up short.

«Parei, Shan! Parei! Gaelen and Farel are friends.»

"Tajik?" Elfeya rose from behind the overturned table, whispering her brother's name.

«Elfeya, get down!» Fearing a trap, Shan thrust the *dahl'reisen* away from him and backed towards his mate,

blades drawn. He'd never betrayed the vel Celay family path—at least not that he remembered—and he didn't think Elfeya had either. But after a thousand years of torture, anything was possible.

And yet, there he was, Tajik vel Sibboreh, Elfeya's youngest brother, appearing inside the room as he shed his invisibility weave. He looked older—much harder and world-worn—than Shan remembered him, but he was still, unmistakably Tajik. Blue-eyed, fire-haired, and staring at his sister like she was the sun and he was a man who'd spent a lifetime in darkness.

Elfeya's empathic senses could never have been fooled by an imposter posing as her brother, so when she abandoned all caution and ran around the table to throw herself into Tajik's arms, Shan knew his eyes must be seeing true.

"Tajik!" Wrapping her arms around her brother's neck, Elfeya wept and laughed in a show of joy too great to be contained. "You are here. It's really you."

Tajik's arms tightened around her. "I thought you were dead," he told her. "I would have ripped Eld apart to find you if I'd known you were still alive. *Sieks'ta.* Forgive me for not coming sooner. I didn't know. I came as soon as I could."

"Las, las, kem'jeto. Ssh." She stroked his hair and kissed him, then drew back to cup his face between her hands. "There is nothing to forgive. I am here, and you are here, and we are together once more. Today, the gods are kind, and my heart is full of joy."

"I don't understand." Shan looked around the room in confusion. He was beginning to think the madness that had haunted him all these centuries had taken fresh root in his brain. Three more Fey had appeared inside the room. Two of them were very distinctive Fey he recognized and remembered. Like Tajik and vel Serranis, Gillandaris vel Sendar and Rijonn vel Ahriman had been his *chadins* at the Warriors' Academy in Tehlas. The third warrior, a Fey with black hair and cobalt eyes, he did not know. Nor did he recognize the two young, unshadowed warriors shrouded in

Mage robes who slipped in after the others and closed the door behind them.

After spending the last thousand years in solitary confinement, the sudden appearance of so many Fey—and so many familiar faces—left Shan feeling overwhelmed. And the fact that these Fey could all be standing there, without a shred of concern for the *dahl'reisen* among them, confused and stunned him. He shook his head, trying to still all the thoughts and questions whirling about in his mind, and fixed his gaze on Gaelen vel Serranis.

"You were *dahl'reisen*," he said bluntly. "Why aren't you still? And why are Fey warriors keeping company with *dahl'reisen*?"

A ghost of a smile played about Gaelen's mouth. "You always were direct, *kem'chatok*." He gestured to the Fey'cha still embedded in his shoulder and thigh. "Do you mind?"

Shan spoke his return word, and the blades he'd sunk into both Gaelen and the *dahl'reisen* returned to their sheaths.

"*Ve ku'jian vallar, Gaelen*," Elfeya said. Allow me to help you. Withdrawing gently from her brother's embrace, she crossed the room to vel Serranis's side and laid glowing hands upon his wounds.

"*Beylah vo, Elfeya-falla*," Gaelen said, as the torn blood vessels and flesh knit back together.

Elfeya glanced uncertainly at the *dahl'reisen*, who had already spun an Earth weave to staunch his wounds and seal the torn flesh until his body's natural healing properties could repair the damage.

The *dahl'reisen* cleared his throat, and said, "I'll go scout the rest of the hall. Forgive me, *ki'falla'sheisan,* for causing you pain." He bowed to her with grave respect before cloaking himself in the best invisibility weave Shan had ever seen. The chamber door opened and closed to mark his departure.

When he was gone, Shan ordered Gaelen to spin a privacy weave on the room and fixed a stern eye on the remaining warriors. "All right, Fey," he declared in a voice that had commanded armies and snapped countless unruly *chadins* to order. "I want answers. How is it that Gaelen vel Serranis is *dahl'reisen* no more . . . and why are Fey warriors keeping company with a Shadowed blade?"

Explanations tumbled out from several of them at once. Time was short, so Shan just let his mind process the overlapping voices, separating and interpreting the individual inputs instantly in his mind—much the way he processed the overload of chaotic information on a battlefield.

"So let me get this straight," he said when they were done. "Our daughter restored vel Serranis's soul. Her mate has allowed *dahl'reisen* to bloodswear themselves to her. And you five"—he gestured to all but the two youngest Fey—"are her bloodsworn quintet, who accompanied her to Boura Fell to rescue Elfeya and me and our daughter's young Celierian sisters. Is that correct?"

Heads nodded, but he could see the four who knew him growing wary at his calm tone. It was a good thing he'd insisted on a privacy weave around the room.

"Then I have only two other questions for you fine warriors of the Fey." Shan straightened to his full height, squared his shoulders and drew a deep breath that expanded his chest. *"What the scorching flames of the Seven Hells do you think you were doing letting her come here?"* he roared. *"And how the flaming Hells is it that you're standing here, still breathing, while my daughter—the woman you swore your souls to protect with your lives—is in the hands of Vadim Maur, the evilest jaffing son of an Elden rultshart ever to be born?"*

"That last part's not their fault," said the young, brown-haired Fey named Kieran. "The Eld knocked them out when they arrived. The High Mage must have used his connection to Ellysetta to—"

Shan pierced him with a glare as sharp as a blade. "The questions, vel Solande, were rhetorical."

Kieran snapped his mouth shut.

Shan turned his focus back to his daughter's quintet. "If we survive this, each one of you five owes me a year's time on the training field. I suggest you come prepared for pain."

Expelling an agitated breath, Shan pivoted on his heel and forced himself to channel his anger, focusing it into grim determination. "For now, however, the only thing that matters is getting our daughter out of this place. Elfeya, can you stand the *dahl'reisen's* presence a while longer?"

"Aiyah. The *dahl'reisen's* pain was terrible, but bearable. I think the old saying is true: That which does not kill you, *does* makes you stronger." She met Shan's eyes in a moment of communion. *«I could not have stood in his presence before these centuries in Boura Fell. But now, I think I could even heal him if he were in need.»*

He nodded. He and pain were old friends. And one of that old friend's harshest but truest lessons was that suffering bred strength.

"All right," he said. "Did you Fey have a plan, or should we adjust ours?"

The seven warriors shared silent looks amongst themselves.

"Lord Shan," Gaelen said, "you and Elfeya-*falla* should get to safety. There is a gateway to the Well of Souls on the level above this one, and it's under Fey control. Go there, and get out of this place. We will find Ellysetta and Rain and bring them home."

Shan exchanged a look with Elfeya. Both their expressions turned to stone. "If you think we are leaving this place without our daughter, vel Serranis," Shan said, "you are greatly mistaken. We have a good idea of where she's being kept. We know all the possible routes we could take and how many guards and wards to expect along the way. You can come with us if you like, but we are going to get our child." Shan's voice dropped to a lethal growl. "And just so we're clear, the High Mage is *mine* to kill."

"Well," Gil said, slapping his hands on his thighs, "I'm glad that's settled. Can we get on with the slaughter?"

"Look how your mate is suffering, Ellysetta." Vadim Maur crouched beside her and grabbed her hair, forcing her to head in Rain's direction. *"Look at him!"* he barked.

His icy voiced throbbed with compulsion, and no matter how hard she tried to defy him and keep her eyes averted, she could not.

Rain was displayed, spread-eagled, on a wooden form shaped like two overlapping crescent moons, his body held in place by a series of *sel'dor* stakes that Den Brodson had hammered through his limbs with grim relish. Every handspan of his once-shining white skin bore signs of brutal abuse. Strips of flesh flayed from his bones. Blistered black char where red-hot brands had scorched deep. Countless *sel'dor* barbs jabbed into his skin and left to fester. Bones broken. Fingers severed.

She'd felt each moment of Rain's torment, each scream, each breathless gasp of stunning pain, just as he'd felt each moment of her helpless horror.

She'd tried to stay strong. She knew her presence—her empathic sharing of his pain—was as deliberate a part of his torture as Den's foul deeds. But she had not been able to stop herself from screaming any more than Rain had. She'd not been able to stop herself from weeping, from begging.

Through it all, Rain had been there in her mind, telling her to stay strong, to be brave, not to give in. As if she, not he, were the one whose body was being shattered and maimed.

"You are a monster," she told Vadim Maur.

"I am a Mage," he countered. "And you can end this anytime you like. You know how. I will get what I want, one way or another. But how many of your loved ones die before that happens—how long they must writhe in agony—is entirely up to you."

Her breath caught on a hiccuping sob.

"I ask you again, Ellysetta Baristani: Accept my Mark." He gripped her head between his icy hands, and the oppressive weight of his Dark magic closed around her, trapping her, squeezing her soul in a vise.

"If you refuse me, your mate will die. When I am done with him, I will put his body on display in the Mage Halls and I will leave it there to rot. The great Rain Tairen Soul,

Worldscorcher, Destroyer of Eld, food for maggots and rot-worms." Then his voice softened, became kind. "But if you submit to me, I will let you heal him. He will live. You can be with him. You can hold him in your arms. Take him into your body."

The pressure of his will receded. Her mind filled with feel-ings of warmth and love. She could almost smell the fresh bloom of spring on the air, the intoxicating scent of Rain's skin. She could almost feel his hands stroking across her body, hear her gasp as pleasure washed over her in waves.

Just as she began to reach for the sweet seduction of the dream, the Mage snatched it away. "But you can have that only when you give me what I want."

«Nei, shei'tani.» Rain's voice whispered on a ragged thread of Spirit. *«Never. You mustn't. Not for me . . . not for anyone . . .»* Each syllable throbbed with pain.

"Every word you speak is a lie, Mage," she rasped. "You'll never let him live. And even if you did, he'd rather die than see me surrender my soul."

"Perhaps, but can you bear to watch it? Can you let him die?" The Mage barked a command to Den, "Do it."

"Nei!" Ellysetta screamed as Den pulled Rain's head back and slashed a blade across his throat. Rain's blood fountained in a scarlet mist.

On the pretext of serving food, Melliandra entered the level where Vadim Maur kept the magically gifted female pris-oners he used in his breeding program. If Lord Death was successful, the High Mage would soon be dead. Melliandra intended to wait for that moment here, close to the warded corridor that led to the nursery where the Mage kept his pro-gram's most promising offspring.

Moving as slowly as possible, she pushed her kitchen cart from cell to cell, opening them with the key the captain of the guard on this level had given to her. He was supposed to walk with her from room to room and watch her as she fed the female prisoners, but she always snuck him a treat from the kitchens and left him to eat it while she made her rounds.

When she reached the cell of the black-eyed *shei'dalin* she'd dragged with her weeks ago to save the life of Lord Death's mate, her nerves were strung tight. The anxiety must have made her careless, because the *shei'dalin* stopped her at the door. "*Sha de dai?*"

"Is it time?" Melliandra repeated. "Time for what?"

"*Dai ve heber eva bebahs.*" She signed the words as she spoke them, poking a finger at Melliandra, rocking her arms in front of her body as if cradling a baby in arms, then walking her fingers. She looked intently at Melliandra, and said, "*Ke am.*" I know.

Melliandra felt her heart drop into her stomach. The *shei'dalin* knew what she was planning. Somehow, Melliandra had given her secret away. She cursed silently and berated herself for the questions she'd asked the other women—questions about how to tend babies. This *shei'dalin* must have overheard and realized what she was planning.

Determined to brazen it out, Melliandra snorted and said, "I don't know what you're talking about." She turned away and reached for the door handle.

The *shei'dalin* caught Melliandra's arm. "*Teska. Ve ku'jian valir eva vo.*" She pressed her lips together and tried broken Elden. "You . . . me . . . go . . . *eva bebahs.*" She rocked her cradled arms again.

"Are you saying you want me to take you with me?"

"*Aiyah!*"

Melliandra held up her hands. "No. I'm not going anywhere, but even if I were, I wouldn't take you with me. No. No!" She pushed the *shei'dalin's* hand off her arm. "You're mistaken. Wrong. *Neida.* Do you understand? *Ve sha neida.*"

"*Teska!*" Though it must have hurt her terribly, the *shei'dalin* spun a Spirit weave showing Melliandra with a screaming baby, a sick baby, a hungry baby. Melliandra all alone, weeping beside a small mound of dirt. "*Ke sha shei'dalin. Ke shaverr vo'vallaren.*" I'm a *shei'dalin*. I can help you.

The images horrified Melliandra as much as the idea of having a healer to help with Shia's son appealed, but she wouldn't be swayed. "No," she said again. "I'm not going anywhere. I'm not taking you anywhere." She turned to leave. She had to get out of here.

"*Wera!*" Wait. "*Teska, wera.*"

The desperation in the *shei'dalin's* voice made Melliandra stop. The black-eyed *shei'dalin* had been battered and raped for weeks on end, and never sounded so frantic as she did now.

Against her better judgment, Melliandra stood by the door and watched the *shei'dalin* kneel beside her bed. She lifted the edge of the pallet and reached inside a slit cut into the bottom of the pallet cover. A moment later she pulled out a small, bruised flower . . . actually, it was the whole flower plant: stem, leaves, roots as well as the distinctive, six-petaled bell-shaped starflowers.

"*De sha Amarynth. Ve am Amarynth?*"

"Yes," Melliandra said, staring at the flower. "I know Amarynth." She lifted her gaze to the *shei'dalin* with dawning comprehension "Are you telling me you're going to have a baby?"

"*Aiyah.*" The woman's expression crumpled, and for a moment Melliandra thought she would break into tears, but this Fey woman was made of sterner stuff. She shook off the emotion and reached for Melliandra's hand again. "*Teska. Ve bos'jian valir eva vo. Ku te kem'behba.*" She laid a palm on her still-flat belly.

Melliandra closed her eyes. If there was one thing she understood, it was the driving need to free an innocent baby from this dark place. "All right. All right, you can come." She thrust her chin out. "But the chime you fall behind, I leave you. Understand?"

The woman nodded, the black tangles of her hair falling

across her face. Tears glistened in her dark eyes. "*Beylah vo. Beylah vo. Sallan'meilissis a vo.*"

"Yes, yes. I get it. You're grateful. Now, stay here and don't say anything to anyone. I'll come get you when it's time." Melliandra turned back to the door. She'd been in here so long, any watching guard would get suspicious.

"*Ke sha Nicolene,*" the *shei'dalin* said in a rush as Melliandra reached for the handle. The *shei'dalin* pressed her palm to her chest. "Nicolene. *Ke sha Nicolene.*"

"Your name is Nicolene." She nodded and pointed to Nicolene to indicate she understood.

"*Te ve?*" Nicolene asked. "*Arast sha ver mana?*" What is your name?

Since the day Shia had gifted a worthless *umagi* with a name, that *umagi* had never shared that name with another. Until now.

"I am Melliandra."

Ellysetta lunged towards Rain, shrieking and writhing like a mad thing when her chains yanked her back. Her hands clawed at the air. Her eyes flamed as her tairen rose, deadly fierce and furious.

She would kill Den and the Mage. She would shred them. She would snap their bones and rip their still-living flesh from their bodies while they screamed and begged for mercy.

Power gathered in a wild, savage rush—only to slam her to the stone floor as her *sel'dor* bonds turned the fullness of her Rage back against her. She lay there, dazed, lungs wheezing, muscles convulsing as she struggled to stay conscious.

The spray of Rain's blood fell upon the faces of the twins, and to her horror the pair of them opened their mouths to catch the droplets on their tongues. Their frozen, doll-like expressions changed. Blood-reddened lips curled into macabre smiles.

Black-eyed and laughing in delight, the twins began to dance in the shower of Rain's blood just like the vision from the most frightening dream she'd ever had. Only now she knew it wasn't their own evil that drove them. It was the Mage's. He was controlling them like human puppets, watching her with his cold, merciless eyes as he did.

Rain's glazing eyes met hers. His lips moved. Though Den's knife had cut clear to Rain's spine, severing his windpipe and making speech impossible, she read the words on Rain's lips. *Ke vo san, shei'tani.*

"*Shei'tan*," she rasped in a broken whisper. "*Stay with me. Stay with me, Rain!*"

She watched in horror as the light in Rain's eyes began to dim, and with it dimmed the silver luminescence of his skin. With each drop of blood that flowed from his throat, more and more of his Light faded. His lashes fluttered closed.

Forgive me, shei'tani. I have failed you. The words brushed across her mind, a whisper of regret sighed on the faltering threads of their bond.

His hands, the hands that had caressed her a thousand times, so broad, so strong, twitched weakly, then went limp. His head fell forward onto his chest, and the long, straight strands of his silky black hair hung down over his face like a shroud.

"*Nei, Rain. Nei!* Stay with me, *shei'tan!*" Tears flooded her eyes, blurring her vision. "*Sterr eva ku!*"

But she had fought enough death to recognize it. His soul had slipped from his flesh and was beginning its descent into the Well. When he reached the Veil and passed through it, no *shei'dalin* in the world would be able to heal him. Not even her.

"*Rain!*" The scream ripped from her throat.

The Mage would not save him. Rain was more useful to him dead than alive, because without Rain, it was only a matter of time before she succumbed to the Mage's sixth Mark.

But if she spun Azrahn to hold Rain's soul to the Light, the Mage would simply Mark her now.

Either way, the Mage would own her, body and soul. And she would become the monster of Elvish prophecy. Ellysetta Erimea, Seledorn's Dark Star, the Light Eater, Corrupter of Worlds.

"Can you let him die?" the Mage had asked.

As Rain's soul fell deeper and deeper into the Well, and the threads of their incomplete truemate bond stretched thin, Ellysetta had her answer. No matter what fates lay in the balance, no matter the cost to her soul or all the souls in the world, when it came to Rain's life, she was as vulnerable as every other truemate who'd ever come before her. Rain was her *shei'tan*, and she could not let him die.

Spurred by Fey instinct, the desperate, driving need to save her mate, Ellysetta spun the only magic her *sel'dor* bonds would let her weave and plunged into the Well of Souls.

«Rain!» Riding an icy wave of pure Azrahn, she dove after his fading Light.

"Hurry," Shan urged as the *dahl'reisen* Farel spun Azrahn to unravel the next layer of the wards securing the chamber against intrusion.

Demonstrating a coordinated precision even Shan had to admire, the bloodsworn *dahl'reisen* and Fey warriors made quick work of dispatching the Elden guards and securing the level without raising an alarm. While the *dahl'reisen* and Shan worked to unravel the wards on this chamber—the only one that had been warded and under heavy guard—the other warriors checked the remaining rooms.

"Nothing," Gaelen announced as they returned. "If they're here, they're definitely in this room."

«Better hurry,» Kiel called from his lookout post near the stairs. *«I hear shouting. I think our secret is out.»*

Swift as a serpent, the High Mage struck. The cold corruption of his magic pierced Ellysetta's soul, its claws sinking deep. His triumph lashed at her mind as his power flooded through her body. His penetrating evil began eating like acid at the truemate threads tying her soul to Rain's.

Chained to the stone floor of Boura Fell, Ellysetta's body thrashed. A howling roar—the cry of a dying tairen—ripped from her throat. Her back arched, and her body went stiff as the first bond thread connecting her to Rain sundered.

"Got it!" Farel crowed. The wards securing the door fell apart.

The chamber door shattered. An explosion of wood and metal shrapnel flew to the opposite side of the room as the Fey burst through. They took in the scene at a single glance: Rain, gutted, garroted, and hanging from the twin crescents like some macabre trophy, Ellysetta prone on the floor with the High Mage crouched over her, Lillis and Lorelle off to one side, and a stocky human standing by a table of bloody torture instruments.

Kieran went left after the human. Kiel went right to get the girls, using his body to shield Elfeya as she raced towards Rain. The rest of them dove for Vadim Maur.

Maur's eyes were pits of darkness. A dark aura surrounded him and around the hand pressed over Ellysetta's heart.

"Maur!" Shan cried. "Get away from my daughter!"

Magic and Fey'cha flew as Shan, Farel, and the quintet attacked. The Mage didn't even have time to react before Shan's red Fey'cha plowed hilt deep into his chest. Six more followed an instant later, and Shan's *meicha* sliced Maur's head from his body.

On the far end of the room, Kieran exclaimed "You!" in surprise as he recognized the blood-spattered human responsible for Rain's torture.

Den Brodson grabbed a pair of bloody knives and raised them threateningly.

Kieran's eyes narrowed. A cold, killing rage iced over his Fey heart, sealing his compassion behind a thick layer of frost.

"Little sausage, you've made your last mistake." In the

blink of an eye, four black Fey'cha flew through the air, sinking into Brodson's body with enough force to send him careening back into the wall. A fifth buried hilt deep in his crotch. Kieran leapt across the distance and grabbed the screaming Celierian by the throat.

"That was for the Feyreisa. This is for Rain." He drove another black Fey'cha into Brodson's belly and ripped it upwards, gutting him like a slaughtered pig. "And this . . . this is for Lillis and Lorelle, you stinking pile of pig *krekk*." His *meicha* swung, metal sparking as it scraped against stone, and Den Brodson's head flew from his shoulders.

"Maybe I shouldn't admit it, but that felt scorching good!" Kieran turned to see how his blade brothers had fared, and his satisfaction over dispatching Brodson to the Seventh Hell turned to dust. *"Krekk."*

Shannisorran v'En Celay held Ellysetta cradled against his chest, her body limp, her head draped over his arm. Her eyes were open but sightless. They had turned completely black, looking like pits of endless darkness in the stark whiteness of her face.

Gaelen knelt beside her. A spiral of Azrahn twirled in his palm, but no shadow darkened the flesh over Ellysetta's heart.

"I don't understand," Gaelen said. "We killed the Mage. Her Marks are gone, just as the Elves said they would be. She should be free."

"Mages incarnate their souls into other bodies." Shan smoothed a hand over his daughter's hair and looked up at the *lu'tan* ringed around him. "He must have transferred some part of his soul into hers before he died. That part of him is inside her now, fighting for dominance. Elfeya says her Light is failing."

"What can we do?"

"Call to her. Help her hold to the Light. I'm going to give what strength I can to Rain. If anyone can help her, he can."

* * *

Darkness surrounded Ellysetta like a suffocating blanket. The aching emptiness where Rain's Light had lived inside her was now a drowning abyss.

She could hear voices calling her name in the distance, but the words did not penetrate the thick fog of despair. She'd failed. She'd failed Rain. She'd failed her sisters. Her parents. Steli. The pride. She'd failed the world.

"You thought we were so different, you and I, but you felt the Darkness awaken inside you. You tasted its power. You liked it." Twined around her, like a serpent wrapped around its prey, the dark sentience of Vadim Maur taunted her.

She wanted to block his voice from her mind, but she could not. She wanted to deny his vile claims, but gods help her, she could not do that either. He was right. There *was* Darkness inside her. She'd been fighting to hide it, to deny its existence all her life, but it was there. Not just the power to enslave, to destroy, to dominate, but the desire to do so. Control—the godlike power to shape the world, and everyone in it, even against their will—that was the true, irresistible seduction of Azrahn.

The Mage drew upon her fears, her moments of rage and savagery, showing them to her, forcing her to relive them. Reminding her of the terrible things she was capable of doing—of the things she had done. Despair swamped her. He was right.

«Nei, shei'tani,» Rain's voice sounded in the Well, much stronger than it had before. *«Do not listen to him. You are bright and shining. What you do, you do for love, to protect the ones you love. That is not evil. And you are loved in return, so very much. Can't you hear them all calling? Can't you feel their love? They know who you are. They know what you can do. And they love you, as I do.»*

The muffled voices became clearer. She heard her parents, calling to her. Her quintet. Kieran and Kiel. Lorelle. Lillis was sobbing, and crying, *«Mama said let love be your guide, Ellie, not fear. Love, Ellie, not fear! All magic comes from the gods.»*

*«Listen to them, shei'tani. Fight for them, for yourself.
Fight for me. Live for me, beloved. I thought my soul was
darkened beyond redemption, but you proved to me that was
not so. Let me do the same for you. Ver reisa ku'chae. Kem
surah, shei'tani. Remember what the Elf queen said. You are
leinah thaniel. You choose your fate. Choose me, shei'tani.
Love me enough to let go of your fear.»*

Once before, in Elvia, as she lay in Rain's arms, she'd
had the strange feeling that Rain—even unarmed and un-
armored—was her living shield against the Dark. Not her
lu'tan, not Hawksheart's Sentinel blooms, not Rain's steel or
even the devastating power of his tairen flame. Rain, himself.

Now she realized how right she'd been. He was her armor.
He was her Light. Just as she was his. With him by her side,
his soul joined with hers, no force in the heavens or the earth
or even the darkest depths of the Seven Hells was stronger.
With him, through him, she *was* the being the Elves called
her: Erimea, Hope's Light, the power that shone brightest
when Darkness reached its peak.

The High Mage of Eld might have made her what she was,
but that did not mean she had to fulfill his purpose.

Desperately, she reached for every ounce of power she
could summon—not just from the vast Source that welled
inside her, but from every loved one, every *lu'tan*, every
person with whom she shared a connection. She channeled
that power, not through the body chained in the physical
world but through her soul deep within the Well.

There was Darkness in her. She could not deny it. But
there was Darkness in Rain, too, and it didn't make him evil.
It didn't make him less worthy of love. All magic comes
from the gods.

She let the Light fill her and released her fear. For Rain's
sake, she forced herself to face everything in her own soul,
the gentleness of the *shei'dalin*, the savagery of the tairen,
the Light and the Darkness. She confronted it, accepted
it. And then she threw open her soul to Rain and let him

in without shame, without reservation, without fear. *«I do choose you, shei'tan. In this life and every life to come. Ver reisa ku'chae. Kem surah, shei'tan.»*

And the blazing strength that was Rain and his love, filled her, tearing through the shadows of her fear. She heard the shrill cry as the darkness that was Vadim Maur lost its grip on her soul.

The broken bond renewed, and with it came a new thread, stronger than all the rest, a bond thread forged of Azrahn and *shei'dalin's* love, strength and gentleness, plaited tight together, blazing with power and strength.

Their joined souls, Light and Dark, soared out of the Well, and in the heart of Boura Fell, their bodies lit up like candle lamps. Their friends and family stepped back as the light grew brighter and brighter, suffusing them with more power than even a Fey body could contain. Their eyes opened, blazing like stars.

«Go, friends. Free the others. Go quickly.»

A golden gray mist surrounded Rain and Ellysetta both, enveloping their bodies in magic, saturating their skin, their breath, their bones . . . filling them until the vast magic already brimming in every cell of their bodies overflowed and merged. Their forms dissolved on an explosion of pain and bliss. Together, the powerful force that was Rain and the brilliant energy that was Ellysetta Changed.

What emerged from the transforming mist, however, was not two tairen but one. A creature of pure Light, as blinding as the Great Sun.

The great tairen's roar was a thunderclap that rocked the whole of Boura Fell.

"Hear us, Mages of Eld!" it cried, and its voice was male and female, tairen and Fey, Rain and Ellysetta, inextricably and forever intertwined, singing a Song so bright the notes illuminated the darkest corners of Boura Fell. "For all those defenseless before your evil, we have come. We are Wrath, the Rage of the living. We are Vengeance, the fury of the dead. We are the Light that will stand forever against your Darkness!" Blazing tairen wings spread wide. "We are Freedom, the hammer that breaks all chains!"

The creature's massive head drew back, jaws agape as fire like the bursting of a giant star spewed from its throat. Rivers of Light swirled around the tairen, spinning faster and faster as the tairen grew ever brighter. The Light expanded in a fiery ball, searing the darkness of Boura Fell, burning away the millennia of pain and evil and anguish. *Sel'dor* melted. Walls and floors turned to brittle char and blew away in the hot, fiery wind of the Light tairen's breath.

Scores of Mages tried to rally a defense, casting Mage Fire and rapid spells at the blazing tairen, but their Fire and their magic and then their bodies dissolved into the consuming expanse of Light.

In the middle levels of Boura Fell, the walls trembled. Choking dust filled the hallways, and chunks of raw *sel'dor* ore fell from the rapidly disintegrating ceilings as Ellysetta's rescuers raced through the bottommost corridors, breaking down cell doors and herding released prisoners towards the Fey waiting to usher them towards the exit through the Well of Souls.

A section of the roof caved in over Gaelen's head, and only Bel's diving lunge saved the former *dahl'reisen* from being flattened like a journeycake.

"You're welcome." Bel grinned, gave Gaelen's lean cheek a slap and hopped to his feet. "We've got to find those women and go, *kem'jeto*," he added as he extended a helping hand to his friend. "This place is coming down around our ears."

"Guess we'd best hurry then."

Bel signaled to the Fey behind them. "You six, take that hallway down there." He pointed several tairen lengths down the hall, where a shadowy corridor headed off from the one they were in. "The rest of you come with Gaelen and me to clear the end of this corridor."

Gaelen was already running towards the end of the hall, leaping chunks of debris like a pronghorn bounding over fallen trees in the forest. "If we're not back in ten chimes, go on without us," he called over his shoulder.

"Ten more chimes, and we'll none of us make it out alive," Bel muttered when he caught up with Gaelen.

White teeth flashed a *sel'dor*-dust-coated face. "Care to make a wager on that?"

Bel laughed in spite of himself. "Ninnywit." They had reached the offshooting hallway. A glance down the sconce-lit corridor revealed only two doors. "You take those. I'll take the doors on the right and work my way back around to you."

Gaelen sped down the corridor. The first door was heavily warded, but one at the end of the short hallway was not. If there had ever been any guards, they had already fled their posts. He flung open the unwarded door and stopped dead in his tracks, shocked by the bright, sunlit beauty of the room. An unexpected paradise in the heart of darkness. More astounding still was the group of weeping, naked women huddled beneath the rocking "sun" suspended from the ceiling painted to look like a sky overhead. The ground beneath his feet was carpeted with small, fragrant white flowers, the blooms' six starry petals shaped like tender bells. Most of the flowers had been crushed by booted feet, but they were still fragrant and still valiantly, stubbornly, clinging to life.

Amarynth. The Fey flower of life, which bloomed only in the steps of a Fey woman carrying an unborn child.

Amarynth. An abundance of it, blooming here in this evil place.

His eyes narrowed at the sight of two blue-robed Primages and several *umagi* trying to force dozens of women into an open portal to the Well of Souls.

«Fey!» he cried on the path the warriors had forged amongst themselves. *«Ti'Gaelen! There are fellanas here!»* Red Fey'cha flew in a lightning-swift strike. The *umagi* dropped like stones, freeing the women who ran, weeping, towards the knot of fellow captives.

Mage Fire blasted towards him. He dodged to one side,

flinging up a swift five-fold weave to meet the lethal Fire and launching half a dozen more Fey'cha in rapid succession. One Primage caught a glancing blow on his upper arm. A look of dismay flashed across his face. A moment later, convulsions racked his body and he collapsed, dead before he hit the floor. The other Mage shot more Mage Fire Gaelen's way and made a threatening move towards the women, but when he saw the reinforcements running into the chamber, he spun around and leapt into the Well of Souls instead. The doorway closed behind him, and Gaelen's last volley of Fey'cha spun harmlessly through the now-empty stretch of air to bury themselves in the trunks of a small grove of trees.

The warriors gathered around the women, Earth masters spinning swiftly to cover them in warm robes. There were thirty or more women in the strange chamber, mostly Celierians, but a dozen or more bore a visible glow of magic in their skins. At least half of the women—including most of the luminous ones—were with child.

Two women, in particular, made the Fey send up prayers of thanks to the gods, while the *dahl'reisen* among them backed swiftly away. *Shei'dalins,* pale and dull-eyed, shackled in *sel'dor.* Two of the three who'd been captured at the battle of Teleon in the fall.

"Nicolene-*falla,*" one of them murmured as Gaelen wrapped a cloak around her shoulders. "They took her."

"Into the Well?" Gaelen asked quickly. Nicolene vol Oros was one of the Fading Lands' most powerful healers, captured along with these two *shei'dalins,* in the battle of Teleon.

"*Nei,* away somewhere else in this place. She would not obey, even to save herself, and they took her away. What they did to her . . ." The *shei'dalin's* voice trailed off and her pale face went even paler. "We felt her pain."

«*Vel Jelani!*» Gaelen relayed the information quickly. «*Nicolene vol Oros is here in this fortress.*»

«*Understood. I haven't found her yet.*»

"What about Lady Darramon?" Gaelen asked the

shei'dalins. The fragile Great Lady Basha Darramon had been captured with these women at Teleon.

The *shei'dalin* shook her head. "Dead."

The ceiling overhead cracked. A massive chunk of rock plummeted from the roof of the cavern and landed in the small lake at the chamber's center with a great splash. Beams of light, far brighter than the false sun that had lit the room, shone through the gaping hole overhead.

Gaelen covered his eyes and looked up, near blinded by the brightness. The hole in the ceiling widened as the *sel'dor* ore simply . . . disintegrated and floated up, towards the light. "*Kem'falla,*" he breathed. He could feel her presence, taste her brightness with every shortened breath. She was the Light. She and Rain. And they were . . . glorious.

Their power pulsed in the air, showered his every cell with dazzling brightness and searing, electric heat. He could feel himself being pulled towards that brightness, wanting to join with it, to surrender up his essence, to be Unmade and transformed, as they had been.

The ceiling overhead dissolved. The blazing tairen bent its mighty head, and from the great, blinding suns of its eyes, a shaft of searing light fell upon him. «*Go, ajian. Go now to the Well.*»

Command and comprehension filled him with equal measure, and his body moved without conscious thought, backing away from the Light, backing towards the Fey and the women they'd come to rescue.

Rain and Ellysetta were glorious, all right. Glorious and unstoppable. What they had begun, they would not—could not—halt.

«*Bel, we're out of time. We have to go.*» He turned to the *dahl'reisen*, who had retreated towards the door. "Go help General vel Jelani. *Fellanas* or not, grab every woman you find and get her out of here." On the path forged between all the warriors who'd come on this mission, Gaelen cried, «*Time to leave, kem'jetos! Head for the Well now!*»

* * *

The power of the great Light tairen had grown to fill four levels of Boura Fell. Tendrils of light spun clockwise around the glowing mass of its center like the whirling silk scarves of Feraz veil dancers. As Mages died and the *umagi* bound by them were freed, the brilliant notes of the Light tairen's Song directed the innocent to the Well of Souls. Those who had willingly embraced the Dark and gorged their souls on evil, however, did not hear the shining notes of the tairen's Song; all they heard was a deafening roar as Light consumed Darkness.

Everywhere the tairen's Light touched, mass dissolved. Steel, *sel'dor*, rock, wood, Mages, and servants of the Dark: everything and everyone who did not flee before the growing brightness burned away as the Light touched them. Glowing sparks—the remnants of their existence—floated up, some small, sparkling white globes, like fairy flies rising from an evening glade, but most were darker red sparks, like the embers that rose on the heat of a bonfire. The sparks floated towards the mass of energy that was Rain and Ellysetta, joining their Light, feeding it. Just as Ellysetta could siphon the energy of those around her and channel it through herself, now she and Rain together absorbed all the evil that was Boura Fell, Unmaking the Darkness and channeling its power into Light.

Their brightness grew brighter. Layer after layer of Boura Fell disintegrated, consumed by their fiery radiance.

The Fey ran through the crumbling corridors of the dissolving Eld fortress, guiding the captive women towards the promise of freedom. The stairwell leading to the level housing the open Gateway to the Well was still intact, and they leaped up the stairs by threes and fours, Air masters helping those who could not manage the stairs themselves.

Gaelen was the last to leave the chamber where the women had been held. Parts of the ceiling of this level were disintegrating. Walls were crumbling. The second door in the short corridor—the one he had not checked because it was closed and warded—now lay in the center of the hallway amid a pile of rubble. As he ran by, a noise made his heart rise up in his throat. A tiny cry. The squall of an infant.

All but a handful of warriors had already left. Only the *dahl'reisen* remained, deliberately hanging back to spare empathic Fey women the pain of their presence.

"Farel!" Gaelen called. "With me!" He pivoted sharply and dove for the hole where the door had been. The opening led to a hallway. Its ceiling—much lower than the cavernous garden room where they'd discovered the women—was still intact, though not for much longer.

The squall of a child sounded again, followed by anxious shushing and soothing murmurs. A woman. Speaking the Elden tongue, telling the child to be quiet, hissing at someone else, "Hurry! Before someone comes!" Gaelen exchanged the red Fey'cha in his hand for black. Fey did not kill women, not if they had any other choice, but he would be spitted and scorched before he let any Eld—woman or not—run off with an innocent child.

He glanced back to see the hard glitter in Farel's eyes . . . and the white-knuckled fingers clenched around a black Fey'cha.

Together, they ran in swift silence down the corridor.

The infant lay in a sling around Melliandra's chest, his brilliant blue eyes watching her with solemn calm as she tied the final knot in the sling holding another baby strapped to the *shei'dalin* Nicolene's chest. The pair of them each carried two infants strapped in crisscrossing slings across their chests. The four infants were the youngest of the children from the High Mage's secret nursery, all blue-eyed, all young enough to be Shia's child. Which child had actually been born to the gentle, loving woman who'd given Melliandra her name, Melliandra didn't exactly know.

It didn't matter. To her, they were all Shia's child, and she was determined to save them.

An explosion rocked the nursery. A fine shower of grit rained down from the ceiling. Time was running out. The battle that had killed the High Mage was still raging—and drawing closer.

Melliandra tried not to look at the other children in the nursery as she and Nicolene gathered their bags of supplies and prepared to depart with their precious burdens.

Four infants. They could save only four. Twenty more children of varying ages lay in cradles or stood clutching the bars of their cribs. She and Nicolene had agreed they would take only as many babies as they could comfortably carry, but one child in particular—a little girl with a cap of wavy brown hair and solemn eyes—made Melliandra ache to change that plan. That child didn't cry or reach for them, as some of the others did. She just stood in her crib, small, baby-plump hands holding the rails, watching them with those unblinking blue eyes—not the pale brilliant blue Shia's eyes had been but a deeper, richer blue, like the sky Melliandra imagined each night in her dreams. Blue sky eyes, the color of freedom.

She couldn't take her, of course. The toddler was too old, too heavy. They couldn't carry the infants and her as well. And if they let her walk, she would slow them down so much, recapture would be all but certain.

Melliandra hardened her heart. She'd known she couldn't save them all. Save as many as she could but leave the rest: That was the plan. It was a good plan, but she hadn't known how hard it would be. Leaving these children here to die— or worse, to live as slaves of the Mages—hurt more than any wound ever had. The children—their eyes so old in faces so young—deserved so much better.

"I'm sorry," she told them. "I'm so sorry."

As if they understood, several of the children began to cry. The sound alarmed Melliandra. This place had been one of the High Mage's most closely guarded secrets. Boura Fell might be falling down around their ears, but other Mages, seeking power of their own, would want to take his treasures for themselves. The crying would lead those Mages straight to them.

"Ssh," she whispered. "Hush, babies. Hush."

"Las, ajianas, las," Nicolene of the Fey soothed.

"We need to go," Melliandra said. "Now." Before the crying brought someone to investigate.

A whiff of an unfamiliar scent raised the hairs on the back of Melliandra's neck. She froze, falling silent. Ears strained. There, beneath the squall of the children, she heard it: a whisper of sound, footsteps in the hall leading to this room.

Someone was coming.

She grabbed the *shei'dalin's* wrist in a steely grip, but the other woman had already sensed something, too. Nicolene pressed a hand to her heart, her face pale as milk. The girl child began to whimper.

"Dahl'reisen," the Fey breathed.

The dread in the woman's eyes told Melliandra all she needed to know. Whoever was approaching was foe, not friend. A threat to their plans of escape. She jerked her head towards the door at the back of the room, the High Mage's secret escape route the *shei'dalin* had pulled from the *umagi* attendant's mind.

They had nearly reached the door when two men rounded the corner. Clad in black leather, and bristling with weapons, the men gripped unsheathed blades in their hands. Melliandra recognized the look in their icy eyes: the promise of death.

Before Melliandra could act, Nicolene gave a cry and flung out her hands. Green sparks shot from her fingertips. The room rocked and shuddered, and the ground beneath the two men gave way. *"Gana!"* she barked. Run!

Shock kept Melliandra frozen in place. She'd heard the *umagi* whisper about Nicolene's fierceness, but she'd thought the Mages had raped and beaten it out of her.

Nicolene scowled. *"Va!"* she commanded. Go! And with

a slash of her hand, an invisible force shoved Melliandra towards the escape route. "*Dai ema!*" Now!

"*Kem'falla, parei!*" The men's magic had stopped their fall. They soared up, out of the hole in the ground. "*Bas shabei mareskia. Bas veli ku'evarir.*" *Mareskia* was the word for friends. *We are friends. We've come to rescue you.*

"*Fossia!*" Nicolene screamed. "*Dahl'reisen fossia!*" *Lies! Dahl'reisen lies!* She flung her hands towards the ceiling. More bright green magic shot from her fingers, plunging into the rock above the *dahl'reisen*. With a shriek, she yanked, and the ceiling came down on their heads.

Nicolene screamed and fell to her knees as if the ceiling had fallen on her as well as the warriors, but she managed to pull herself back to her feet and stumble towards Melliandra.

"*Sal ne shabei desrali, to ke war desral,*" she cried, waving her hands in a frantic gesture.

Melliandra didn't catch half the words, but it was something about the *dahl'reisen* not being dead.

Sure enough, the pile of rubble was already shifting, starting to bulge upwards as the buried *dahl'reisen* fought their way to the surface. Instinct kicked in. Melliandra bolted for the High Mage's emergency exit, pausing only when the *shei'dalin* snatched the little solemn-eyed girl from her crib and shoved her into Melliandra's hands.

"What are you doing? We agreed—"

"*Seya veli eva bos! Ke nei suya heberi eva dahl'reisen.*" Melliandra's mind filled with an image of the baby screaming in torment in the hands of *dahl'reisen*. The vision winked out. The *shei'dalin's* jaw set, and she glared at Melliandra, daring her to object.

"All right!" Melliandra capitulated with a show of ill grace, even though she was secretly glad not to abandon the child with eyes the color of freedom. "Now, let's go! *Veli!* And stay out of my mind, do you hear?"

Together, they raced into the narrow tunnel the High

Mage had built as his secret escape route. Nicolene pulled the walls and ceiling down behind them as they went.

The last thing Melliandra saw before the cave-in blocked the path to the nursery was one of the *dahl'reisen* rising from the rubble, his eyes pinned on her. In that one moment, as their gazes clashed, a bolt of recognition shot through Melliandra, stabbing straight through to her heart.

His eyes. He had pale, brilliant ice blue eyes, ringed by cobalt. Just like the woman who had given Melliandra her name and her first taste of kindness and love.

Shia's eyes.

Gaelen spat an oath and lunged towards the rubble-filled ruins of the caved-in passageway. Green Earth blazed in his hands as he began to form the weaves to clear the passage, but before he could release his weaves, another section of the ceiling caved in. He had to leap to one side to avoid being buried again.

Farel started to clear the fresh pile of rubble, but Gaelen waved him off. Bits of the ceiling overhead were already starting to crumble and float upwards.

"Leave it," he said. "We're out of time. Wherever Nicolene-*falla* has gone, she'll have to look after herself until we can come back for her. We've got to get these children to safety." He called for more of his men and reached for one of the toddlers standing in the cribs.

"Sieks'ta, General," Farel said as the others arrived and they began handing off children. "It's my fault she ran. If I hadn't been with you—"

Gaelen shook his head. *"Nei*, the fault is mine. I should have considered there might be a *fellana* inside." He clapped Farel on the shoulder and handed him a small, unsmiling boy with dark brown eyes. "Quickly, *kem'maresk*. We need to go." The room was very bright now, forested with shafts of light shining through the disintegrating ceiling overhead. He snatched the last child from the crib beside him and followed Farel and the others down the crumbling corridor.

At the opening to the short hallway, Gaelen paused for a final look back at the blocked passage where the girl accompanying Nicolene vol Oros had stood. Who was she? Not Fey or Elvish. Not Celierian, either, with that milky white skin that had clearly never seen the sun. And those eyes. Huge silver coins, framed by sooty lashes. They unsettled him in a way he could not explain.

With a rumbling crack the rest of the nursery ceiling dissolved. Blinding light filled the room. Gaelen flung up a hand to shield his eyes.

"General!"

Farel's shout spurred him to action. Whoever or whatever Nicolene vol Oros's disconcerting companion might be made no difference now. Gaelen spun on his heel, hunched his body to protect the child in his arms from falling debris, and raced after his fellow *lu'tan*.

The *dahl'reisen* guarding the gateway to the Well of Souls began herding all the rescued captives and refugees into the portal. "Into the Well!" they cried. "Everyone into the Well now!"

"But the wounded," one of the *shei'dalins* exclaimed.

"Seal what you can't heal! We're out of time! Go! Go! Go!"

Vadim Maur's escape tunnel led up and away from Boura Fell. Melliandra and Nicolene ran as quickly as they could, the *shei'dalin* pausing every few seconds to bring down the ceiling behind them. Each time they came to a fork in the tunnel, Melliandra and Nicolene followed whichever path led up, towards the surface of Eld. Up was where the sky was. Up was where the Mages were least likely to be. And so, up they went.

At last they arrived, out of breath, legs burning from the uphill run, at a winding stair that led to a closed door. Melliandra turned the knob and carefully pushed the door slightly ajar.

She braced herself for a flood of bright white light coming

from the burning ball called the Great Sun that traveled across the sky. Sunlight, Shia had called it. But there was no burning ball of light. And the roof of the world—the thing Shia called the sky—was not the bright, beautiful blue Shia had described. It was black and scattered with tiny silver flecks—like *sel'dor* ore sprinkled with tiny crystals of mirror stone.

Melliandra's hand began to shake, and her stomach did flips inside her belly.

"Arast sha neida?" What's wrong?

The sound of the *shei'dalin* Nicolene's voice made Melliandra jump. *"Neitha,"* she answered brusquely. Nothing. Maybe this was just another big room, like the garden room, and they were still inside Boura Fell. But when she forced herself to shove open the door and saw the immensity of the alien landscape stretched out before her, she knew the truth.

This—this dark place—was the world. Tall, soaring spires of things Shia had called trees surrounded the doorway, but something was wrong with them. Half of the trees were gray, barren bones, like the skeletons of trees. At her feet, what should have been the soft, slender blades of the ground cover called grass were brown, brittle stalks that crackled when she poked them with a tentative toe.

This world above was dead. And *cold*—as cold as when Mages spun their dark magic. Despair swamped her. Where was the warm, bright, green-and-blue world Shia had sung of? Had the Mages destroyed it?

She turned to Nicolene. "I'm sorry," she said. "This was a mistake. This is not what she told me it would be. The sun is gone. The world is dead. I think the Mages killed it." To Melliandra's horror, tears sprang to her eyes, and her voice cracked. She hugged Shia's son to her chest. What were they going to do now?

Nicolene smiled, but there was such compassion in her eyes, Melliandra couldn't take offense. *"Nei, kaishena,"* the *shei'dalin* soothed. *"Nei desrali. Nei Magia. De sha eilissei."* Not dead. Not Mages. It is *eilissei*.

"I don't know *'eilissei.'* "

"Sa Dol liath." Nicolene tilted her head to one side with her hands beneath her cheek and pretended to sleep. *"Cordai Sa Dol liath, de sha eilissei."*

The Great Sun is sleeping, she'd said. When the Great Sun sleeps, it is *eilissei*. Melliandra hadn't known that the Great Sun needed to sleep, but a little of her tension faded away. Although the world was so different than Shia had described, it was clear Nicolene was not alarmed—not by the dead trees nor the dark nor the coldness of this place.

"Bas arrisi atha legan." Green Earth spun in powerful waves that sent tingles across Melliandra's skin, and the tattered threadbare rags of her clothes thickened to dense, warm fabric, so plush she could barely feel the cold. Something equally warm encased her bare feet and ankles. Shoes. The first she'd ever worn. When the green weave faded, all seven of them, Melliandra, Nicolene, the four babies, and the little girl, were bundled warmly against the cold.

The *shei'dalin* gave a gentle push. *"Va, kaishena. Nei siad."* Go, young one. Don't be afraid.

With Shia's child and one other cradled against her chest and a little girl with eyes the color of a not-*eilissei* sky clinging tight to her hand, Melliandra Maureva, descendant and slave of the High Mage of Eld, drew a shaky breath and took her first, hesitant step into freedom.

As Nicolene and Melliandra began their trek towards the Mandolay Mountains in the north and the refugees from Boura Fell made their way through the Well of Souls, the ground over Boura Fell began to shift and bulge. It rose upward, slowly swelling into a large dome of earth and rock and toppling forest.

Then, abruptly, the dome burst, and a brilliant tower of white light shot into the sky.

All across Eld, the tattered remnants of Vadim Maur's great Army of Darkness turned in surprise as the sky over the dark forests of Eld flared ultrabright. Hundreds of miles away, on the battlements of Orest, and all along the mighty Heras River and the northern provinces of Celieria, the world fell into awed silence. All activity ceased. Fey, Celierian, and Elvish faces alike turned to the north.

The tower of light burned for a full chime, turning darkest night to brilliant day, before it collapsed in upon itself with a soundless boom that shook the core Eld. In the wake of that brightness, a great, glowing light shot up and streaked westward across the Elden sky.

From a distance, the streak of light looked like a giant shooting star racing across the night sky. But for years to come, those close enough to see what lay at the heart of the brightness would speak of a magnificent tairen made completely of light that flew across the skies of Eld. It dipped down and breathed the fire of the gods upon Koderas and Boura Maur, turning both into smoking craters, before continuing westward to disappear high in the Rhakis mountains. What became of that Light tairen, none could say, but soon after its disappearance into the Rhakis, the waters of the Heras once more ran rich with the magical power of *faerilas*.

And in the place that had been Boura Fell, where the Light tairen first appeared, what remained was a great monument of shining crystal, shaped like a enormous, six-pointed crown—a beacon of Light in the dark heart of Eld. And within the haven of the crystal crown's radiant golden white light, no Darkness would ever again endure.

CHAPTER TWENTY-ONE

Blazing radiance to the Plains of Corunn
Fly high, flame strong; roar far, reign long

Feyreisa, Feyreisen; magic and might
Two Souls, side by side, in tairen flight

Majestic Flight,
a poem by Belliard vel Jelani of the Fey

19th day of Seledos
The Fading Lands ~ Wingshadow,
Shellabah of the Daris Line

Purple silk caressed creamy marble columns, fluttering on a gentle breeze redolent with the aromas of burning fireoak and cinnabar. Outside, a light snow blanketed the northern fields of the Fading Lands, but within the magic-warmed luxury of Rain's palatial *shellabah*, the only chill came from the cone of packed snow melting down Ellysetta's naked stomach.

She closed her eyes and stretched like a cat as the heat of Rain's tongue followed the path of the ice, drowning in sensation as Rain's lips and hands slid across her skin, stroking, caressing, worshipping with humbling reverence. There was nothing like this feeling, this wholeness. This completeness. His mind and hers, one. He touched her, and she felt the caress with both her senses and his. An overload of emotion, of sensation. A harmonic that built upon itself again and again with each shift of his silken skin, each flex of corded muscle, each warm breath and stir of flesh.

Her hands tightened, fingers digging into the hard blades of his shoulders, holding him close.

He lifted his head, burning lavender eyes gleaming through a tangle of silky black hair. His mouth curved, and he held her gaze as he licked and kissed his way down her body.

She was him, all burning stone and heady desire, on fire with want, dizzy with the sweet aroma of her scent and the taste of her flesh on his tongue. She knew what he saw, what he felt, when he held her, when he kissed and caressed her.

She arched her back, thrusting her breasts upwards, glorying in the hot rush that consumed him at the sight. Everything about her gave him pleasure. Her helpless abandon to his tender assault made the blood pound in his veins and the tairen in his soul roar with possession and triumph.

«Aiyah, fellana, you do make me roar.» He was touching her, skin to skin, and their bond was at last complete. Her thoughts were as open and accessible to him as her emotions had been, as her body was now. There was no part of her he did not know as well as he knew himself. No Shadow, no Light, no thought, or hope that he could not share.

Once, that would have alarmed her. To be so . . . naked. So utterly vulnerable, even to him. Now, it filled her with joy, a warm, radiant happiness like a sun shining forever in her soul.

She smiled into his eyes, loving him with a completeness she'd never dreamed possible. There was no part of her that did not belong to him, no part of him that did not belong to her. They were now one soul, shared between two bodies. One soul existing in a state of grace so perfect, so complete, it was as close to feeling the hand of the gods as a living creature could experience.

Her fingers traced the smooth, proud lines of his face and

neck, caressed the breadth of his shoulders, marveling at the softness of the Fey skin that covered such indomitable strength. "You are my strength, *shei'tan*."

"And so I will be for all eternity, Ellysetta *shei'tani*." He caught her hand and pressed a smiling kiss into her palm. The tip of his tongue touched her skin in a small, catlike lick. The glow kindling in his eyes turned the tiny, feline caress into an erotic promise. "Wilt thou join thy beloved, *shei'tani*?"

Her lips curved, lashes lowering in a simmering look. "Always, *shei'tan*."

His mouth touched hers, and heat bloomed in instantaneous response. She arched against him, purring in her throat as his hands smoothed down the sides of her body and tracked trails of fire and longing in their wake.

"Mrowr?"

A rush of cold air swept into the protected warmth of the *shellabah*. Ellysetta's eyes flashed open, as a familiar voice sang, *«No, no, kitling. When the Feyreisa and Feyreisen are mating they like 'privacy.' You must knock before entering their lair.»*

She and Rain groaned together and turned towards the purple silk drapes—one of which now sported the face of an inquisitive tairen kitling poking through at the bottom. "Mrowr?" Hallah said again, twitching her black ears.

«Knocking! Knocking!» three kitling voices chimed with delighted exuberance. Hallah squawked as the silk drape over her head ripped from its moorings and three kitlings tumbled into the *shellabah* on top of her. Fuzzy and adorable, their wings still sporting downy fur, Letah, Sharrah, and Miauren clambered to their feet, and promptly lost all interest in Steli's lessons about knocking in favor of chasing the pretty, fluttery purple thing now tangled in their wings and tails.

Watching them, Steli purred in maternal contentment then told Ellysetta and Rain, "Steli is teaching the kitlings to do knocking."

"So we see," Rain said drily. "Thank you so much, Steli-*chakai*."

Steli snickered, twitched her nose, then gave a great, feline yawn and fluttered her wings. *«Hunting tomorrow.»*

"Somewhere other than here, I hope." Ellysetta sat up, spinning a gown to cover herself.

«Hunting?» The kitlings stopped chasing the silk drape and perked up. *«Pouncing!»*

Pouncing was apparently a lesson Steli had already taught, because all four kitlings immediately began hunkering down, growling in their throat, then leaping at one another, crying. *«Pounce! Pounce! Pounce!»*

Ellysetta squealed and leaped out of the way as Sharra came tumbling past, crashing into the chaise and sending it skittering across the *shellabah's* warmed marble floors.

«Very good pouncing, kitlings,» Steli purred in approval. *«But be careful of the pride-kin. In this form, they break.»*

«Sorry, sorry,» Sharra mumbled, then she growled and threw herself on her siblings again.

As Ellysetta laughed and rolled her eyes, a second interruption ended any hope of shooing out the tairen and returning to the peace and privacy she and Rain had been enjoying since returning to the Fading Lands.

A private Spirit weave arrived from Dharsa. *«Rain? Ellysetta?»*

«Marissya?» Rain answered instantly, all humor wiped away by concern. Marissya would not have intruded except for good reason. *«What is it? What's wrong?»*

«Neitha,» she assured him. *«Nothing is wrong. But we have found something in the Hall of Scrolls. I think you both should come.»*

The Fading Lands ~ Dharsa

The Hall of Scrolls had been badly damaged in the attack on Dharsa, but its Keeper, Tealah vol Jianas, had insisted that all homes and the palace be restored before the Fey diverted any of their efforts to repairing the Hall. Consequently, it was only now, a full week after the battle, that the rubble was cleared. And in doing so, the Fey had uncovered a secret stair that had been hidden behind a thick, solid wall of stone.

At the sight of the broken rock and the gaping, jagged edges of the dark hole that led down below the Hall, the hairs on the back of Ellysetta's neck stood up. Her hand reached for Rain's.

"There is a mirror down there," she said. "Like the Mirrors of Inquiry here in the Hall." All but a few of those Mirrors now lay smashed and shattered in the rubble.

Marissya looked at her in surprise. "*Aiyah*, there is a mirror. But how did you know?"

"I have seen it before. In my dreams." She released Rain's hand and ducked into the jagged doorway, summoning a ball of Fire to light her way. The stair curved down into a small, windowless stone chamber beneath the Hall of Scrolls, and there, in the center of the room, just like her dreams, sat the dark, oval mirror perched on a stone column.

As she approached it, the mirror began to glow a phosphorescent blue, and a face appeared in the center of the glowing light. Blond hair billowed gently around the stern, Fey-beautiful masculine face from her dreams. Green eyes shone like stars. The mouth opened, and a voice spoke, deep and resonant.

"I am the Mirror of Knowledge. I wait for the one foretold to restore all that was lost."

"That's all it's been saying since we found it," Marissya said. "We've asked it every question we could think of, it won't tell us who the one foretold is, what it will restore, or how to restore it."

Ellysetta remembered her last dream of the mirror, the intricate weave of *shei'dalin's* love and Azrahn that had spun from her hand. "I think I know." She glanced at Rain. "I think I am the one foretold, and I think this is the key." She showed the others the weave in Spirit. She no longer feared Azrahn—with her soul now joined to Rain's, Darkness would never again threaten her—but she didn't want to just impulsively start spinning.

He nodded. He knew every dream she'd ever had as intimately as she did. "Go ahead, *shei'tani*. Though perhaps, to be safe, the other *fellanas* should leave the room?"

"Are you joking?" Tealah sputtered. "This room has been hiding beneath the Hall of Scrolls for who knows how long. Whatever happens, I'm not going to miss it."

Marissya didn't want to leave, but as she carried the only other Tairen Soul in the Fading Lands beside Ellysetta and Rain, she chose caution over curiosity.

When she was gone, Rain and Ellysetta wove protective weaves around the stone chamber and then Ellysetta spun the weave from her dream. Azrahn and *shei'dalin's* love poured from her fingertips, looping and twining in a perfect reproduction of the weave from her dream. The blue glow behind the mirror's face began to swirl and brighten, and the mirror man's eyes flashed with sudden green sparks that flew out of the glass.

Rain shoved Ellysetta and Tealah behind him. Magic flared to life in his hands, but the green sparks had already stopped and begun to swirl in a cone of light that became the figure of a Fey king standing tall and proud before them in the golden war armor of the Fey. He had gold-shot chestnut hair and eyes like burning flame. When he spoke, his voice shimmered with gold and silver sparkles, like tairen speech. "I am Tevan, called Fire Eyes, born of the Fey king Sevander and his queen Fellana the Bright, Lady of Light, she who was once tairen and *makai* of the Fey'Bahren pride."

"Oh. My. Gods." Tealah covered her mouth with her hands, her eyes huge as saucers. "He was real. The legend is true."

"I offer greeting to the one who was foretold, the daughter of my line—the line of Fellana the Bright—who carries within her the magic of Fey and Elfkind, tairen and Mage. May the memories I once erased from the world to save it, now be yours to use for the good of all, in keeping with the will of the gods. May the Light always shine on your Path, daughter of Fellana, and may you be as bright a beacon for our people as she who gave me life."

"Rain," Ellysetta breathed, reaching for his hand.

"I know," he murmured, equally as dazed.

The image of Tevan disappeared, and the face in the mirror began to speak. "I am the Mirror of Knowledge, created by command of the Fey King Tevan Fire Eyes, to hold all knowledge that was removed from the world so that it could one day be restored."

Much later, as night descended over Dharsa, and the Mother and Daughter moons rose to add their brightness to that of the winter star called Erimea, Rain and Ellysetta gathered in the palace with Ellysetta's parents, her quintet, and the members of the new Massan to share the incredible secrets revealed by the Mirror of Knowledge. Water master, Loris v'En Mahr, had accepted the role as the leader of the Massan. Eimar remained as its Air master, while Dax joined as the new Earth master. Bel and Tajik had agreed to stand as acting Spirit and Fire masters, until Rain decided which Fey Lord should replace Tenn and the deceased Spirit master, Nurian.

"The Time Before Memory was the time when Fey used Azrahn freely," Ellysetta told them. "According to the Mirror of Knowledge, the Fey did not come with the prides to this world. Only the Elves did. When Lissallukai breathed her magic across the Bay of Flames, a tribe of mortals living by the bay were the first to swim in its waters and they were transformed by her great magic, just as the legend claimed. Only because they were the first, their gift was the greatest—that gift was the six branches of Fey magic, the power over the four elements and the two mystics. Those mortals became the Fey."

Ellysetta hid a smile as several of her quintet shifted in discomfort. Though far from mortal now, the ancestral link didn't sit well with them. These Fey had much to learn. Mortals might not be magical, but they had their own special gifts, and she intended to see the friendship between Fey and Celieria blossom once more.

"Of those six branches of magic, the greatest was the gift of Azrahn, the soul magic," Rain added, "which has both a Light and a Dark side to it. The Light side, the Fey have spun without fear since the Time Before Memory—it is the power we know as *shei'dalin's* love."

Now it was Marissya's turn to flinch in surprise.

"The Dark side," Rain continued, "what we know as Azrahn, is very powerful in its own right, but also dangerous. It is a force of destruction and force, rather than healing and peace. Together in its wholeness, Azreisenan, the soul magic, is the true source of our power . . . of our immortality, of our fertility, of our magic. And in giving the Fey power over the Dark side of Azrahn, as well as the Light, the gods gave the Fey a gift they never gave the Elves—freedom. Freedom to choose our path. But that gift is also our test."

"All great gifts come with a great price," Bel murmured.

"*Aiyah*," Ellysetta agreed, "and the price of the greatest gift ever given to the Fey—the gift of Azrahn—is the temptation of the Dark Path. No Elf will ever fall to Darkness. They are incapable of it, because the gods never gifted them with the fullness of Azrahn. But the Fey can, because we can choose to wield our magic for good or evil."

"If Azrahn is such a boon to the Fey," Tajik interrupted, "why would it be outlawed and why would its use be wiped from the memory of the world?"

"Because in Sevander's time—and Tevan's own—many of the Fey began seeking ever greater and greater power— especially those who were strongest in Azrahn, including Sevander's uncle. They began to focus exclusively on the Darkest powers of Azrahn. They became the Mages. Sevander's uncle was, in fact, the Mage who transformed Fellana into a Fey."

"And then used the tairen's power he'd gotten from her to wage war against the Fey," Dax said.

Rain nodded. "And his descendants continued his work, raising an even greater army. A force the like of which the world had never seen."

"The Army of Darkness," Gil said.

"*Aiyah*," Rain agreed. "And it was as devastating a force as the legends portray—much worse than the revenant army this Mage put together. It was so devastating in fact, that after he defeated it, Tevan Fire Eyes and his tairen and Elvish advisors decided the Fey were not ready for the great and dangerous power of Azrahn. With their help, he wiped all knowledge of its use from the world. In doing so, he robbed the Mages of all the secrets of their Dark magic and created the Time Before Memory."

"He and his advisors thought that by outlawing the use of the Dark side of Azrahn, they would spare the Fey the greatest temptation of the Dark Path," Ellysetta concluded. "And they did. The world entered a time of great peace—the golden years of the First Age. But over the millennia, the Mages began rebuilding their lost knowledge. And as generation after generation of Fey banished their most powerful masters of Azrahn for weaving it, the Fey unknowingly drained their own bloodlines of the magic most essential to their survival." She glanced at Gaelen. "That's why the *dahl'reisen* thrive while the Fey wither. Because so many of them are still powerful masters of Azrahn—and because between the High Mage's breeding efforts and the remnant magic of the Mage Wars, the Light and Dark sides of Azrahn were being combined again."

"So are you saying the *dahl'reisen* are the real key to returning fertility to the Fey?" Eimar asked, looking troubled at the thought. He had fought with *dahl'reisen* as his allies, and approved their bloodswearing to Ellysetta, but cozying up to warriors who'd chosen the Shadowed Path still did not sit well with him.

"*Nei*, not the *dahl'reisen*," Rain corrected. "Azrahn. Azrahn is the key—and the connection between the tairen and the Fey, not only because our magic sprang from Lissalukai's great fire, but because every Tairen Soul starting with Tevan Fire Eyes are the descendants of Fellana, who was the last of Lissallukai's bloodline. That's why our fates are so closely entwined. The Tairen Souls keep Lissallukai's blood—and, with it, her greatest magic—alive and strong. And Ellysetta, who combines Fey, tairen, Elvish, and even Mage powers, is the most powerful master of Azrahn born since Lissallukai herself. It is Ellysetta—both through the children we will bear, and every child conceived as a result of her fertility weaves—who will return the fullness of Azrahn back to the tairen and the Fey."

Ellysetta curled her fingers around his and smiled. One day in their lifetime, they would see the skies over the Fading Lands once more filled with tairen and hear the streets of Dharsa ring with the laughter of Fey children. Her children— their children—would be powerful Tairen Souls, just as they were, raised in love amid the Fey and the pride. And that was reward enough to make the great price of her gifts worthwhile.

"The Elf king of Tevan's time Saw what would happen," Rain concluded, "including the fact that Ellysetta would be born to bring the fullness of Azrahn back to the tairen and the Fey. So upon his advice, Tevan ordered the creation of the Mirror of Knowledge and the Elf king told his descendants to watch for her birth."

"You really were born to save us," Marissya said.

"And so she has." Rain raised a glass of chilled *faerilas*. "To the treasures of the past, my friends, and to the joys of a bright future."

27th day of Seledos

Rain stood on the balustraded terrace just outside the ballroom of the Dharsa's newly restored royal palace and looked out at the gleaming gold-and-white beauty of Dharsa nestled in the forested hills. He closed his eyes and inhaled the aroma of jasmine and honeyblossom and the sweet, intoxicating fragrance of Amarynth that wafted on the cool evening breeze.

For a thousand years, the world behind the Faering Mists had been his prison. Now, at last, the Fading Lands was home once more, and for the first time in centuries—perhaps for the first time in his entire life—he was truly at peace.

His quest to save the tairen and the Fey was complete. He had found the woman Shei'Kess had sent him to find, and together they had saved the tairen and the Fey and brought the promise of life back to the Fading Lands.

Rain drew in his breath again, and a slow smile curved his lips as a new scent, familiar and beloved, danced across his senses like a warm caress. Turning, he held out his hand.

As it always had—and as Rain knew it always would—his heart leapt at the sight of her. She was a vision in white and silver and stunning flame.

Her white silk gown—overlaid with Elvian lace and studded with tiny diamonds like morning dewdrops caught in a spider's fine web—whispered across the marble terrace stones as she crossed to his side. Rajahl vel'En Daris's crystal gleamed at her wrist, while Rain's crystal hung from a platinum chain around her neck. Her hair tumbled about her shoulders and down to her waist like a cloud of tairen fire.

Her fingers slid across the back of Rain's wrist, but he turned his hand to thread his fingers through hers and hold her hand the way Celierians—and now he, as well—preferred.

His thumb brushed across hers in a tiny caress, and he smiled into Ellysetta's bright Fey eyes. "*Beylah vo, shei'tani.*"

She tilted her head to one side. "For what?"

"For . . . everything." The Eye of Truth had sent him to Ellysetta to find the salvation of his peoples. But in her, he had also found the salvation of his own soul.

He had longed for death until she renewed his fierce desire for life. She had smashed countless Fey traditions and taboos, and forced him to rethink everything he believed of the world as she forged her own, unique path with quiet but relentless courage. He had thought all *dahl'reisen* were beyond redemption, yet she had restored Gaelen's soul and won the bloodsworn loyalty of the Brotherhood of Shadows and brought the gift of their powerful magic and fertility back to the Fey. He had thought Azrahn was evil, yet even before the Mirror of Knowledge had revealed its secrets, she had proven the forbidden magic could be just as powerful a force for good.

She'd made the world beautiful and wondrous once more, as it hadn't been for him since he was a boy. She made him believe the Fey would again become the great, shining Light they had once been to this world. A beacon of hope and freedom and strength that would forever stand fast against the Dark.

She smiled at his thoughts and shook her head. "You give me too much credit. Most of that is not my doing."

"And there you are wrong. Without you, *shei'tani,* none of this would have been possible." He waved his hand to indicate the rebuilt beauty of Dharsa with its fully restored Hall of Scrolls and the crowds gathering at the foot of Dharsa's central mount. Fey, Elves, Celierian friends and dignitaries, all standing side by side in the heart of the city, garbed in splendorous raiment as they attended Rain and Ellysetta's truemating celebration and the coronation of the Fading Lands' new queen.

"He is right," Marissya said, as she and Dax joined them on the terrace. Like dozens of other mates of the Fey, the pair were garbed in the verdant green-and-white hues they would both wear until the birth of their child. The heady scent of Amarynth perfumed the air around them, blooming in abundance from every bower and garden in Dharsa. "You have changed our world."

"I never meant to."

Marissya smiled. "The gods weave as the gods will, Feyreisa."

The breeze blew a wayward curl against Ellysetta's cheek.

Rain reached out to brush it back out of her face. "Where are your parents?"

"With Tajik and Papa, keeping Lillis and Lorelle out of trouble until the ceremonies begin. Papa has been regaling them with stories of my childhood." She laughed, but a sheen of tears glimmered in her eyes. Despite her overwhelming joy at freeing her Fey parents, he knew she still sorely missed her adoptive mother. Today's bonding ceremony would be the second time Ellysetta and Rain had celebrated the joining of their lives. Mama's absence, and the absence of other dear friends lost to the evil of the Eld, was a somber Harmony to the now-joyous verse of her Song.

Happiness was hers, but as with all great gifts of the Fey, that happiness had come at a steep price.

"I think Lauriana would have liked Shan and Elfeya," Rain said.

Ellysetta nodded, as she thumbed away her tears. "*Aiyah.* I know she would. And I know they would have liked her, too."

"How could we not?" A warm, vibrant voice replied. "She is the woman who kept our daughter safe and guided and loved her in our stead."

Rain and Ellysetta both turned to the open archway leading from the ballroom as Shan, Elfeya, Sol Baristani, and the twins stepped outside to join them.

Smiling, Elfeya v'En Celay approached to embrace her daughter and her daughter's mate. Ellysetta's birth mother looked every inch the powerful *shei'dalin* she was, in a gown of stunning scarlet and gold with her truemate's *sorreisu'kiyr* set in a golden torque at her throat. Her Light was nearly as bright as Ellysetta's, setting her skin aglow so that she shone like a star. She resembled her daughter in so many ways—the fiery hair, the gentleness, the steely will that lay beneath her vast compassion and empathic gifts. It was that steel that had enabled her to survive her thousand years of torment. That steel that had made her the indomitable truemate of the legendary warrior standing at her side.

Rain held out his hand to clasp the forearm of Shannisorran v'En Celay, the warrior once known as Lord Death. He flinched slightly at the acid burn of the *sel'dor* bands lining the thick golden cuffs at Shan's wrists. Shan might be free from the High Mage, but he was not free of the man's dread gifts. The tairen's soul Vadim Maur had tied to Shan's was with him still—and just as wild and savage as it had been during his captivity in Boura Fell.

He wouldn't allow Elfeya or Ellysetta to risk themselves trying to undo what the Mage had done, and he wouldn't risk the Fey by giving the beast its freedom, so he had willingly bound himself in *sel'dor*. To his mate's objections, he had replied, "Pain is life, *kem'san*. I accepted that long ago. We are together, and we are free. That is joy enough for me."

The Fey Lord's face was carved from stone, but his granite jaw softened, and the hard glitter of his green eyes warmed when he turned his attention to the daughter he'd suffered decades of torture to protect. "Blessings of the day, *ajiana*. *Miora felah* to you and your mate. May Shadow always fall short of your Path and your days be filled with joy."

Ellysetta embraced him. "*Beylah vo . . . Gepa.*"

His arms clutched her close. "You do us proud, *kem'nessa*." He bent his head to her ear, and added in a hoarse whisper, "You were worth every moment."

The tears she'd been fighting squeezed out between her lashes. When her father released her, she begged again, "Won't you change your mind and stay with us here in Dharsa?"

Shan smiled and shook his head. "*Nei*, child. Tehlas is our home. It is where we belong."

Rain had asked Shan and Elfeya to take Tenn and Venarra's place on the governing council, but they had declined. After their centuries of confinement, the bustle of Dharsa unsettled them—and disturbed the tairen tied to Shan's soul. They both believed the solitude of their now-abandoned home city would suit them much better and grant them both the time they needed. Time to live together in peace, without pressure or restraint. Time to walk the silvery beaches of Tairen's Bay, or turn their faces up to the sun, or lie on the rooftop of their old home at night and make love beneath the stars. Time to heal and to learn what it was to be free once more.

"But you will visit us, of course," Elfeya said. "You and your mate . . . and your papa and sisters, of course." She sent a fond glance at the twins, who both already bore smudges of dirt on their pristine white gowns. The two girls had captivated Shan and Elfeya with their laughter and mischievous antics, and most of their time since returning to Dharsa had been spent in the company of the twins, watching over them and spoiling them as they had not had the chance to watch and spoil their own child. Elfeya lifted her hands to spin a quick weave. The smudges vanished and the slightly askew bouquets of Amarynth nestled in the twins' mink brown curls straightened neatly. "And perhaps one day, their mates as well, hmm?" she added, as Kieran and Kiel joined the group on the terrace.

Rain's brows drew together. Elfeya was looking at Kieran and Kiel when she spoke, and there was a very Elvish look in her eyes.

Before he could comment, Bel appeared in the arched doorway and signaled to him. Rain nodded an acknowledgment. "*Kabei.* Our final guests have arrived. With them is someone I think you and your daughters will want to meet, Master Baristani."

They turned their attention to the arched doorway just as Gaelen and Rijonn ushered in two dozen of the women and children from the *dahl'reisen* village and Farel's white-haired, silver-eyed hearth witch.

"Sheyl." With a happy smile, Ellysetta greeted the woman who had helped save their lives and enveloped her in a warm hug. "*Meiveli ti'Dharsa.* Welcome to Dharsa. Welcome to the Fading Lands."

"Thank you." Sheyl nodded at Rain. "Thank both of you for your kindness and generosity in offering us shelter and a new home. Farel sends his greetings and bids you both much joy."

Despite the lingering concerns of some Fey, Rain had

granted safe harbor in the Fading Lands to the refugees from the Verlaine Forest—including every *dahl'reisen* who had sworn a *lute'asheiva* bond to Ellysetta. As few as the Fey had become, there was more than room enough for the *dahl'reisen lu'tan* to live in one of the abandoned Fey cities without inflicting their pain upon the vulnerably empathic women of the Fey.

Farel and most of his men had refused. Even without the Mists to bar their return, they would not step foot in the Fading Lands while they still bore their *dahl'reisen* scars. They chose instead to settle in Orest and Dunelan, to serve as the guardians of the Fading Lands they had always been. Many of the villagers had refused as well—like Sheyl, who would not leave her chosen mate and several non-*dahl'reisen* men who preferred to fight alongside their friends, fathers, and brothers. The rest had made the woodland city of Elverial their home, though there was talk of resettling in Lissilin. Thanks to Tealah's tireless efforts to recover all the lost knowledge retained in the Mirror of Memory, Rain and Ellysetta now knew how to restore magic to the dead Source there. Life would bloom in the desert again.

"*Sha vel'mei,* Sheyl," Ellysetta said. "Though I do wish for both your sakes that Farel had accepted Rain's invitation. I would gladly restore his soul, Sheyl."

"We both thank you, but he could never accept the pain it would cause you. Despite what some Fey may still think, he is too honorable a Fey to ever let you suffer on his behalf." Sheyl forced a smile. "Enough sad talk. This is a day of joy. And there is someone who would like to meet your father and sisters." She gestured, and the woman standing in the shadows of the archway stepped out onto the terrace.

Lillis's eyes widened briefly, but then a slow smile spread across her young face. "Your name is Bess." She walked across the terrace and hugged the aunt she'd never met as if they were old friends. "Hello, I'm Lillis. Mama loved you very much, and so will I. I'm so very glad you've come."

Ellysetta tilted her head to eye her young sister in amazement. "How did you know that, Lillis?"

But all Lillis would say was, "Mama told me." Shock gave way to warm welcome as the other Baristanis stepped forward to greet Lauriana's long-lost sister.

A handful of chimes later, a distant roar rumbled through the air and a triumphant, welcoming cheer rose up from the gathered crowds of Fey. Silhouetted against the deepening twilight of the eastern skies, the Fey'Bahren pride soared across the sky towards Dharsa. The whole pride had come—including the kitlings who had only recently learned to fly and were now gamboling across the sky like rambunctious kittens.

Now, at last, everyone was here. Now, at last, Dharsa could celebrate Ellysetta's coronation and the first *shei'tanitsa* bonding ceremony to be held in over a thousand years.

In the golden Hall of Tairen, tairen, friends and family and countrymen had gathered. Spirit masters positioned around the great hall began to weave as Ellysetta began her slow march down the center of the hall towards the dais, where Rain, Loris v'En Mahr, and two gleaming tairen thrones awaited. The Spirit masters spun detailed images of each moment out to several locations in the sky over Dharsa, so that all the gathered throngs could watch the ceremonies

Steli, blue eyes whirling with pride, stood behind the throne that would be Ellysetta's. Sybharukai lent the support of the tairen by standing behind Rain's throne. The four tairen kitlings sat with the rest of the pride off to one side, wide-eyed and taking everything in. Their long tails curled in front of them, and the tips flicked with interest as they looked around. An occasional furtive glance at Sybharukai made them straighten up and quit fidgeting.

Over her white, diamond-encrusted gown, Ellysetta had donned a long silver cape woven from the bloodsworn blades of her *lu'tan*. The cape trailed a full tairen length behind her, its gleaming length sewn with the thousands of Soul Quest crystals of the warriors who had fallen in her service. As she passed Shei'Kess, the great oracle began to glow with soft radiance, as if acknowledging and welcoming her.

Dorian XI, garbed in resplendent Celierian blue, nodded as she passed. Next to him stood Illona Brighthand, and though Galad Hawksheart had been invited to attend, he had sent Fanor Farsight to represent the Deep Woods elves in his stead. Queen Annoura, who had gone into seclusion to await the birth of her child, had not come. But Gaspare Fellows, his eyes damp with happy tears, stood proudly beside his king. Lord Teleos, Ellysetta's distant cousin, stood beside Shan and Elfeya.

Tenn and Venarra had come as well. No longer serving on the Massan, they remained reluctant to embrace the many changes that Ellysetta, Rain, and now the Mirror of Knowledge had brought about, but Ellysetta was determined to put the past to rest. They had feared Ellysetta's power, just as she had. And as Illona Brighthand had pointed out, without Tenn's stubborn refusal to join the war, there would not have been enough warriors in Dharsa to repel the Elden invasion. The gods had woven as they would, and Ellysetta chose to make the best of it.

She smiled at her family, her quintet, Kieran and Kiel, the other familiar, now-dear faces of those gathered here. And as she swore her oath and accepted the responsibilities of becoming Ellysetta Feyreisa, Queen and Defender of the Fading Lands, she imagined that Mama and the many beloved friends who had perished were watching her, too, and smiling with approval.

Nalia, Loris's *shei'tani*, carried Ellysetta's crown, and Rain placed it on her head. A six-pointed crown of platinum, topped with six clear crystals from Lissalukai's *kiyr*. As the crown touched her head, the crystals began to glow, circling her head in an aura of radiant light.

Finally, before the assemblage, Rain and Ellysetta, truemates and Tairen Souls of the Fey, pledged the fullness of their immortal lives to one another. With great dignity,

Loris v'En Mahr, the newly instated leader of the Massan, called forth Tealah, the Keeper of the Hall of Scrolls, who delivered to him a large and ornately wrought golden scroll.

"By the grace and Light of the gods, Rainier vel'En Daris, son of Rajahl and Kiaria vel'En Daris, and Ellysetta Baristani vol Celay, daughter of Shannisorran and Elfeya v'En Celay, adopted daughter of Sol and Lauriana Baristani of Celieria, have joined their souls as one in *shei'tanitsa.* Henceforth and forevermore shall they be known as Rainier and Ellysetta v'En Daris, truemates of the Fey, Feyreisen and Feyreisa of the Fading Lands. So let it be written in the Scroll of Life. May your Light always shine, and joy be your constant companion." Magic flashed at the bottom of the scroll, and the words Loris had just spoken appeared in gleaming golden letters.

When Rain and Ellysetta turned to the crowd, cheers arose in a great, joyous roar. "*Mioralas!* Rainier v'En Daris! Ellysetta v'En Daris! Feyreisa! Feyreisen! *Miora felah ti'vos!*" Air masters spun and showers of fragrant petals rained down in the Hall and across the city as Fey voices rose in joyous song. Outside, the tairen leapt into the air and circled the city, roaring and filling the sky with celebratory flame.

The city's celebration continued into the night, Fey and Elves and Celerians dancing and singing and feasting together as they had not done in a thousand years. As the star the elves called Erimea rose into the night sky, the tairen gathered on the golden rooftops of the restored palace crowning Dharsa's central mount.

«It is time, Ellysetta,» Steli called.

Rain turned and held out his hand to his truemate. "Are you ready, *shei'tani?*"

Ellysetta took his hand. "*Aiyah.*" Rich, vibrant music played in her mind: the pride song of the tairen. An answering song rose up within her, filling her soul with soaring joy. Her steps quickened as she and Rain ran up the hill to the courtyard outside the Hall of Tairen, where the pride was waiting. The kitlings were perched on the golden eaves, while the adults had alighted on the grassy expanse of the courtyard and formed a loose circle.

"This is a great honor, you know," Rain whispered, as they entered. "By bringing the pride here, rather than having you to come to Su'Reisu, Sybharukai acknowledges you a queen and *makai* in your own right."

Steli huffed and nudged Ellysetta with her head. *«You are all surprises, kitling.»*

Ellysetta laughed ruefully and rubbed the great cat's silky white jaw. "To myself also, Steli." A tingling spread through her limbs.

A growl rumbled in Sybharukai's throat, and her tail lashed at Steli's haunches.

«Sybharukai-makai says time to sing, not talk. Go, kitling. Find your wings so we can fly and hunt together.» Steli pressed her furry white nose to Ellysetta's back and nudged her into the center of the tairen ring.

«We hear your song, Ellysetta-Azreisa.» Sybharukai opened her mouth and deposited three very large crystals on the ground near Ellysetta's feet. One was a clear, colorless crystal that shone with a bright, silvery white glow, as if the light of a star had been captured in stone. The second was a deep, dark red sparkling with a kaleidoscope of rainbowed lights. And the third, though obviously Tairen's Eye, didn't shine with the inner radiance of normal crystals. It was dark, lifeless, looking more like *selkahr* than Tairen's Eye.

"Sybharukai?" Rain frowned. "What is the meaning of this? Where is her Soul Quest crystal?"

«Those are her crystals, Rainier-Eras. She does not sing one song but many. She sings the song of all the prides, but the strongest of them are the songs of Reikaia, one of Cahlah's kitlings stolen in the egg, the song of Fellana, mother of the first Tairen Soul, and the song of Lissallukai, Light of the Gods, makai of all the prides and the first tairen who sang magic into this world. That is the Old Magic we smelled in her.» Sybharukai's great, pupilless eyes fixed on

Ellysetta. *«Take them, kitling. Make them yours. Join them, as you have joined us all.»*

Ellysetta reached down and scooped up the dark crystal. It filled one palm entirely, and at her touch, it warmed with sudden heat. Images flashed through her consciousness, familiar images from the dreams of fire and blood she'd had so often, only this time she wasn't afraid. This time she understood. They weren't all evil Mage-sent dreams. Many were the cries of tairen whose souls were tied to her own, the memories of their own battles against Darkness and their own memories of grief and rage and loss.

Unlike the rest of the highly empathic Fey women, she was not helpless to defend herself against the evil of others. She was a Tairen Soul, a queen, a young *makai* of the prides. And though she'd been born to Fey parents and a stolen tairen's soul had been grafted to her own by the High Mage of Eld, she was something much more than the sum of her parts, and something much more than Vadim Maur had ever intended.

Ellysetta picked up the other two crystals: the starry crystal of Lissallukai and deep red crystal of Fellana. Each began to shimmer and swirl at her touch, the essences of the long-dead tairen recognizing the part of themselves that had been born to live again in her.

Just like them, she was a creature of Light and Shadow, capable of giving life or death, of creating or destroying. She was the living embodiment of the greatest magic of all: Azrahn, the soul magic, in its devastating entirety: the golden *shei'dalins'* love wielded by the strongest Fey women, and the shadowy power of destruction and control wielded by the Mages and spun by those warriors of the Fey who dared to use it. The Maker and the Unmaker. The Healer and the Destroyer.

She was the will of the gods made flesh, a living Tairen's Eye crystal sent to restore balance and strength to the Fey by bringing back into their world the powerful magic their ancestors had surrendered: Azrahn, the double-edged sword. The magic from which all other magic sprang, which was both the greatest gift and the greatest curse the gods had given to the Fey. In Azrahn lay the power of the divine, and the gods' eternal test of the worthiness of the Fey . . . for only a soul dedicated to Light could resist the lure of Azrahn's Darkest and most powerful secrets.

Ellysetta cupped the three Soul Quest crystals in her hands and closed her eyes. Power gathered in her belly. She knew what to do—not by instinct, as so many of her greatest weaves had been in the past, but thanks to the vast repository of knowledge stored in the Mirror of Knowledge and the pride memory it had returned to her.

She closed her eyes and focused the power. *«Shei'tan, will you help me?»*

«You need never ask.» Instantly, his power joined her own.

She reached for more, and it came freely, from every soul that shared a connection with hers. Bel, Gaelen, her *lu'tan*, Dax and Marissya, Kieran, Kiel, the twins, Aunt Bessinita, the tairen, the astonishing well of power that belong to her Fey parents, Shan and Elfeya, and finally, the power of every soul, living or dead, whose Light shared a bond with her own. Their power poured into her, and she absorbed it into herself without hesitation or fear, concentrating the magic of their Light inside her until her skin began to glow bright as a star. She gathered their power until she could hold no more, and the electric burn danced across her skin like fire.

Then she began to spin. Not Earth, nor Water, nor Air, nor Fire. Not Spirit either.

She spun Azrahn—pure, unfettered, powerful Azrahn—woven in an intricate pattern of Light and Dark. A weave of Making and Unmaking, of Destruction and Healing.

A weave of magic and creation.

As the magic gathered and swirled around her hands, she cried, "I am Lissallukai, Light of the Gods, against whom no Darkness shall endure. I am Fellana, bringer of life, mother-kin of all *feyreisen*. I am Reikaia, the tairen whose death gave another soul life. I am Ellysetta-Azreisa, Tairen Soul of the Fey, and I sing the Song of the living and the dead. I sing the Song of Souls."

Ellysetta's eyes flew open, blazing with the intensity of her magic. In her hands, the three crystals—stones that no other power but tairen fire could destroy—dissolved, then re-formed as a single solid jewel, a shining cabochon of deep ruby Tairen's Eye filled with starry white drops that looked like clusters of Amarynth blossoms.

Light gathered in the heart of the crystal, not some dim glow, but a dazzling radiance. Within moments, the crystal blazed like the sun, sending beacons of light radiating outward in all directions.

The song of Ellysetta's soul grew louder, insistent, almost frantic. She could feel the wind on her face, brisk and icy as if she were soaring through the high reaches of the sky. Urgency and longing drew her tight, setting her muscles trembling with anticipation.

Sybharukai settled a radiant eye upon her. *«And now, Ellysetta-Azreisa, will you let your tairen at last find her wings?»*

"Aiyah," Ellysetta agreed. Her fingers closed around the newly forged Soul Quest crystal. She brought it tight against her chest, holding it to her as if she could embrace Lissallukai and Fellana and the infant tairen whose soul had been stolen and tied to hers. "*Aiyah*," she said again. Her chin lifted, and she held Sybharukai's whirling gaze. "Help me set her free. Show me how to let her fly."

«Rainier-Eras,» Sybharukai commanded, *«join us to sing your mate through her First Change.»*

A rush of magic washed over Ellysetta as Rain's body took its other form. Her heart pounded like a bass drum against her chest as the black tairen completed the circle of great cats ringed around her. The tairen sat back on their haunches, and with a great rustle, their wings spread wide, blocking out all sight of the world. Even the kitlings joined their elders, stretching their much smaller wings as far as they would go.

A low, rumbling purr began. Softly at first, then growing louder as the first, clear, crystalline notes of the song pealed in Ellysetta's mind.

It wove around her in intricate plaits, the notes shimmering red, blue, white, green, lavender, and black. Fire, Water, Air, Earth, Spirit, and Azrahn, that much-maligned magic so essential to them all. Azrahn, the soul magic, the Shadow and the Light, the Maker and the Unmaker. The song showed her the pattern and urged her to embrace the magic of the Change.

The notes saturated her senses, wrapping her tight in glorious flows, invading her flesh and setting her body aflame. Pleasure so intense it could scarce be borne flooded her body and unmade her. She flung her head back and cried out, a cry of joy and surprise that deepened to a sound no mankind, human or Fey, called their own.

With a roar, Ellysetta found her tairen form.

Fur sprouted where flesh had been. Her limbs grew long, and her fingers curved into lethal claws. Fangs lengthened in her mouth. Wings unfurled, their undersides shining gold in the fading light of day.

Ellysetta took an experimental step in her new, unfamiliar body. She felt the earth beneath the pads of her feet, claws sinking into dirt and rock. And then, because she could, she rose on her hind legs and breathed fire into the sky, laughing at the hot rush and searing taste of it.

«Shei'tani.»

Her great head swung round to meet her mate's glowing pupilless tairen gaze. She saw herself in his mind, sleek and powerful, with fur the color of cinnamon and flames, eyes whirling with bright rainbowed radiance of Tairen's Eye crystal that was even now calming to vivid, crystalline green. Ellysetta breathed deep, marveling at the acuteness of her senses. Scent, taste, sight, sound: All were clearer now, sharper, and visible radiant flows of magic overlay everything, giving the world a constant, shifting glow.

Tairen song—*her* song—hummed through her veins, resonating in every cell. Not separate songs as once they had been, but one song: the bright, fierce blaze of tairen forever and inextricably tied with the deep, cool well of feminine Fey power. And through the wholeness of her song, tied in bonds that would last all eternity, every part of Ellysetta's soul was joined with the majesty, the honor, the fierce strength and the limitless, everlasting love of Rainier-Eras, Tairen Soul, King of the Fey.

«Will you dance the skies with me, beloved?» he asked.

«Yes! Yes! Let us fly!» her tairen half cried with sudden eagerness.

Rain poured images into her mind, directing her new tairen body in the age-old intricacies of tairen flight. She gave herself over to him without reservation, and her body processed and followed his instructions without conscious thought.

She crouched, great muscles bunching in her hind legs, magic gathering, then sprang. Her wings shot out, fully extended, and Air swept up to fill them, snapping the membranes taut. She pumped her wings, gaining loft and speed, propelling her tairen body higher and faster until the air grew brisk and cold, and the ground raced far, far beneath her.

«Rain!»

«I am here, beloved.»

And he was. He always would be.

Together, Rain and Ellysetta, truemates and Tairen Souls of the Fading Lands, raced across the sky, their mighty wings spread wide.